BIG SPLASH

"Ready?" Frank asked Nancy. She nodded. In front of her, Joe jumped into his inner tube. Shouting a war whoop, he plunged down the falls.

Nancy was next. The ride assistant held the tube while she climbed in. Holding on to the handles, she pushed off. Instantly, a smile lit up her face as she sailed down the first fall into churning rapids.

"Ayyy! Yahoo!" Nancy added her shouts to Joe's hoots. Spinning wildly, she hit the next fall, which splashed into a swirling pool.

As Nancy's tube rushed toward a thick grove of ferns, a movement on the bank caught her eye. Snapping her head around, she saw a man crouched in the brush. He was dressed in camouflage clothes, a bandanna tied around his nose and mouth.

Surprised, Nancy grasped the handles of the tube more tightly. Was he on the staff of Jungle Falls? Suddenly, he lunged wildly at her, a knife clutched in one hand!

Nancy Drew & Hardy Boys SuperMysteries

DOUBLE CROSSING
A CRIME FOR CHRISTMAS
SHOCK WAVES
DANGEROUS GAMES
THE LAST RESORT
THE PARIS CONNECTION
BURIED IN TIME
MYSTERY TRAIN
BEST OF ENEMIES
HIGH SURVIVAL
NEW YEAR'S EVIL
TOUR OF DANGER
SPIES AND LIES
TROPIC OF FEAR
COURTING DISASTER
HITS AND MISSES
EVIL IN AMSTERDAM
DESPERATE MEASURES
PASSPORT TO DANGER
HOLLYWOOD HORROR
COPPER CANYON CONSPIRACY
DANGER DOWN UNDER
DEAD ON ARRIVAL
TARGET FOR TERROR
SECRETS OF THE NILE
A QUESTION OF GUILT
ISLANDS OF INTRIGUE
MURDER ON THE FOURTH OF JULY
HIGH STAKES
NIGHTMARE IN NEW ORLEANS
OUT OF CONTROL
EXHIBITION OF EVIL

Available from ARCHWAY Paperbacks

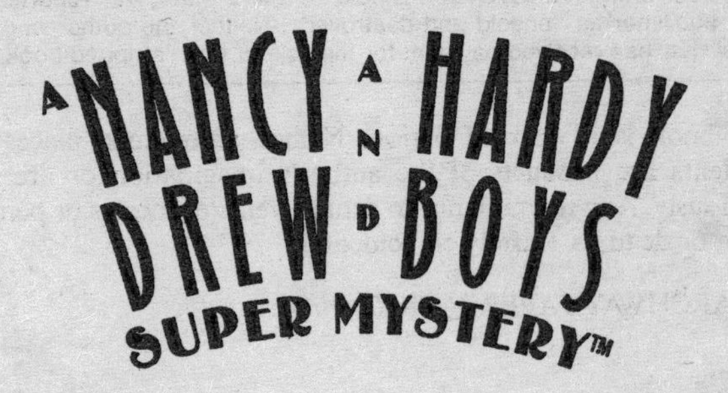

EXHIBITION OF EVIL

Carolyn Keene

AN ARCHWAY PAPERBACK
Published by POCKET BOOKS
New York London Toronto Sydney Tokyo Singapore

AN ARCHWAY PAPERBACK *Original*

An Archway Paperback published by
POCKET BOOKS, a division of Simon & Schuster Inc.
1230 Avenue of the Americas, New York, NY 10020

Produced by Mega-Books, Inc.

ISBN: 0-671-53750-4

First Archway Paperback printing August 1997

10 9 8 7 6 5 4 3 2 1

Cover art by Franco Accornero

Printed in the U.S.A.

IL 6+

Chapter One

FIRST WE'LL SPEND the day at Big Splash Water Park," Bess Marvin told her best friend, Nancy Drew. "I want to ride the Triple Thrill Turbo Pipeline, and Jungle Falls looks totally cool, too."

"Bess." Nancy shifted her eyes from the Virginia highway to glance at her friend. Bess was sitting in the passenger seat, a dozen colorful brochures scattered on her lap.

"Next we'll head to Jamestown for some history," Bess continued, waving one of the brochures. The windows of the Mustang were down, and the humid air had blown her hair into a blond whirl. "Then off to Busch Gardens for pure fun."

"Bess!" Nancy tried again, louder this time. The humming tires and rushing air made it hard to hear.

Bess looked startled. "What?"

"Aren't you forgetting something?"

Bess's blue eyes widened. "No! Don't tell me I forgot my bathing suit!"

Nancy laughed at her friend's horror-stricken expression. "No. I mean, aren't you forgetting that we're going to Williamsburg, Virginia, on a case?"

"Oh, *that.*" Bess waved her hand in dismissal.

"Yes, *that.*" Pulling a scrunchie off her wrist, Nancy bunched her reddish blond hair into a ponytail with one hand while steering the Mustang into the slow lane with the other. Both girls were dressed casually in shorts and T-shirts. Still, Nancy didn't want to arrive at Big Splash Water Park looking completely disheveled. "Mrs. Somers wants us to keep an eye on her daughter, not ride the waves."

"True, but your father said that Mrs. Somers can be overly dramatic," Bess reminded Nancy. "I bet that when she told you someone was sending letters to Dana, she just meant an overzealous fan."

Nancy shook her head. "An overzealous fan wouldn't send a threatening letter that said, 'Hotshot divers lose.' "

"Maybe not," Bess agreed. "But Dana is the

star of the diving exhibition, so she's bound to attract attention—good *and* bad. We just need to solve this case in a jiffy so we can start playing tourist."

"I hope it's that easy." A sign caught Nancy's eye. "Our exit's coming up. Do you think you can put away your brochures for a second and get out the map?" she asked, a teasing glint in her eye.

"Sure." Bess unfolded the map of Virginia and peered at it. "Uh—where are we?"

Nancy laughed. "You're holding it upside down."

"Oh, right." Bess flipped the map over.

"Wait, there's a sign for Big Splash and Virginia Gardens." Nancy steered the car down the off ramp and into traffic. Up ahead she could see a billboard with a picture of a water slide and an arrow pointing to the entrance of Big Splash.

Bess bounced in her seat. "Ooooh. I can't wait to hit the Paradise Wave Pool."

"Unfortunately, you're going to have to wait," Nancy said. "Our first job is to meet Dana and her mother. Dana's afternoon diving show is at one o'clock, so we should just make it."

"That sounds like fun, too." Bess plucked at the front of her T-shirt. "Only I want to change into my bathing suit first. These clothes are too hot."

Nancy followed the line of cars into the parking lot. Behind a high wall, she could see the tops of brightly colored slides and tubes. At the gate, Nancy flashed a special pass that Mrs. Somers had sent her.

She pulled into a reserved parking slot near the main entrance, then turned off the car. She checked her watch. "The show starts in twenty minutes. I'm curious to see what the star of a diving exhibition does."

"Probably all sorts of daring flips and somersaults," Bess mumbled, hanging over the back of the seat and searching through her beach bag. "I've got lotion, an extra suit . . ."

"Sunglasses," Nancy interjected. When she climbed out from the Mustang, she found the glare from the asphalt blinding. Like Bess, she felt hot and sticky from the long car ride.

"There!" Bess stood up, her arms overflowing with stuff. "I'm ready."

"For what? A week in Hawaii?" Nancy laughed as she pulled her neatly packed beach bag out from the backseat. She locked the car doors, then went around to join Bess, who was bent over, trying to retrieve a dropped sandal.

"Here, let me take something," Nancy offered.

"Thanks." Bess plopped two beach towels into Nancy's free arm, then topped it off with her purse.

Nancy shook her head, her blue eyes twinkling. "Let's hope they have lockers."

"And someplace to eat," Bess said over her shoulder as they headed for the entrance. "I'm starving."

They showed the guard their passes, then followed the arrows and crowds to the locker rooms. By the time Nancy had changed into her bathing suit, perspiration dotted her forehead.

"You're right, Bess, the wave pool sounds great."

"Good. Let's take a quick dip." Bess stuffed her shorts and shirt into her bag. She was wearing a red-striped bikini that accented her curves.

Nancy found an empty locker. "First, Dana's show. Second, meet Dana and her mom."

"Third, go swimming?" Bess asked hopefully.

"Right." After taking out a towel, Nancy shoved her bag into the locker. She had opted for a figure-hugging one-piece suit in bright blue. Around her slim waist, she belted a fanny pack that held her money.

"The Splash-a-Rama Theater is to the left," Nancy said, consulting the brochure as they left the locker room.

Bess pointed to a concession area. "And burgers and fries are on the right."

The girls grabbed a quick bite, wolfing down their food as they filed into the theater with the gathering audience. Nancy chose seats close to the front so she could watch Dana.

While she sipped her lemonade, Nancy

glanced around the Splash-a-Rama. It was an outdoor amphitheater with curved rows of seats overlooking two circular pools and a trampoline. A ten-meter platform towered over one pool. Two springboards jutted out over the other.

When the music started, six divers—three guys and three girls—jogged in from a building behind the platform. Smiling and waving, they lined up in front of the pools and bowed. Their slim, tanned bodies were clad in red, white, and blue Speedo suits.

Nancy recognized Dana from the photo Mrs. Somers had given her. She was petite, with sun-streaked short brown hair and a confident smile.

Earlier, when Mrs. Somers met Nancy in River Heights, she had not only referred to Dana as the "star of the show," but she'd boasted of her daughter's many wins at collegiate and national competitions. As Nancy checked out the other team members, she wondered if maybe Dana's achievements had rubbed some of them the wrong way.

The six divers split up and jogged around the pool to the tune of "Yankee Doodle." Bess leaned closer to Nancy. "Look how skimpy those guys' suits are," she whispered. "Do you think they'll stay on?"

Loud clapping drowned out Nancy's laughter as the divers took their positions. "Big Splash Water Park is proud to introduce our diving team," the announcer said over the loudspeaker. "Team captain Tommy Waldhauser partnering with Susan Li on the springboards. Grant Homan and Angelina Regalio on the trampolines. And climbing the ten-meter tower is Dana Somers, with Phil Yancey waiting below. Give them a big hand, folks. Tommy and Susan will now wow you from the springboards."

"Wow me is right!" Beth said breathlessly. "That Tommy Waldhauser is cute with a capital *Q.*"

"Bess." Nancy bit back a grin. No matter where they went, her friend managed to fall for some guy. "We're here to keep our eye on Dana, not the team captain."

"Right," Bess murmured, her gaze glued to Tommy as he and Susan simultaneously bounced high on the springboards, somersaulted, and shot like arrows into the pool.

Next a drum roll sounded, and a blue and red spotlight focused on Dana. She looked tiny, perched high on the tall tower, but she had a confident smile. Nancy held her breath. The platform Dana stood on was thirty-three feet above the pool.

"That's as high as a three-story building," the announcer said. "Which means our divers will hit the water at speeds of more than thirty miles an hour."

Gasps rose from the crowd. Bess clutched

Nancy's arm. Even Nancy's mouth went dry. No wonder Mrs. Somers was worried about the threatening letters. The slightest slip, and Dana could be injured seriously.

The music broke into a popular tune. Nancy's gaze was riveted on Dana, who was poised high above the pool. For a second, Dana stroked the pendant she wore around her neck. Then, with one last wave, she raised herself on her toes in preparation for her dive.

As she stepped gracefully to the end of the platform, her right foot suddenly shot out from under her. Arms flailing, Dana flew awkwardly off the tower and plunged toward the pool below.

Chapter Two

NANCY JUMPED FROM her seat as Dana plummeted into the pool, striking the water sideways. Bess screamed, and a horrified gasp rose from the crowd.

Nancy had to find out if Dana was all right. She ran toward the pool, reaching it at the same time as the other divers. Through the clear water, Nancy could see Dana clawing her way to the surface. Tommy and Susan vaulted into the pool. Grabbing their teammate's arms, they pulled her to the side.

Dana hung on to the edge. Water streamed down her face, and her chest heaved.

"Are you all right?" Tommy asked. He still held one arm around her waist to support her.

Dana nodded. Suddenly, a shrill scream pierced the air. Nancy whirled around in time to see Dana's mother hurtling from the building behind the tower, her permed brown curls bouncing as she ran.

Nancy hurried forward to intercept her. "Mrs. Somers, Dana's all right." Nancy took the woman's hand and squeezed it reassuringly. Tears filled Mrs. Somers's eyes. "I knew something like this was going to happen."

"Take a deep breath. You need to get yourself under control before you can help Dana."

Mrs. Somers gulped and nodded. She was wearing a white dress that matched the pallor of her face at that moment. A purse hung from her shoulder, and despite the heat and casual atmosphere, she wore nylons and heels.

"I'm fine." Mrs. Somers pulled away from Nancy and hurried toward Dana. Angelina and Phil were helping her from the pool. Mrs. Somers enveloped her daughter in her arms.

Abruptly, Dana pulled away. "I'm all right, Mother," she snapped.

"But you could have been killed!"

"No. Accidents happen." Dana took a ragged breath, her fingers working her pendant. Nancy looked closer. It was a dolphin arched over a wave.

"What happened?" Tommy asked. "You've done that opening dive a hundred times."

Nancy glanced over at him. She'd been wondering the same thing.

In the background, Nancy could hear the announcer telling everyone that Dana was okay. Then the music started again, and he directed the audience's attention to Angelina and Grant on the trampolines.

"I slipped," Dana said matter-of-factly.

"Slipped?" Tommy frowned as he followed Dana's skyward gaze. "On what?"

Anger sparked in Dana's eyes. "How should I know? I was too busy falling thirty feet."

Tommy opened his mouth as if to say something, then clamped it shut, but not before Nancy saw irritation flash in his eyes.

"Maybe someone should check it out," Nancy said.

"Who are you?" Dana asked.

"Oh, Dana, this is Nancy Drew." Mrs. Somers introduced them.

Dana's eyes narrowed. "You mean the detective? Mother, I told you not to hire anyone. Everything's all right. Now, if you'll excuse me, I've got a show to do."

Before Mrs. Somers could protest, Dana marched over to the springboards.

"I'm sorry, Nancy. She told me not to call you," Mrs. Somers said. "She's so stubborn. I can't believe she's diving so soon after falling. I'd better keep an eye on her." Clutching her purse to her side, she bustled toward an empty space in the first row of seats.

"Will someone tell me what's going on?" Tommy asked.

Nancy turned to the team captain. He was about five feet nine, with the broad shoulders, slim hips, and lean muscular build of a swimmer.

"I'm a private detective," Nancy answered. "After Dana received those threatening letters, Mrs. Somers asked me to come to Big Splash."

"Good. Someone needs to figure out what's going on—before a diver gets hurt." Tommy ran his hands through his short blond hair. "Look, I'm going to inspect the platform. Dana didn't just slip."

"I'd like to know what happened, too." Nancy walked with him to the back of the tower.

"There's only room for one of us up there," Tommy said as he started up the narrow ladder. Nancy turned her attention back to the divers. Since the platform was off limits, she knew they had to be ad-libbing routines. But they were all pouring so much energy into twisting, bouncing, diving, and splashing that she doubted the audience could tell.

Amazed, Nancy watched Dana jump high on the trampoline, do a triple somersault, then soar like a bird into the pool. Next, Susan flipped off the springboard. At the same time, she flipped a baton in the air and caught it before shooting into the water.

As Tommy climbed down the ladder, Grant and Phil were doing a series of slapstick punches, kicks, and dives to the theme song from *Rocky*.

"What did you find?" Nancy asked Tommy.

"Petroleum jelly." He held up one finger, which was covered with grease. "Smeared all over the end of the platform."

Nancy furrowed her brow. "But who? And when?"

He shrugged. "Anyone. Anytime. It's not as though we have security guards. I've worked here every summer since I started college, and we've never had anything like this happen, until Dana."

"What does that mean?"

"Nothing." He wiped his finger on his suit. "Look. I've got to join the show. Maybe we can talk later."

"Okay." Nancy watched Tommy jog to the trampoline. Leaving the stage area, she sidled past the row of onlookers and sat down next to Bess.

Her friend's eyes were wide with curiosity. "What happened?"

"The platform was sabotaged," Nancy whispered. "Which means whoever sent Dana those threatening letters is serious, Bess. Deadly serious."

"First-class accommodations," Joe Hardy announced as he stepped back to check out the interior of the A-frame tent.

His older brother, Frank Hardy, chuckled. "I've never heard of a first-class hotel that didn't have beds, plumbing, or maid service."

"True, but we have our comfortable mattresses of straw." Joe rustled the fluffy pile with the toe of his boot. "Warm wool blankets, haversack pillows, and sweet-smelling grass under our feet."

"Fortunately, I don't think we'll need those itchy blankets in this heat," Frank pointed out. He was bent over, placing a candle in a small brass holder. "And after a couple nights of camping, the ground is going to feel like bricks."

Joe grinned and punched Frank on the arm. "Hey, we're supposed to be Revolutionary War soldiers, not modern-day wimps."

The two brothers had finished setting up camp in a grassy field at Virginia Gardens, a theme park that showcased Virginia history. That noon they'd arrived with the Second New York Regiment, a group of Revolutionary War buffs.

Joe and Frank belonged to Company C, one of three companies that made up the regiment. Their whole regiment had been invited to join other reenactment groups for a few days to perform the Battle of Yorktown for the throngs of tourists who visited the park every summer.

When they first arrived, the Hardys had to shed their shorts and T-shirts for white linen shirts and overalls, tight-fitting pants that buttoned down the insides of their ankles. They looked like authentic Revolutionary War soldiers.

"It's neat that the park does a reenactment every year," Joe said as he slipped on buckled leather shoes. "People today need to know how important the Battle of Yorktown was to our country."

Frank stashed his haversack underneath his blanket. "Right. It marked the end of the war and of British rule—something we Americans should never forget."

"You guys ready?" a cheery voice called in a British accent. A hand pushed back the tent flap, and Colin MacDonald, Frank's pen pal from England and an avid reenactor, ducked and entered.

He was in full dress uniform, wearing the colors and stripes of the British Light Infantry. His shoulder-length hair was pulled back in a short ponytail called a queue and tied with a rag.

"A redcoat!" Frank picked up his musket from the straw and pretended to take aim. "It's good it's not 1781. I'd have to shoot."

Colin patted the saber hanging by his side in its scabbard. "I think I would have run you through first, Hardy," he joked.

"Aren't you going to get hot in that wool coat?" Joe asked Colin.

"Yes, but there's so much to see, I didn't want to have to rush back to change. My group's gathering in an hour to plan our battle strategy."

"Plan all you want." Joe's blue eyes twinkled. "The patriots are still going to whip the redcoats."

"Yeah, yeah. I know history can't be rewritten." Colin waved his fist. "But this time we're going to give you a fight!"

The three boys laughed. Frank had been corresponding with Colin for a month, so he knew how zealous the young Brit was about English history. Even though the Revolutionary War had been fought more than two hundred years ago, feelings could still run high between the reenactment groups.

"Before the battle, I want to show you guys some authentic weapons," Colin said. "A relative of mine, Major Fergus MacDonald, was an aide-de-camp to British General Cornwallis. He was headquartered right here."

Joe pointed to the ground. "Here?"

"At the Frobischer House," Colin said, clarifying. "Come on. I'll show you."

He snapped his heels, saluted, then spun

around. Frank couldn't help but shake his head as he picked up his tricornered hat and followed his friend into the sunlight.

The camp consisted of ten A-shaped tents pitched in two rows, plus two larger tents for the commanders. As they passed through the camp, Frank and Joe greeted the other soldiers in the regiment. Some sat on logs, cleaning muskets, while others stacked wood for an evening fire. Many wore uniforms similar to Frank and Joe's. Others wore hunting shirts and breeches. There were no boom boxes, cars, or modern conveniences. Only an occasional glimpse of a tourist reminded Frank that it wasn't really 1781.

When they left the encampment and approached the park's main attractions, the noise grew louder and the crowds bigger. The park had been built to celebrate Virginia's history from prehistoric times to the present.

Frank had read in a brochure that just past the park's entrance was a marsh, then deep woods filled with native plants and animals. Next was Powhatan Indian Village, a 1780s farm, and a theater showing the film *Exploring the Blue Ridge Mountains.* At the end of the park were the exhibits of the future. "I can't wait to tour the park," Frank said. "Drink up a little history."

"Pretty neat place, huh," Colin agreed. "And what's really great is that the Frobischers, the family that owns the park, is descended from original settlers."

"How do you know all this stuff?" Joe asked.

"Major MacDonald, my many greats grandfather, was headquartered at the Frobischers' house in Yorktown. You see, during the siege of Yorktown, the British took over most of the homes, ousting the families who lived there."

"Wow!" Joe said. "So this really is a trip to the past for you."

"About five years ago, the Frobischers reconstructed the house and turned it into a museum for American and British artifacts from the Yorktown battle," Colin added. "When they did, they helped preserve our family history, too."

Colin pointed to a two-story clapboard home built in the original Williamsburg style. "They moved it board by board and brick by brick. Dashing, isn't it?"

As they went up the hard-packed dirt walkway, a cute teenage girl standing on the stoop greeted them. She wore a linen shift, a long, dark blue skirt, and a linen apron. Her glossy chin-length auburn hair was covered with a mob cap.

"Welcome to Frobischer House," she said, her green eyes merry at the sight of the soldiers. "I'm Regina, and I'll be your guide."

With a big grin, Joe linked arms with her. "A patriot sympathizer, too, I gather."

"Oh, yes!" Regina gave Colin and his uniform

the once-over. "Redcoats be hanged!" she said in a mock-angry voice.

"Not until we put you colonial upstarts in your place," Colin joked right back as the four went into the museum. "Can you point out Major MacDonald's pistols?" he asked her.

"Of course." Holding her skirt with both hands, Regina swept down a dark hallway.

"I'd like to look at everything," Frank said as they passed framed documents and old prints.

Colin checked his pocket watch. "I've got to get back to my regiment, so I don't have much time."

"I'm sure our guide would be happy to show us around the rest of the museum," Joe said.

Regina flashed Joe a smile over her shoulder. "It would be my pleasure."

Frank grinned to himself. Knowing Joe, he'd be back to visit Frobischer House—and the lovely guide—many times.

When they reached what looked like the old parlor, Regina turned to face them. "Each room is filled with authentic artifacts from the war," she said, waving her hand at the weapons and uniforms in glass showcases. "In the kitchen you'll find old kettles, utensils, and examples of food and how it was prepared. Upstairs is a bedroom right out of the 1700s."

Frank nodded, interested in everything. Beside him, Colin was busily glancing around.

"There are the pistols." Colin strode over to a rectangular case where two pistols were displayed on red velvet. "These are the weapons I was telling you about. They belonged to my ancestor, Major MacDonald."

"You're related to Major Fergus MacDonald?" Regina exclaimed. Frank turned to look at her. She was staring at Colin, a mixture of shock and anger in her eyes.

Colin puffed out his chest and saluted. "Indeed I am, ma'am."

Regina's cheeks flushed bright red. "Well, I'm glad to have finally met a MacDonald," she spat like a furious cat. "I've waited a long time to deliver this message!"

Regina raised her hand. She looked as if she was about to strike Colin!

Chapter Three

REGINA SLAPPED Colin's cheek so hard that his head jerked back. "That's for killing my ancestor, Mary Frobischer, who died defending this house against you English!"

Colin's hand flew to his cheek. "What are you talking about?"

Without another word, Regina lifted her skirt a couple of inches and flounced from the room.

"Boy, you sure make an impression on the ladies," Joe said.

"What was she talking about?" Frank asked Colin. "Major MacDonald killed someone in her family?"

Colin shrugged. "I guess so. Though it's the first I've ever heard about it." He flexed his jaw.

"And I'm not sure why she whacked me. It was a war, you know. A lot of people died—on both sides."

"It was two hundred years ago," Joe pointed out. "I think our guide is carrying a grudge a bit too far."

Colin faced the display case. "Anyway, before I was so brutally attacked, I was going to tell you about the pistols." After sticking his hand inside his wool coat, he pulled out a sheet of paper.

Frank turned his attention back to the weapons. They were flintlock pistols with walnut butts and ornate silver side plates and butt caps.

"Look, there's the MacDonald coat of arms on the escutcheon," Colin said, pride in his voice.

Frank bent closer and studied one of the pistols. On the top of the grip, a silver shield was divided into fourths. Each fourth had a design etched in it. "It's a thistle and a cross?"

"Yes. The thistle is for MacDonald. The cross is for my mother's family." Colin held the paper to the glass. Frank noticed the same shield design drawn on it.

"My parents made a copy of the coat of arms from our genealogy book." Colin glanced from the paper to the pistols and back to the paper. "Wait a minute. Something's wrong. Really wrong."

Abruptly, he folded the paper and tucked it under his coat lapel. "Frank, Joe, I've got to check on something." Turning, Colin fled from the museum.

"Colin, wait!" Frank started after him, running into a crowd of entering tourists. Something had upset his friend, and he wanted to find out what it was. When he finally made it to the steps, Colin was gone.

"Whew, am I glad the diving show's over with no more accidents," Bess said to Nancy.

"Me, too." Nancy took a deep breath. She hadn't realized how tense she'd been during Dana's last dive—a reverse one-and-a-half layout. The dive required Dana to flip backward toward the board. Though Dana had made it look effortless, Nancy had kept her fingers crossed until it was over.

Wild clapping brought Nancy's attention back to the stage. The six divers were bowing in unison. Nancy joined the enthusiastic applause. Despite Dana's fall from the platform, the team had pulled off a terrific show.

The music turned into a rousing march as the divers jogged offstage toward the building behind the tower. Nancy stood up just in time to spot Mrs. Somers chasing after her daughter. The other two women divers, Susan and Angelina, stood talking outside the building.

"Come on, Bess," she said. "We need to speak with Dana."

Nancy worked her way through the crowd, trying to catch up with Mrs. Somers. When they passed the pool, Bess slowed down to peer into it.

"The water isn't even very deep," she said. "I don't know how they have the nerve to dive into it."

"Me, either." Nancy continued down the ramp leading to the building. It had two doors. Men was written above the door on the left, and Women above the door on the right. She smiled and said "Good show" to Susan and Angelina, who nodded and moved off to the side of the building.

Nancy stopped and glanced back at the pool area. It was only about fifty feet away. The tower was hidden by a row of trees. Tommy was right, she decided. Anyone could have sabotaged the platform between shows.

"I think we use the door on the right," Bess teased. "You know, the one marked Women."

When they entered the locker area, steamy air enveloped them, despite a ceiling fan whirling. The room was empty, but from a doorway on the right, Nancy heard the spray of a shower and people arguing.

"I told you no detectives, Mother." Nancy recognized Dana's furious voice.

"Well, I'm sorry, but I'm not going to stand by

and wait for you to get hurt!" Mrs. Somers's shrill voice replied.

The shower abruptly went off. "I can handle it, Mother. So tell that Drew person to go back to River Heights."

"Sounds like Dana isn't too happy to see us," Bess whispered.

"Oh, you are so selfish!" Mrs. Somers snapped. Seconds later she barreled through the doorway. When she saw Nancy and Bess, she jerked to a halt. Droplets of water clung to her curls, and the skirt of her dress was soggy and limp.

"Oh!" She patted her damp hair as if to hide her embarrassment, then waved to the shower area. "I suppose you heard everything."

"I'm sorry Dana doesn't want us around," Nancy said. "Because I think she may be in real danger."

"Danger!" Dana appeared in the doorway, a beach towel wrapped around her, her brown hair plastered to her head. Her eyes were bloodshot, though she didn't seem to have been crying. "What are you talking about? Not that silly accident, I hope."

"It was no accident," Nancy explained. "Tommy checked the platform. Someone greased it with petroleum jelly."

Dana's brows shot up, and one hand flew to her throat. Nancy noticed the pendant wasn't around her neck. "But . . . but . . . who? And why?"

"That's what I hope to find out." Nancy smiled reassuringly. "If you'll let me help."

"Please, Dana," Mrs. Somers pleaded.

Dana let out a big huff of air. "All right, but investigate quietly. And no police. I don't want the show interrupted again." She lowered her voice to a whisper. "The team's already mad at me for . . ." Her voice trailed off.

"For what?" Nancy prompted.

"Nothing." Dana shrugged and went over to her locker.

"I'll tell you why they're mad." Mrs. Somers pulled two sheets of paper from her purse. Nancy recognized one as the threatening letter Mrs. Somers had shown her. "Hotshot divers lose" was pasted on it with letters cut from a newspaper.

"The team's mad that Dana's the big star. So mad that one of them sent her another message this morning." Mrs. Somers handed Nancy the second sheet. After unfolding it, Nancy read the words out loud: " 'The next dive may be your last.' "

"Wow!" Bess looked over at Dana, who was slipping on shorts and a T-shirt. "Whoever sent the message must have put petroleum jelly on the platform!"

Mrs. Somers waved her hands in the air. "Now

you see why I was so hysterical when Dana slipped!"

"May I keep the two notes?" Nancy asked.

Mrs. Somers nodded. "Yes. And I'll help in any way I can, Nancy. Dana's so talented that she could go to the Olympics, but not if she has an accident or loses her nerve. So find whoever's trying to hurt her, please."

"Do either of you have any ideas about which team member could be sending the notes?" Nancy asked, her gaze traveling from Mrs. Somers to Dana.

Dana shook her head. "No," she said brusquely. "And I don't think it is a team member. That's my mother's theory. They might be miffed that I'm the star, but they're all used to competition. I think it's someone else."

"Like who?" Nancy asked.

"Kirby Harliss," Dana replied.

"Kirby Harliss?" Mrs. Somers repeated in a surprised voice. "What's he got to do with you?"

Dana pulled a comb from a purse sitting on the bench and impatiently pulled it through her short hair. "I told you about him, Mother. He's that guy who keeps hanging around, watching me."

"Watching you?" Nancy prompted, hoping Dana would clarify.

"Well, maybe *watching* isn't the right word. But he's always hanging around. He's a lifeguard at the Happy Hippo Pool, but half the time he's in the audience during our shows or outside the locker room when I'm leaving."

"Has he ever approached you?" Nancy asked.

"No. That's what's so weird." Dana shivered involuntarily. "He just stares."

"I bet he's got a big crush on you," Bess said.

"Bess is right," Mrs. Somers said. "You know who's really behind those threats, Dana. You just don't want to face it."

Just then Susan Li strode into the locker room from the front entrance. A towel was draped around her shoulders, and her damp black hair was held back with barrettes.

Mrs. Somers twirled and pointed an accusing finger at Susan. "That's who's behind the letters," she declared. "She's the witch who wants my daughter dead!"

Chapter Four

"WHAT ARE YOU talking about?" Stopping in her tracks, Susan stared at Mrs. Somers with a startled expression.

"Admit it, Miss Li." Mrs. Somers's hand was shaking with fury. "You're the one who's sending those nasty letters."

"Mother!" Dana exclaimed with horror. "Why are you accusing Susan? She's my friend."

"Because she's the one who's really jealous of you. She's the one you always beat in competitions." Mrs. Somers faced Nancy. "Susan and Dana have been on competing teams since high school," she explained. "Maybe they're on the same team now, but Dana's still winning the applause of the audience."

"That's crazy!" Susan snapped. "We aren't in a popularity contest."

"Oh, really?" Mrs. Somers stepped toward Susan, her finger still leveled at the girl. "Then why are you working so hard to perfect that pitiful twirling act?"

Dana gasped. "Mother! Why are you being so rude?"

"Please, Mrs. Somers." Nancy put a restraining hand on the older woman's arm. "Let me handle this."

Mrs. Somers's arm dropped like dead weight. "You're right." Pulling a tissue from her purse, she dabbed at her nose. "That was uncalled for."

"I'm sorry about the outburst," Nancy told Susan, who stood frozen by the entrance. "Mrs. Somers is upset because of the threatening letters Dana's been getting." Nancy held out the two messages. "One came this morning."

Susan barely glanced at them. "That's terrible! Who would send these?"

"That's what Nancy's going to find out," Bess said. "She's a private detective."

"A detective?" Susan echoed. Nancy noted the hint of fear in her voice. Then Susan's cheeks colored, and she spun toward Dana. "How dare you hire someone to spy on the team!"

"I didn't," Dana said defensively. "My mother was just worried."

"Worried about what? That her precious

daughter might get upstaged?" Suddenly Susan whirled around to face Nancy. "I think I'd better set you straight, Ms. Drew. The only person who thinks Dana is a big star is her mother. No one on the team is jealous. And that goes for me. My new baton act has been blowing Dana out of the water. So I think you've got your suspects dead wrong!" Throwing down her towel, Susan stormed out of the locker room.

Mrs. Somers turned to Nancy, a triumphant gleam in her eyes. "Did you hear that? Did you see her rush off? I know she's guilty."

Dana slammed the door of her locker. "She rushed off because you called her a witch, Mother!"

Bess put her two fingers in her mouth and whistled shrilly. When Dana and her mother turned to her, she said, "Would you two quit arguing and let Nancy handle this?"

"Bess is right," Nancy said. "If Dana is in danger, we need to work together."

Mrs. Somers bristled. "Of course Dana is in danger."

"Mother, for once keep your nose out of my business!" Dana snapped. Then her shoulders slumped forward, and tears filled her eyes. "I'm sorry. I've been trying not to let the threats get to me, but after that fall . . ." Her voice cracked.

Mrs. Somers rushed forward to hug her. "There, there. I'm sorry, too. I can't imagine the stress you've been under, wondering and worrying if someone is out to get you."

"You know what we need?" Bess suggested cheerfully. "We need to do something fun. Dana, when's your next show?"

"This evening."

"Then let's play tourist for a while," Bess said.

Mrs. Somers brightened. "I think that's a great idea."

"Okay." Dana nodded. "I haven't taken any time off lately, and this afternoon at Virginia Gardens there's a reenactment I'd love to see. I have free passes."

"Ooh. Virginia Gardens." Bess pulled a brochure from her beach bag. "That sounds like a great way to relax!"

"I agree," Nancy said, though she knew she wouldn't be doing much relaxing. Her mind would be spinning, trying to figure out who wanted to hurt Dana. Because one thing was certain. Whoever had greased the diving platform had put Dana in danger.

"Now I know why so many soldiers died in the Revolutionary War," Joe said as he ran his finger around his tight collar. "They boiled to death in their uniforms."

Frank chuckled but kept facing forward with his back ramrod straight. The two brothers were marching in the front rank of their platoon to the slow beat of the drum. They wore long-sleeved linen shirts with military collars, linen waistcoats, and blue wool uniform coats with buff facings.

On Joe's right hip, a cartridge box hung from a linen shoulder strap that crossed diagonally over his chest. On his left hip, his bayonet scabbard hung by a second strap. Joe's musket rested on his left shoulder, the butt in his hand. His right arm was at his side.

Without moving his head, Joe directed his gaze to the large crowd standing on both sides of the field, watching the demonstration. Ahead of him was British redoubt number ten, a mound of dirt with a trench in front. The earthen works was fortified with palisades—sharp stakes set in rows. On top of the mound stood two light cannons manned by blue-coated cannoneers. In back of them, Joe could just make out the red line of British infantry.

Sweat broke out on his forehead—not only from heat but also from tension. He knew this wasn't really war. His musket was loaded with a blank charge and no musket ball, and his bayonet was rubber. Still, the *rump, rump* of the drums, the thud of marching feet, and the orders of the sword-wielding commander were real.

As the battalion drew closer to the redoubt, a

cannon boomed and gray smoke filled the air. Rushing ahead, the sappers and miners used axes and saws to clear the stakes from the redoubt. The leather-aproned soldiers were called "the corps of forlorn hope" since they made perfect targets for the enemy. Joe hoped none of them would get shot.

The boom of gunfire increased. A miner fell. Joe's fingers tensed on the butt of his gun. They were close enough for a bayonet charge. When would the commander give the signal?

"Charge!" Joe heard Colonel Winters finally yell.

"Charge!" echoed Reggie Hartman, the division captain.

Joe sprang into action. Lowering his musket waist high, he ran across the field, into the trench, and up the side of the redoubt. The second cannon boomed, and a soldier fell at his feet. Joe darted around the last of the palisades. Muskets cracked, and two more patriots fell. A redcoat charged him. Joe thrust his bayonet at him. The soldier grabbed his chest and crumpled.

In the noise, smoke, and confusion, Joe couldn't find Frank. Not that he had time to look. The butt of a gun slamming against his chest forced him down the embankment.

"Got you!" someone hollered. Joe looked up to see Colin grinning triumphantly.

With a roar, Joe sprang back up the hill. Colin dropped his musket and reached for his saber. Joe lunged with his bayonet. With a cry, Colin staggered, then fell, his saber clattering to the ground.

"No, I got *you,*" Joe corrected. When he straightened up, the redcoats had been driven back. Their musket butts were down, their cannons silent.

A cheer went up, and the color bearer, the young soldier who carried the battalion flag, waved his flag over the redoubt. The British were defeated!

Joe slapped a fellow patriot on the back, then went to find his prisoner. Colin still lay on the trampled dirt, eyes open, one arm awkwardly bent beneath him.

"Okay, redcoat"—Joe prodded him with the butt of his musket—"the British surrendered. Time to march to our tune." Bending at the waist, Joe held out his hand to help Colin up. His friend didn't stir.

"Colin, the battle's over. Time for the parade of the victors and the vanquished."

When Colin didn't move, Joe frowned. He knew the Brit was into realism, but this was carrying it too far.

"Hey." Joe knelt and gave Colin's shoulder a shake. Suddenly a cold chill raced up his spine.

Blood was seeping through the front of Colin's waistcoat.

Fingers shaking, Joe felt for Colin's neck pulse. "Come on, come on," he chanted, hoping Colin was only pretending. He couldn't find the beat of a heart.

His friend was dead.

Chapter Five

COLIN'S DEAD? Joe thought in disbelief.

No way. This was a demonstration. No one had loaded weapons. How could Colin be dead?

Frantically, Joe searched for a pulse. Finding none, he tried CPR for several fevered minutes. When there was no response, he jumped to his feet. "Frank!"

His brother was rounding up several redcoats with the point of his bayonet. "What?" he hollered back.

"It's Colin! Come quick!"

Lowering his musket, Frank came running, the division captain, Reggie Hartman, right behind him.

Joe knelt by Colin's side. "I can't get a pulse."

"What!" Frank hunkered down and felt Colin's neck. "Call park security and nine-one-one," he quickly told Reggie. By then, several other soldiers, both patriots and redcoats, had come over, too.

"Joe—what happened?" Frank asked him in a troubled voice.

Joe swung his head from side to side. "I don't know. The last time I saw Colin, I pretended to stab him with my bayonet, and he fell." When he realized what he had said, Joe sucked in his breath. "You don't think—"

"No way." Frank bent closer to study the front of Colin's waistcoat. His coat had fallen open, revealing the widening stain of blood. "Your bayonet's rubber."

"Then how was he killed?" Joe asked.

"I'd like an answer to that question, too." Carefully, Frank took Colin's arm and tipped him sideways. The carved handle of a knife was sticking out of Colin's back. Joe couldn't believe his eyes. . . .

Colin had been stabbed.

"That was amazing," Bess said from the edge of the field where she stood with Nancy and Dana. "I've never seen a reenactment before."

"Me, either." Nancy shaded her eyes. The cannons were silent, and a soldier was waving a flag on top of the redoubt. "I'm glad the patriots won." The three girls had arrived at Virginia Gardens with Phil Yancey and Angelina Regalio just in time for the demonstration. It had been so realistic and exciting that Nancy had momentarily forgotten why she was in Williamsburg.

"Well, I'd better get back to Big Splash," Dana said. "For the evening show." She sighed. "I enjoyed the break, Bess. Thanks for suggesting it."

Bess smiled. "You know what they say about all work and no play."

"And the diving shows have been a lot of work," Dana admitted. "But, hey, tomorrow night the owners of Big Splash are giving a party for staff and friends. It should be a blow-out, and you two are definitely invited."

"Will all the divers be there?" Bess asked eagerly. Nancy had to laugh. Bess was obviously thinking about Tommy.

Suddenly, a cry rang out across the field. Nancy started. Was it her imagination, or was that Joe Hardy's voice, calling for his brother, Frank?

She turned to Bess, her brow furrowed. "Did you hear someone yell 'Frank'?"

"Frank?" Dana looked totally puzzled.

Bess laughed. "Nancy obviously has a certain guy on her mind."

"I just thought I heard Joe." Nancy stood on tiptoes, trying to see over the dispersing crowd.

"She means Joe and Frank Hardy," Bess explained to Dana. "They're friends and fellow detectives. But I don't know why they'd be at Virginia Gardens."

Sticking her sunglasses on top of her head, Nancy scanned the redoubt. The British and American soldiers were milling around on top. Nancy knew that Joe and Frank were history buffs. Still, Bess was right—it would be an unlikely coincidence if the Hardys were in Williamsburg, too.

"Why don't you two play tourist for a while?" Dana said. "I can catch a ride with Phil and Angelina."

"I'd love to see the rest of Virginia Gardens," Bess said. "Nancy?"

Nancy turned her attention away from the battlefield. "Maybe we'd better stick with you, Dana."

"No way," Dana protested. "I'll be fine. And knowing my mom, she'll have checked every inch of the water park for booby traps."

"Okay. But be careful," Nancy cautioned. "We'll meet you after the show."

Dana waved and headed off to meet Phil and Angelina.

"At least she seems a little more relaxed," Bess commented as she watched Dana leave.

"And she seems to have accepted the fact that I'm investigating," Nancy added.

Just then she saw a soldier in blue race down the side of the redoubt. On top of the earthen mound, a group had clustered around two kneeling patriots. Something was wrong.

"I'm going closer," Nancy said. She took off across the field. Behind her, she could hear Bess calling, "Hey, wait for me."

Nancy reached the redoubt at the same time as park security. Heart hammering, she climbed the steep hill after them.

When she reached the top, she stopped dead. Two soldiers were stooped over a third lying in the dirt. Nancy recognized the two patriots immediately—they were Frank and Joe Hardy.

"Stand back! Stand back!" The two security guards began herding the people back from the scene.

Sirens whirred in the distance as Bess came puffing up the hill. "What happened?" she asked.

"Looks like someone got hurt during the reenactment," Nancy told her. Hurrying over to Frank, she put her hand on his shoulder. "Hey, soldier, what's going on?"

Frank glanced up, his expression startled when he realized who it was. He rose to his feet and put his arms around Nancy's shoulders, hugging her almost desperately.

"Nancy! What in the world are you doing here?"

"That's just what I was going to ask you."

Nancy leaned back so she could see Frank's face. Tears blurred his eyes. "What happened?"

"It's my friend Colin from England," Frank explained, his voice hoarse with emotion. "He came to Virginia for the reenactment, and now he's—he's dead."

Nancy's hands tightened on Frank's waist. "Dead?"

"He was stabbed in the back."

The sirens grew louder as an ambulance and two police cars roared across the field.

"Stand back, please." A security guard tapped Nancy on the arm and gestured for her and Frank to move away from the body. "Give the medics room to work."

"I need to talk to the police," Frank told the guard. "Colin was my friend, and my brother was the first to find him."

The guard nodded tersely. "Wait over by the cannon."

Nancy took Frank's hand and led him to where Joe was already standing next to Bess. Joe had set the two muskets against the wheel and was leaning wearily against the barrel. His face was ghostly white, and he was shaking his head as if in a daze.

"What happened?" Nancy repeated.

As Joe retold the story, Nancy, Bess, and Frank kept their eyes on the medics who had rushed to Colin's side. It didn't take long for them to determine what Joe and Frank already knew—Colin was dead.

By then several more police had arrived and were taking names of the reenactors. A woman in a pants suit with an ID and badge clipped to her coat pocket was taking notes. She approached the four teens and introduced herself as Detective Burnett. "The park guard told me you two were the first to reach him," she said to Frank and Joe. "I need to speak with you both."

Frank nodded. Nancy knew the Hardys were used to helping investigators. But she also knew how difficult it was when the victim was someone you knew.

Half an hour later, both Joe and Frank had finished talking with Detective Burnett. The county medical examiner had finished checking over Colin, and the police were zipping his body into a body bag.

Nancy took Frank's hand. "I'm sorry."

Shoulders slumped, Frank stared into space. The sun was setting, and Nancy shivered despite the heat. "The police told all the reenactors to stay nearby." Frank shook his head. "It's going to take forever to interview everybody. And so far, no witnesses have come forward."

"Which means they'll never figure out who killed Colin," Joe said as he came over with the two muskets. Bess was behind him, carrying his cartridge box and canteen. "There were at least fifty people involved in the reenactment. In all the confusion and excitement, any one of them could have killed him."

"Except there must be a reason Colin was killed," Nancy pointed out. "All fifty didn't have a motive."

Frank snorted. "Oh, that should make it easier." Instantly, he squeezed Nancy's fingers. "Sorry. I didn't mean to bark at you. Colin had been so excited about coming to the States for the reenactment." He told Nancy and Bess how he had been writing to Colin after meeting him in England during a summer visit. "He was especially keyed up because his ancestor was a major at the siege of Yorktown, and now"—his voice broke—"now he's been murdered."

"Couldn't it have been an accident?" Bess asked.

"No way," Joe declared. "We're all super careful during reenactments. And Detective Burnett said the ME reported that the knife had been forcefully plunged into Colin's back."

Nancy shuddered. "But who would want to kill your friend? Did Colin say anything?"

"No," Frank said, but then he frowned. "Wait a minute. There was something." He turned to Joe. "Remember when Colin ran out of the museum?"

"Right." Joe nodded. "After that guide slapped him across the face."

Frank told Nancy and Bess about Regina, the two pistols, the MacDonald coat of arms, and Colin's hurried departure.

Nancy cocked her head. "Sounds like you may be onto something."

"I think you're right," Frank agreed. "In fact, I'd like to get hold of the copy of the coat of arms." Joe gestured to the zipped-up body bag. "Uh, if the piece of paper is under Colin's coat, it's police evidence now."

"Maybe we'll get lucky and find it in his tent." Frank reached for his musket. "Come on, let's head to the British encampment."

"How about if Bess and I take the weapons back to our tent?" Joe suggested. "Then we'll meet you."

The four teens agreed, then hurried down the side of the redoubt. As Nancy strode beside Frank, trying to keep up, she thought about the crazy events of the afternoon—Dana falling from the tower, Frank and Joe with a dead buddy.

She shuddered. Evil was definitely lurking in Williamsburg.

"There's Colin's tent," Frank said, pointing to the fourth one in the line. By now it was dusk. Fires crackled, and the aroma of stew wafted from iron kettles.

"He was bunking with some guy named William." Frank stopped to check out the tent. The flap was down, and there was no candlelight inside. "It looks like no one's there."

"Maybe we'd better ask someone before we barge in," Nancy said. "You look a little suspicious in your Continental uniform."

Just then, a *clunk* sounded from inside the tent. Frank froze.

He put a finger to his lips. "If someone's in there, it might be Colin's murderer," he whispered to Nancy.

She nodded. Silently, they crept to the closed tent opening. Frank paused, listening. He could hear muffled sounds, as if someone was moving around slowly, trying not to be heard.

Frank's heart hammered. His fingers clenched into fists. Lunging forward, he pushed the flap aside. A dark figure was kneeling in the middle of the tent. When the flap flew open, the person sprang to his feet.

Before Frank could open his mouth, something whacked him hard on the side of his head.

Chapter Six

FRANK KNOCKED into Nancy, and they both fell awkwardly to the ground. Frank staggered to his feet first and rushed into the tent. "Hey!" he hollered angrily, but he was too late. The shadowy figure had wriggled under the back of the tent and was gone.

Frank dashed out of the tent. "He's getting away," he shouted to Nancy as he raced around the back, stopping to glance right, then left. A buffer of trees separated the camp from the rest of the park. Where had the intruder gone?

"There he goes!" Nancy cried, pointing toward the woods.

Frank took off just as a dark shadow darted from the barricade of trees and raced toward the bright lights of the park. Frank wound his way through the tangle of limbs and vines, finally bursting into the confusion of the Powhatan Indian Village.

He skidded to a halt. Before him stretched a half acre of tourists milling around dome-shaped dwellings. To his right, a group of elderly tourists were shooting pictures of the ceremonial dance circle. To his left, a guide in a leather-fringed dress was demonstrating hide tanning to a troop of Girl Scouts.

Frank exhaled loudly. The intruder was nowhere in sight. He'd lost him again.

"Frank! I found something!" Nancy called out.

Frank turned. Nancy was at the edge of the woods, gesturing for him to join her. She held a piece of white paper in her hands.

"It was on the ground." She handed it to him. "Our mystery person may have dropped it."

Frank recognized the copy of the shield that Colin had stuck under his coat. "This is what I was looking for—the MacDonald coat of arms. But why would someone steal it?"

Nancy tapped the paper. "Answer that question, and you may find your murderer."

Frank thought a minute. "When we were at the museum, Colin compared the coat of arms on the paper to the one engraved on Major MacDonald's pistols. That's when he got an odd look on his face, told us something was wrong, and left."

"Strange," Nancy admitted.

"Now we just have to find out what Colin meant by 'something's wrong.'" For the first time, Frank felt his spirits rise, even though he knew that finding Colin's killer wouldn't bring back his friend.

"Did you get a glimpse of the person at all?" Nancy asked.

Frank shook his head. "I couldn't even tell if it was a man or a woman. Too dark. Too fast." As they headed back through the woods to the tent, Frank touched the side of his face. "Plus, whoever it was whacked me a good one."

"With a haversack," Nancy added. "It looked like the person had been rifling through it."

"Colin probably had the paper in it." Grabbing Nancy's hand, Frank pulled her through tangled brush and into the British camp. "Come on. Let's meet Joe and Bess, then head to Frobischer House. We have some pistols to look at."

"What do you think, Frank?" Joe asked as he stared first at the coat of arms drawn on the piece of paper and then at the ones etched in silver on the pistols.

Nancy and Bess had left for Big Splash, after they'd told Frank and Joe why they were in

Williamsburg. Joe thought it sounded like a tricky case, and he understood why Nancy was reluctant to leave Dana unguarded.

Since the museum closed at eight, Joe and Frank had had to hurry. Joe was glad to have an excuse to see Regina again and had been disappointed when she didn't greet them at the door.

"Colin was right," Frank said. "Something is wrong." He pointed to the picture. The shield was divided into fourths. Thistles were drawn in the top left and bottom right sections. Crosses were drawn in the top right and bottom left sections.

Joe glanced from the picture to the pistols, not noticing anything different. Then, all at once, he saw what was wrong.

"Now I see. The thistles and crosses are reversed. Which may not mean anything," Joe added quickly.

"I think we need to talk to the curator or the person in charge of the museum," Frank said. "It seems odd that he or she wouldn't be aware of the discrepancy."

"Are you thinking the curator might know something that would lead us to Colin's murderer?" Joe shook his head. "That seems like a long shot."

Frank headed out to the hallway. "Maybe, but right now it's the only thing we have to go on."

When they went into the hall, Joe looked

around, wondering if Regina was talking to a group in one of the other rooms. Not that he wanted to get slapped, too, but she might know to whom they could talk.

He peered into the kitchen and spotted a woman dressed in colonial garb. She was short and pudgy and appeared to be in her thirties. Definitely not Regina, Joe thought, remembering how she had managed to look sexy even while wearing a skirt to her ankles.

Joe approached the woman. "Marge" was printed on her name tag. "Excuse me," he said, "but we were wondering if we could speak to someone in charge of the museum."

Marge's brows shot up to the ruffles of her mob cap. "Is there a problem?" she asked in a Southern drawl.

"Oh, no. My brother and I are collectors," Joe fibbed smoothly. "And we'd like some more information on some pistols we recently purchased."

Marge studied him. "You're here with the reenactment group?"

Joe nodded.

"All right, then, you can talk to Mrs. Grant, our curator. Luckily, she's working tonight." Marge pointed out the kitchen door to the narrow wooden stairs. "Her office is on the second floor."

Motioning for Frank to follow, Joe led the way

upstairs, his buckled shoes clunking hollowly on the wooden steps. A group of tourists stood in the hall, peering into a room on the right. When Joe passed by, he glimpsed a four-poster bed covered by a quilt. He stopped in front of an open doorway on the left. It was an office crowded with desks, file cabinets, and a huge computer terminal. Every available space was piled high with artifacts—rusty pots, chipped stoneware, and dirt-caked knives.

"Mrs. Grant?" Joe knocked on the doorjamb.

"Is she in there?" Frank asked.

"It's hard to tell. There's so much junk lying around."

A woman popped up from behind the computer. "Yes?" The woman's glasses were perched on the end of her nose, a spray of graying hair hanging across her forehead. "I'm Emily Grant. How can I help you?"

Frank elbowed his way past Joe. "We were hoping to ask you something." He briefly told Emily about Colin's relationship to Major MacDonald and his shock at finding the difference in the coat of arms.

While Frank talked, Joe leaned against the doorjamb. The musty smell of mildew filled his nose, and he sneezed loudly. Behind him, he could hear visitors murmuring in the hall.

"Your friend Colin showed me this," Emily was saying when Joe turned his attention back to the curator. She was studying the paper. "And I told him he was right. It is a mistake." She pointed at the shield. "The thistle is the sign of the man's family, the MacDonalds, so it should always be in the left corner of the shield just as it is on the paper. The cross was the sign for the wife's side of the family, so it should always be in the right corner."

Emily gave the paper back to Frank. Joe thought she looked genuinely puzzled. "I don't know why they're reversed on the pistols. Everything in the museum has been carefully authenticated."

"By you?" Frank asked.

"I didn't authenticate Major MacDonald's pistols. I was hired only last year, and the pistols were already on display. But the Frobischers pride themselves on their collection. And when I came, I rechecked every letter of authentication."

"I'd like to see that letter," Frank said. "Because we think the pistols may have something to do with our friend's murder."

Emily Grant's eyes widened behind her glasses. "Murder!" she gasped. Clasping her hands in front of her, she slowly stood up. Joe thought that Emily's initial look of puzzlement had turned to one of fear.

Frank nodded as he carefully folded the paper and slid it under his wool uniform coat. "Yes.

Colin was stabbed in the back during the reenactment."

"B-But . . ." Emily Grant stammered. "What connection could there be between his murder and the pistols in this museum?"

Frank leaned closer. "I'm not sure. But I think *you* might have an idea, Mrs. Grant."

Her mouth dropped open. Then, just as quickly, she snapped it shut. "I've never heard anything so absurd in my life. I think you'd better leave," she declared, pointing toward the door. "And take your accusations with you."

Frank straightened. "Fine. But we're going to find out why there's a discrepancy between the pistols and the MacDonald coat of arms. And then, Mrs. Grant, we'll be back."

"Finally, we get to go swimming," Bess said as she and Nancy headed down the sidewalk toward the Paradise Wave Pool.

It was Tuesday evening, the night of the employee party at Big Splash. Nancy and Bess had spent the day keeping an eye on Dana. Fortunately, she had received no new threats, and the shows had gone off without a hitch.

Throwing back her head, Nancy let the sun caress her cheeks and the warm breeze ruffle her hair. Big Splash was closed, and the crowds were gone, so it was easy to pretend that she and Bess were vacationing in a tropical paradise.

When they reached the wave pool, groups of employees were hovering around tables filled with food or relaxing on lounge chairs, talking. Potted palms lined the huge rectangular pool, and the setting sun reflected off the glassy water.

The far end of the pool was bordered by a wall with a long building on top and deep woods behind the building. Nancy knew the waves were generated from the building. At the near end of the pool was a wooden sun deck and a white sand beach that sloped into the water.

Stopping next to a lounge chair, Bess dropped her beach bag onto it. "Dana didn't say it was going to be a Hawaiian luau. Do you think the Hardys will come?"

"I hope so. I left a message for them. There was no way to get to talk to them directly. I imagine they're knee-deep in sleuthing." Nancy laid her beach towel on the chair. "Do you see Dana?"

"No, but I see Tommy Waldhauser," Bess whispered. "And guess what, he looks as good in jeans as he does in his bathing suit."

Nancy followed Bess's gaze. Tommy was standing with two other divers drinking sodas. When he caught Bess's eye, he waved to her. "Gee, Bess, why don't you keep a close watch on the team captain tonight?" Nancy teased. "After all, he and the other divers are our main suspects."

Bess smiled happily. "I'd like that job. Though after poking around all day, I agree with Susan. None of the divers seems to have it in for Dana."

"Or at least they're good at hiding it," Nancy reminded her. For a second, she scanned the crowd. "I wonder if our mysterious Kirby Harliss will show up tonight," she mused out loud. "I'd like to talk to him and find out why he's so interested in Dana."

The lights around the pool switched on, and a motor began to hum. Waves formed at the wall end of the pool and slowly drifted toward the beach. A cheer went up, and everybody began shedding cover-ups and running into the water, carrying noodles, tubes, and floats.

"Last one in is a rotten egg," Bess said as she pulled her T-shirt over her head.

"Go on in. I want to find Dana first." Nancy watched as Bess waded into the pool until she was waist deep, then dove into a wave. Seconds later Tommy Waldhauser shed his jeans and splashed in after her.

Nancy grinned, glad that Tommy was interested in Bess, too. She wandered over to the lavish buffet. Absently, she picked up a paper plate, her mind intent on locating Dana. She spotted Mrs. Somers talking to an older couple. Dana wasn't with her. Had she gone into the wave pool?

Nancy checked out the beach, her gaze resting

briefly on Susan. The petite girl stood off by herself under a palm. A paper cup was clutched in one of her hands, and she was staring intently at the swimmers.

Nancy threw a few appetizers onto her plate and went over to Susan. "Hi. Great show today," she told her.

Susan shifted her eyes to Nancy's face. "Thanks."

Nancy speared a chunk of cantaloupe with her toothpick. "You're right, Susan," she said. "Your baton act *is* blowing Dana out of the water."

Susan snorted. "Who noticed? After this morning's show, there were a dozen reporters crowded around the locker room, wanting to interview 'poor' Dana about yesterday's accident."

Nancy's hand froze halfway to her mouth. "Really?" She set the cantaloupe back on the plate. The reporters must have come while Bess was watching Dana and Nancy was talking to Mrs. Somers.

"Which means Dana will be tonight's headlines," Susan added. "And tomorrow's audience will be packed with people wanting to see her. Not that *I* care," she declared hotly. Tossing her cup into a trash can, she strode off.

Nancy could tell by the tone of Susan's voice that she did care—a lot. She wondered why Dana and Bess hadn't mentioned anything about the reporters. She also wondered who had tipped off the newspaper. Dana's mother?

A shrill scream broke through the air, and Nancy whirled around. It was Mrs. Somers. Nancy saw the older woman rush toward the water, her heels sinking into the sand. "It's Dana! Help her!"

Dropping her plate, Nancy raced down the beach. Mrs. Somers was pointing with both hands to the crowd of swimmers. "Dana needs help!"

Nancy's heart quickened as she splashed into the water, trying to see over all the bobbing heads, rafts, and tubes. There was so much laughter and squealing, she couldn't hear. Was Dana really in trouble, or was Mrs. Somers overreacting?

But then she heard a piercing scream, and Nancy knew Mrs. Somers was right. Dana *was* in trouble!

"Help!" Dana's voice floated over the pool, weaker this time. Diving headfirst into the waves, Nancy swam toward the far back wall—the direction of the scream.

The giggling, splashing swimmers didn't seem to notice as Nancy surged past. If Mrs. Somers hadn't alerted her, Nancy might not have heard Dana. The rush of the waves, the laughter, and the chatter of the guests almost drowned out Dana's cries.

Nancy's powerful crawl stroke carried her swiftly through the waves. Lifting her head, she tried to spot Dana. A wave broke over her. Water streamed into her eyes and nostrils. With one hand, she brushed her hair from her face as she glimpsed two figures about fifteen feet in front of her.

One was a guy with a long ponytail, his face hidden by a scuba mask. The other was Dana. The guy had both his hands around Dana's throat, and though she was hitting him, he was forcing her under the water.

"Stop!" Nancy hollered.

Startled, the guy looked up. Letting go of Dana, he lunged toward a ladder about twenty feet behind him.

Kicking with all her might, Nancy swam for him, reaching the ladder just as he was climbing out. She grabbed his ankle. Cursing, he kicked at her, but Nancy jerked his leg so violently he was thrown off balance and fell into the water.

Determined not to let him get away, Nancy hurled herself on top of him and threw her arms around his neck and shoulders. With a grunt of anger, he flung himself backward against the ladder. Nancy gasped as her head struck a rung. She released her grip on him as she slipped under the water.

Nancy forced her eyes open. Bubbles filled the water, and she couldn't see. Then strong fingers clawed at her hair, grabbed a hunk, and began dragging her away from the ladder into deeper water.

Nancy flailed wildly. The person holding her head under was strong, and as her breath exploded in her lungs, a thought flashed through Nancy's mind—she was going to drown.

Chapter Seven

"OH, MY GOSH, it's Nancy!" Joe Hardy dropped his towel onto the sand and raced down the side of the wave pool, his eyes on Nancy's head as it went under. A girl in the water near Nancy was screaming to save her. Several people were rushing toward Nancy.

As Joe barreled through them, he had no idea what was going on. He and Frank had just arrived. Frank had headed for the buffet, while Joe had aimed for the water. Then the screams had caught his attention. All Joe could see was Nancy in the water, fighting with some guy wearing a mask.

By the time he reached the ladder, a girl in a string bikini had already grabbed a life ring from the guard tower and was diving in. Without hesitating, Joe dove in after her.

When he surfaced, he was about ten feet from the guy in the mask. Joe saw Nancy's face break the surface for an instant, only to be shoved under. The creep was trying to kill her!

Furious, Joe launched himself at the guy. "Hey!" he hollered, and when the guy snapped his head around, Joe rose out of the water so he had the leverage to clobber him on the jaw. The guy fell back and released Nancy. The girl in the bikini grabbed Nancy's arm, hauled her to the surface, and gave her the life ring.

Nancy was choking and gasping, but as soon as Joe saw she was all right, he growled and turned toward the creep. Behind the scuba mask, the guy's eyes were wide with fear, and blood streamed from his lip.

Shooting away from Joe, the guy struck off for the opposite side. In two strokes, Joe had him by the ponytail. "Get back here, jerk." For a second, the guy flailed at Joe, then suddenly fell limp as if all the fight had gone out of him.

By then a crowd had gathered on the side of the pool. Joe saw Frank standing next to several men in security uniforms.

"This guy tried to drown Nancy!" Joe called.

"And me!" A girl who looked like a soggy rat was climbing from the water. "That's Kirby Harliss. He was trying to kill me, too."

When Joe reached the ladder, the guards bent down and grabbed Kirby's arms. Joe released him and swam back to Nancy, who clung to the ring while the girl in the bikini pulled her to the side. Nancy's breathing was ragged, but she smiled weakly at Joe.

"Thanks . . . both of you." She directed her last words to the girl, whom Joe recognized from somewhere. Then the girl turned green cat's eyes his way, and he knew who she was—Regina the guide.

Regina helped Nancy float to the ladder. Reaching down, Frank pulled Nancy out. The guards were holding Kirby, who was slumped between them.

"You need to arrest him," Dana, the drowned rat, was saying.

Joe followed Regina up the ladder, taking a moment to appreciate the great legs she'd been hiding under her long skirt at the museum. Then his attention was diverted to the more pressing problem of who Kirby was and why he'd been trying to drown two girls.

"Dana! Dana!" A woman rushed up, adding to the confusion. Her pearl necklace and dressy skirt and blouse made her stick out among the swimmers. Behind her, a gray-haired couple dressed in matching white pants and navy blazers elbowed their way through the crowd.

"What's going on here?" the man demanded

in an authoritative voice. His hat decorated with a nautical crest made him look as if he'd just stepped off a yacht.

Everyone started talking at once.

Joe went over to Regina, who stood dripping at the edge of the crowd. "Can you tell me what's going on or at least who's who?" he whispered.

She smiled. "Only if you lend me a towel."

"Sure. My pleasure." Joe hustled back to retrieve the towel he'd dropped on the sand. When he hurried back, Regina reached for it, gratefully draping it around her shoulders.

"The person you punched is Kirby Harliss," Regina explained. "He's a lifeguard at the Happy Hippo Pool."

Joe snorted. "I thought lifeguards were supposed to save people, not drown them."

"And the girl accusing him of trying to drown her is Dana Somers, one of the park's divers."

"And where do you fit in?" Joe gazed into Regina's eyes. "I thought you worked at Virginia Gardens."

"I belong to the gray-haired pair in matching suits." Regina nodded to the older couple. "I'm their granddaughter."

Joe cocked one brow. "They look important."

"They are. They're the owners of Big Splash and Virginia Gardens."

Joe whistled. "The Frobischers."

"Right. I'm Regina Frobischer."

Joe feinted playfully. "The guide with the great right hook."

Regina looked embarrassed. "I'm so sorry for that. I realized later how out of line I was. But when I went to apologize to your friend, you had already left the museum." She glanced around the crowd. "Is your friend here now?"

Joe blanched. "No, he's not here. He—um . . ." He hesitated, clearing his throat. "Colin was murdered last night. At the reenactment."

All the color drained from Regina's face. "The one who was killed was your friend?" she gasped. "But why?"

"We don't know why. When we talked to the police this morning, they showed us the murder weapon. It was a reproduction of a dagger used in the Revolutionary War. The grip was interesting because it was made from silver and it was inscribed with a date."

"A date?" Regina's eyes widened.

"Seventeen sixty-eight. The police aren't too hopeful the dagger will help them catch Colin's killer. Anyone could have made it."

"Seventeen sixty-eight? A silver grip?" Regina clapped a hand to her mouth. She was staring at him as if she'd seen a ghost.

Joe was surprised by her reaction. "Yes. Do you know something about it?"

"No!" Regina shook her head, her wet hair

slapping her cheeks. Whipping the towel from her shoulders, she thrust it into Joe's hand. "I've got to go."

Joe caught her wrist. "Wait. You do know something. What?"

"I don't know anything!" Regina yanked her wrist from Joe's grasp. "So thank you for the use of your towel, and goodbye!" Twirling on bare feet, Regina pushed past the onlookers.

"Regina, wait." Joe started after her, slowing at the edge of the crowd.

Regina paused to grab a beach bag from a lounge chair, then jogged up the sidewalk. Joe watched her go, trying to decide if he should chase after her. She obviously knew something. But what?

Then angry voices made him turn. The two security guards were heading toward him, with Kirby firmly held between them. Kirby's long hair drooped in wet tangles. The scuba mask was gone, and he stared at the ground with a vacant expression. His body and limbs hung slack, and he stumbled as they led him past.

Joe frowned, confused. Kirby Harliss hardly resembled a crazed killer. What had made him go after Dana and Nancy?

"Okay, back to the party, folks," another guard said, trying to disperse the gawkers. Behind him, Frank, Nancy, and Dana were still clustered at the edge of the pool. Dana was gesturing angrily as she talked to Mr. and Mrs. Frobischer.

Suddenly, Kirby jerked his left arm from the guard's grasp and spun around. "You've got it all wrong!" he shouted, his voice quivering. "I wasn't going to hurt Dana. It was all an act. And Dana put me up to it!"

Chapter Eight

"I WAS SUPPOSED TO attack Dana from behind and pretend to drown her," Kirby continued, his words taut with emotion.

Stunned by the outburst, Nancy turned toward Kirby. The crowd had frozen. Everybody was staring at him in shocked silence.

Catching Kirby's arm, the guard tried to drag him away. But Kirby kept yelling, his face growing redder. "Dana told me that when I saw someone coming, I should let go of her, swim to shore, and escape into the woods behind the wave generator."

Nancy inhaled sharply. Was Kirby accusing Dana of plotting the whole thing? She turned back to Dana. The diver stood rigid with fury.

"He's lying!" Dana screamed.

"No. I'm not." Tears sprang into Kirby's eyes. "You told me I wouldn't get caught. Don't you see, everybody?" he pleaded to the crowd. "Getting caught wasn't part of the plan!"

"That's enough, Harliss!" Mr. Frobischer thundered. "Take him to my office," he said to the guards.

"Wait!" Clutching Frank's towel around her shoulders, Nancy approached Kirby. "If Dana *did* plan the attack, then what was her reason?"

"She wanted the publicity," Kirby said. Blood oozed from the cut on his lip, and his eyes were vacant and staring. "She wanted to be the big star, but Susan's new act was getting all the applause."

Which is just what Susan had suggested, Nancy thought, remembering their initial confrontation.

"Dana's the one who dreamed up the threatening letters," Kirby admitted. "She's the one who told me how to grease the plat—"

A shrill screech cut off his words. Curving her fingers into claws, Dana threw herself at Kirby, attacking his unprotected face with her nails. Throwing off the towel, Nancy grabbed Dana's wrists. At the same time, Frank circled Dana around the waist with his arms. Then he picked her up and pulled her off Kirby.

"He's lying!" Dana screamed again as Frank

held her back. "He's been stalking me for days! He's the one who greased the platform."

Kirby shook his head sadly. A bright red scratch on his cheek stood out against his skin's pallor. "No. The only thing I'm guilty of is being stupid enough to do what you asked me to do, Dana, because I loved you."

All eyes turned to Dana. Her body shook with fury.

"Dana, is this true?" her mother finally asked in a small voice.

"No!" Dana insisted, but her protest sounded hollow. Breaking free from Frank, she stormed through the crowd. After saying "I'm sorry" about ten times, Mrs. Somers hurried after her.

For a few minutes, no one said a word. Even Nancy was too shocked to talk. Why hadn't Dana stayed to defend herself? Unless Kirby was telling the truth.

Then Mr. Frobischer cleared his throat. "Well, I'm going to instruct the guards to let you go, Kirby. But I'm sure you realize I cannot tolerate this kind of behavior from one of my employees. Get your things from your locker. You can come by the office for your pay."

Kirby nodded. When the guard dropped his hold, Kirby touched the scratch on his cheek. Then he left, his head hanging.

Nancy's shoulders slumped with exhaustion.

Frank put an arm around her, and she leaned against him. "You okay?" he asked.

She nodded. "Considering I swallowed a gallon of water."

"I guess that means you'll be too full to eat dinner," he teased.

"What's going on?"

Nancy turned to see Bess and Tommy rushing up. The two were wet, and they were holding hands. Their cheeks were flushed with excitement.

Nancy grinned. "Where have you been?"

"Big Mama Falls!" Bess exclaimed. "It's the coolest."

Tommy gestured toward the departing guards. "What happened?"

"Oh, nothing much," Frank joked. "Just that Kirby Harliss tried to drown Dana but Nancy saved her. Only she didn't really have to save her because Kirby was only pretending."

Tommy and Bess stared at Frank in total confusion. "Huh?" they chorused.

Nancy and Frank burst out laughing. When Nancy explained what happened, Tommy got a funny look on his face. "I didn't know Kirby well," Tommy said. "He was kind of a loner. Still, what could have possessed him to do such a stupid thing? And I knew Dana would do almost anything for attention, but I didn't think she'd stage her own drowning."

"Which explains the reporters this morning," Nancy added. "Dana must have called them herself." She glanced around for Susan. "I think I owe Susan an apology."

"Maybe we can find her," Tommy said. "Bess and I are headed for the buffet. We worked up an appetite at Big Mama Falls. If we see her, I'll let her know you're looking for her."

Tommy and Bess went off just as Joe came up. Nancy gave him a big hug. "Thanks for saving me."

"Except I should have punched Dana, instead of that Kirby guy."

"Probably. Though I think Dana's going to get her punishment." Nancy brushed strands of wet hair off her forehead. "I have a feeling the Frobischers will fire her, too." For a moment, Nancy felt sorry for Dana. Had her mother pushed her too hard into being a star?

"Well, enough about Dana." Nancy heaved a sigh. "How's your case, guys? Any new developments?"

Joe snorted. "Yeah. My suave brother practically accused Mrs. Grant, the museum curator, of being involved in Colin's murder. It's a wonder she didn't stab him with a rusty bayonet."

"It wasn't quite that bad," Frank protested. He told Nancy about the pistols. "The coat of arms on the escutcheon definitely doesn't match the

MacDonald coat of arms. When we asked Mrs. Grant about it, she didn't have an explanation. Then I mentioned Colin's murder and told her I thought it was linked to the pistols."

"And she got really scared, Nan," Joe said. "Like we'd hit a nerve. That was when Frank suggested in his subtle way she might be involved."

Frank chuckled. "Okay, it wasn't the coolest approach. But I did it for a reason. I wanted to see how Mrs. Grant would react."

"And?" Nancy prompted.

Joe laughed. "She kicked us out of the museum."

"So you really think Mrs. Grant might be involved?" Nancy asked.

"I don't know. But it's the only lead we have," Frank replied, running his fingers through his hair. Nancy could tell that Colin's death and the investigation were really stressing him out. "The murder weapon was a dead end," he continued. "Colin was stabbed with a reproduction of a British dagger. A date inscribed on the silver grip was unusual, but so far, the police can't link it to anyone."

Joe snapped his fingers. "I almost forgot. When I mentioned the date to Regina Frobischer—you know, the guide from the museum—she turned white as a sheet and took off."

"Regina was here?" Frank asked.

"Yes. She was the one who helped Nancy," Joe explained.

"Regina Frobischer." Nancy searched her mind. "Is she related to the Mr. and Mrs. Frobischer who own both Big Splash and Virginia Gardens?"

"Their granddaughter," Joe said. He looked at Frank. "Don't you think it's strange that she should take off when I mentioned the date and the silver handle? Unless it was my subtle charm that made her run like a rabbit."

Nancy laughed at Joe's joke, but when she glanced at Frank, her smiled faded. He was frowning.

"That's interesting about Regina," he said, tapping his cheek with one finger. "Maybe it's not just a coincidence that she works at the museum with Mrs. Grant. Maybe the two of them are in it together."

"In *what* together?" Joe asked impatiently. "So far, we don't have a clue how the pistols relate to Colin's death."

"Then we'd better find a clue." Turning to Nancy, Frank put his hands on her shoulders. "Your mystery may be solved, Nan, but I think tomorrow's going to be a busy day for Joe and me now that we finally have some suspects."

"Hey, I'll be happy to interrogate the lovely

Regina Frobischer," Joe offered, rubbing his hands together.

Frank grinned. "Then you'd better learn how to duck her right hook."

"I'll be glad to help, too," Nancy said as the trio sauntered slowly back to the beach. She was glad Frank had finally cracked a smile. Maybe they could join Tommy and Bess and enjoy the rest of the evening.

The music over the speaker system was lively, and people were swimming and eating as if nothing had happened. Nancy wished she were in the mood for partying, but something was nagging at her—maybe her case wasn't solved. She still had to confront Dana and Mrs. Somers. And she had a good idea that neither mother nor daughter would be eager to tell the truth.

"Boy, what I wouldn't give for a big bowl of corn flakes," Frank said. He was hunkered next to the fire, stirring oatmeal in an iron kettle that hung from a pot hook. Smoke stung his eyes, and hot flames toasted his cheeks. "With ice-cold milk and blueberries," he added, licking his lips.

"Hey." Joe poked his brother's thigh with the butt of the musket he was cleaning. "Quit complaining, or we'll be forced to eat fire cakes."

"Ugh." Frank wrinkled his nose. "Not those things. They taste like burnt shoes."

It was the next morning. Frank had spent a restless night thinking about Colin. Finally, he'd sat by the fire, falling asleep under the stars. Now his neck had a major kink in it, and his ribs were bruised from lying on a rock.

And worst of all, he still had no idea who killed Colin.

"Oatmeal's ready," he announced to any interested soldier. No one rushed over.

Joe laughed. "I think they all sneaked out to McDonald's this morning."

"I always knew Company C was a smart bunch." Frank chuckled. "So tell me again what Detective Burnett said when you called this morning."

"She said there were no fingerprints on the dagger. And in the confusion of the reenactment, not one person saw Colin being stabbed."

"Which is what our murderer intended," Frank said.

"Still, it's hard to believe the murderer killed Colin in daylight without anyone seeing him."

"Him?" Frank glanced up from the fire. "Aren't you forgetting our only two suspects are female?"

Joe propped his musket against his leg. "No. It would be impossible not to notice that Regina Frobischer is female. But I want to say right now, big brother, *I* don't think she's involved."

"Once again, little brother's mind is clouded

by a pretty face," Frank joked as he spooned a glob of lumpy oatmeal into a wooden bowl. He stared at it, his appetite suddenly gone. "Uh, we have a couple of hours until our first demonstration. Maybe we can swing by a restaurant before we confront Emily Grant again."

Joe grinned. "I always knew you were full of good ideas."

An hour later the Hardys entered Frobischer House. The park had just opened, and they were the first visitors to the museum.

"Let me do the talking," Frank told Joe as they went up the stairs.

"So we can get kicked out again?"

"No," Frank replied. "I've got a plan to help us find out what Emily Grant is hiding."

Joe rolled his eyes. "Great. A plan."

The office door was open, and Mrs. Grant was sitting at a table, studying a green bottle with a magnifying glass.

Frank announced them with a sharp rap on the doorframe. "Mrs. Grant, we'd like to talk to you again about Colin."

"I have nothing more to say," she declared without taking her eyes off the bottle.

"Good. Then just listen." Frank took a deep breath, hesitating as he hunted for the right words. Emily Grant was hiding something, and Frank was determined to find out what it was.

"Two days ago Colin showed you his picture of

the MacDonald coat of arms and told you of his concern that it didn't match the coat of arms on the pistols."

Frank paused. Emily hadn't moved, but Frank could tell her attention was no longer riveted on the glass.

"I think Colin discovered that the pistols in the display case were fakes," Frank went on. "I think when he spoke with you, he accused you of selling the real ones and replacing them with copies."

The curator sat frozen, her fingers gripping the bottle tightly. Frank had hoped that he might get her to listen.

He took a step forward. Putting his hand on the back of her chair, he bent closer. "So, to protect yourself and your reputation, you murdered him."

The bottle dropped from the curator's hand, shattering on the floor. When she spun around, her face was white with fear.

Why would she act so afraid, Frank thought, unless she was guilty of Colin's murder?

Chapter Nine

JOE STRAIGHTENED UP. Frank's accusation had worked. The expression on Emily's face telegraphed one thing—guilt.

"Call Detective Burnett, Joe," Frank said. "Tell her we found Colin's killer."

"No, wait!" Emily stood up so fast that her chair fell over. "Don't call the police. It's not what you think. I didn't kill your friend."

Joe frowned. "Then what's going on? Why the guilty expression?"

Emily took a deep breath. Taking off her glasses, she polished them slowly on the hem of her shirt. When she put them back on, tears glimmered behind the round frames.

"Because I am guilty—of not telling you the

truth." Turning, she picked up a dustpan and brush, knelt on the floor, and began cleaning up the broken bottle.

Joe glanced at Frank, who lifted one brow. The curator was obviously ready to tell them something. But what?

"When Colin showed me the paper, I knew right away it was proof that the pistols were forgeries," she explained as she carefully swept the broken glass into the dustpan. "But I didn't tell him that."

She looked imploringly at the Hardys as if trying to make them understand. "I *couldn't* tell him. There was more to it than just the pistols."

"What do you mean?" Frank prompted.

Emily stood up with an effort. "When I first came to the museum, I suspected there were fakes here. Only I couldn't prove it. For every item I thought was suspect, I found letters of authentication from the best sources. The previous curator had been very thorough."

She dumped the glass in the trash can, then turned to face the two Hardys. "But after I talked to Colin, I knew my hunch was correct. He said he was going to take his genealogy paper to Mr. and Mrs. Frobischer and tell them what he thought. I asked him to wait. In the meantime, I faxed a letter to the person who supposedly authenticated the pistols."

Joe's brows shot up. "And did you get a reply?"

"Not yet. Look, I'm feeling guilty because you may be right—the pistols may have something to do with your friend's death. And maybe if . . ." Her voice broke. "Maybe if I had told Colin what I knew, he wouldn't have been killed." Putting her hands to her face, Emily began to cry softly.

Frank patted her awkwardly on the shoulder. "No. It sounds like someone else found out about Colin's discovery. But who?"

"Did you tell anyone else about this?" Joe asked.

"No. Except for sending the fax . . ." Her voice trailed off. "You don't think—"

Frank nodded firmly. "Yes. If the letter of authentication was bogus, your fax could have tipped someone off. Who did you send it to?"

Mrs. Grant rummaged around her desk, finally pulling a piece of paper from under a stack of books. "Professor John Wykowski, Lowland College in Ohio."

"I think we'd better give this information to Detective Burnett," Joe told Frank. "They can track down this professor faster than we can."

"It sounds as if the previous curator had to have been in on it, too," Frank said. "He would have to have known that the real artifacts were being replaced by fake ones."

Emily nodded in agreement. "That had

crossed my mind also. But I'm afraid you won't be able to question him. Dr. Chan was an older man, and right after he retired, he died of a heart attack."

"You're right. It would be tough to interrogate him," Joe murmured. Moving from the doorway, he paced down the hall, trying to absorb all the information. Emily seemed to be telling the truth, and what she said made sense.

If the real artifacts were being sold, Joe mused, then whoever was behind the scam could be making big money. And that might make him or her ruthless enough to kill Colin.

But who was involved?

Stopping in the hall, Joe glanced into one of the exhibit rooms. It was a bedroom furnished with period furniture and household items. A velvet rope was stretched across the doorway to keep tourists out.

Joe looked into the stark bedroom. It contained a small four-poster bed covered with a tattered quilt, a washstand, and a fireplace. An exhibit label propped on a wooden table by the doorway explained the importance of the room and its contents. But what caught Joe's eye was the dagger housed in a glass case on the same table.

Joe peered closer, and his heart began to pound. The dagger had a silver grip and an inscription.

Ducking under the velvet rope, Joe went into the room. Bending over, he studied the inscription through the glass. There were four numbers engraved on the grip, and though they were worn, he could still read them: 1-7-6-8.

Joe snapped upright—1768! It was the same date that was on the dagger that had killed Colin.

Joe's gaze darted to the exhibit label. "In the fall of 1781," it read, "when the British army took over Yorktown, Major Fergus MacDonald, Cornwallis's aide-de-camp, was headquartered in the Frobischer House. Mary Frobischer and her husband, Josiah, a Yorktown merchant, were forced to serve Major MacDonald.

"On the night of October 13, as Washington's cannons boomed in the distance, Mary Frobischer, patriot and fighter for freedom, tiptoed into Major MacDonald's bedroom. She was hunting for an important map she'd seen the major working on earlier, a map that detailed the location of British and German troops.

"But Major MacDonald awoke and, thinking he was being attacked, whipped this dagger from under his pillow and stabbed Mary. She died of her wounds."

Wow, Joe thought. He whistled under his breath. No wonder Regina had run off when he mentioned the dagger. She had to know that the dagger that killed Colin was identical to the one that killed Mary. Joe wondered what kind of message the culprit meant to send by killing Colin with an identical dagger.

Of course, the daggers being the same could be a coincidence. But Joe doubted it. He also doubted that Regina had been involved in Colin's murder. But was she involved in the forgeries?

Joe shook his head, wanting the answer to be no. Since the date inscribed on the silver handle was unique, Joe had a strong suspicion there must be a connection between the two daggers.

Which meant Regina Frobischer had some explaining to do.

"Do you think Dana and her mother will talk to us today?" Bess asked Nancy as they walked across the parking lot. It was early, and Big Splash hadn't opened for tourists. Still, cars were already lining up to get in.

Nancy shrugged. "Who knows? They sure didn't want to talk to us last night. But I hate leaving without some explanation. After all, Mrs. Somers did ask us to come to Williamsburg."

Bess beamed. "And thanks to her, I met Tommy."

"At least you two had fun last night." Nancy stopped at the ticket booth to show their passes.

The woman in the booth stared at her curiously. "Hey, you're that lady who saved Dana," she said.

"Yup, that's my friend, Nancy!" Bess piped up. "Always saving people."

The woman shook her head. "I always knew that Kirby Harliss was no good. I'll be glad when he leaves."

"You mean he's still at the park?" Nancy asked, surprised.

"Yeah. Came in early to pick up his check and clear out his stuff." She made a *tsk*-ing noise. "Imagine him accusing Dana of planning the whole thing."

"Thanks." Nancy grabbed the passes and hurried into the park. She wanted to catch Kirby before he left.

"Gee, it sounds like that woman thought Dana was totally innocent," Bess commented as she trotted alongside Nancy.

"Yeah. I wonder what the other employees think."

"Oh, we know what Tommy and Susan think," Bess said. "They pegged Dana for a publicity hound from the beginning."

Nancy stopped in front of the women divers' locker room. "Do me a favor—go in and see if you can find Dana or her mom. Tell them I'd like to talk with them. I'm going to the Happy Hippo Pool to find Kirby. There are some unanswered questions lurking in my brain."

"Like what?"

"Like, was Dana really the mastermind? Or

was she a victim? Kirby's performance last night could have been great acting."

Bess plopped her hands on her hips. "You think he's going to tell you the truth?"

Nancy grinned slyly. "Oh, I've interrogated tougher guys than him."

Bess laughed. Then, waving goodbye, she disappeared into the locker room. Nancy headed down the sidewalk toward the Happy Hippo Pool, hoping she could get Kirby to talk. Yesterday, he'd been ready to blurt out everything. But after a night of thinking about what he'd done, he may have decided to clam up.

The Happy Hippo Pool was the playland for younger kids. Nancy had passed by it yesterday, noticing how much fun the children were having *whooshing* down slides, shooting water cannons, climbing on the big hippo, and splashing under the waterfall.

Now it was deserted. Nancy hunted for signs of Kirby. On the far side of the pool was a small building. The door was hanging open. Was Kirby inside, clearing out his things?

"Hello?" Nancy called as she started around the pool. The waterfall was on, muffling her voice.

Nancy glanced around the pool, wondering where Kirby could be. Just then she spotted something bobbing beneath the cascading water.

It was a body.

Heart hammering, Nancy jumped into the shallow pool. The water sloshed against her knees as she waded to the falls. The person was lying facedown, fully clothed, pants puffed with air, long hair floating in the water like seaweed.

Nancy swallowed hard. Goose bumps pricked her skin. Reaching under the flowing water, she grabbed the back of the pants and pulled the body away from the falls. Then she steadied herself and rolled the body sideways.

It was Kirby. His mouth hung open, and his long hair clung to his pale cheek. A bloody gash gaped at the side of his head.

A sob caught in Nancy's throat. She splashed back to the edge of the pool, falling into the water.

She stood up again and inhaled slowly, trying to calm down and think clearly. She had to call the police. She had to tell them that someone had hit Kirby on the head.

Nancy shivered, then willed herself to move. A few feet in front of her, something glistened at the bottom of the pool. She reached into the water and pulled it out. Her eyes widened.

It was a silver chain. Dangling from the chain was a dolphin leaping over the waves. Nancy recognized it instantly—it was Dana's pendant!

Chapter Ten

"I DIDN'T KILL KIRBY," Dana Somers sobbed into her hands. She was sitting in one of the offices at the Williamsburg police station.

Detective Burnett sat behind a cluttered desk. Her partner, Saul Cohen, stood behind her, an elbow propped on the top of a file cabinet. Nancy stood by Dana's side, her hand resting on her shoulder. Mrs. Somers sat rigid in a chair next to her daughter. Bess was waiting outside.

"Dana, you don't have to say anything if you don't want to," Nancy said. "The police only want to ask some questions."

Dana nodded. She'd thrown a hooded terry-cloth jacket over her bathing suit. The police had brought her to the station right before her afternoon diving show.

"Miss Somers, we're not accusing you of murdering Mr. Harliss," Detective Burnett said patiently. "We just want to know about the pendant."

Nancy squeezed Dana's shoulder reassuringly. Earlier, Nancy had talked to Detective Cohen, answering his questions about finding Kirby. By now both Burnett and Cohen knew all about the incident last night at the wave pool, and about Kirby's accusations against Dana.

"I don't know why my pendant was in the kiddie pool," Dana choked out. "Someone must have stolen it from my locker."

She looked up, her eyes glittering with tears. "Look, I'll admit that Kirby and I planned those fake threats. I know it was a stupid way to get attention. We didn't want to hurt anyone!"

"My daughter is telling you the truth," Mrs. Somers said indignantly. "So why don't you let her go?"

"But someone did get hurt, Mrs. Somers. Murdered, in fact," Detective Cohen said brusquely. "Kirby was hit on the head, then drowned. And it seems more than a coincidence that he was involved in a tacky scheme with your daughter."

"I didn't kill him!" Dana insisted. She stared

pleadingly at Nancy. "Tell them, Nancy. Tell them I couldn't kill anyone."

Nancy took a deep breath. Dana's tears seemed genuine, but after all her other convincing performances, Nancy wasn't sure what to believe. Especially since Dana's pendant *was* at the scene of the crime.

"I think you'd better get a lawyer, Dana," she said instead.

Mrs. Somers picked up Dana's limp hand and squeezed it. "We'll get the best lawyer around," she promised. "Don't you worry, sweetheart. We'll prove you didn't do it. Your diving career won't be ruined. You can even make the Olympics."

Nancy was startled by Mrs. Somers's last statements. How could she be worried about Dana's diving career at a time like this?

"Miss Drew, we need to ask you to leave." Detective Cohen walked over to the office door and opened it.

Dana clutched at Nancy's shirt. "You'll help me, won't you, Nancy?"

Reluctantly, Nancy nodded. Then she quickly slipped through the door.

As soon as Bess saw Nancy, she rushed up. "What happened?"

"The police are questioning Dana," Nancy explained. "After the incident last night, they figure Dana has a motive. Kirby did expose her scheme in front of everyone. And, of course, there's the pendant."

Bess shook her head. "Wow. And to think we thought the mystery was solved."

"It turns out it's just the beginning." Nancy felt incredibly tired. Leaning against the wall, she went on. "Mrs. Somers is calling a lawyer. I'm pretty sure the police are going to charge Dana with murder."

Bess's brows shot up. "That's terrible!"

"You want to hear something else terrible? Mrs. Somers seemed most worried about what an arrest would do to Dana's diving career."

Bess raised one brow. "No wonder Dana sent herself those threatening letters. With Mrs. Somers for a mother, she must have been under tremendous pressure to succeed."

"You're not kidding. Now what we need to figure out is how far would Dana go to get ahead. Would she murder someone?"

"She *was* pretty angry last night," Bess said. "Maybe Kirby blurting out their scheme pushed Dana over the edge."

"I don't know if Dana is innocent or guilty," Nancy admitted. "But I'm going to find out who killed Kirby Harliss—even if it means implicating Dana."

* * *

"Wow," Joe said as he pulled into the Frobischers' driveway. "Emily Grant didn't mention that the family lived in a castle."

Frank leaned forward and looked through the windshield of their van. "It *is* rather impressive. But I imagine that Big Splash and Virginia Gardens are real moneymakers."

"And the family's been in the area since the sixteen hundreds. I guess you'd call that old money."

Joe drove slowly down the asphalt drive, admiring the view. The stately three-story brick home had been built on the banks of the James River. Willows, pines, and cottonwoods dotted the manicured lawn, which sloped to a dock jutting into the brown, gently rolling water. Two large powerboats were moored to the dock.

"Emily said Regina lived in a carriage house," Joe said, looking around. "There." He pointed to a quaint clapboard cottage partially hidden by overgrown bushes and flowering vines. Joe parked in the drive curving in front of the cottage.

Frank unbuckled his seat belt. "Let's find out why Regina called in sick today. My bet is that it has to do with our case."

"Maybe." Joe opened the car door. After spotting the dagger, he had to agree with his brother—Regina *was* hiding something. Still, he couldn't see her as a cold-blooded murderer.

"My hunch is that Professor Wykowski, who supposedly authenticated the pistols, is going to be the key to cracking our case. So let's hope the police can track him down."

"If there is a professor. What if he's part of the hoax? Anyone capable of replacing real weapons with replicas could also be capable of forging a letter of authenticity."

"True," Joe agreed. "Which means we still have to cover every lead. And I guess that means talking to Regina."

Not that Joe minded seeing Regina again. He just wished he were picking her up for a romantic picnic by the river instead of interviewing her about a murder.

Climbing from the van, he eyed the carriage house. A small, bright red sports car was parked by the side of it, but the curtains were drawn as if no one was home.

Frank was already striding up the two steps to the front door. He knocked, then rang the bell. Joe peered in a window, trying to spot a light or some movement behind the curtains, but the interior was dark.

"I hope nothing's wrong." Joe walked around to where the sports car was parked. A crumpled fast-food bag lay on the passenger seat.

Frank pounded on the door again, louder this time. "Regina?" he called. "It's Frank and Joe Hardy. We met you at the museum."

"I'll check to see if there's a back door," Joe said, growing worried. Had something happened to Regina?

"Wait, someone's coming." Frank gestured for him to return.

Joe bounded up the front steps. The door opened an inch, and Regina Frobischer peered through the crack.

"What do you want?" she asked warily. She looked sharply at Joe. "I told you I don't know anything about Colin's death."

"But we think you do," Joe said. "It's not just a coincidence that he was stabbed with the same kind of dagger that killed Mary Frobischer."

Regina's green eyes popped open, and she gasped. "How'd you—?"

"The museum exhibit," Frank told her.

For a second, Regina stood frozen, her face half hidden by the door. Joe knew he and Frank could go inside. All it would take was one good push. But Regina had to let them in. If she was going to tell them anything, she had to trust them. Finally, she opened the door, then stepped back into the shadows. As Joe passed by, he noticed she was bundled in a velour bathrobe, even though the house was warm. She wore no makeup, her auburn hair was tousled, and her eyes were bloodshot as if she'd been crying. Still, her smooth skin and long eyelashes reminded him of those of an antique porcelain doll.

"Are you all right?" he asked.

She nodded, then shook her head. "No. I called in sick because—because—I am *sick*. Sort of." She shut the door behind them. "I had a rough night and just woke up. I need breakfast. Would you like some? I have cereal and fresh blueberries."

Joe's mouth began to water. In all the excitement, they'd forgotten to eat. "That sounds terrific."

Regina led the way down a narrow hall into a tiny kitchen. Here the curtains weren't drawn, and sunlight flooded the room. It was filled with hanging plants and vases of flowers. A parakeet chirped from its cage.

Making kissing noises, Regina walked over and opened the cage door. "Good morning, Walter. Are you happy to see me?"

The parakeet hopped onto Regina's shoulder and nuzzled her cheek with its beak. Joe grinned, wishing he could trade places with the bird.

Frank was staring skeptically at Walter. "Gee, does Walter always sit on your shoulder when you make breakfast?"

"Only when we have company." Regina opened the refrigerator door. "Usually he walks around the table, eating my cereal."

Frank curled his lip. Joe slapped him on the back. "Hey, are you forgetting what you cooked us for breakfast? Toxic oatmeal."

"Here. Make yourself useful, soldier." Regina thrust a container of milk and blueberries into Joe's arms. Joe wondered why she'd decided to invite them in and fix them breakfast. He hoped it meant she trusted them enough to reveal her secrets.

"Does this mean you're going to tell us about Mary Frobischer and the dagger?" Frank asked as he sat in a kitchen chair.

Leaning forward, Regina pulled several boxes of cereal from a bottom cupboard. "Yes, though I still don't know how that will help you find your friend's killer." She straightened abruptly. "But that's why I tossed and turned all night." Her gaze darted from Frank to Joe. "I was trying to decide if there was a connection. I mean, Mary was killed more than two hundred years ago. So how could the identical daggers be a coincidence?"

"Good question." Joe dumped the blueberries into a colander and rinsed them off.

"Maybe together we can figure out the answer," Regina said. Joe thought she sounded sincere.

"Tell us about Mary," Frank prompted.

For a second, Regina stared out the window, and the only sound in the kitchen was Walter's throaty chirps. Joe finished rinsing the berries and set them on the kitchen table when he sat down.

"When the British occupied the city of Yorktown," Regina began, her eyes still riveted on the window, "they took over all the homes, including Mary and Josiah Frobischer's. Both were fierce patriots, but they stayed, pretending to be Tories so they could spy on MacDonald and his men. Mary would serve them dinner or clean their rooms, listening for any bit of information. She'd pass it on to Josiah, who had been forced to live in the stable. He'd then smuggle the information to General Washington."

Turning, Regina set the cereal boxes on the table along with bowls. Joe's stomach started to growl, but he hated to interrupt Regina's fascinating tale.

"One night Mary sneaked into Major MacDonald's bedroom to steal an important map. Only he woke up and caught her and brutally stabbed her in the back."

"With a dagger engraved with the date 1768," Joe said solemnly. "Just like the one that was used to kill Colin."

Regina frowned and bit her lip. "Yes," she whispered, sitting slowly in the chair next to him as if she were in a daze. "Just like Colin."

"Which can't be a coincidence." Frank propped his elbows on the table and leaned closer to Regina, his eyes narrowed.

Oh no, Joe thought. Frank had the same relentless look in his eye that he'd had when he first questioned Emily Grant. Joe knew his brother was wound up tight over Colin's murder, but he hoped Frank could remain cool. Otherwise, he'd blow this interview with Regina.

"Do you know what I think, Regina?" Frank asked. "I think you're guessing that someone in your family has killed Colin for revenge!"

Chapter Eleven

"No!" Regina jumped up from her seat, knocking over the colander of berries. Her cheeks were red with anger. "You're wrong—both of you!" She glared at Joe as if he'd betrayed her. "No one in my family murdered Colin."

"Then how do you explain the identical daggers?" Frank demanded.

"I can't!" Regina shouted, so loudly that Walter fluttered in the air before settling back on Regina's other shoulder.

Joe stuck his face in his brother's. "Back off, Frank," he growled. He couldn't believe that Frank had accused a Frobischer of murdering Colin. His brother was usually more levelheaded.

Frank put up his hands. "Okay. I apologize. But it's the only link I can see. After all, Regina, you were angry enough at Colin to slap him the other day. Maybe someone in your family was angry enough to kill him."

"Slapping Colin was impulsive and stupid," Regina said. "It's hard to explain why I did it."

Frank crossed his arms against his chest and leaned back in his chair. "Try."

Regina exhaled. Sitting down, she began picking up the blueberries and plopping them into the colander. Joe glared at Frank before he started to help her.

"Usually I live with my parents in California," Regina said. "I've visited my grandparents before, but this is the first time I've spent a whole summer with them. As I'm sure you've guessed, my grandparents are obsessed with their family history. I never paid much attention to it until I started working at the museum. Then I became fascinated, too. Especially with Mary Frobischer, who wasn't much older than me when she died. I'd fantasize about what it would be like if I was living during the siege of Yorktown. Would I have been brave enough to be a spy? Would I have risked my life for my country?"

"So when Colin told you he was related to the person who had killed Mary, you took it personally," Joe guessed.

Regina nodded. "Very. But that doesn't mean

someone in my family would kill anyone over the past. It was war. People died on both sides."

"But someone in your family could still hold a grudge. After all, not only was your ancestor killed, but your family home was devastated, too," Frank reminded her.

"True," Regina agreed. "But after the war, General Washington deeded five hundred acres to Josiah in return for the family's war contributions. The signed document is hanging in the museum."

"Is that how the Frobischers got the land for Big Splash and Virginia Gardens?" Joe asked.

"Yes," Regina replied. "Initially my family farmed the land, but then they helped make the whole Williamsburg area a prosperous tourist attraction."

"See, Frank." Joe punched his brother on the arm. "The Frobischers made out okay. Why would any of them hold a grudge?"

Frank exhaled slowly. "Still, I can't help but think that the identical daggers are a clue."

Joe reached for a blueberry, unable to ignore his rumbling stomach any longer. "I'm sure if Regina discovers anything that might help us catch Colin's killer, she'll tell us." He grinned at her over a box of cereal.

She grinned back. Walter ruffled his wings, and a blue feather floated to the table. Picking it up, Regina tucked it behind Joe's ear.

"Of course I will," she said. "I promise." She held up a box of cereal. "Now, how about breakfast?"

Twenty minutes later the Hardys headed to their van. Joe patted his stomach. The cereal and blueberries had tasted great.

Hesitating by the van door, Joe jingled his keys. He wished he'd lingered to say goodbye to Regina—and maybe ask her for a date.

"Start the van, Frank." Joe tossed him the keys. "I want to invite Regina for a camp dinner of burnt beef jerky and charred biscuits."

"No way." Frank tossed the keys right back. "She's still a suspect."

"A suspect!" Joe glowered at his brother. "You heard her explanation."

Frank opened the van door. "Maybe she didn't kill Colin for revenge. But aren't you forgetting she works at the museum? She could be in cahoots with the forgers."

"That's a stretch, Frank."

"No, it's not. You're just swayed by her big green eyes." Grinning, Frank stepped into the car.

"Don't forget her great legs," Joe muttered. He jerked open the door. A piece of folded paper was lying on the driver's seat. "Hey, what's this?"

Joe climbed into the car, then opened the paper and skimmed the message. "Hey, Frank,"

Joe said, waving the paper. "A visitor left us a note while we were inside. This might be the breakthrough we've been looking for."

"What's it say?"

"'If you want to find out who killed your friend,'" Joe read out loud, "'meet me on the *Godspeed* at the Jamestown Settlement this afternoon at four. P.S. I'll find you.'"

Frank jumped out of the van and began looking around.

Joe climbed out, too. Except for a flock of geese on the lawn, the place appeared deserted. "Whoever it was is hardly going to stick around. And since we were in the back of the cottage, we wouldn't have heard a car drive up."

"True." Frank continued to scan the grounds. "But I don't like the idea of someone following us. That means the person knows we're investigating Colin's death."

"Then we'd better go to Jamestown," Joe told his brother. "And find out if this mystery person really knows who killed Colin."

"Do you really think Dana might be innocent?" Bess asked Nancy as they walked along the second-floor balcony of a motel.

"I believe a person is innocent until proven guilty. And besides, I promised Dana and her mother I'd help." Nancy found the room she was looking for—number 216. It was Kirby's room—where he'd been living for the past month. Nancy hoped she and Bess might find some clue that pointed to a killer other than Dana.

Glancing nervously around the seedy motel, Bess shivered. "I hate it when you do this kind of stuff," she whispered. "What if somebody catches us snooping in his room?"

"If we work quickly, nobody will." A maid pushed a cleaning cart around the corner. "Excuse me, miss," Nancy called. "We locked our key inside. Can you open the door for us?" Reaching into the pocket of her shorts, Nancy pulled out five dollars and held it up.

Without even looking at them, the maid unlocked the door.

"So much for security," Bess said under her breath.

"Thank you." Nancy pressed the five dollars into the woman's hand, then pushed the door open. The room smelled musty and damp, and even though the air conditioner was blasting away, it was warm and sticky.

"Ugh." Bess wrinkled her nose as she surveyed Kirby's room. "How can anyone live in a motel room for a summer?"

"For the great room service?" Nancy joked. Pulling latex gloves from her purse, she slipped them on. "Here, put these on." She handed Bess another pair, then went over to Kirby's dresser.

Pulling open the drawers, she rifled through his clothes, which were mostly shorts and T-shirts. "Why don't you check the closet? We've got to work fast—before the police show up."

Bess gasped. "The police?"

"Yeah. They might decide to get a search warrant."

"Oh, great," Bess muttered to herself as she opened the closet door. "Yuck. What a mess. What are we looking for, anyway?"

"I'm not sure," Nancy replied. "We know Dana and Kirby worked together. But maybe there's something to suggest that Kirby had another enemy. Someone else who might have killed him."

"Hey, here's a stack of magazines," Bess called, squatting on the closet floor. "They've got letters cut out of them."

"Dana and Kirby must have used them for the threats." Nancy closed the drawers and crossed the room to the bedside table. A slip of paper was tucked underneath the telephone. She pulled it out, her breath catching when she read the message: "Meet Susan 7."

Meet Susan?

"Bess! I found something!"

"What?" Bess closed the closet door and came over. "What do you think it means?" she asked after reading the message.

Nancy tapped the paper on her palm, then slid

it back under the telephone. "I'm not sure. Maybe Kirby met Susan this morning at seven."

Bess's mouth dropped open. "You mean *Susan* murdered Kirby?"

"Or maybe she met him last night at seven, before the pretend drowning, or else she was supposed to meet him tonight."

Slowly, Bess closed her mouth. "Wow. Confusing, huh."

Nancy nodded. "Yes. I think my apology to Susan might have been a bit hasty. She could have swiped Dana's pendant from her locker and left it in the pool to frame her. With Dana out of the way, Susan would have gotten what she wanted—to be star of the show." Nancy pulled off her gloves with a snap. "Come on, Bess, let's go find her. She has some explaining to do."

Half an hour later, Nancy and Bess wound their way through a crowd of spectators leaving the diving show.

"I hope she hasn't left already," Bess said as they entered the amphitheater. Nancy and Bess went down the steps to the stage, which looked empty. Then Nancy spotted Tommy hurrying down the walkway toward the locker room.

Bess waved and called his name, but he didn't turn around. "I guess he didn't hear me," she said with a shrug.

"It's just as well," Nancy said. "We're here to talk to Susan, not flirt with Tommy." Nancy grinned at Bess when she noticed her blush. Bess had talked nonstop about the terrific time she and Tommy had had at the party the other night.

As they rounded the pool, passing beside the tower, a *whooshing* noise made Nancy glance up. A baton was hurtling from the tower's platform, pointed right for Bess's head!

Chapter Twelve

"LOOK OUT!" Nancy shoved her friend with both hands, sending her sprawling. The baton missed Nancy's shoulder by an inch, bounced to the concrete, then rolled to the ladder.

"What in the world!" Bess exclaimed as she pushed herself into a sitting position. Her eyes widened when she saw the baton. "Where did that come from?"

Nancy pointed to the top of the tower, then reached down to help Bess to her feet. "Luckily, I heard it coming."

"That's for sure." Bess wiped her palms on her shorts, then leaned back, looking skyward. "Do you think it's Susan's? And if so, what was it doing up there? How did it fall?"

"Good questions, Bess." Nancy handed Bess her purse. "Hold this while I climb up to see if I can find some answers. That baton didn't just fall by accident. Someone was aiming for us."

Grabbing the rung above her head, Nancy started to climb the tower. When her head finally rose above the platform, she heaved a sigh of relief—she'd reached the top. But her relief didn't last long. Looking over the edge, she caught her breath as she noticed how high up she was.

Gripping the sides of the ladder tightly, Nancy peered across the flat platform. At the edge, she spotted a blob of gray the size of a silver dollar. A smooth tubular-shaped crease was in the middle, as if the baton had been shoved into it. When she touched the blob, it felt sticky. Putty?

Nancy craned her neck. She could easily see the amphitheater's entrance. Someone coming into the theater, unless he or she was intentionally looking at the top of the tower, would not notice her.

That meant someone could have spotted them, rigged the baton, and climbed down the ladder. A hard shake on the tower would have dislodged the baton at the right moment.

Tricky, but possible.

As Nancy climbed down, she remembered seeing Tommy run off. Was he involved with

Kirby's murder? And if so, how did he get Susan's baton?

Instead of answers, I now have more questions, Nancy thought. But then, solving a murder was never easy.

"I'm glad our mystery writer invited us to meet him at the Jamestown Settlement," Frank said as the two brothers strolled through James Fort. It was a re-creation of the English fort built by the first settlers in 1607. "This is really interesting."

"Virginia Gardens doesn't have any exhibits on Jamestown," Joe said. "Though the Powhatan Indian Village is similar."

Lifting a reproduction of a military helmet from a hook on the wall of the guardhouse, Joe put it on. It was dome-shaped and made of a heavy gray metal. "Good protection," Joe said, rapping on the top. Pretending to hold a musket, he marched back and forth in front of Frank. "Though it weighs a ton. I bet the English soldiers got some major headaches." Taking off the helmet, he handed it to an interested group of kids.

Frank glanced at his watch. "It's about a quarter to four. Let's head to the ships."

The Hardys hurried to the fort entrance, past thatched houses made from wattle and daub.

"How will we know our contact?" Joe asked.

"We won't." Frank scanned the three ships tied to the wharf on the James River. "He'll know us. I wonder which ship the *Godspeed* is."

Joe opened his visitor's guide. "It's the middle ship. 'The *Susan Constant,* the *Godspeed,* and the *Discovery* are reproductions of the three vessels that brought the first settlers to Virginia in 1607,'" he read aloud as they strode down the walkway.

"'The voyage took two to four months. Because of overcrowding and poor nutrition, many of the crew and passengers suffered illnesses or died.'" Joe grimaced. "Gee, sounds like fun."

When they reached the wharf, the wooden planks thudded under their feet. It was packed with camera-toting tour groups, and the late-afternoon sun was hot and bright. Frank stopped in front of the *Godspeed,* gazing up at the high masts. The ship was almost seventy feet long, with a mainmast about fifty feet tall. Rigging crisscrossed the boat from stern to hull and mast to deck.

"Let's spread out," Frank suggested. "Just in case our mystery person has something in mind besides a friendly meeting."

Frank boarded the boat, joining the group on the main deck who were listening to a young guide dressed in a seafaring costume from the 1600s. Joe had climbed a set of stairs leading from the main deck to the stern, which rose fifteen feet from the river. Holding on to some rigging, he was gazing over the water like a navigator directing the ship's course.

"Moldy biscuits, watery beer, and maggoty beef," the guide was telling someone who'd asked a question about food. "Occasionally, the ships stopped in the Caribbean, where they picked up wild boar, sea tortoises, and fresh fruits."

The guide moved toward an arched doorway. "Now let's go down to the 'tween deck. That's where the passengers spent most of their time."

Frank waved his hand to catch Joe's eye, then pointed below. He thought the mystery person might want to make contact in a less conspicuous place.

He climbed down the steps behind a woman carrying a tired toddler. It was darker below the main deck, and he had to stop to let his eyes adjust.

Someone jostled him roughly, then thrust a piece of paper into his hand. Frank fell against a cannon. When he righted himself, he saw a guy about his age hurrying up the steps to the main deck. Frank glanced quickly at the paper.

"I think I'm being followed," the note said. It had been scrawled on a page ripped from the visitor's guide. "Meet me at the Powhatan Village. Be careful."

Whirling around, Frank sprinted up the steps.

A new group of tourists was boarding the ship. He strained to see around them, but he couldn't find the guy he was looking for anywhere. Frank glanced again at the note. If someone was following the mystery man, that person could be watching him, too.

Nonchalantly, Frank made his way to the Great Cabin as if to inspect the captain's sleeping quarters. He glanced around at the stern, wondering where Joe was. They needed to get to the Powhatan Village.

"Joe!" Frank called, trying to find his brother among the tourists. Suddenly, he heard a strangled cry. At the same time, a guy flew overboard, arms spread-eagled.

It was Joe!

Chapter Thirteen

"JOE!" FRANK RAN to the side of the ship and watched in horror as Joe plummeted fifteen feet, disappearing into the greenish brown water below.

Panic seized him. Frank knew Joe was a strong swimmer, but he had no idea how deep the water was. What if his brother had plunged headfirst into a muddy river bottom?

Around him, the crowd chattered excitedly as they pointed toward the water. Frank kicked off his shoes and, grasping a line, climbed onto the ship's railing. He was ready to jump in after Joe, when he saw bubbles rise and the top of Joe's head bob to the surface.

"Are you all right?" he called down.

"Don't worry about me!" Joe sputtered. "Get the guy in the yellow T-shirt. He pushed me overboard!"

Frank spun around. Barefoot, he tore across the main deck and over the gangplank, then scanned the wharf for a guy in a yellow shirt among the tourists.

The guy was gone. Angrily, Frank smacked his fist against his palm. Two sailors jogged down the wharf toward a ladder between the ships. Frank retrieved his shoes, then hurried after them. Joe was swimming around the hull of the *Godspeed,* heading toward the ladder.

He climbed up, dripping wet and mad.

"Are you all right, sir?" one of the sailors asked nervously. Grabbing Joe's elbow, he helped him onto the wharf.

"He's fine," Frank assured him. "Don't worry, we're not going to sue or anything."

The two sailors looked at each other with relieved expressions. "I must say, we've had people slip on steps and gangplanks, but you're the first person to fall into the water." One of the sailors handed Joe a towel.

Frank bit back a grin. "Yeah. My poor brother's definitely got two left feet."

Joe shot him an annoyed look. When the sailors went back to the ship, Joe turned to Frank. "I can't believe I let the guy get the jump on me. One second I'm gazing across the water, pretending I'm captain of the ship, and the next I'm freefalling into it."

"You didn't recognize the guy?" Frank asked.

Joe shook his head. "I glimpsed a yellow shirt and two hairy arms, then *wham,* I was flying overboard. You didn't see him run off?"

"No. The place was too crowded. And I lost the mystery man, too." Frank handed him the note.

"What!" Joe skimmed it, then crumpled it in his fist. "Come on, let's get to the Powhatan Village. Maybe it's not too late for our rendezvous."

The Hardys jogged up the hill, past the rest rooms and gardens, and into the woods. The Powhatan Village consisted of several dome-shaped longhouses spread out among the towering trees.

"They're called *yehakins*," Joe read from the guidebook. "They were made by bending saplings and covering them with mats woven from reeds. Maybe our man's hiding out in one of them."

"Interesting," Frank murmured, though he was only half listening. He desperately wanted to find the guy who'd given him the message.

He went into one of the *yehakins*. It was cool and dark, with a dirt floor. Low wooden frames covered with furs lined the inside walls.

"Hey, Frank, get a load of this," Joe said,

holding up a skunk pelt. "They must have used this thing for a pillow."

Frank couldn't help but laugh as he ducked through the open doorway and left the longhouse. In the shady hamlet, several guides dressed in Native American costume talked with a few scattered tourists. The mystery man was not among them.

He must have been scared off, Frank thought. Not that he blamed the guy for being cautious. Obviously, someone was after the Hardys, and the mystery guy didn't want to get caught.

Joe joined Frank. "You know what I think?" he said. "I think the whole thing was a setup."

"A setup?"

"I think our man lured us to Jamestown so the thugs could rough us up," Joe said. "A warning to quit nosing into Colin's murder."

"I don't agree," Frank said. "For one thing, you were the only one 'roughed up.' If our letter writer was in on it, why didn't he whack me when he had a chance?"

Joe shrugged. "I don't know. But whoever the mystery guy is, he's giving me the creeps. Why is he so afraid to contact us? Why the secrecy?"

"Because obviously someone's after him, too." Frank scanned the peaceful hamlet. A sparrow hopped into a basket of ground corn, stole a crushed kernel, and flew off. "But one thing's for sure," he added in a low voice. "Someone's getting mighty edgy. That means we must be on the right track."

Nancy twirled the baton as she headed for the divers' locker room. It was late afternoon. Bess was waiting outside to meet Tommy and confirm her dinner date with him. Nancy was hoping to catch Susan before the last diving show.

Pushing open the door of the women's locker room, she smiled to herself. Nancy couldn't wait to see Susan's reaction.

"Where did you get that?" Susan asked when Nancy handed her the baton.

"You don't know?" Nancy asked.

"It was in my locker. I put it there after my last show." Susan jumped up and opened her locker door. "At least it *was* in here. How did you get it?"

Nancy cocked an eyebrow. Either Susan was a great actress, or she really hadn't known it was missing.

"Bess and I discovered it when we passed by the tower earlier. It was hard to miss since it was falling from the platform—heading straight for Bess's head."

Susan inhaled sharply. "What are you talking about?"

"Someone rigged it to fall off the platform."

"But who? Why?"

Nancy narrowed her eyes. "I was hoping you might tell us."

Susan gasped. "You think I put it up there? No way! Someone must have stolen it. My combination's no secret. Hey—" Susan's puzzled expression suddenly turned to anger. "Now I get it. You're trying to get me in trouble—to frame me so you can get dear Dana off the hook. Well, if you ask me, after that scene at the party, she was the only one who had a reason to kill Kirby."

"Oh, really?" Nancy smiled innocently. "Then how come Kirby was supposed to meet *you* at seven?"

The blood drained from Susan's face. "What are you talking about?"

"I'm referring to the note in Kirby's motel room." Nancy propped her arm against the locker. "A note the police would love to see. Tell me, Susan, why did you meet Kirby that morning? To murder him?"

"Murder him!" Susan choked out. "No. And I didn't even meet him that morning. It was the night before."

Nancy held her breath. So she was right about one thing—Susan and Kirby had been in contact. "You met him at seven the night Kirby tried to drown Dana?"

Susan slumped to the bench. "Yes."

Nancy slowly sat next to her. She pressed her lips together, waiting for Susan to speak first.

Just then, a door swung open. Bess walked in, a silly grin plastered on her face.

Susan glanced up, then stared back down at her bare feet. "It's not the way it seems," she said dejectedly. "I didn't have anything to do with Kirby's murder, or with the baton falling on you. It's just that . . ." She hesitated.

"It's just that you were jealous of Dana?" Nancy suggested.

Susan nodded. "She's an excellent diver. And she did beat me this spring—regularly. The other day, I caught Kirby sneaking into the locker room to put something in Dana's purse. When I confronted him, he told me the whole story of how he and Dana had cooked up the threatening letters and the accident during the show. I promised not to tell on him, because—"

When she looked up at Nancy, tears glittered in her eyes. "Because I figured I could use Kirby, too. To *really* scare Dana. He was lonely and gullible. It didn't take much to convince him that Dana was only using him. I told him that she thought he was a dork and that she'd dump him once she was a big star."

"Do you really think that was true?" Nancy asked.

"Of course. Dana thought she was better than everybody. The night of the party, I met Kirby at seven. I told him the best way to get back at Dana was to really scare her during the pretend drowning. Then, later, we could stage another near-accident—make her really lose her nerve."

"Only Kirby got caught," Nancy guessed.

"Right. Afterward, I called Kirby and told him to forget our plan. It was too risky to stage another accident. Only he wouldn't listen. He was furious at Dana for turning on him at the party, and he was determined to get back at her."

"Did he say how?" Nancy asked.

Susan shook her head, her shiny hair swinging over her cheeks. "No. I hung up. I wanted nothing more to do with him." She looked up at Nancy, her eyes pleading. "You've got to believe me. I was only playing Dana's game. I didn't think anyone would get hurt."

"Or murdered," Bess added grimly.

Nancy stood up. "You know the police are going to find that note in Kirby's motel room."

Susan's face went white with fear. "No! Can't you get the note for me?" She grabbed Nancy's hand and pressed it between her palms. "I'll do anything!"

With a frown, Nancy withdrew her hand. "No, I can't get the note. And the best thing you can do is tell the police the truth."

Susan jumped up, her cheeks flushed angrily. "You witch. I can't believe you'd help that murdering Dana but not me."

"We don't know she's a murderer," Bess declared.

"Oh, really?" Susan smiled smugly. "She had tons of motivation. In fact, I bet she killed Kirby when she found out he turned against her. Plenty of people know how spiteful she can be. Just ask Tommy Waldhauser—the other boyfriend she used, then dumped. He'll tell you that Dana would do anything to get ahead. *Anything!*"

"Tommy?" Bess cried out. "Tommy was Dana's boyfriend?"

Susan nodded. "Yeah. Hot and heavy. Until he figured out Miss Ambition only liked him because he was the team captain. When he told her he wasn't going to give her special treament, she dumped him like a bag of stinky garbage."

Nancy frowned. The more she heard about Dana, the more she sounded guilty. *If* Susan was telling the truth.

"Tommy vowed to get even," Susan added. "In fact, framing her for a murder would be a great way of getting even, don't you think?" She looked at Nancy with a cocky grin.

Bess's cheeks burned red. "Tommy wouldn't do that," she sputtered.

Nancy wasn't so sure. Dana was in jail, so obviously she couldn't have rigged the baton. That meant somebody else was involved in Kirby's murder. Did Tommy hate Dana enough to set her up? Nancy eyed Susan. No matter how hard the diver protested her innocence over

Kirby's death, Nancy couldn't ignore the fact that she had conspired with Kirby to scare Dana during the fake drowning. Susan was ambitious, too, and she clearly had her own dark side.

"I don't believe you about Tommy," Bess declared. Turning, she headed for the exit. "Come on, Nancy. Let's get out of here."

"Yes, please leave." Susan took the baton from Nancy and twirled it expertly. "I have to rehearse."

Without a word, Nancy left. She hoped her silence would make Susan nervous and show her that she wasn't off the hook yet. If Susan was guilty of something besides jealousy, she just might become anxious enough to make a mistake.

Once outside, Bess whirled to face Nancy. "You don't believe her about Tommy!"

"Bess," Nancy said with a sigh, "you know when I'm on a case, I suspect everybody. After the show, we'll talk to Tommy and see what he has to say about Dana. Aren't you meeting him for dinner?"

Bess nodded glumly.

"Don't worry," Nancy said reassuringly. "If he's innocent, he won't mind my questions. And I promise I won't hang around. I've got a dinner date myself—with Joe and Frank."

Bess rolled her eyes. "All right. But what a

romantic way to start a date—pumping someone about a murder!"

"Are you still convinced that forged Revolutionary War artifacts are the key to Colin's murder?" Joe asked Frank. He was headed for the motel bathroom, a towel wrapped around his waist.

Joe was sweaty from the reenactment. His mouth tasted like dust, and his eyes stung from the smoky gunpowder. A hot shower was going to feel great.

The Hardys had finished their last demonstration at Virginia Gardens. Instead of going back to New York with the rest of their battalion, they had checked into a motel. Joe knew that Frank wasn't about to leave without solving his friend's murder. Emily Grant had called earlier, and they'd set up a meeting with her. Joe hoped she would have some more information for them.

"Yup," Frank said, answering Joe's question about the artifacts. "I bet someone operated a black market ring using the Frobischer museum as a front." Frank pulled clean shorts and shirt from his suitcase—he'd already showered. "That's why this meeting with Emily Grant is important. She may have uncovered something. Then we've got to meet Nancy at Big Splash. I'd like to discuss the case with her. Maybe she can look at all the evidence with a fresh mind."

Joe snorted. "What evidence? Me falling into the James River? She already knows I'm a nut for cheap thrills."

"You're right," Frank said, frowning. "We don't have much to go on." Frank tugged on a T-shirt, messing up his damp hair. "Let's just hope Emily has some good news."

Half an hour later, the Hardys were crammed into Emily Grant's messy office. The museum curator was shaking her head in disbelief.

"I don't believe it." She held several pages from the fax machine in her hands. "I've had five responses from experts at different colleges and museums. Not one of them authenticated artifacts from this museum. That means the letters of authentication were forged. The signatures were forged."

Disgusted, she threw up her hands, and the pages went fluttering to the dusty floor.

"You mean Professor Wykowski from that college in Ohio never even saw Major MacDonald's pistols?" Frank asked.

"That's correct." With a weary groan, Emily slumped into her desk chair.

Joe scooped up the papers. After skimming the faxes, he handed the one from Wykowski to Frank. "According to Wykowski," Joe explained, "he has no idea what Emily Grant is talking about. He never received pistols from the museum. In fact, he's never even heard of Frobischer House."

"What a nightmare. That means everything in the museum could be fake!"

Looking as dejected as Emily, Frank crossed his arms over his chest and leaned against a file cabinet. "The former curator, Dr. Chan, must have been as phony as a three-dollar bill," he grumbled. "Only how did he get away with it? And who was he working with?"

"Since the good doctor is conveniently dead," Joe pointed out, "we can't ask him. That's going to make tracking down our bad guys tough."

Emily sighed. "I'll help any way I can. I mean, obviously my career is over." Removing her glasses, she carefully polished them, her brow furrowed. "My colleagues will laugh themselves silly when they find out I've been in charge of a collection of fakes."

"What are you going to tell the Frobischers?" Joe asked her.

"Nothing!" Frank said vehemently, answering for her. "We've got to keep this to ourselves. We can't even tell the police. If the information leaks out that we're onto their scheme, the culprits might run. Then we'll never find Colin's killer."

For a second, Joe and Emily were silent. Joe couldn't help but think that Frank was wrong. If Colin was killed because he discovered that two pistols were fake, what would the murderers do to a curator who suspected an entire collection was filled with fakes?

"The police *should* know, Frank," Joe told his brother. "At least they can give Emily some protection."

"Don't worry about me," Emily said, putting on her glasses. "We probably should contact the police, but I want to catch these—these"—her voice was full of anger as she groped for the right word—"deceivers! In fact, I'm going to go through every folder, file, and shelf. There's got to be some clue here."

Frank patted her shoulder. "Thanks. We need all the help we can get."

Reaching forward, she pulled a musket off a pile of papers stacked on her desk. "What's really sad is that I've found forgeries sprinkled throughout every display. Here, let me show you."

Joe moved closer. The musket was similar to the replicas carried during the reenactment. But since it came from the museum collection, it was supposed to be more than two hundred years old.

"Beautiful, isn't it?" Mrs. Grant ran her fingers down the barrel. "Only this morning, when I took it to a friend of mine who's a firearms expert, he quickly pointed out that the wood on the grip has been chemically aged."

Joe whistled. "Wow. I never would have guessed. The forger must be an expert."

"How much would an authentic musket from the Revolutionary War sell for?" Frank asked.

"A collector might pay more than seven thousand for one in excellent condition, while this replica would be worth about five hundred."

"That's more than six thousand dollars in profit," Joe said, sauntering back to the doorway and leaning against the jamb. "Just on one item. Imagine the profit from—"

Behind him a floorboard squeaked in the hall. Joe fell silent. A group of tourists? He glanced over his shoulder just in time to see someone dressed like a rifleman whirl away from the office door.

Instantly, Joe tensed. Someone—not a tourist—had been listening!

"Hey!" he called, taking off down the hall. "Wait a minute!"

The rifleman hit the stairs at a dead run. As Joe ran after him, his heart raced with excitement. It had to be the person behind the forgeries. Maybe even Colin's murderer! Who else would be spying on them?

With a burst of speed, Joe leaped to the bottom of the steps. The rifleman tore through a crowd of tourists, pushing them aside rudely.

"Stop!" Joe hollered. When the rifleman paid no attention, Joe gritted his teeth and went for it. Diving forward, he tackled the rifleman around the legs. They both went down, sprawling at the feet of the confused, milling tourists.

"Gotcha!" Joe scrambled to his knees, straddling the rifleman. Reaching up, he grabbed the guy's shoulder and flipped him over roughly.

The rifleman's tricornered hat fell off, and auburn hair spilled out from it. Joe jerked upright in surprise. It wasn't a *him* at all. It was Regina Frobischer he'd tackled to the ground!

Chapter Fourteen

"Get off me, Joe Hardy, you big creep!" Regina pummeled his chest with both fists.

Joe was so shocked to see Regina in the rifleman outfit that he almost sputtered an apology and jumped up. Then he remembered why he'd been chasing her in the first place.

Grabbing her wrists, he held her flailing arms still. "Not until you explain why you were snooping around Emily Grant's office."

"I was not snooping!" Regina spat out, furious. "I work here, remember?"

"Regina? Joe? What's going on?" Emily Grant hurried down the steps, with Frank right behind her. Joe glanced up at them, noticing that the tourists were hovering around.

"We're just acting out a page in history," he told the curious group. Nodding and chattering excitedly, several people quickly raised their cameras to shoot pictures.

Regina craned her neck to see the photographers. "I want copies of those pictures for evidence!" she shouted.

"Joe, would you let her up?" Frank said.

"Sure," Joe answered. "As soon as she tells me why she was listening in on our conversation."

"I'm not saying a word until you let me up." Pressing her lips together in a tight line, Regina scowled at him.

Joe scowled back. Regina Frobischer had to be the most stubborn girl he'd ever met. Exhaling loudly, he stood up, offering her his hand. "All right. I'm sorry I knocked you down."

Ignoring his outstretched hand, Regina sat up. She plopped her hat back on her head, adjusted her fringed hunting shirt, then gracefully got to her feet.

Now that Joe had a chance to look at her, he couldn't believe he'd mistaken her for a guy. Even the baggy shirt couldn't hide her petite, curvy build.

"Well?" Joe prompted.

Regina set her hands on her hips. "I don't have to explain any—"

"Regina," Emily Grant cut in, her tone no-nonsense. "Come upstairs to my office."

Startled by the sharp voice, Regina closed her mouth and followed the curator up the steps. Joe glanced at Frank, who shrugged and headed after them.

"Now, what's this about listening in on our conversation?" Emily asked as soon as the four of them were jammed in her office with the door shut. Joe found himself squashed against Regina—not that it was such a terrible place to be, he decided. He was especially enjoying the scent of her perfume mixed with the smell of her leather shirt.

"I wasn't listening in," Regina protested. "I came up to talk with you about scheduling a large group."

Joe cocked one brow. "Sure. Then why did you run off like a scared rabbit?"

"Because . . ." Regina began, but then her voice faltered. Her eyes darted to Emily, then Frank. "Okay. I did overhear parts of your conversation. I was about to knock when I heard Emily say that the letters of authentication were bogus. I heard her tell you about the musket. And I especially heard the part where *you"*—she pointed an accusing finger at Frank "—told Emily not to tell my grandfather and grandmother that stuff in the museum is fake."

"Then you heard my reasons, too," Frank said.

Regina nodded. "But my grandparents still need to know about something that affects them so deeply. Frobischer House is their pride and joy!" Her voice rose, and her green eyes snapped indignantly.

Joe realized he was wrong to accuse Regina of spying. She had overheard accidentally, and she was right—the Frobischers should know about the forgeries.

"But that would blow our whole investigation," Frank said, his voice deadly serious. "And right now, I couldn't care less about a ruined museum collection. The important thing is to find my friend's murderer."

"Oh." Regina's anger dissolved instantly. "I didn't look at it that way. I was being selfish. Still, maybe my grandparents could help? They left the operation of the museum to Dr. Chan, but they might know something."

Frank shook his head. "They might, but I don't want to talk to them yet. I'm afraid if too many people get involved, we're going to scare off the killer."

"He's right," Joe said. "But I agree with you also, Regina. Your grandparents should know as soon as possible."

"That will be my job, though, young lady." Emily shook her finger at Regina. "Since your grandparents hired me to oversee their collection, I'll explain what's happened when I have all the proof in my hands."

"Okay." Regina seemed mollified. "But I want

to be there when you explain it to them. They're going to be devastated when they hear that their prize collection has been replaced with fakes." With a sigh, she stroked the barrel of the musket lying on the desk. "Ever since I was little, they've told me stories about Josiah and Mary Frobischer and how they risked their lives during the Revolutionary War. Frobischer House and its contents are a memorial to them."

"Hey, maybe when we crack this case, we'll find the original artifacts. Until then"—Joe took Regina's hand between his palms—"thank you for keeping this mum. Would dinner and an evening at Big Splash help you feel better?"

Frank groaned, then grinned. "Romeo to the rescue."

"I'd love dinner." Regina laughed. "Actually, when you tackled me, it was pretty funny." She looked up at him with her big eyes. "And the tourists loved it. Too bad you weren't wearing a redcoat uniform. We could have put on a great act!"

"Tommy will be here. He just got delayed," Bess insisted as she paced in front of the outdoor eating area at Big Splash. She was dressed for her dinner date in a miniskirt, a scoop-necked blouse, and sandals. Seashell earings dangled to her shoulders, and her hair hung soft and shiny against her neck.

It was a hot night, so Nancy had worn shorts and a tank top over her bathing suit. Her hair was pulled loosely up in a barrette so the breeze could cool her neck.

"He will!" Stopping in her tracks, Bess shot Nancy an angry look, as if daring her to disagree.

Wisely, Nancy kept her mouth shut. Tommy was already twenty minutes late. Glancing around the umbrella-shaded tables, she searched one more time for the team captain, but he was nowhere in sight.

Had Susan told him about the conversation in the locker room? Had Tommy split because he knew Nancy wanted to talk to him?

"Nan!" Frank Hardy waved as he came down the walkway. He wore jeans shorts and a blue T-shirt with a picture of a surfer on the front. Behind him, Joe walked hand in hand with a girl. Nancy recognized her immediately. It was Regina Frobischer, the girl who had rescued her the night Kirby attacked her in the wave pool.

Nancy waved them over to an empty table, then sat down in one of the chairs. It was a sticky night. A swim later on would feel great.

After the five teens had ordered, Frank filled Nancy and Bess in on Emily Grant's news.

"So you were right about the pistols being fakes," Nancy said. "But are you sure that what's going on at the museum is connected to Colin's murder?"

"I'm not positive. But what else could it be? The police interviewed everybody in the British reenactment group. Colin was well liked and squeaky clean. He didn't even owe anyone money."

"We still haven't accounted for our mystery man," Joe said.

"Mystery man!" Regina's eyes lit up. She wore a lemon yellow beach shift over her swimsuit. Nancy could see why Joe was attracted to her, but was it safe to tell her everything?

Joe described the encounter at the Jamestown Settlement with such dramatic flair that he had everyone laughing, including Bess, who had been gloomily biting her fingernails. Nancy was glad to see that Tommy wasn't going to ruin Bess's whole night.

"After a dunking in the James, I guess you won't want to swim tonight," Regina teased.

Joe grinned. "You mean try the water rides? I can't wait."

"I think that's a good idea," Nancy agreed. "We need to take our minds off murder—and other things." She looked pointedly at Bess.

"Yeah," Bess said, slumping lower in her seat. The waitress came over and set a huge plate of french fries in front of her.

Bess frowned. "I didn't order fries. They must be someone else's."

"They're yours. Compliments of the guy over there." The waitress jerked her thumb over her shoulder.

Bess spun around in her chair. Tommy waved from the counter. Shoving his hands into his jeans pockets, he came over, a sheepish grin on his tan face.

"Hi." Standing next to Bess's chair, he nodded to the group. Bess was smiling so hard that Nancy thought her friends cheeks would snap.

"Uh, Bess, how about introducing us?" Joe said, chuckling.

"Oh, right. Umm, guys, this is Tommy Waldhauser, captain of the diving team." After Bess had introduced everybody, Tommy pulled up an extra chair and straddled it backward. The waitress brought food, and for the next few minutes everyone was passing ketchup and munching burgers.

Finally, Tommy cleared his throat. "I guess I owe you an explanation," he said, directing his words to Nancy and Bess. "Susan told me about your conversation in the locker room. She said you're determined to find someone besides Dana to pin a murder rap on."

"That's not true," Nancy protested. "I'm just trying to sort out the facts."

"Whatever." Tommy plucked a fry from the plate and slowly chewed it. "Well, I was with Phil

Yancey the morning Kirby was killed. My car's in the shop, and he gave me a ride over here—picked me up at my apartment at seven. We went to HoJo's for breakfast and arrived at Big Splash the same time as the police."

Nancy dabbed her lips with her napkin. "So, why didn't you just tell me?"

Still chewing the fry, Tommy glanced sideways at Bess, a guilty expression on his face. "Because most of what Susan said was true. At a party one night, Dana dumped me—big time—right in front of everybody. Told me I dove like a pelican with a busted wing." His gaze shifted to Nancy. "She made me so mad, I did threaten to get even with her."

"And did you?"

He didn't look away. "No. The next morning, I woke up to the fact that she had been using me. She thought since I was team captain, I'd give her more stage time. Well, I wouldn't. That's why she dumped me. I was mad, but I also knew I was better off without her. Besides, I barely knew Kirby. Why would I want to kill him?"

Nancy wondered the same thing. She turned her attention back to Regina, Joe, and Frank, who were discussing the water rides. Out of the corner of her eye, Nancy saw Tommy take Bess's hand.

"Sorry I was late," he apologized in a low

voice. "But I had to think things through. Dana and I had had an ugly fight. I knew, sooner or later, that someone would interview me."

Bess smiled and whispered something back to him, and Nancy knew he was forgiven. But was he telling the truth? His explanation seemed almost too neat and well rehearsed.

Suddenly, Frank nudged her with his elbow. "Eat up, Nan, and quit worrying about your case. Tonight we're going to cut loose and try Jungle Falls."

"Jungle Falls?"

"You'll love it!" Regina exclaimed. "A half mile of twists and turns through a tropical jungle filled with real animals and birds. My grandparents designed it for me. When I was little, I loved to visit the zoo."

Joe grinned. "Nothing like having grandparents who grant your every wish," he teased.

Regina threw a french fry at him. "Watch it, Hardy," she said playfully, "or you might find yourself face-to-face with a real tiger."

"Well, I'm ready to try Jungle Falls," Nancy said. Frank was right. She needed to push sleuthing from her mind—at least for the night.

Forty minutes later the teens had on swimsuits and were standing at the head of the line for Jungle Falls. A warm, sticky breeze rustled the palms.

Tilting her head back, Nancy tried to spot the parrots and monkeys she could hear squawking and chattering in the treetops. Finally, she caught a glimpse of a furry animal scurrying down a limb, but only a glimpse.

They're as hard to see as the solution to my mystery, she thought as she stepped closer to the rushing water. Most of the rides at Big Splash consisted of flowing water plunging down slides or tubes. But Jungle Falls had been constructed of man-made rocks so it looked like a real stream complete with rapids and waterfalls.

"Ready?" Frank asked behind her. She nodded. In front of her, Joe jumped into his tube. Shouting a war whoop, he plunged down the falls after Regina.

Nancy was next. The ride assistant held the tube while she climbed in. Holding on to the handles, she pushed off. Instantly, a smile lit up her face as she sailed down the first fall into churning rapids.

"Ayyy! Yahoo!" Nancy added her shouts to Regina's screams of delight and Joe's joyous hoots. Spinning wildly, she hit the next fall, which splashed into a swirling pool.

As Nancy's tube rushed toward a thick grove of ferns, a movement on the bank caught her eye. Snapping her head around, she saw a man crouched in the brush. He was dressed in camouflage clothes, a bandanna tied around his nose and mouth.

Surprised, Nancy grasped the handles of the tube more tightly. Was he on the staff of Jungle Falls? Suddenly, he lunged wildly at her, a knife clutched in one hand!

Chapter Fifteen

NANCY KICKED OUT with her foot, hitting her assailant's knee and propelling her inner tube into a spin. The knife missed her face, slicing the tube instead, and she heard the hiss of air.

With a curse, the man stepped into the water and grabbed Nancy's wrist with one hand. The knife blade flashed wickedly, missing Nancy's cheek by inches. Furious, she attacked, sinking her teeth into the fleshy part of the man's thumb.

Screaming, he jerked away. Nancy threw herself off the tube, flopping sideways into the water. The current sent her whirling down the rapids.

"Argh!" Nancy heard the man's cry of frustration before she spilled over the next set of falls. Swirling and spinning, she bumped along the stream's rocky bottom, finally dropping over the last fall into a deep pool.

Gasping, she bobbed to the surface. She looked up, expecting to see the knife-wielding man plunge after her. Her tube plummeted over the falls, but the man had disappeared.

"Miss!" someone hollered. "You need to get out of the way."

Nancy turned to see the ride attendant wading in after her. He picked up the partially deflated tube, then came over.

"Are you all right?" He held up the tube. "I see your tube isn't. What happened?"

Nancy coughed. "It must have sprung a leak." She grinned weakly. "I'm okay, but it was kind of a wild ride."

He grinned back, his teeth white against his dark tan. "Got your money's worth, right?"

"Nancy!" Frank called as he floated to a stop next to her. "What happened?"

"Did you see him?" Nancy splashed through the water to Frank. "Did you see the guy with the knife?"

Frank jumped out of his tube. "He had a knife?"

"Yes. Fortunately, he slashed my tube instead of me."

"I saw you bail out. Then I saw this figure vanish into the jungle. But he was gone before I could get a good look at him."

"Come on." Nancy glanced up the falls into the thick growth. "He's got to be up there. I want to catch him." She started to climb from the pool, but Frank stopped her.

"No. Let's tell park security." When Nancy opened her mouth to protest, he added, "He's dressed in commando gear and has a knife, Nancy. We're in bathing suits. It's not exactly a fair fight."

Nancy let out her breath. "You're right. Except by the time we contact security, the creep will be long gone."

The two made their way to the exit. Just then Bess, Tommy, Regina, and Joe came up.

"What's going on?" Joe asked. "You two look really stressed out. Was the ride too wild?"

Frank told the others about Nancy's being attacked.

Regina looked intrigued. "Gee, I didn't know they'd added a knife attack to the jungle ride. Sounds cool."

"Sounds real," Nancy countered. "It was no rubber knife."

"Do you think it has to do with Kirby's murder?" Bess asked anxiously. "Like Susan's baton barely missing our heads?"

"Wait a minute," Tommy said. "That's what you confronted Susan about? What happened?"

Before Nancy could caution Bess, her friend blurted, "Nancy and I were walking across the stage of the amphitheater, and Susan's baton fell from the tower. It almost hit us!"

Nancy grimaced. She wished Bess hadn't told Tommy. Even though he acted as if he knew nothing about the baton, Nancy couldn't forget seeing him hurry off the stage right before it fell. Since Tommy had come with them on the Jungle Falls ride, he couldn't have been the culprit who had attacked her. Still, Nancy didn't trust him one hundred percent.

Tommy gave a low whistle. "I'm glad no one got hurt."

"Nancy and I are going to report this attack to park security," Frank said. "Why don't the four of you meet us at one of the other rides?"

"How about the Lemon Drop?" Regina suggested.

"Okay," Bess agreed, but she gave Nancy a worried look. "Will you be all right?"

"Sure." Nancy squeezed her friend's hand reassuringly. But she was worried, too. The knife-wielding guy had looked serious—and professional. For the first time, the thought flashed through Nancy's head that spurned lovers and jealous divers had nothing to do with Kirby's death. Something else was going on.

Something big.

Frank clenched one fist, ready to hit the uniformed security guard. He and Nancy had been in the office for half an hour, waiting to report the attack. But when the guard finally talked with them, Frank could tell by the smirks on the man's face that he didn't believe Nancy's story.

Maybe they *were* bombarded with fun-crazed teenagers reporting everything from lost children to missing wallets. That didn't mean they shouldn't take Nancy seriously.

"O-o-okay," the officer said as he finished writing the report. "We'll keep an eye out for a soldier who took a wrong turn on his way to the army base." He kept a straight face, but Frank could almost hear his silent chuckle.

"Thank you, sir," Nancy said politely. Grasping Frank's elbow, she whisked him from the office.

"Told you so," she muttered when they stepped out the door. "Now we'll never catch him."

"Sorry, Nan. You were right. We should have gone after him back at the ride."

"No, *you* were right." Nancy linked elbows with Frank as they walked from the small building that housed the offices. "It would have been stupid to chase down an armed assailant."

Frank frowned with mock seriousness. "Oh, I don't know—we could have smothered him with our beach towels."

Nancy started laughing, but soon her smile died, and she became tense. "You know, Frank, the attack changes things."

"How?" Frank stopped and faced her. She was tapping her lip with one finger, her brow furrowed in thought. Frank had seen that look many times.

"My gut feeling tells me the attacker was no amateur. That means something else is going on at Big Splash. Something bigger than ambitious divers. Plus, Dana's in jail, Tommy was with us, and I can't picture Susan hiring a professional to scare me off."

"I don't think the guy was just trying to scare you, either," Frank said solemnly.

A slight tremor shook Nancy's body. Frank cupped his hand behind her neck and pulled her close. He and Nancy had been friends forever, and he hated to see her so upset.

Nancy tilted her head back to look at him. "The problem is, if we eliminate the divers, I don't have a clue who killed Kirby. Except—" She snapped her fingers and felt her heart race. "Except that the person responsible *has* to be a park employee. Someone who has easy access to all areas of Big Splash—day and night."

Frank nodded. "Good point."

Nancy sighed and laid her head against Frank's chest. "Gee, that narrows it down to about two hundred employees."

"Hey. I thought you two detectives were chasing bad guys, not swooning in each other's arms," Frank heard Joe say. Nancy pulled away as Joe and Regina walked up, hand in hand, with Tommy and Bess right behind them. The two couples were soaking wet and grinning from ear to ear.

"That Lemon Drop was out of sight!" Bess exclaimed.

Tommy ran his fingers through his short, damp hair. "Scary, too. Every day I dive thirty feet into a tiny pool, but that's the first time my stomach met my throat."

Everybody laughed. Then the loudspeaker announced that the park would be closing in twenty minutes.

"Just enough time for one more ride," Regina said. "And I know just the one—the Roaring Twenties." Grabbing Joe's hand, she started to lead him away. "Twenty hairpin curves through a pitch-black tunnel," she added gleefully.

Frank glanced at Nancy before following them. "Game?"

"Sure." She grinned. "No jerk in camouflage is going to scare me away."

At the ride, Frank and Nancy were first to climb onto a two-person raft, with Frank behind Nancy. Bess and Tommy were in the chute beside them. Each chute of running water disappeared into the mouth of the pitch-black tunnel.

The attendant shouted for them to go. Frank released the side of the chute, and the raft shot forward into the dark. Nancy screamed as they raced through the surging tunnel of water, bumping and twisting around curves so sharp that the raft threatened to tip over with every turn.

Minutes later, they burst out the end of the tunnel, landing with a *splat* in a quiet pool. The raft flipped over, dumping them into the water. Sputtering and laughing, Frank surfaced just as Bess and Tommy jetted from the tunnel's mouth.

Nancy was already dragging the raft to the side. "Wow, that was great!" she whooped.

"That *was* fun," Frank admitted, smiling. The four teens climbed from the pool and grabbed their towels to dry off. Frank heard a loud rebel yell as Joe and Regina came flying out the end of the tunnel.

"The park will be closing in five minutes," the loudspeaker announced.

"Rats. And I was just beginning to get into these rides," Frank said.

"How about continuing the fun at Virginia Gardens?" Tommy suggested when Joe and Regina joined them. "There's a late-night fireworks show."

Bess raised her hand, waving it eagerly. "Count me in."

"I think I'll pass," Nancy said. "It's been a long day. But you two go on ahead."

"Joe?" Regina prompted.

He arched one brow. "I was thinking of something a little more romantic. Like a walk along the James River."

Regina smiled coyly and nodded her agreement. Biting back a grin, Frank shook his head. No matter how frustrating the case or exhausting the day, his little brother was always up for romance. Still, he wished Joe would stop being quite so candid with Regina.

Since Regina was a guide at the museum, Frank mused, she had access to all the artifacts. That meant she could be working with someone to switch them.

As the group gathered their belongings and left the Roaring Twenties, Frank decided that Regina Frobischer was a prime suspect. Before Joe went for a moonlight walk with her, Frank needed to warn him to keep his mouth closed and his eyes open.

After the teens changed into their clothes in the locker rooms, they walked to the parking lot. Frank trailed behind with Nancy.

"You know, Frank, it's beginning to look more and more like Dana is innocent," Nancy said. "I mean, she's overly ambitious and spoiled rotten, but I don't think she killed Kirby."

"Then who did?" Frank knew he was echoing what was in Nancy's own mind. "And why was Dana framed?"

"Because she set herself up with the perfect motive. Everybody at the employee party knew she was furious at Kirby. She makes a perfect scapegoat."

When they reached the parking lot, Frank walked with Nancy toward the van. Bess and Tommy headed over to Tommy's car to leave for Virginia Gardens. Joe and Regina had slowed so that Joe could fish the van keys from his knapsack. The parking lot was starting to empty for the night, and a long line of cars crawled toward the exit.

Just then Nancy stopped dead. "Frank." She touched his arm.

Frank snapped his head around. Nancy was staring at the van. Beside it, four shadowy figures seemed to be dancing. Then Frank heard a muffled "oof" and the sound of blows and knew that the figures weren't dancing. Someone was getting beaten up.

"Fight ahead!" he yelled, and took off. As he ran closer, he could see the figures more clearly.

It was definitely a fight—and not a fair one, either. A guy in a white shirt was being held by two others while a third punched him.

As Frank raced toward the van, he heard the smack of fists against flesh and then a muffled groan.

A rush of adrenaline surged through Frank's body, giving him a burst of speed. He had to get there in time—before the guy in the white shirt was mashed to a pulp!

Chapter Sixteen

THREE AGAINST ONE, Frank thought as he sprinted toward the van, his gaze riveted on the four figures. Time to make the odds a little fairer.

Behind him, he could hear Joe and Nancy's shoes pounding the asphalt. Good. He'd need backup. "Hey!" he yelled when he reached the van. "How about making this a fair fight?"

The two guys threw their victim to the asphalt and turned on Frank. He threw a punch at the closest face.

Whap! The force threw the guy against the side of the van. He hit it hard, sliding down against the tire. The second guy took off. When Joe and Nancy ran up, the third one took off, too. The fallen one sprang to his feet, then followed the others. Cutting through the line of cars, they disappeared into the darkness.

"Come on, let's go after those creeps," Joe said, his chest heaving and his eyes glittering.

"Let them go." Frank turned and saw Regina kneeling next to the guy in the white shirt. He was sitting up, clutching his stomach.

"Are you all right?" Frank asked. The guy's nose was bleeding, and one eye was swelling shut, but Frank knew who he was—the mystery man who had tried to contact him on the ship.

"Here, put this under your nose." Regina pulled a towel from her beach bag. "And lean forward. Do you think it's broken?"

The guy shook his head.

"Then pinch your nostrils shut and apply pressure for about five minutes."

"Thank you for rescuing me," the guy mumbled from behind the towel.

Frank squatted next to him. "No problem. I'm Frank Hardy, but I think you already know that."

Still pinching his nose, the guy nodded. "I'm Tye Gwynn," he said in a nasal voice. "I was waiting for you and your brother by your van, hoping to talk to you finally, when those three gorillas jumped me."

"Why are they after you?" Joe asked.

Tye heaved a sigh. Lowering the towel, he

looked up at them and asked, "You got an hour? Because it's a long story."

Forty minutes later, they were all in the Hardys' motel room. Nancy dabbed Tye's cut with a sterile guaze pad as she listened to Joe and Frank fire questions at him.

"Were you the one in the tent?"

"Did you put the note in the van?"

"How did you know—"

Suddenly, a shrill whistle rang through the room.

"Time out!" Regina said as she handed Tye a towel with some ice wrapped in it. "This isn't a police interrogation. Besides, you're not letting Tye answer your questions."

"You're right." Joe went over to a chair and dropped tiredly into it. "It's just that this is the first real break we've had."

Frank continued to pace between the two double beds. "Sorry, Tye. We were just so eager to meet you at Jamestown, and when that didn't work out . . ." He stopped in midsentence. "What did happen at Jamestown? Why did you run off?"

"Frank!" Nancy and Regina chorused.

Frank threw up his hands. "All right! No more questions."

Nancy smoothed the ends of a bandage over Tye's cut. Gently, Tye touched his nose, which had turned black and blue. Then he carefully held the icy towel against it.

"Thanks." He gave Nancy a lopsided smile. Already his lips were starting to swell.

"I'm thirsty," Regina said. "Anyone else want a soda?" All four teens nodded. After Joe handed Regina some money, she left the room.

Frank sat on the edge of the bed. "Ready to tell us what's going on?" he asked Tye.

When Tye nodded, Nancy kicked off her sandals and leaned against the headboard. It sounded as if it was going to be a long—and revealing—story.

"It all started this spring when I did some research for a history course," Tye began.

While he talked, Nancy had the chance to study him. He was about her age, with close-cropped black hair. The cuffs of his button-down shirt were rolled casually past his wrist, and he wore chino pants and loafers without socks.

"One of the assignments was to write a genealogy," Tye was saying when Nancy tuned back in. "My grandmother had a lot of family records. In them was a document deeding one of my ancestors, Amos Gwynn, land in Yorktown."

Joe shifted restlessly in his chair. "I don't see how—"

Tye raised one hand, wincing as he did. "Be patient. After the Civil War, the land was deeded to Amos by his former master, Charles Wine.

Mr. Wine was a rich plantation owner, a northerner who'd bought the land to grow tobacco. When the war was over, the house had been burnt to the ground and the lands ruined. Disgusted, Mr. Wine not only gave Amos Gwynn his freedom, he gave him the land."

"Wow. That was quite a gift," Frank said. "Though I'm sure the story doesn't end there."

"That's right," Tye said. "When I asked my grandmother what had happened to the land, she said it was old business that didn't need bringing up." Tye rubbed his temples tiredly. "But I couldn't let the subject drop. I kept digging around in the files until I found a court order from 1872 giving three hundred acres, the same land that had been deeded to my family, to the Frobischers."

Both Frank and Joe perked up as soon as they heard the name Frobischer. Just then Regina knocked on the door. Jumping up, Frank let her in.

"You're just in time," he said, opening the door wide. Regina came in, clutching five soda cans. "Tye's telling us about your ancestors."

Tye suddenly looked wary. "What are you talking about?"

"Meet Regina Frobischer," Frank said.

Tye dropped the towel from his nose. "Why didn't you tell me?"

Now it was Regina's turn to look confused. "What's going on?"

"Tye's about to relay some of your family history," Joe said.

"That's fine with me," Regina said. "I'm interested in learning everything I can about my ancestors."

"Maybe you can answer some of my questions then," Tye said. "Anyway, I kept bugging my grandmother—why did Amos Gywnn lose the land? What happened to it? Finally, she got angry and handed me a stack of letters written in 1872. The letters were from Amos Gwynn to his sister in South Carolina. He wrote that the Frobischers had taken the land from him through 'cunning and thievery'—his exact words."

Regina had been handing out sodas, but when she heard Tye, she whirled around. "That's a lie!"

"Maybe, maybe not," Tye countered. "After all, black people suffered many injustices after the Civil War. The South was devastated financially, and many whites banded together in an effort to keep freed slaves from settling and prospering. It was just a fact of that time."

"But, but—" Regina stammered. "What proof do you have that my family stole the land?"

Tye hung his head. "None. That's the problem. And that's the reason I came to Yorktown. I was hoping to find something that proved the Frobischers illegally took possession of the land. I even talked to your grandparents. They told me to check the courthouse records."

"And it was all legal, right?" Regina asked.

"Yes. I found records from 1872 that deeded the three hundred acres back to the Frobischers after they showed a document signed in 1781 that proved ownership."

Joe frowned. "I don't get it. I thought the land had belonged to that Charles Wine guy."

"Oh, I can explain all that," Regina cut in. Plopping down in front of Nancy, she sat cross-legged on the bed. "You know I've told you lots about Josiah and Mary Frobischer and how they aided General Washington during the Revolutionary War."

"Yeah, but what does that have to do with my family acquiring land during the Civil War?" Tye asked, puzzled.

"It'll be clear in a minute," Regina said. "Anyway, in return for service, General Washington often gave loyal patriots land."

"That's true," Frank said. "I've read it in history books. But usually the land was in unsettled areas, like Ohio."

Regina nodded. "Right. But since Mary was killed 'in the line of duty' and their house in town almost destroyed by shelling, General Washington awarded Josiah farmland outside

Yorktown as a way of thanking the family. The letter Washington wrote deeding the land to my family is hanging in Frobischer House right now."

"You mean the land that Virginia Gardens and Big Splash is built on was given to your family by George Washington?" Nancy asked.

"Right. Only my family didn't claim the land until after the Civil War," Regina explained.

"Why not?" Joe asked.

Regina frowned. "I'm not exactly sure, but somehow the document from Washington was lost. You have to remember that right after the Revolutionary War, Yorktown was in ruins. Families were torn apart. Mary was dead, and her sons were sent to live with relatives out west until the war ended and Josiah could send for them. Josiah had died when the boys came back East as young men. They couldn't find the document from Washington anywhere. All that was left was the shell of Frobischer House and a few possessions."

Regina paused and took a sip of her soda. "Josiah's youngest son, Samuel, decided to settle in Yorktown. He was a skilled jack-of-all-trades. My grandfather is descended from him. Samuel rebuilt Frobischer House, married, and had a son, Franklin. Franklin had a son, James, and it was his family that was living in Yorktown during the Civil War. James found the lost document from General Washington where Josiah had hidden it in the back of an old clock. It wasn't until the clock was being repaired that it was found—almost a hundred years after it had been written!"

"Wow, that's quite a story," Nancy said. She glanced over at Tye, wondering what he was thinking. His brows were knit in an expression of intense concentration. Nancy knew it was a lot to take in.

"James immediately took the document to the county courthouse," Regina said. "When the magistrate saw the signature of General Washington, he knew that the property outside town, which then must have belonged to Amos Gwynn, rightfully belonged to the Frobischers." Regina turned her big green eyes to Tye. "Of course, no one ever told me about the people who lost the property. I'm sorry it was your family, Tye. I hope this explanation answers some of your questions."

Tye nodded once, though he kept his eyes on his soda can.

"So the property that was once a tobacco farm belonging to a freed slave is now a multimillion-dollar theme park," Frank commented.

"Right. My grandparents had always wanted to do something to celebrate their family's contribution to the Revolutionary War. When they built Virginia Gardens, they moved the original family home to the park and made it a museum."

"Well, all that explains how the Frobischers got the land," Frank said. "But I still don't know why you were trying to contact us, Tye. What does your family losing your land have to do with Colin's death?"

Tye fidgeted uncomfortably on the bed. "Because even though I checked the records, I wasn't convinced that the transaction was legal. I mean, why would Amos Gwynn write that the land was taken through cunning and thievery?"

"Because he was furious at losing the farm," Regina said matter-of-factly.

"That's what I thought, until after I contacted Mr. and Mrs. Frobischer and someone started following me, which again aroused my suspicions." Tye's dark eyes darted to Regina's face. She was staring at him, her lips parted, a look of astonishment on her face, but she didn't say anything.

"So I decided to go to Frobischer House to check out the document from General Washington," Tye went on. "That's when I overheard Colin talking to Frank and Joe about the pistols."

"You were at the museum that day?" Frank asked.

"Yes. When Colin ran off, I followed him. I

told him who I was and asked him about the pistols. He showed me the coat of arms and explained that he thought the pistols were forgeries. He said he was going to talk to the Frobischers about it."

Frank's brows shot up. "He what?"

"He was going to talk to the Frobischers," Tye repeated.

Frank and Joe gave each other surprised looks.

"Emily told us she asked Colin not to see the Frobischers until she'd checked on the authentication," Joe said. "Why would she lie?"

"Maybe she didn't. Colin might have felt it was too important to wait," Frank suggested. "He was pretty upset."

"Well, he told me he was going to see them," Tye added. "And that he'd meet me at his tent after the reenactment to tell me what the Frobischers said."

"So that was you at the tent," Frank said. "Why did you run off?"

"I thought you were the goons who had been following me," he explained. "I waited at the tent for Colin, and when he didn't show, I asked one of the guys in his regiment where he was. He told me he'd been murdered!" Tye dropped his head in his hands. "I freaked out. Later I pretended to be an out-of-town reporter, and a police officer told me you were friends of Colin's as well as detectives. That's why I'd been trying to contact you. I thought we could work together to find out what's going on."

"Why did you think Colin's murder had anything to do with your family losing their land?" Nancy asked.

"I wasn't sure," Tye answered. "I just thought something fishy was going on—something that had to do with the Frobischer family."

Regina jumped up, her eyes stormy. "No way! You're making all this up, trying to drag my family into Colin's death."

"I'm not making this up," Tye insisted. "Joe and Frank can tell you what happened at Jamestown Settlement. The same goons who followed me there attacked me tonight." He smacked his palm with his fist. "I'd recognize that gorilla in the camouflage outfit anywhere. He was the one punching me."

"Camouflage!" Nancy inhaled sharply. Was it the same guy who had attacked her in the jungle? Leaning forward on the bed, she touched Tye's arm. "Describe him."

"Big guy." Tye held his arm up high. "When he first confronted me at the van, he had a knife. He held it in his right hand, which was wrapped with some dirty gauze."

Nancy's mouth fell open. "Frank, it must be

the same guy who attacked me at Jungle Falls! But why? Unless—" She took a deep breath, her mind racing as she tried to put it all together. Then the connection dawned on her. "Unless the same people who killed Colin murdered Kirby, too!"

Chapter Seventeen

"DON'T YOU SEE, Frank?" Nancy said excitedly. "If the same guy who attacked me also attacked Tye, it proves that Kirby's murder has nothing to do with Dana and her scheme for publicity."

"You could be right, but I still don't understand how Kirby's murder ties in with Colin's," Frank said. He agreed with Nancy that maybe Dana didn't kill Kirby, but as far as he was concerned, the two cases were totally separate. "And how does either murder relate to Tye?"

Joe shook his head. "You guys have me totally confused."

"Me, too!" Regina hopped off the bed, her mouth pursed in anger. "Except I'm not confused about one thing: I keep hearing the Frobischer name linked in the same breath with goons and murderers. Well, leave my grandparents out of this. The only thing they're guilty of is working hard to make Virginia Gardens and Big Splash successes. *And"*—she paused to take a ragged breath—"they'd want to be the first to know if something illegal was going on."

With her hands on her hips, Regina fumed for a second more. Then she plopped back onto the bed, crossed her arms, and glared silently at the floor.

Nancy cleared her throat. "Regina's right. I'm making a lot of wild accusations with no proof. The only thing I know for sure is that one of the goons who roughed up Tye also went after me. But why?"

"We know one other thing," Joe reminded her. "Emily Grant has definitely proven that Frobischer House is filled with fakes and that someone forged the letters of authentication. The question is, who?"

Tye raised his hand. "Wait, we know one more thing. My family *did* lose their land."

"Legally!" Regina huffed.

"Then why did someone try to scare me off when I started asking question about it?" Tye countered.

Groaning under his breath, Frank rubbed his hands over his face. His brain was in overdrive and going nowhere. Blocking out the arguing, he tried to concentrate on what they knew so far.

Suddenly, a link between Kirby's and Colin's deaths came to him. He thought back to Nancy's earlier conclusion that Kirby's killer *had* to be a park employee.

Frank pressed his fingertips to his eyes, putting it all together. The person who killed Colin had blended in with the reenactors, then disappeared without a trace. It made sense that he or she was a park employee, too.

"Regina," Frank said, catching her attention, "do some employees work for both Big Splash and Virginia Gardens?"

"Only the security guards. The same company, Protect U, Inc., hires and trains the guards for both the parks."

Frank punched his fist in the air. "That's it!" he exclaimed. "That's why security laughed at us when we reported the guy in camouflage. That's why it was so easy for someone to sneak in and kill Colin and Kirby, and attack Nancy and Tye. Because it's not only an inside job, but park security is behind it."

Regina looked so astonished she couldn't speak, while Joe and Nancy nodded excitedly.

"But what does that have to do with my family losing their land?" Tye asked.

"Let's tackle one thing at a time," Nancy suggested.

"I'll bet park security is running the forgery ring," Joe said. "Being on the inside would make it easy to switch the artifacts."

"Maybe Kirby found out about it," Nancy cut in. "He was always slinking around. He could have overheard two guards discussing the black market ring. So they murdered him to shut him up."

Suddenly, Regina moaned. Joe scooted behind her on the bed, putting a hand on her shoulder. "Are you all right?"

"Forgeries. Murder. This is terrible," she choked out, her eyes brimming with tears. "We've got to tell my grandparents."

"No!" Frank was adamant. "If security *is* running a black market ring, telling your grandparents might tip the culprits off. Then we'd never catch Colin's killer."

He stood up. "What we need to do is talk to Emily Grant. If we tell her we suspect a park employee, she may be able to narrow down who it is. Maybe someone who regularly comes into the museum."

"Frank!" Joe bolted straight upright in his chair. "What if Kirby's and Colin's killers know Emily is helping us? She could be in danger."

"Joe's right." Frank grabbed the van keys off the TV. "We've got to get to the museum."

* * *

Joe cast a sidelong glance at Regina. During the ride to Virginia Gardens, she'd held his hand tightly but hadn't said a word.

Not that he blamed her. No one was doing much talking. They were all too worried about Emily and too stunned by their discussion at the motel.

Joe's own mind was spinning, so he knew that Regina had to be totally confused. Even though her grandparents weren't being accused, Regina knew that the fact that their employees were suspected of illegal activities meant big trouble.

When they reached Virginia Gardens, Frank slowed the van. Most of the cars were leaving the theme park, which meant that the fireworks show was over. Frank steered through the outgoing lines of traffic and parked in the lot, which was nearly empty.

"Come on, I'll take you in the back way," Regina said. Holding Joe's hand, she led the group through an open gate and down a dark sidewalk. When they approached the security booth, the uniformed guard glanced up.

Joe's stomach twisted into a knot. He hoped the guard wasn't one of the bad guys. If he was, he'd surely recognize one of them.

"Hi, Miss Regina." The guard nodded. Joe was relieved to see he was an elderly man with a kind smile. "You're here kind of late."

"Uh, we're going to F-Frobischer House," Regina stammered. "I left my purse there."

Joe cocked one brow. Regina's purse hung from her shoulder. He hoped the guard didn't notice.

"Go on in." He buzzed the gate open. Regina rushed through, dragging Joe with her.

"Whew. That was close," Tye said behind them. "I kept waiting for Mr. Camouflage and his knife to appear."

"If he does, I get first swing at him," Nancy joked, but Joe could hear the tension in her voice.

As the five teens rushed to Frobischer House, they passed stragglers leaving Virginia Gardens. Joe wondered if Tommy and Bess had had a good time. Then he wondered briefly if he and Regina would ever get their moonlight walk.

Suddenly, Regina stopped dead. "I smell smoke," she whispered.

Joe raised his head and sniffed. "Me, too. Do you think it's from the fireworks?"

"No! Look!" Regina pointed straight ahead. Joe could just make out the dark shape of Frobischer House half hidden by trees. Smoke rose from an upstairs window.

"It's coming from the upstairs," Joe said. "If Emily's still in her office, we have to get her out!"

"I'll run back and alert security and then call the fire department," Nancy said.

Joe raced toward the museum, Regina beside him with Tye and Frank steps behind. Smoke billowed from both upstairs windows. Joe halted by the front door.

"I'm going to go in," he said, leaping up the one step. He felt the wooden door. It was hot, and when he slowly opened it, a cloud of smoke fanned out into the night air.

"This way's too dangerous." Stepping back, Joe scanned the second story. Since there were no lights on in the building, he hoped that meant it was empty. "Emily!" he hollered at the upstairs windows.

"Tye and I will check around back," Frank said as he sprinted around the corner.

"The first floor isn't on fire yet," Regina said, panting. "I've got to get in there."

"No!" Joe grabbed her arm. "It's too risky. And it doesn't look like anyone's in there."

"But the letter from General Washington is there. It's the only proof that my family didn't steal the land!" Yanking her arm from Joe's grasp, Regina ran to the front door.

"No!" Joe screamed.

Before he could stop her, Regina pushed the open door and disappeared into the smoke-filled museum.

"Regina!" Joe yelled. Without hesitating, he plunged in after her. A gray haze enveloped the hall. He tried to picture where the document was hanging and finally headed to the old parlor where the pistols were displayed.

"Regina!" Joe called again. The smoke was thicker in the back room, and for a second Joe couldn't see a thing.

Then, through the wall of gray, he spotted a splash of yellow—Regina's yellow beach shift. When he reached her, she was frozen in place, staring at the bare wall.

"It's gone!" she cried. "The document's gone!"

"Then let's get out of here!" Wrapping his arm around her shoulders, Joe propelled Regina toward the front hall.

Together, they stumbled past a glass display case. An explosion made them both jump, and when they reached the hall, Joe saw that the stairs had fallen in in a fiery heap.

"Oh, I hope Emily's safe!" Tears made a trail down Regina's sooty cheeks. Joe turned her away from the stairs and toward the front door. At least, he hoped it was toward the front door. The smoke was blinding.

Yanking up his shirt, he covered his nose and mouth. Regina hid her face in his chest. Joe knew that in a fire, most people died from smoke inhalation. That meant they had to get out—fast.

"The front door is this way." Regina tugged on Joe, pulling him ahead. The air was hot, and Joe's throat stung. He doubled over, coughing.

When he looked up, he was disoriented. Was Regina leading them the right way? Just then, cool air brushed his cheeks.

"Straight ahead!" Joe choked out, the smoke filling his eyes, nose, and mouth. A crackling noise above his head made him freeze. He looked up and saw a black splotch spread across the ceiling like spilled paint.

Regina screamed and threw herself backward, knocking Joe into the wall. The ceiling collapsed in a roar of smoke and dust, crashing to the floor in front of them.

Forced back by the intense heat, Joe and Regina spun around, but a wall of smoke blocked the hallway. Adrenaline shot through Joe's body, and his fingers felt numb. They were trapped—and the fire was getting hotter every second!

Chapter Eighteen

"JOE!" REGINA SCREAMED. "We're going to burn!"

Panicking, Joe spun toward the front door. "This is the only way out!" he shouted. "We have to jump over the burning rubble. Can you do it, Regina?"

Regina nodded, then doubled over in a fit of coughing. Joe eyed the smoldering pile. So far, there weren't any visible flames, but he knew it could flare up at any second.

Straightening, Regina drew a strangled breath. "Let's go." She coiled, then leaped, landing safely on the other side. Joe could barely see her in the thick smoke. Turning, she gestured frantically for him to follow.

Joe jumped. The instant he dropped on the other side, the pile burst into flame. Regina grabbed his hand and yanked him out the front door. The two stumbled down the steps, rolling in a heap on the brick sidewalk.

"Regina! Joe!" Nancy, Frank, and Tye ran over to them. Frank grabbed Joe under the arms and dragged him down the sidewalk. Nancy and Tye helped Regina to her feet, then hustled her to safety.

Joe watched in horror as the entire upstairs collapsed in an inferno of noise and flames. With a moan of dismay, Regina sank down beside him. Joe reached for her hand. They had escaped just in time.

Sirens rang through the air. Two pumper trucks roared across the lawn, while several security guards ran to meet the firefighters.

Frank squatted next to Joe. "Are you all right?" he asked.

Joe glanced at Regina, who was leaning against his shoulder. Her face was streaked with soot, her bangs singed. But when she smiled and gave his fingers a squeeze, he knew she was all right.

"Why did you guys decide to go in there?" Nancy asked.

Regina wiped her palm across her eyes. "To get the document from General Washington," she answered. "I wanted to prove to Tye that this is our land."

Tye shook his head. "It's not worth dying for, Regina."

"Emily!" Regina burst out. Raising her head, she glanced around wildly. "We didn't check to see if she was in there. Since there weren't any lights on inside, I hoped she'd gone home. Have you heard any news about her?"

"She's safe," Nancy said, quickly reassuring Regina. "The security guard said she left the park about an hour ago."

Regina sank back against Joe. "Thank goodness."

The firefighters had turned their hoses on the museum, but the fire proved to be too hot. Joe grimaced as the flames devoured the clapboard walls.

"It's awful!" Regina moaned. "Frobischer House was so old and historic, and it was moved with great care from its original site in town. It's terrible to think that all that history's now up in flames."

"I bet our culprits set fire to the house on purpose," Joe said angrily. "To destroy evidence. Without the faked artifacts and forged letters Emily collected, there's no way to prove a black market ring was operating."

Still hunkered down beside Joe, Frank nodded wearily. "Which means it will be tough to link the members of the ring to Colin's or Kirby's murders."

"Don't give up yet," Nancy said. "Emily might have made copies of the forged letters. Maybe she even took some of the artifacts home with her for safekeeping."

Joe's brows shot up. "That's right. Emily's a smart lady, and she was determined to uncover the culprits. She may have taken precautions."

Just then two paramedics came up, their emergency bags in hand. "We hear you two were trapped in the fire," one medic said.

"Yes," Joe told him. He had enough emergency medical training to know they would want to check Regina and him for burns and smoke inhalation.

"That looks like a nasty burn on your arm," the other medic said to Regina. Opening his bag, he squatted next to her.

Joe caught Nancy's and Frank's eyes. "Find out where Emily lives," he said in a low voice. "We need to head over there—pronto."

"Joe, when the medic is done with you, you and Frank take the van and go on ahead," Nancy suggested. "Tye and I can stay with Regina."

Joe and Frank nodded their agreement. Joe's gaze focused on the milling security guards. If any of them was responsible for setting fire to the museum, he would also know that Emily Grant had left. Joe didn't want to leave Regina, but if

Emily did have important evidence, she could still be in danger.

Half an hour later, Nancy sat on the grass beside Regina. The medic was gently cleaning her arm. Tye was standing by a rescue vehicle, watching the crew douse the flames.

As Nancy stared at the fire, she realized that all thoughts of Kirby's death had vanished from her mind. Too much had happened in the last couple of hours.

"Ouch!" Regina jerked her arm away.

"Hurts, huh?" the medic said. "You're lucky, though. Your lungs are clear, and this is just a first-degree burn, like a bad sunburn. Keep it clean and cool, and in time it will heal." He started repacking his bag.

"Thanks," Regina said. She turned to Nancy. "I wish I knew what happened to that document. It was always hanging on the wall." For a moment, she stared ahead, lost in thought. "Let's hope Emily took it home with her."

Unless whoever started the fire took it, Nancy thought. She didn't want to voice that possibility to Regina, who was already upset. If the arsonist stole the document, Regina's family might never get it back.

"Look, Regina, Tye's right," Nancy said gently. "The document wasn't worth losing your life over."

Tye came up and stood beside Regina. "If we can't find it or if it did get burned, I'll figure out another way to answer my questions about Amos Gwynn."

"Since the document is so valuable, maybe your grandparents had a copy made," Nancy suggested.

"No. All our family heirlooms were displayed in Frobischer House," Regina said dejectedly. She sighed as she looked at what was left of the museum—a smoldering mound with a brick chimney sticking up from the middle. "Our entire history has been wiped out in one catastrophe."

Abruptly, she spun to face Nancy and Tye. "Wait a minute, not our *entire* history. My grandparents have some letters stored in their safe, letters dating from the Revolutionary War." Regina's eyes gleamed. "I've never read them, but I bet there are letters that will tell us about General Washington deeding the land to Josiah!"

"I have to admit, that would clear things up once and for all," Tye said.

"Nancy! What's going on?" Bess and Tommy came running through the crowd.

Nancy and Regina jumped up. "Bess? What are you doing here?" Nancy asked.

"We were getting into Tommy's car when we heard the sirens," Bess said, breathing rapidly from her run. "Tommy stopped someone to ask what was going on, and we learned that the museum was on fire."

"I can't believe it," Tommy said, studying the charred remains of Frobischer House. "What happened?"

"I'll tell you on the way to my grandparents' house," Regina offered. "Come on." Waving for her friends to follow, she headed quickly away from the burning museum.

Nancy, Tye, Bess, and Tommy exchanged puzzled glances, then trotted after her.

"Where are we going?" Nancy called.

"My grandparents' house," Regina called out over her shoulder. "To find those letters!"

Twenty minutes later Tommy steered his car down the Frobsichers' long driveway. Replicas of old-fashioned gas lamps lined the drive, and in their light Nancy could see flowering bushes, roses, and fruit trees. When Tommy rounded a bend, his headlights shone on Regina's grandparents' stately mansion.

Spotlights illuminated the Williamsburg-style brick house, which was beautifully landscaped with large boxwoods, holly, and azaleas. The house was three stories tall, with a steep slate roof. Five dormers jutted out from the top story, and sturdy chimneys rose skyward from both ends.

"This place looks like a page out of a history book," Nancy said.

"It's supposed to," Regina said with a smile. "My grandparents researched Williamsburg architecture before having the house built five years ago."

Tommy swung around the drive, stopping at the front door. Regina hopped out of the car in a flash and headed straight into the house without waiting for her friends.

"The museum isn't the only thing on fire," Bess commented. "Regina's hot to find those letters."

On the way over, Nancy had introduced Tye and explained to Tommy and Bess all that had happened.

"She's obsessed with proving to Tye that her ancestors didn't steal his family's land," Nancy said as she climbed out from the backseat. "Not that I blame her."

Nancy ran lightly up the brick stairway. Regina had left the front door hanging open. Nancy wondered if the Frobischers were home. If they were, she and Regina would have some explaining to do when Regina started rifling through their old family letters.

Not that the Hardys could hope to keep their investigation a secret any longer, Nancy mused. The torching of the museum had definitely brought things to a head, and it was clear that the culprit knew that the investigation was heating up. But the Frobischers had already talked to Tye once and sent him to the county courthouse, where he'd found documents that showed the land was legally the Frobischers'. Unlike Regina, they might not feel an urgent need to offer further proof.

"Regina?" Nancy called in a low voice as she entered the central hall. For a moment she stared in awe at the curved staircase, the painted molding, the crystal chandelier, and the wide-plank flooring. Large oil paintings of a grim-looking man and woman hung over an antique chest.

"Wow!" Bess gasped. "This could be a museum, too. Just like the original Frobischer House."

A clunking noise made Nancy turn. "Regina?"

"In the library!" Nancy heard her call out.

Nancy, Bess, Tye, and Tommy hurried down the hall and into a spacious room. On two sides, bookshelves rose from floor to ceiling. In the middle of the room, several cut-velvet upholstered chairs were arranged around a walnut table. Three Oriental rugs were scattered around the wood floor.

Regina had pulled a framed painting off the wall behind a desk. Standing on a footstool, she was fiddling with the dial of a safe.

"I've seen my grandparents do this before," she said, her gaze riveted on the dial. "There!" As she spoke, the safe door swung open. Reaching in, Regina pulled out a manila envelope.

Unclasping the envelope, she pulled out several stacks of yellowed papers. "Here," she said, waving a packet at Nancy. "Start looking through these letters for any mention of the document from Washington."

Nancy hesitated. "Are you sure we should be doing this without your grandparents' permission?"

"Really." Bess glanced nervously over her shoulder. "If they wanted you to see these, why didn't they show you them before? Why were they locked up?"

"They're locked up because they're priceless to my family," Regina explained as she jumped off the footstool. She thrust a pile of letters at Bess and Tommy, then Tye. "This summer, they offered to show them to me one day, but I was heading off to the beach with some friends—I didn't want to see them at that time. Now I do, and I know my grandparents would want me to clear up this matter with Tye."

Sitting behind the desk, Regina began leafing through the letters. Nancy picked up a packet and sat in one of the straight-backed chairs. So much for a cozy reading chair, she thought. Its back was so stiff and high that there was no way she could get comfortable.

"The letters you gave Tommy and me are dated from the early nineteen hundreds," Bess said.

Tye waved two letters he held. "And most of these are from someone named Sasha in South Carolina."

"That's my aunt Sasha," Regina explained.

Glancing through her stack, Nancy noted that most letters had fairly modern stamps and postmarks. Then she opened a legal-size envelope and pulled out half a dozen yellowed sheets of folded, crinkly paper. She carefully unfolded one of them, noticing the faded ink and the *s*'s that looked like *f*'s, which was typical of the writing style in colonial days.

Suddenly, Nancy jolted to attention. "I think I've got something," she said.

"Good!" Regina popped her head up. "Choose a letter, and read it out loud."

" 'Dear Mary,' " Nancy began.

"Mary Frobischer," Regina explained excitedly. "This is what we're looking for."

" 'Washington is set to shell redoubt number nine at dawn. Pass this on to MacDonald. Then burn this letter. Josiah.' " Puzzled, Nancy reread the contents to herself. Regina had said that Mary and Josiah were loyal patriots. Then why were they passing on information to Major MacDonald, a British officer?

Regina looked confused, too. "That doesn't make sense," she said, furrowing her brow. "Are you sure that's what it says?"

Nancy nodded. "Positive. Let me read another. 'Dear Josiah, John is suspicious that I'm passing information to MacDonald. Stay away for a day. Your loving wife and fellow Tory, Mary.' "

When Nancy looked up, Regina was biting a nail and frowning. "A Tory! That couldn't be right," she exclaimed. Jumping up, she bounded around the desk and grabbed the letters from Nancy. As she flipped through them, pausing to read to herself, the color in her face slowly drained.

After a moment her hands dropped to her sides. Her eyes glazed over. Opening her fingers, she let the letters flutter to the carpet.

"Regina?" Bess prompted.

"According to these letters, Mary and Josiah were Tories," Regina whispered in a stunned voice. "Josiah would spy on Washington's army, then bring the information back to Mary to pass on to Major MacDonald. MacDonald didn't kill Mary, this John Goode guy did—when he found out she was betraying her country!"

Raising her head, Regina stared at Tye with a shocked expression. "If my ancestors were traitors, General Washington would never have deeded them land. That means the document is one more forgery, and my family's history, plus all this"—she waved her hand around the mansion—"is a lie!"

"We wondered when you'd find out, Regina," a silky-smooth voice said.

Nancy whirled in her chair. Mr. and Mrs. Frobischer stood in the library doorway. Mrs. Frobischer was dressed for a formal evening in a blue satin cocktail dress, high heels, and a sapphire necklace. In her hand she held a pearl-handled revolver, and it was aimed at her granddaughter's head.

Chapter Nineteen

REGINA GRABBED the back of Nancy's chair to steady herself. Slowly, Nancy stood up to face the Frobischers. She couldn't believe her eyes. Had Regina's grandparents been guilty all this time?

"Wh-what is going on?" Regina stammered. "What are you doing with that gun?" She clapped a hand over her mouth. "You! *You* killed Kirby and Colin?"

Mrs. Frobischer *tsk*-ed. "Oh, no, dear. We would never do anything that gruesome. We had Jason kill them."

"Jason Cavanagh?" Tommy exclaimed. "Isn't he head of security at Big Splash and Virginia Gardens?"

"Yes. He's a loyal employee, and he's Regina's cousin," Mr. Frobischer said in his deep baritone. He was dressed in black tie as if just coming home from an evening at the opera. "Come here, Jason, and introduce yourself."

A beefy guy with big arms stepped into the doorway. He wore a baseball cap and a camouflage shirt and pants. A knife sheath hung from his belt.

Nancy caught her breath. It was the guy who'd attacked her at Jungle Falls.

"Grrr!" Nancy heard a low growl, and Tye lunged forward. Instantly, Jason whipped his knife out of the sheath. "Back off, punk," he said, his voice steely, his eyes cold. "Or I'll finish what we started in the parking lot."

"Take it easy, Tye," Nancy murmured. She knew from her encounter with Jason that he wouldn't hesitate to use his knife.

"Jason is not only skilled with a knife," Mrs. Frobischer said. "He's also a master of disguise. Dressing as a redcoat to kill Colin during the reenactment was his brilliant idea."

Nancy was stunned. The Frobischers were talking about Colin's death as if it had been a scene from a play.

For a second, Mrs. Frobischer pursed her lips sadly. "Though it was a terrible thing to kill a fellow British officer," she said thoughtfully, "even if it was all in the name of war."

"War?" Regina scoffed.

"A fight for our lives, Regina," Mrs. Frobischer explained. "And for our family's heritage and history."

Regina bristled. "Which history? The one you made up about Mary and Josiah, the loyal patriots? Or the real story about a family of traitors, murderers, and thieves?"

Mrs. Frobischer paused a second, as if thinking. Nancy kept her eye on the gun barrel, which had lowered. Then her eyes shifted to Jason. His beefy arms were crossed in front of his chest, and his gaze was murderously intent, as if he was just waiting for a chance to pounce.

"Now, dear, 'murderers and thieves' is a harsh phrase," Mrs. Frobischer finally said. "In fact, you should be proud of your ancestors. We've been master con artists and forgers since the beginning of time. In fact, the fakes in the museum were so good that no one ever would have discovered them. That's why we had to kill Colin when he came to us with this story about the pistols' being fake. We knew that once he'd made the forgery public, it was only a matter of time before the rest of the collection would get scrutinized. And we couldn't let that happen." Mrs. Frobischer shook her head, her sapphire necklace glittering.

"Because then the letter from General Washington deeding the land to Josiah would be checked out," Tye cut in. "And when that was discovered to be fake, the whole world would know that you stole the land from *my* family."

Mrs. Frobischer arched one brow. "I wouldn't use the word *stole,* Mr. Gwynn. Frobischers came to Virginia on one of the first ships from England and helped found Yorktown. It was *General Washington"*—she spat out his name contemptuously—"and his troops who destroyed the town. Everything we had was wiped out. We deserved that land."

Regina pressed her hands to her temples. "I don't believe what I'm hearing. You mean none of those stories about Mary and Josiah is true?"

"Oh, Mary was brave and dedicated, all right," Mrs. Frobischer said, nodding her head. "It's just that she was on the side of the British."

"And what about the exhibit in the museum?" Regina asked. "Obviously, Mary wasn't stabbed by Major MacDonald, since she was spying for him."

Mrs. Frobischer smiled proudly. "Wasn't that exhibit clever?" She patted her husband's arm. "It was your grandfather's idea, actually. And part of it was true. Mary was killed with Major MacDonald's dagger. John Goode, another Yorktown resident, was forced to care for the major's horses. One day, he stole the dagger from the major's saddlebag. When he discovered that

Mary and Josiah were traitors, he stabbed Mary with it."

"Why did you use the same kind of dagger to kill Colin?" Nancy asked.

"That must have been another one of Jason's 'brilliant' ideas," Regina said sarcastically.

"We thought that using a replica of Major MacDonald's dagger to kill another MacDonald was a nice touch, too." Mrs. Frobischer beamed at Jason. "You're so clever, dear."

"A nice touch"! "You're so clever"! Nancy was astounded at the Frobischers' ability to rationalize every cruel deed their family had done.

"Not clever," Regina retorted. "Joe Hardy figured it out. It immediately made him suspicious of *me.*"

"Well, we hadn't counted on Colin having two nosy teen detectives for friends." Mrs. Frobischer sounded peeved, and she narrowed her eyes as her gaze flitted around the room.

Nancy could only hope that the two nosy detectives were uncovering information that would lead them to the Frobischers. Otherwise she shuddered to think what "brilliant" idea Jason would come up with to get rid of the five of them.

"Since John Goode was the only person who knew the truth about Mary and Josiah," Mr. Frobischer continued, as if he were giving a history lesson, "Josiah killed him, then told everybody in Yorktown how Mary was stabbed by Major MacDonald."

"But Major MacDonald knew the truth," Nancy said. "Why didn't he come forward?"

"The British had just been soundly defeated," Mr. Frobischer explained. "The war was lost, and hundreds of soldiers were dead or wounded. Major MacDonald had more important things to worry about than the poor residents of Yorktown."

Mrs. Frobischer humphed. "Poor is right. For the next hundred years, Josiah barely eked out a living."

"Is that why you stole my family's land?" Tye said in a challenging tone. "Greed?"

Mrs. Frobischer raised her brows. "Of course," she replied coolly, as if surprised by such an obvious question.

"But why wait until after the Civil War to go after the land?" Regina said, puzzled. She held out her hands in a pleading gesture, as though wanting to know the whole truth. "Why didn't Josiah try to get land after the Revolutionary War?"

"Good question, sweetheart," Mrs. Frobischer said. "It would have been more convenient if Josiah had thought about acquiring land back then. But he had more immediate things to think about—like burying his wife and making enough money to send to relatives to raise his motherless sons."

Mr. Frobischer continued. "It was Franklin and his son James who were the real schemers. Even before the Civil War, they had dozens of scams going. But they knew there was no way they'd be able to take land from rich plantation owners like Charles Wine."

Tye snorted angrily. "So you waited until a poor freed slave owned it."

Mr. Frobischer smiled loftily. "That's right. After the Civil War, the South was in turmoil. Franklin and James saw their chance. They forged a letter from General Washington and hid it in the old clock. Inspiring, don't you think?"

"Inspiring," Mrs. Frobischer said with a nod when no one else agreed. "When our family took over the farm, they made a small fortune growing tobacco. And, of course, you can see what we've contributed to the history of colonial America. Yorktown and Williamsburg are prosperous tourist meccas thanks to our multimillion-dollar theme parks."

"Which were all acquired through deceit," Nancy reminded them. She couldn't believe the Frobischers were boasting about their lurid past. "That's why you sicced your goons on Tye. His claim threatened to topple your empire."

"Yes, he and those Hardys were pesky." Mrs.

Frobischer humphed again. "Then Kirby stuck his nose into our business when he overheard Jason, T.C., and Leo discussing how to get rid of them. He demanded hush money, so Jason hushed him up forever."

"Leo and T.C.!" Tommy exclaimed. "They're the security guards for Big Splash."

So that's how they were able to rig the baton and steal Dana's necklace from her locker, Nancy thought. "And Dana's scene at the party the night before gave you the idea to frame her," she guessed.

"It was all Jason's idea," Mrs. Frobischer said, smiling proudly at Jason. "He did inherit the Frobischer blood." Arching one brow, she looked at Regina. "And what about you, dear? I know all this is a shock, but are you with the rest of us? Family needs to stick together, you know. We hope you won't betray us."

All eyes turned to Regina. Raising her hand, she wiped the tears from her eyes. Nancy held her breath. The saying "Blood is thicker than water" flashed through Nancy's mind. Still, how could Regina side with a family of cutthroats?

Slowly, Regina nodded. "I'm Frobischer blood through and through," she told her grandparents. "And I'll do whatever it takes to protect the family."

Nancy was stunned. Behind her, she heard

Bess gasp. Beside her, Tye and Tommy stared in shocked silence as Regina strode across the library floor and embraced her grandmother, then her grandfather.

"Well, that's one problem out of the way," Mr. Frobischer said heartily. "Now we just have to dispose of the rest of you."

"Dispose of us?" Bess squeaked.

"What are you going to do?" Nancy demanded, trying not to sound worried, though her heart was racing.

"Your ashes will be found floating on the James River," Mrs. Frobischer explained. "Victims of an unfortunate boating accident. Of course, a few empty beer bottles bobbing by the burnt wreckage will convince the authorities that the boat crashed and exploded because of your speeding and wild partying."

Jason jerked his head down the hallway. "Leo and T.C. are getting the boat gassed up now."

"I'd better check on them," Mr. Frobischer said. "This accident has to look perfect."

"Go ahead, dear. Regina can help Jason and me." Reaching into her sequined shoulder bag, Mrs. Frobischer pulled out another small pistol and handed it to Regina.

"You're not going to get away with this," Tye warned when Mr. Frobischer left.

Mrs. Frobischer grinned. "I hate to disappoint

you, Mr. Gwynn, but we will get away with it. In fact, we've been getting away with it for more than two hundred years."

"Grandmother," Regina said in a clear voice. "We do have some other loose ends to tie up—Joe and Frank Hardy, and Emily Grant. They need to be part of this boating accident."

"Oh, my." Mrs. Frobischer fingered her sapphires nervously. "You're right about the Hardys. But don't worry about Emily. Paul and Steve took care of that interfering woman earlier."

Nancy started. What did that mean? What had they done to Emily?

"Then we need to lure the Hardys over here," Regina said with an evil smile. "And I know just how to do it."

When they reached Emily Grant's house, Frank rapped loudly on the front door. There was no answer, so he pressed the buzzer hard. Joe stood on the lawn and surveyed the windows.

"No lights on inside," Joe said. "And the curtains are closed."

"She's got to be home," Frank said impatiently. "We need to tell her about the fire and warn her that she may be in danger."

"What we need to do is go to the police," Joe countered.

"Let's check around back," Frank suggested. "If Emily is here, something could be wrong."

Joe nodded. The two Hardys jogged around to the back of the old clapboard home to a modern deck built off the first floor. A sliding glass door opened onto the deck. While Joe checked an outside window, Frank bounded onto the deck and tried the door. It was locked, and the floor-length curtains were closed.

Bending, he shut one eye and peeked through a slit where the curtain didn't quite meet the wall. Chills ran down his spine when he spotted a hand, palm up on the tile floor. It looked as if someone was lying dead inside!

Chapter Twenty

"JOE!" FRANK CALLED hoarsely, waving at his brother. "It's Emily! We've got to get in there!"

Joe leaped onto the deck. Searching his pockets, Frank found his lock-picking kit. Luckily, the sliding glass door didn't have a security bar.

"Got it." Frank slid the door open. Then, pushing the curtains aside, he hurried into the house. Emily Grant was sprawled on the kitchen floor. Frank immediately smelled gas. Rushing to the stove, he found that the pilot light was out and the valves were on full blast. By the time he turned the valves off, Joe was dragging Emily across the kitchen floor toward the open door. Frank hurried over to Emily. Picking up her legs,

Frank helped his brother carry her onto the deck and place her on a lounge chair.

"I'm going to use the cell phone in the van to call nine-one-one. She needs oxygen," Joe called over his shoulder as he sprinted down the steps.

Frank sat on the edge of the lounge chair and tried to remember what to do for inhaled poisons. Just then Emily began to moan and toss her head.

"Emily? It's Frank."

Her eyes fluttered open, and she blinked in confusion. "Frank?" Reaching up, she touched her temple. "Where are my glasses? I can barely see."

"They're probably inside. We found you unconscious on the floor. The gas in the stove was on. What happened?"

Shutting her eyes, Emily groaned. "They stole the things I'd brought home from the museum."

"What things?"

"The MacDonald pistols, a musket, and the document signed by General Washington deeding the land to the Frobischers," she answered in a groggy voice.

"Do you know who it was?" Frank asked.

She nodded, then rubbed her forehead. Frank knew she must have a pounding headache from the poisonous carbon monoxide in the gas. "I knew one of them, Paul Kovak," she went on.

"He's the security guard at Virginia Gardens who locks the museum every night."

And switches forged objects for the real ones, Frank guessed. Was he the one who had killed Colin?

Tears filled Emily's eyes. "That's why I let them in. They told me the museum had burned and they wanted to make sure I was safe. I had no idea they were the black market thieves we were looking for."

Frank patted her arm. "Don't worry. Joe's calling the police. You need to give them names and descriptions. They'll catch them."

"They'd better," Emily said, gasping. "The document they stole might be the key to everything."

"What do you mean?"

"It's forged," Emily said quietly.

Frank's brows shot up. "You mean the letter deeding the Yorktown land to the Frobischers is a fake?"

Emily nodded weakly. "Yes. I checked and rechecked it. Which means that the land may not even belong to them. Can you imagine if anyone found that out? The Frobischers would be in court for the rest of their lives."

"Wow." Frank exhaled slowly. "Do you think they know?"

Emily nodded, this time forcefully. "The more I thought about it, the more I realized that if there was a black market ring in operation, then Mr. and Mrs. Frobischer had to be aware of it. After all, the museum housed their family heirlooms, their history. How could they not realize the artifacts were being replaced with fakes?"

"Unless they were in on it," Frank murmured.

"Or"—Emily took a shaky breath—"unless there were never *real* ones in the first place."

"You mean they stocked the museum with forgeries?" Frank asked, his brows shooting up in surprise. "But why?"

"False pride, perhaps." Emily slumped back onto the lounge chair. "I don't know."

Just then Joe came running around the house. "Frank! Regina called on the car phone. She told us to come quick. They've found Colin's murderer!"

"I've got a funny feeling about this," Frank said as he steered the van down the Frobischers' driveway half an hour later. The Hardys had waited until Emily was in safe hands with the paramedics before leaving. "Why would Regina call us instead of Nancy?"

Joe shrugged. "Don't be so suspicious."

"I'm being cautious," Frank replied as the Frobischers' mansion loomed up ahead of them. It was all lighted up like a Christmas tree, and everything looked calm and peaceful. "If Emily's theory is right, the Frobischers are in this scam up to their eyeballs."

"No way," Joe scoffed. "They're pillars of the community. Little old grannies and grampies. Emily was just grasping at straws. It's those security goons who are guilty. You wait and see."

"I don't know, Joe," Frank said doubtfully.

"You should be glad we're wrapping this up," Joe added. "The medic said Emily will be fine. And with Emily's description, the police should be able to nab that Paul guy and his buddy fleeing with the things they stole from her house. I bet when the police search the goons' vehicle, they'll find evidence to link them to the arson, too."

Frank snorted. "What I want is to nail them for Colin's murder."

"Well, according to Regina, she and Nancy are going to hand the killer to you on a silver platter."

"Yeah?" Frank said skeptically. "Then why didn't Regina tell you who the killer was over the phone?"

"I don't know," Joe said with a shrug. "Maybe she was so excited she forgot."

Frank glanced out the window at the house. "Unless she's leading us into a giant trap. At least you told Regina we couldn't find Emily."

"Yeah. I lied to her big time—just in case her family is connected with the forgers."

"And you said you weren't suspicious." Frank gave his brother a wry grin as he pulled the van up behind a green car parked at the mansion. "Whose car is that?"

"It looks like the one Tommy and Bess took tonight when they left Big Splash." Joe punched his brother lightly on the arm. "Come on, let's go in and get our bad guy."

Opening the van door, Joe climbed out. Frank hesitated before stepping out. His gut told him not to trust Regina Frobischer—to be prepared for anything.

The Frobischers' front door was halfway open.

"Regina? Nancy?" Joe called out, peering inside.

"Come on in!" Regina answered.

Frank followed Joe down the hall toward a lighted doorway. When the Hardys stepped into what looked like a library, Regina greeted them with a strained smile. She was sitting in a high-backed chair, with her hands hidden behind her.

Regina slowly moved her hand from behind her back, and Frank heard Joe catch his breath. Still smiling, Regina was pointing a revolver straight at their heads.

A big guy dressed in camouflage stood behind her. Frank froze—it was Nancy's attacker. He'd expected that Regina had something up her sleeve, but not this.

"Regina?" Joe said in a puzzled-sounding

voice. "What's going on? I thought you were going to tell us who Colin's killer was."

"Change of plans," Regina said cheerfully. "We're going to have a boating party instead. Only you and your friends aren't coming back."

Frank saw Joe's shoulders tense. "What?" Joe blurted. "Don't tell me your grandparents are in on this forgery scam!"

"They're the masterminds," Regina declared, her tone serious. Slowly, she stood up, the gun never wavering.

"But you couldn't . . ." Joe's voice trailed off. He lifted his arms and then dropped them in a gesture of despair.

"No, I wasn't in on it," Regina told him. "But now I am. This is my family. This is my home. I'll kill before any of it is taken away." She gestured to the right with the gun. "Now, go on down the hall to join your friends, and don't try anything funny."

This may be the only chance I have to make a break for it, Frank thought as he slowly turned around. But he immediately heard the thud of boots on wood and felt the sharp prick of a knife blade in his back.

"I wouldn't try anything if I was you," a deep voice said.

Frank looked over his shoulder. The hulk in camouflage gear grinned nastily at him.

"Don't worry. I'm just in a hurry to get to that boating party," Frank quipped.

"Save the wisecracks for when you're sinking to the bottom of the James River," the guy said. "You'll need something to laugh about then."

With Regina on one side and the goon on the other, Frank and Joe were herded down the hall. When they reached the kitchen, Nancy jumped up from where she, Tye, Tommy, and Bess were sitting around a table.

"Frank!" she exclaimed, her voice shaky with fear.

"Sit down!" a guy with another gun barked from behind her.

Frank recognized the goon he'd punched in the parking lot. The guy must have recognized him, too, Frank thought, since his eyes narrowed and he shot Frank a wicked-looking grin.

"Well, I think introductions are in order," Mrs. Frobischer said brightly from over by the counter, where she and her husband were sipping something in wine glasses. Dressed in formal wear, they did indeed look like pillars of the community. Only now Frank knew they were ruthless criminals.

Pointing with her glass, Mrs. Frobischer introduced the goons—T.C., Leo, and Jason—to Frank and Joe as if they'd just arrived at a cocktail party.

"Jason was the one who killed your friend, you know," Mr. Frobischer bragged.

Jason smiled smugly, and Frank's hands clenched into fists. If there hadn't been a gun aimed at his head, he would've wiped that grin right off Jason's face.

Mr. and Mrs. Frobischer clinked glasses. "To our clever, rich family and our lovely granddaughter," they toasted. "And now that we all know each other," Mrs. Frobischer announced, "let the party begin!"

Jason began to chuckle. "And it'll be a bang of a party, too, since we've got the boat rigged to blow sky high. Boom!" Curling his fist, he punched the air hard, and Bess screamed.

Jason lowered his arm, then gave the teens a look so cold that it chilled Frank's insides.

"In fact, the party will be such a *blast,"* Jason hissed, "that you'll all die laughing."

Chapter Twenty-One

FRANK LOOKED at Nancy. She was staring at Jason in sheer terror. But then he noticed the determined set to her mouth. Nancy wasn't nearly as frightened as she was pretending to be.

Not that she shouldn't be scared. The whole Frobischer family was obviously crazy enough to kill anyone who got in their way.

Their only hope was that Detective Burnett had caught Paul and his cohort. If either of them ratted on the Frobischers, the police might get to them in time.

"Let's get going," Jason ordered with a wave of his knife. "Single file and no funny business."

As Frank shuffled out the kitchen door behind Joe, he tried to assess the situation. Right now, they were outnumbered. But that could change at any time. When it did, Frank knew that they would have to be ready to fight for their lives.

As the group went down the grassy slope to the dock, Nancy tried her best to look cowed. She wanted Jason and the others to think she was overcome with fear, so that when she, Joe, and Frank did strike, they'd take them by surprise.

A gentle breeze wafted off the James River, and Nancy could hear the soft lap of water against the dock pilings. It was a gorgeous night, and she had no intention of ending it by getting blown up in a boating accident.

"Leo, T.C.," Mrs. Frobischer called to the two security guards. "Go on down to the boat and make sure there's enough rope to tie everybody up. Also, make sure the second boat is gassed up. You'll have to follow us out to the middle of the river."

When Leo and T.C. hustled off, Nancy caught Frank's eye. He nodded as if reading her message. When the two left, the odds would be in their favor—except for the guns. Still, it might be their only chance.

With a cry, Nancy pretended to trip. When she did, she fell against Mrs. Frobischer. Slicing down on the older woman's wrist, Nancy knocked the gun from her grasp. Frank dove for it. At the same time, Joe spun and karate-kicked Mr. Frobischer in the chest.

Nancy whipped around to confront Regina, but suddenly an arm wrapped around her neck in a chokehold and slammed her backward against a hard chest.

Frank jumped up, the gun in his hand. But Jason had been quicker. He had Nancy in a deathlock. She gasped, barely able to breathe. The blood rushed to her head, and she felt herself growing faint.

"Drop it, punk," Jason told Frank. "Or I'll break her neck with one snap."

Frank, Tye, Joe, Tommy, and Bess froze in their tracks. Mr. Frobischer was kneeling on the ground, holding his chest and coughing. Regina had gone into a shooter's stance, her gun pointed at Frank.

"Do what he says, Frank," Regina said. "Jason means it."

Frank's face turned ashen. Don't drop the gun! Nancy wanted to scream, but all that came out was a gargling sound as Jason tightened his hold, and she almost passed out from the pain.

Frank dropped the gun. Tears filled Nancy's eyes. She should have known there was no way they could go up against cold-blooded murderers.

"Kill him, Regina," Mrs. Frobischer said in an

icy voice. Stooping, she picked up the dropped gun. "Then he can't make any more trouble."

Bess clapped a hand over her mouth, muffling a scream. Joe, Tommy, and Tye stood rigid with anger and helplessness.

Nancy's eyes widened. No! she silently pleaded.

"No, Grandmother." Regina swung the gun around, aiming it at Mrs. Frobischer. "This has gone far enough. *You* put down your gun. Then call off my cousin the gorilla. If he doesn't let Nancy go, I'll kill you."

All the blood drained from Mrs. Frobischer's face. "Regina!" she gasped. "What is the meaning of this? You're one of us!"

"No," Regina declared, her voice steady. "I'm not one of you. I only pretended to be, so that I could call Frank and Joe and warn them. But Jason foiled my plans. He listened in on the phone conversation. So I had to continue my charade. I hoped that once the Hardys arrived, they'd even the odds. I was going to warn you, Joe, as soon as you came, but—"

"But I knew she couldn't be trusted," Jason cut in. "That's why I decided to be part of the welcoming committee."

Regina tipped her chin up. "I won't be part of a family that cheats and murders to get what it wants."

"Oh, Regina." Mr. Frobischer shook his head

as he staggered to his feet. "And all this time we thought you had what it took to be a Frobischer."

Regina smiled coolly. "I do have what it takes. It's just not your idea of what a Frobischer should be. Now drop the gun!" she commanded.

Mrs. Frobischer opened her fingers and let the gun slip to the ground. Tye lunged for it, then aimed it at Jason. "He's mine," he growled.

"Give it up, Jason. Let Nancy go," Frank said calmly.

Just then police sirens blared in the background. Nancy felt Jason's grip tighten.

"No way! She's my ticket outta here," he shouted, dragging Nancy backward toward the boat. "And no one's going to stop me!"

Nancy cried out as she stumbled over his feet. Pain shot up her neck. Suddenly, she felt Jason's arm shift lower around her throat.

She gulped a mouthful of air. Mustering all her remaining strength, she stomped down on the arch of Jason's foot.

"Ow!" For an instant, his grip loosened. That was all it took. Reaching up with both hands, Nancy tore his arm from around her throat. Whirling around, she stabbed her thumbs into his eyes. At the same time, Frank, Joe, Tye, and Tommy jumped Jason. The knife fell from his grasp, and Bess snatched it up.

Nancy slumped to the ground, gasping. When she looked up, Jason was flat on his back, struggling against Tye, Tommy, and Joe, who were holding him down. In the distance, Nancy heard a powerboat motor rev up. When she looked toward the river, T.C. and Leo zoomed away from the dock.

"They won't get far," Frank said, coming over and kneeling next to her. He pointed toward the mansion. Detective Burnett and half a dozen police officers were rounding the corner. "Are you all right?" Frank asked as he inspected the bruises on Nancy's neck.

She nodded. "Thanks to Regina." She smiled at the other girl, who aimed the gun steadily at her grandparents. "That's twice you've saved my life."

"All in a day's work," Regina replied. "After all, I'm a Frobischer."

"This is the life—finally," Bess announced as she speared a chunk of fruit from Tommy's plate.

The seven teens were sitting around a table at the Paradise Wave Pool eating a sumptuous lunch—compliments of Mrs. Somers.

"Sun, sand, swimming. You can't beat them," Joe said. He was sitting next to Regina, his arm around her shoulders. "Williamsburg is a lot more fun when you're playing tourist rather than detective."

Tye lifted his soda can. "Here's to summer and a much-needed vacation. Which will definitely be more fun than trying to solve a two-hundred-year-old mystery."

Nancy had to agree. Leaning back in her chair, she closed her eyes and let the sun warm her face. Her throat was bruised and sore, but otherwise everything had turned out all right.

The police had arrested Paul and recovered several stolen artifacts and the forged Washington document. When the coast guard had picked up Leo and T.C., the two had promptly ratted on Jason, accusing him of murdering both Colin and Kirby. With the list of crimes against them, the Frobischers and their goons would be in jail forever.

"Is Dana going to say goodbye before she leaves?" Bess asked Nancy.

Nancy lifted her head. "I think so. But she's pretty embarrassed about everything that's happened."

"Why is she leaving?" Tommy asked. "The diving team still needs her, and the Frobischers could hardly fire her."

"Not from jail, anyway," Joe agreed. "Which is where they'll be forever." He gave Regina an apologetic smile.

"Don't worry. That's where they belong," Regina said with a sigh. "Even if they are my grandmother and grandfather." For a second she stared down dejectedly at her sandwich. "I felt terrible turning on them, but I had no choice."

"It's a good thing you did," Frank said, "or we might all be fish food at the bottom of the James River." He had been sitting quietly next to Nancy. She knew he was exhausted, too. Plus, he was still grieving for his friend.

"I just wished you hadn't taken so long to turn the gun on them," Joe teased. "I was starting to get a tiny bit worried."

"With Jason hovering over me, I had to wait for the right time." Tipping her chin up, Regina looked at Joe from under her long lashes. "Do you mean you doubted me, Joe Hardy?"

"Well, you are a Frobischer," Joe countered. "Family ties can be pretty strong."

"You know, I always wondered why my father moved as far away from my grandparents as he could," Regina said. "He never would talk about it, but before I came out here for the summer, he tried to dissuade me. Of course, that only made me more determined to come. When I phoned my dad and told him everything, he was almost apoplectic."

Lifting her head, Regina squared her shoulders. "So if my dad wanted nothing to do with the scandalous Frobischers, there must be other law-abiding relatives in my past. And I aim to find them."

"Here! Here!" They all lifted their juice glasses in a toast. Then Nancy turned to Tommy.

"Dana says she needs some time off from

diving," she told him, answering his original question. "She doesn't like the person she was turning into, with all that competing she had to do."

Bess snorted. "Thanks to her pushy mother."

"I think she's taking time off from her, too," Nancy said, glancing over at Regina, who was talking quietly with Joe.

That afternoon Regina's parents were arriving from California. Joe was taking Regina to the airport to meet them. Nancy knew the family would have a lot to sort through.

"So, what do you think, Tye?" Nancy turned to him. "Do you think you'll ever unravel the truth about who owns this property?"

He shrugged. "I told my family that the Frobischers' letters could prove the land was stolen from them, but they said it would take years in court and be a huge legal mess."

"I'm hoping my parents and Tye's family can work something out," Regina said. "Though even now, the ownership and running of the parks is up in the air."

"Whew. I'm glad I can now sit back and enjoy the rides and sun," Frank said with a laugh.

"Me, too!" Bess piped up. "I'm ready to relax."

Pushing back her chair, Nancy jumped up. "There's no time for relaxing!" she exclaimed to Frank and Bess.

"No, not another mystery!" Bess groaned as she rolled her eyes.

"Oh, come on, you wimps," Nancy teased, her blue eyes gleaming wickedly. "An even bigger challenge awaits us at Big Splash Water Park. We still haven't ridden the Triple Thrill Turbo Pipeline!"

"Valencia."

Her name sounded like a warning and a plea at the same time.

Although maybe she only heard those things because she felt equal parts danger and desire herself. Just then, something heavy crashed into the door at the top of the stairs. A big tree limb, maybe. Or a part of the house?

The roof?

"Please?" She clutched the blanket around her like a cape, wishing she could crawl into his lap and stay there until the tornado ran its course.

Instead, she pressed closer to him, hip to hip, her thigh squeezing against his.

Lorenzo made a ragged sound of protest, but at the same time, he encircled her shoulders with his arm, tugging her nearer. For a moment, he rested his cheek against the top of her head.

"Maybe you could suggest an appropriate distraction," he urged. "Because my thoughts are all running in the wrong direction."

* * *

Trapped with the Texan
by Joanne Rock is part of the
Texas Cattleman's Club: Heir Apparent series.

Dear Reader,

What fun we writers have cooking up these stories for you! I love writing the Texas Cattleman Club stories because the connected plotlines always provide opportunities to chat and brainstorm with writer friends. For *Trapped with the Texan*, I dreamed up a whole family full of Cortez-Williams brothers with Barbara Dunlop, and then we browsed Texas properties online to find the perfect inspiration for the Cortez-Williams Ranch. The process is kind of like seeing a movie with a good friend. It's more fun when shared!

So settle in for the high drama of another trip to Royal, Texas. There's a storm brewing in this story, and all the careful planning for an arts festival on Appaloosa Island is at risk. I'd love to hear what you think of *Trapped with the Texan*. You can find me online at joannerock.com or Harlequin.com!

Happy reading,

Joanne Rock

JOANNE ROCK

TRAPPED WITH THE TEXAN

Special thanks and acknowledgment are given to Joanne Rock for her contribution to the Texas Cattleman's Club: Heir Apparent miniseries.

Recycling programs for this product may not exist in your area.

ISBN-13: 978-1-335-73504-1

Trapped with the Texan

This edition published by arrangement with Harlequin Books S.A.

For questions and comments about the quality of this book, please contact us at CustomerService@Harlequin.com.

Harlequin Enterprises ULC
22 Adelaide St. West, 40th Floor
Toronto, Ontario M5H 4E3, Canada
www.Harlequin.com

Printed in U.S.A.

Joanne Rock credits her decision to write romance after a book she picked up during a flight delay engrossed her so thoroughly that she didn't mind at all when her flight was delayed two more times. Giving her readers the chance to escape into another world has motivated her to write over eighty books for a variety of Harlequin series.

Books by Joanne Rock

Harlequin Desire

Brooklyn Nights

A Nine-Month Temptation

Dynasties: Mesa Falls

The Rebel
The Rival
Rule Breaker
Heartbreaker
The Rancher
The Heir

Texas Cattleman's Club: Heir Apparent

Trapped with the Texan

Visit her Author Profile page at Harlequin.com, or joannerock.com, for more titles.

You can also find Joanne Rock on Facebook, along with other Harlequin Desire authors, at Facebook.com/harlequindesireauthors!

For Patricia Savery,
whose strong spirit inspires me.
Thank you for reading as long as I've been writing!

One

Earbuds in place, Valencia Donovan cranked up the volume of her music while she rocked out discreetly in the parking lot of the Texas Cattleman's Club. Seated in the driver's seat of her late-model pickup truck, she sang along to her personal playlist labeled "Game Time Hype," even though her appointment within the walls of the prestigious, members-only club was no game.

Fiery girl-power anthems weren't anything she'd normally listen to at home or while working at her ranch. But as a dedicated overachiever, Valencia appreciated the ferocity of the lyrics before she had to give an important business pitch. She might be well beyond the age of her high school basketball days when she'd first started the playlist, but she wasn't about to mess with her winning streak now. Not when she really, *really* needed an investment from Lorenzo Cortez-Williams to expand her horse rescue operation.

Closing her eyes, she pumped her fist and let the final strains of the song flow over her while she visualized her success.

Slam. Dunk.

Smiling, she turned off the music once her energy fired to life. And yes, maybe she glanced around the parking lot just a smidge self-consciously to see if anyone noticed her antics. But she'd parked in the farthest corner of the lot. Now, tossing the earbuds aside, she slid out of the truck and locked the doors behind her. She paused long enough to check her reflection in the side mirror, smoothing down a few curls that had sprouted in the humidity.

Her pre-meeting routine might be on the corny side, but the outfit she wore was conservative enough. A navy blue sheath dress with a matching jacket and nude sling-back pumps. She wasn't a member of the TCC herself, but she knew how the other half lived. Her adoptive family had raised her to be comfortable in this world, and Valencia had shaken off the dirt of her roots a long time ago. Her unhappy early childhood did *not* define her.

Checking her watch as she entered the dark-stone-and-wood historic building, she noted that she was precisely on time for her meeting. Which would undoubtedly work in her favor. The retired rancher whom she was meeting was a septuagenarian with deep pockets and a reputation for philanthropy. She intended to dazzle him with her business plan for Donovan Horse Rescue, and solidify the final necessary funds to expand the rescue so she could develop an equine therapy component in the form of a summer camp for kids. Her charitable foundation had already been promised a portion of the funds raised by the ticket sales to Soiree on the Bay, an upcoming food, art and wine festival on Appaloosa Island.

Today's meeting could yield the rest.

"Miss Donovan?" a man's warm baritone greeted her.

Valencia glanced up from her watch to meet the intent regard of a wildly handsome man. He had dark brown hair and dark eyes framed by heavy brows. A deeply tanned complexion that she guessed was more due to heritage than the sun. And his gray pants and black shirt were tailored in such a way that she couldn't help but notice how broad-shouldered and fit he was. Valencia sighed appreciatively as she continued to drink him in. Well over six feet, this guy loomed over her, and she was *not* a petite woman. Even without the expensive-looking boots he wore, he would still be tall.

Yikes! How long had she been standing there ogling him?

Her manners returned along with a hint of dismay. Since when did a hot-looking man turn her head? Especially when she had just played her game-time hype playlist and needed all her focus?

"Yes. I'm Valencia Donovan." She gave him a polite smile while hoping her racing thoughts didn't show on her face.

Dressed as he was, he couldn't possibly work at the Texas Cattleman's Club, but she also couldn't imagine who else would greet her by name.

"Lorenzo Cortez-Williams." He extended his hand. "A pleasure to meet you."

"Oh." Confused, she clasped his palm automatically upon hearing the name. But hadn't her meeting been with a much older man? The extremely compelling rancher whose hand enveloped hers couldn't be more than thirty-five years old. "I'm sorry. I thought—"

"You were expecting someone else?" He smiled warmly while gesturing her ahead of him. "Our table is this way."

Knocked off her game, Valencia took a deep breath as he relinquished her hand. She'd been too rattled to enjoy the touch even though her palm retained a hint of his warmth. Of course, she shouldn't be enjoying skin-on-skin contact with a potential investor. Berating herself for the slipup, she shoved aside thoughts of her companion's potent sex appeal and focused on business as she followed him through the dark wood-paneled corridors into the high-ceilinged dining area. Hunting trophies and historical artifacts provided understated decor where some of the most influential residents of Royal, Texas, enjoyed a meal.

"I read your bio to prepare for the meeting," she admitted as he showed her to a quiet table in the back. "And the photo of Lorenzo Cortez-Williams showed a man closer to my grandfather's age."

"*My* granddad, no doubt. That's the problem with inheriting the family moniker. There are two other formidable Lorenzos still bearing the same name. I'm Lorenzo the third." As he withdrew a high-backed leather chair for her at the round table, she couldn't help but notice the ring finger on his left hand remained bare. "My father is Lorenzo Junior. Gramp is the original."

"Of course." She lowered herself into the chair he indicated, even as she struggled to recall what else she'd read about the Cortez-Williams family on their charitable website. "Will either of them be joining us?"

He slid her chair into place before taking the seat across from her. A waiter arrived to greet her at the same moment, bringing a carafe of water and pouring two glasses while taking their drink orders. When the server left, Lorenzo leveled that piercing brown-eyed gaze her way again. His full focus on her.

"It will be just us today, Miss Donovan."

"Please call me Valencia."

"Only if you pay me the same courtesy." He lifted his glass of water and clinked it softly to hers before taking a sip. "And I have taken over my grandfather's former duties. Gramp has grown a soft heart for causes, and a few months ago we discovered he was on track to donate most of the family fortune."

She hid her renewed sense of dismay by taking her time spreading her napkin over her lap. Did the man seated across from her need to reel in the spending now? She wished she could go back in time and prepare for this meeting differently.

"That must have been upsetting for your family," she murmured, before lifting her eyes to his. "Was he aware that he was in danger of overextending? I hope his health is still sound."

Lorenzo was still regarding her steadily, his dark gaze unnerving her a bit. If they'd been in a dimly lit bar for drinks, she would have felt a feminine thrill at whatever chased through his brown eyes. But now, with the success of her dream on the line, it was distracting.

"Gramp is in excellent health, thank you." He

shuffled aside his menu. "But we thought it best if I took over the vetting process for charitable donations. You'd be surprised how many con artists are out there."

Bristling at the implication, she forced a cool smile. "I assure you, my efforts to rescue horses are very real. I can provide you with references. People who can vouch for my character."

"I'm not questioning your integrity, Valencia. But as a representative of my family, I need to exercise caution since all of those things can be faked." There was a somberness in his expression that told her he'd had firsthand experience with those kinds of people.

The knowledge soothed her a bit, even as the last of her plans for this meeting crumpled under the need for a new approach.

"I'm sorry to hear that there are folks who take advantage of your family's generosity that way, but I suppose I shouldn't be surprised." She waited while their server returned with the iced tea she'd ordered. Then, listening to the waiter reel off the lunch specials, she chose the carne asada while Lorenzo asked for his "usual." After he departed, Valencia returned to her subject with renewed determination. "So tell me, how can I convince you that Donovan Horse Rescue is legitimate? Rest assured that I am emphatic about transparency with my finances."

The spark of interest in his smoldering eyes told her that he appreciated the approach.

"For starters, just meeting you in person is helpful. I like to size up who I'm dealing with face-to-face." He took a pull from his longneck, his expression thoughtful.

"I can't argue with that. I rely on my instincts, too. What else can I tell you about the rescue?"

"I look forward to hearing all about it over lunch," he murmured, setting down the dark bottle. "But I won't be relying solely on my instincts when making my final decision. If I like what I hear today, I'll want to visit Donovan Horse Rescue in person. Tour your facility and see what I think."

"Fantastic." She welcomed the chance to have him see the ranch for himself. She was proud of what she'd built, and knew every detail of her expansion plan by heart so she could explain it to him while looking at the footprint of the anticipated new additions. "I realize it's short notice, but are you available after lunch today?"

A shiver ran through her as she awaited his response. Because, as much as she anticipated selling him on her foundation, she also felt slightly wary of having this extremely compelling rancher walking around her personal space. She had the feeling Lorenzo Cortez-Williams would leave his mark somehow.

Which meant she needed to tread warily with a man who held the future of her mission in his hands.

"Unfortunately, I have another appointment this afternoon." His words disappointed her more than they should have, making her aware that the undercurrent of sizzling attraction she felt hadn't eased since they'd sat down. "Are you free tomorrow, perhaps?"

The smoky quality of his voice made the proposition feel more personal.

"For the prospect of showing you my operation, I would gladly clear my schedule. But as it happens, I'm free all day."

She couldn't have held back her grin. Strictly because she knew the rescue was impressive and would make her case for her. *Not* because she was already looking forward to seeing him again.

The rapid tattoo of her heartbeat, however, already called her a liar.

Business and pleasure don't mix.

Lorenzo Cortez-Williams should have been the last man in Royal, Texas, who needed to repeat those words like a mantra. They'd been branded into his skin by his restaurateur fiancée, who'd targeted him for his wealth, ran up his credit cards and then disappeared from his life five years ago. *After* she'd signed his family's beef company to a cut-rate deal for her restaurants, a deal that had seared more resentment into him with each passing year until it was done.

So why did he need to pull into a local coffee shop to remind himself of the necessary separation between work and play, lest he show up at Donovan Horse Rescue too early for his appointment with Valencia Donovan? Probably because the woman attracted him like no one else ever had. Ex-fiancée included. Valencia had impressed him with more than her smarts even though her business acumen came across immediately during their meeting. There'd been a warmth of spirit about her obvious love for horses, a commitment to her mission that practically shone out of her eyes when she spoke. He'd been…captivated.

Tightening his grip on the take-out cup from the drive-through, Lorenzo steered his truck back onto the county route that would lead to Valencia's place, reminding himself that he wouldn't be seeing her again after today. He'd already taken the liberty of ordering an investigation of her and her business, a practice that he'd leaned on after discovering how many scammers had shaken money out of the family's charitable fund in the past. Not to mention the fiasco with Lindsey that had made him question his own judgment. His private investigator was discreet. Thorough. And Lorenzo now had a detailed report on Valencia that showed her in a favorable light. At only thirty years old, she'd already blazed quite an illustrious path for herself. She'd aced high school and college, accumulating awards and honors for her community involvement even as a teen, before going onto tremendous success in the corporate world during her eight-year stint with an agricultural company based in Dallas.

Valencia's early childhood was a gray area since she'd been adopted when she was young and there was little information available about her formative years. Yet considering all she'd accomplished since then, Lorenzo was prepared to move forward with her request if he liked what he saw at the rescue today.

Assuming he could look at anything but her. How many times had he thought about her intelligent brown eyes taking his measure when she first saw him? There'd been a moment before she realized that she'd be meeting with him, when her response to him had been purely feminine. She'd hidden it fast and thoroughly once she'd recognized her error, but he couldn't get that look out of his head. Last night, he'd spent far too long letting their innocuous encounter spin out into other, more provocative scenarios in his mind.

Now he turned into the gravel drive that led to her place, his oversize pickup truck dipping into an uneven patch despite the high-grade suspension. Settling his drink into the cupholder so he could keep both hands on the wheel, he noted the creek's proximity and an equipment barn that looked like it had been recently upgraded. An unassuming one-story stone house sat on a low hill overlooking the creek, but the simple landscaping and unfinished garage told him that Valencia had put her finances into the horses instead of the home.

Something he could appreciate, having been raised on a ranch himself. He parked off to one side of the driveway between the house and the barn, then took a last bracing sip of his coffee before exiting the truck.

The scent of pink briar hung in the air, the driveway partially lined with the airy flowers that closed up when you brushed against them. Lorenzo skirted a thick patch of them to head toward the house. Before he'd gone three steps, a sorrel Belgian came into view as it jumped a low hedge behind the house, carrying Valencia Donovan on its broad back at a lengthened trot.

Dressed in faded jeans and boots, she was even lovelier today. Well-worn denim hugged her thighs while a flowy pink blouse rippled in the breeze around her shoulders. A buff-colored hat kept the sun from her delicate features, long blond waves trailing down her back. She rode with ease that went beyond good horsemanship that was common enough around this part of Texas. The animal's gait was one of the toughest to sit gracefully, especially on such a huge draft horse that would have a powerful trot. Yet her hips moved with practiced grace, the rest of her body still, a feat that spoke of long hours of training and muscles attuned to the work.

Damned if that display didn't jolt him right back into wayward imaginings about the woman he'd thought of far too often since their meeting the day before.

"Good morning," she greeted him on a breathless laugh as she swung down from the mare, her cheeks flushed with color. "I hope I haven't kept you waiting. Sapphire has taken a few days to settle in here, and she was in such good spirits on our morning run that I found it hard to turn her around."

Another woman—a ranch hand, he guessed—approached to take the mare's reins from her. But Valencia took an extra moment to tip her head to the Belgian's neck and croon softly at her before handing them over. Her compassion was obvious. After Lorenzo had been taken in by a false-faced woman in the past, he liked to think he had a better radar for deceit now. Valencia's love of the horses definitely wasn't fake.

"Sapphire is one of your rescues?" he asked, forcing himself to think like an investor in her foundation and not a man wildly enamored by a woman.

He really needed to start dating more. He didn't normally get sidetracked this way.

"Yes." Valencia's gaze followed the Belgian for a long moment before turning her pretty brown eyes to him. "Her owner died a few weeks ago and the man's nephew contacted me about taking her in. Some animals have ended up here because of neglect or unsuitable living conditions, but Sapphire has been well cared for." She gestured toward a stable he'd noticed when he drove in. "Would you like to see the facilities we have so far?"

"Very much." The more they kept the focus on the rescue, the less attention he'd pay to the woman herself. "It looks like you've recently upgraded the outbuildings."

"I have." She headed in the direction of the stable. "I saved every cent from my job in the corporate world to put toward start-up costs for the rescue. My plan began with the right facilities that could expand as we grow."

"I read your three-phase business model." He'd been more than a little impressed with the level of detail. She'd anticipated every potential expense. "You should be able to afford the adjoining parcel of land next."

She needed more space before she could move

into the next phase—an immersive equine therapy camp for troubled kids. The end goal had made him all the more curious about the unknown portion of her background—her birth parents and early home life. What struggles had she faced before her adoptive parents came into the picture?

"Yes. If the ticket sales to Soiree on the Bay are as robust as we all hope they will be, I'll be able to buy the land at the end of the month." As they passed the stone house, she excused herself long enough to dash up the front steps and open the front door so a black-and-tan dog—a border collie mix was his guess—could bolt down the stairs and run ahead of them. "That's Barkis, by the way."

"Barkis?" he laughed. "A funny name for a dog when he didn't even make a sound at seeing me."

"Barkis was a package deal along with the first horse I rescued." Her smile faltered a little as she spoke. "I learned about the animals from an eleven-year-old girl living next door to them. She'd drawn a crayon sketch of the horse and the dog and walked into a gas station to post it on their community notice board while I was buying a bag of chips for a road trip."

He heard the echo of some painful memories in the story, and felt a new wave of admiration for this beautiful, caring woman who not only abhorred suffering, but who felt called to help in a deeply personal way.

"You intercepted her sign?" he guessed.

"I was still working at my job full-time, even though I'd already started the business plan. I was on the road that day to see one of our more remote equipment dealers. But when I spoke to the little girl about the animals who needed help—neglected, hungry animals she petted and consoled through a rusted barbed wire fence every day—I recognized that moment was going to be my beginning." Her voice had gone fierce during the story, but she paused now to draw a breath as they reached the stable. "She didn't know the animals' names, but privately called the dog Barkis and the horse Tuxedo. I still give her updates about them."

Valencia nodded toward the stable door as she preceded him inside. It took him a moment to regain his composure after the story, though, envisioning her dressed in her business suit and heels in some ramshackle gas station, taking the time to listen to a passionate kid with a crayon drawing.

She'd somehow ditched her job and saved the animals, no doubt earning hero status in the kid's eyes. He followed her into the stable, his gaze drawn to the sway of her hips before he remembered himself.

If Valencia Donovan was putting on an act to entice funds out of the Cortez-Williams family, it was a damned good show. But with every moment he spent in her presence, even the most cynical part of himself found it tougher to believe. Which meant he'd have to try twice as hard to stick to his guns and avoid the potent temptation that dogged him every moment he spent with Valencia.

Two

Determined to prove her ambitions for Donovan Horse Rescue were very real, Valencia took Lorenzo through each building and introduced him to every horse on her property over the next two hours. She refrained from sharing more personal stories after accidentally confiding the way she'd leaped into the rescue work that first time. After that slipup, she stuck to the scripted details that were available on the rescue's website, unwilling to give a potential investor any reason to think she led with her heart and not her brain.

She could share heart-tugging stories. Just not the details that crawled under her skin and made her care on a deep level. Those dark eyes of his saw too much already.

As they turned away from Buttercup, the last of the horses in the new stable, they left the second stable building and skirted the paddock. The sun had risen to its zenith, making her aware how much time she'd spent showing him around.

"Your operation is impressive," he observed, reaching to give Barkis a scratch around the ears since the dog was circling him, tail wagging in double time. "And the website does an effective job of making the animals sound appealing to potential supporters and adopters."

Lorenzo straightened from where he'd pet the pup. He was dressed more informally today in dark jeans and a more casual button-down, but his boots were still hand-tooled leather, the kind that rarely saw ranch work. And why did he have to look even more appealing to her this way than he had over their business lunch? Yesterday, she'd met the businessman. Today, she was seeing the rancher, and yes, she liked that side of him.

She'd read more about his family after their lunch meeting, and learned that Lorenzo was not only the third to bear the name, but also the oldest of his siblings. It made her wonder how he felt about being the heir to the family legacy.

"Thank you. I'm hoping Soiree on the Bay not

only brings added funds, but also more public visibility and traffic to the site."

"I'm sure it will." He slowed his pace as they neared his pickup truck, a beast of a model with a turbo-charged diesel engine, built-in winch and all the extra features that were still on Valencia's wish list. "But once you start your summer camp, will you keep some horses stabled here permanently? When you find animals who are a good fit to work with camp goers, I assume you'd want to keep them here."

Pleasantly surprised he'd given that much thought to her expansion project, she hoped that meant he was seriously considering financial support.

"Absolutely. And even though the campers would only ride trusted mounts under the guidance of a certified instructor, I hope the attendees could be involved with caring for the rescues." She'd been certified after working with an equine therapy center during college, and she missed it. For that matter, she missed the atmosphere of healing and community that went hand in hand with an equine center, much like the one her adoptive parents had sent her to as a child. "Giving troubled kids another creature to care for allows them to feel rewarded and accepted for simple acts of kindness."

He nodded while she spoke, as if her words had

affirmed something he'd been thinking. Had she somehow revealed too much again?

"Your passion for the project is clear," he said gruffly, tipping his head toward her and making her realize how close they stood.

Her heart beat faster and she wondered if she'd been the one to venture so near to him, or if he'd been the one to trespass on the businesslike boundaries they'd silently agreed on. Swallowing a flash of nervousness, she folded her arms around herself to add a barrier between her and the dark, masculine appeal of the man in front of her.

"May I ask what drew you to this kind of work?" he prompted when she remained silent.

Normally, she had a scripted answer, but she wondered how much he already knew about her personal history. How well had he researched her and her organization? She didn't like the idea of anyone circling around the wounded parts of her past, and it bothered her all the more to think of this successful, formidable man seeing that side of her.

"Barkis wasn't incentive enough?" She raised an eyebrow, allowing her lips to quirk, and hoped he'd give her a pass on sharing anything more personal. He knew her business plan. She shouldn't have to bleed on the proposal, too.

"He's a damned fine dog," Lorenzo agreed a

moment later, taking a step backward with a laugh and effectively breaking the tension of the moment.

She breathed a relieved sigh that he'd let her off the hook. Before she could reply, he continued speaking.

"Thank you for taking so much time to speak with me today, Valencia. I enjoyed the tour and wish you well with the rescue either way, but I'll speak to my family about your project and get back to you within the week."

She forced a smile, hoping she hadn't blown her chances to sell Lorenzo on the idea of her horse rescue with her need for privacy. Already a pang of regret twisted inside her that she hadn't been more forthcoming about her past. But then again, sharing those darker details could have come across as too much.

Too *needy*.

And she had to keep those vulnerabilities hidden at all costs. Especially when her feelings were already so complicated when it came to him.

"The pleasure was all mine," she assured him, her eyes darting to his as the word *pleasure* tripped off her lips accidentally. Perhaps she'd spent too much time in close proximity to him to be second-guessing her language choices and cherry-picking what details to share with him. Valencia sighed. Why couldn't she have met with his gray-haired grandfather about the donation? Because Lorenzo the third was a temptation she did *not* need in her life right now. "I look forward to hearing from you."

With a tip of his hat, he walked away, his broad shoulders holding her gaze. For all his wealth and refined manners, Lorenzo had an ease around the ranch that had made it easy for her to talk to him today. And yes, she could admit she admired that in a man.

As he drove off, her canine woofed a goodbye. For her part, Valencia knew she'd have only herself to blame if the Cortez-Williams family wasn't ready to invest. The only good part about that? At least she wouldn't have to blush and stammer her way through any more parting words with the gorgeous rancher. Pressing a cooling hand to her still-warm cheek, she was heading back to the house for a bite to eat when the sound of tires crunching through the gravel on her driveway made her turn around again.

Her pulse quickened at the thought of Lorenzo returning, but the vehicle that rounded the bend could never be mistaken for a pickup truck. The sleek Aston Martin could belong only to an Edmond, one of Royal's wealthiest families.

And, sure enough, as the sports car drew nearer she could see the oldest of Rusty Edmond's sons behind the wheel. The Edmond siblings, Ross, Asher and Gina, together with Ross's friend Billy

Holmes, were the driving force behind Soiree on the Bay. The Edmond family also owned Appaloosa Island, the site of the festival. Normally, Asher was Valencia's contact when she had festival questions, so she was a little surprised to see Ross here today.

Even more so to see him heft a toddler from a car seat in the back of the coupe, carrying the curly-haired boy in his arms as he ambled toward her. They were an appealing pair. No matter that Lorenzo was the only man who turned her head lately, she couldn't deny that seeing handsome Ross with his chubby-cheeked son in his arms was enough to make any woman's ovaries hum.

"Hello, Ross," she called, striding closer. "And hello to this adorable young gentleman you've brought with you."

She'd heard that Ross had a child with Charlotte Jarrett, his fiancée and the executive chef of Sheen, a popular restaurant in Royal. But she hadn't met the little one before. She opened and closed her fist in a baby-wave she thought most toddlers would recognize.

"My son, Ben," he announced, the pride shining in his blue eyes as he looked down at the boy. Ben smiled shyly at Valencia before bouncing in his father's arms with toddler joy. "I was just on my way to Sheen to see Charlotte, and since we were driving past your place, I thought I should drop by to share an update on the food and wine festival."

His tone grew serious as he spoke, drawing Valencia's attention from Ben to his father's face.

"I hope everything is still on track for the event at the end of the month." Valencia had attended all the meetings of the festival advisory board. She and Charlotte were both members, along with Lila Jones, who worked for the Royal Chamber of Commerce. Rancher Brett Harston had initially been on the board, too, but he'd been booted off by Rusty for having the audacity to sweep Rusty's ex-wife Sarabeth off her feet. "I know at the last meeting, we talked about some funds that were unaccounted for—"

"It's a bigger problem than I first realized." Ross hitched Ben higher against his chest to combat the boy's wiggling. "A more significant amount of money is gone than what I initially believed."

Valencia stilled, a chill running through her in spite of the July heat. "But there's a chance it's a mistake, right? A bookkeeping error?"

Ross shook his head, but seemed to hedge answering the question directly. "I just thought you should know since you were counting on those funds for your horse rescue."

It took a moment for her to absorb the full import of his words. When she did, she felt her dreams rumble unsteadily. She'd worked so hard to make the summer camp a reality. To create the equine therapy component that would give troubled kids the chance to bond with animals the same way she once had.

"Are you saying that the ticket money is gone?" Her voice didn't sound like her own.

How could it be possible? The people involved with the festival were some of the town's most upstanding citizens. She'd enjoyed working with them to make Soiree on the Bay a reality.

"I'm saying we can't account for all of the income, and it's a significant amount." He scrubbed a free hand through his hair, looking weary. "I hope we'll get this figured out. But just in case, it's only fair that you know."

"I understand. And I—" She nodded, her movements jerky and abrupt since it still felt like someone had pulled a rug out from under her feet. "Thank you, Ross."

"Of course. I'm sorry I didn't have better news, but I'll stay in touch." He turned to leave, little Ben waving bye-bye at Valencia over his father's shoulder as he walked away. Valencia waved back at him, smiling at the boy in spite of her inner turmoil.

She'd pinned so many hopes on the ticket sales from Soiree on the Bay. If Ross's fears were realized and she didn't receive any supporting funds for the horse rescue as promised, how could she possibly support the next phase of making the equine therapy camp a reality?

One thing was certain. She needed the help of the Cortez-Williams family—most especially its darkly cynical heir—now more than ever.

Seated on a leather couch inside the Cortez-Williams ranch office, Lorenzo cross-checked the information on his tablet screen, reviewing files from three different agencies on Donovan Horse Rescue.

Occasionally, while scrolling through the text, he'd pass a photo of Valencia—her pretty face smiling out at him from the screen—and feel a jolt of lust. Along with a surge of guilt about how thoroughly he'd had her investigated.

But he suppressed the guilt each time, more than bolstered by the reminder of Lindsey's faithlessness. If anything, he needed to exercise all the more caution when reviewing Valencia's horse rescue because of the pull of sizzling attraction he felt toward her. His ex-fiancée's treachery had forced him to be more careful with anyone who stirred the kind of response that Valencia had. Considering how much Valencia affected him, triple-checking the references was hardly overkill.

But he'd already floated the files past an overseeing committee earlier in the week, and they'd given her project a unanimous thumbs-up, so it wasn't just his say-so that would result in a donation. Impartial outsiders had been consulted, too.

"Lorenzo?" his ranch manager called from somewhere deeper in the building. "The vet arrived a few minutes ago. She's in the cow barn now."

He glanced up from his tablet, accustomed to interruptions in the office since it was a casual shared space for ranch paperwork, really just a corner of the equipment barn. On the other side of a big filing cabinet and bookshelf, there were trucks and tractors. Beyond that, a small mechanic shop for simple repairs. Mostly, the place was air-conditioned against the heat of a Texas July, with round-the-clock access to a good coffee machine and fridge full of cold drinks.

"Thanks," he called, returning his attention to his work. "I'll head over there before she finishes."

The veterinarian's visit was a routine check since the ranch didn't employ their own. Lorenzo wanted her to look at one of the horses before she left. But right now, he had no reason to delay calling Valencia any longer. He knew he'd done his due diligence where her rescue was concerned. And couldn't justify withholding funds she deserved just because he'd been fooled by a woman before.

Valencia did have a connection to a shady character in her past, but considering it was her birth father and she'd been taken away from her parents at an early age, Lorenzo could hardly hold that against her. Her school and work records were pristine. Her horse rescue mission a noble one that she pursued tirelessly.

And damn, but she'd been in his thoughts nonstop since meeting her. Not just because she was undeniably sexy. She was also warmhearted, hardworking and sharp as hell. He'd been even more drawn to her after seeing her with her animals. Her ease in riding, her passion for rescue and her obvious bond with every creature she cared for were all compelling to a man born and raised to ranch. Underneath her corporate polish, there beat the heart of a bona fide cowgirl.

Lifting his phone, he placed the call. In two rings, she answered, her voice a little breathless.

"Hello?" she huffed lightly into the speaker, the sound making him all but feel the rush of her exhale on his skin.

"Hello, Valencia. It's Lorenzo." Shutting off the tablet, he set it aside on the leather couch. Then, tipping his head back, he closed his eyes and imagined her on the other end of the call. He could indulge that desire now when she couldn't see him. "I have some news to share with you. Would you be able to meet me for dinner tomorrow?"

Strictly for business purposes, he reminded

himself. After all, she deserved to celebrate the approval of funds from his family, and he wanted to be there to share that with her.

"Of course. Where should we meet?" she replied in a rush, perhaps to hide the moment's hesitation before her response. No doubt she'd picked up on the vibe of molten-hot attraction as clearly as he had. If anything, it was a relief to know she was conflicted about that, too.

"How about Sheen?" he suggested. The food and service were excellent, and he wanted to show her a good time if only just this once. "I can make reservations for seven o'clock."

He'd almost offered to pick her up, but he'd remembered himself just in time. This wasn't a date. But he refused to miss out on this last opportunity to see her. She was a vibrant, memorable woman, and if he hadn't met her on a professional basis, he would definitely pursue her.

The realization surprised him. He hadn't felt that kind of connection—a *need* to see a woman again—in five years. His dating life since Lindsey had been superficial, something he'd undertaken only for expediency's sake.

"That sounds great." Her voice was warmer now. Hopeful. "I'll look forward to it."

Disconnecting the call, Lorenzo shut down the tablet with the files full of information about Valencia Donovan, more excited about the prospect of seeing her than he should be. He didn't need the information anymore now that the decision was made to help her charity. She'd never know how thoroughly he'd investigated her, and it didn't matter anyway since it had been strictly for business purposes.

He'd never allow himself to have a liaison with anyone remotely connected to his family's business. Not after the last time he'd misjudged a woman. So after tomorrow night, he wouldn't be seeing Valencia Donovan ever again.

Three

No matter how many times Valencia told herself that dinner with Lorenzo would be purely professional, she'd still ended up changing outfits twice. Overthinking her clothes was *not* a good sign.

Hurrying up the sidewalk in front of Sheen, the popular new Royal restaurant, Valencia straightened the strap of her white crepe dress and told herself it was appropriately conservative. Even though she couldn't recall baring this much shoulder in her corporate job. She was just off her game tonight because she didn't know what to expect from the meal, and so much rode on Lorenzo's decision.

A gust of wind hastened her pace up the walkway, and she clutched the loose waves of her hair to keep them from blowing around. Before she reached the front door of the all-glass building, it swung open from within. Lorenzo stood on the threshold, dressed in a sharp dark suit with a pale blue Oxford shirt open at the collar. He looked... like a man she wished she were meeting under different circumstances. That must be why her heart rate jumped.

"Hello, Lorenzo." She smiled widely to cover the rush of nerves, still holding her hair in one hand. "It's windy all of the sudden."

"It's good to see you, Valencia." His gaze dipped over her once—briefly—yet she was so hyperaware of him, she couldn't help but notice. "You look lovely."

The words were easily spoken. Gentlemanly. That didn't stop the rush of pleasure she experienced. Forcing herself not to dwell on that, she murmured a thank-you and let go of her hair as he ushered her inside the cool interior, his hand finding the small of her back to help her navigate through the evening crowd hoping for a table.

The warmth of his palm sent tendrils of pleasure curling through her, heightening her awareness of him. She caught the barest hint of his spicy aftershave when they were forced closer together because of a group hurrying past them. Valencia inhaled deeply, trying to place the subtle blend of scents that made her want to lean closer.

Following his lead, she moved with him through the main dining area to a table in a corner. White candles on every table, tucked into hurricane lamps and surrounded by white flowers, gave the room an ethereal glow. Shades had fallen over some of the exterior walls to give the diners privacy, but the glass divider separating the kitchen remained visible. She wondered if Ross's fiancée, Charlotte, was cooking tonight. She'd heard the woman was extremely talented. The complex aromas—cooking spices and the yeasty scent of freshly baked bread—made Valencia eager to taste the fare.

"We're sitting right here, if this is okay with you?" Lorenzo moved around her to withdraw an upholstered chair for her.

"Of course. It's perfect." She took a seat, knowing this flattering attentiveness was probably the byproduct of good Texas upbringing and not anything personal. But it felt really nice. "I appreciate the chance to visit Sheen. It's all the more welcome this week after hearing the troubling news about Soiree on the Bay."

Worries about the food and arts festival—and developing a plan B for her horse rescue—had never been far from her mind since Ross's visit.

Lorenzo's expression turned grave as he took

the seat across from her. "I heard rumors about missing money from the advance ticket sales, but I hoped they were just gossip. Anything involving Rusty Edmond seems to attract public speculation."

"I believe this is more serious than that." Valencia hesitated, wondering if Lorenzo might perceive her broaching the topic as a way to add pressure to solicit a donation from the Cortez-Williams family. But it was too late to backtrack now. "Ross Edmond paid me a visit the same day you toured the ranch. He wanted to warn me there might not be any funds from the ticket sales."

Scowling, Lorenzo shook his head. "It has to be an accounting error. And if it's not, there are only so many potential parties to blame considering the small group involved with the festival." He gave her a level stare. "You're on the festival advisory board, aren't you?"

She bristled, even as she told herself he wasn't accusing her of anything.

"I am. And I still can't wrap my head around any other possibility than a bookkeeping mistake," she concurred.

Lorenzo appeared thoughtful, but the sommelier's arrival at their table ended the discussion. Valencia gladly deferred to his preference for a bottle of wine. From the exchange between them, she suspected the vintage was something much better than anything she'd had before.

"We're celebrating, after all," he announced after the woman left their table, clearly shifting the tone of their conversation.

She was only too happy to focus on why he'd asked her to meet him tonight. Anticipation tingled through her, even as she tried to keep her hopes in check.

"Are we?"

"Definitely." His dark eyes glittered with mischief, almost as if he enjoyed keeping her guessing. "I shared your proposal for Donovan Horse Rescue with the committee that makes the final decision on donations from our family's business." He paused, the moment of suspense drawing out before he smiled broadly. "They unanimously voted to approve it."

Relief surged through her and a happy squeal she couldn't quite suppress bubbled up in her throat.

"Thank you." She reached for him in her excitement, covering his forearm and squeezing. "Thank you so much! You have no idea how much this means to me."

Even through the lightweight jacket he wore, she felt his muscles flex beneath her fingers. Her eyes darted to where she touched him...and she would have pulled away, except that at the same moment, he covered her fingers with his. Warmth flowed through her as she met his gaze again.

"You're welcome," he assured her, tightening his grip for a moment before relinquishing her. "Although it was your hard work that impressed the committee. It's clear you have a well-developed plan for making the rescue a success. Your commitment to the cause—and a worthy cause at that—came through in every page of your pitch."

Her throat had gone dry at the feel of his hand over hers, the memory of that brief touch still humming in her skin. Belatedly, she realized her hand lingered on his forearm and she snatched it back a little too quickly.

What was it about him that knocked her off balance?

She licked her lips and tried to regain her composure.

"Yet the proposal wouldn't have made it that far if not for your help. I really appreciate you taking the time to see the operation in person." Recalling his earlier concerns about con artists and shady requests for funds, she added, "To see for yourself that I *am* a legitimate businesswoman."

A shadow chased through his expression. Had she said something wrong? Or had he somehow read a hint of feminine interest in her eyes and retreated from that?

The sommelier returned, along with their server, giving Valencia a window of time to cool the heated impulses. She just needed to make it through this meal without touching Lorenzo again, and she would be home free. There would be no more cause to interact. No more temptation to throw caution to the wind with someone she would always feel indebted to.

Just get through dinner.

On the surface, it sounded simple. But considering the magnetic draw of the man, Valencia knew the challenge was very real.

By the time dessert was served, Lorenzo had stored away plenty of new information about his sexy and intriguing dinner companion. And learning about her this way was far more satisfying than the private investigator's report he'd read on her business.

But for all that he'd learned about Valencia, she still danced around the particulars of her childhood. Perhaps that was because they hadn't known one another long. Yet the studious way she avoided any talk of her own experience with equine therapy, despite the obvious relevance to her current path in life, heightened his curiosity about the notes in her background file. Especially those pertaining to her biological father—a convicted felon.

He recognized that he was particularly wary around women who might get close to him only for the sake of his bank account. But as much as he wanted to shut off that part of his brain that forced him to remain on guard, he couldn't help but watch for any signs that Valencia would leverage their mutual attraction for financial gain.

Now, as she speared a bite of shortbread with her dessert fork, she fixed him with a playful gaze. "You realize you've pried out all my secrets over dinner while telling me very little about yourself."

Startled that she'd noticed, he tried to force aside his reservations.

"Me? I'm an open book." He pushed back from the table, tossing his napkin on top of his empty dessert plate, his gaze dropping to her mouth. "A side effect of having four brothers is that nothing remains secret about me for long."

She blinked, brown eyes wide with surprise. "There are *five* Cortez-Williams brothers in all?"

"After me, there's Matias, Rafe, Tomas and Diego. Hellions all in their own way, while I—as the oldest and bearing my father's name—have had no choice but to rein in all hell-raising impulses." He was only partly kidding. "So it follows that I have less interesting secrets."

Her mouth curved into a sad smile. "As an only child who owes my adoptive parents everything, I empathize." She chewed thoughtfully on her lower lip for a moment before returning her gaze to him, a spark of flirtation in their dark depths. "But despite your skillful deflection, I still think you owe me at least one provocative factoid about yourself."

If this had been a date and not a business dinner, he would have slid his chair closer to hers so he could touch her while he imparted some of the wicked thoughts he'd had about her over the course of their meal.

For a long moment, he let the heat of that fantasy sizzle over him. But then, knowing he couldn't possibly respond the way he wanted, he settled for leaning forward so he could speak to her confidentially across the table.

"Between you and me? If I hadn't been destined to be a rancher, I would probably be Royal's resident auto mechanic."

Her eyebrows lifted in surprise, a genuine smile hovering around her lips now as if the news delighted her. "Really?"

"Really. I've wanted to fix cars—fix anything mechanical—since I got a toolbox under the Christmas tree when I was thirteen." He watched her expression carefully, searching for any hint of dismay at the hobby that still brought him as much satisfaction—more, if he was honest—as overseeing his family's ranch. Lindsey had laughed outright about his preferred pastime when he'd mentioned it to her, but she'd been outright appalled when she'd arrived early for a date and found him still underneath a tractor in the equipment barn, his coveralls greasy.

Valencia, on the contrary, appeared fascinated. "I envy you possessing that skill." She traced her index finger idly up the stem of her wineglass. "Although I'm not sure a hidden mechanical talent qualifies as an overly provocative secret."

His brain was still stuck on the first part of what she'd said. "Envy?"

Had he heard her correctly? That certainly wasn't the mindset of his father, who viewed the work Lorenzo enjoyed as somehow "beneath" him.

"Do you know how much money I would save if I knew the first thing about engine repair? I just traded in my old truck for a new one after I got a sky-high estimate to repair an oil leak that was supposedly so buried in the engine as to make it not worth fixing." Her brow furrowed. "And don't get me started on the equipment needed around the rescue."

He hated the idea that he might have been able to save her a significant amount of money on the truck and hadn't known about the problem. It surprised him how much he wanted to offer his help and know-how in the future. And yet, she wasn't his responsibility. Hadn't he told himself tonight would be the last time they spent together?

Besides, helping a woman financially had been his Achilles' heel with Lindsey.

While he wrestled with that notion, both of their phones went off. Not with ringtones—he'd most certainly turned his to silent—but the strong vibration of a local public safety alert.

Frowning, he reached for his phone, and noticed many of the restaurant patrons doing the same thing.

"Tornado alert." He read the words aloud, his attention shifting to the glass windows of the restaurant while murmurs of alarm traveled around him. With the linen shades blocking most of the view, he couldn't see what the weather looked like outside. "I need to get you home."

All around them patrons were collecting their things, calling for their checks. The residents of Royal took tornado warnings very seriously. Especially after a twister had touched down close enough to the Texas Cattleman's Club to do some serious damage less than ten years before.

Lorenzo reached for the leather binder containing the bill, thankful their server hovered at the ready. Only then did he notice Valencia had gone pale. Eyes fixed on the windows at the front of Sheen, she swallowed hard, with visible effort.

Concerned, he didn't hesitate to slide his chair

closer to her now. He laid his palm on her shoulder. "Hey. Are you okay?"

She gave a jerky nod, but he thought he felt her trembling beneath his palm. "Fine. Just—you know. Worried about my animals. My ranch hands only work part-time. They've gone home for the night."

"I can help secure them when I take you home," he assured her, understanding her anxiety. Property damage was one thing, but harm to living creatures in your care was another. "We'll be on the road in no time."

She turned wide eyes toward him, but there was no mistaking the look of gratitude in her expression. "Are you sure? What about your ranch? Shouldn't you—"

"We have staff on-site that will ensure their safety. It's no trouble for me to give you a hand." Glimpsing the server returning with the leather folder containing his receipt, Lorenzo had a generous tip added and the bill signed in another moment. "Do you have a storm shelter at your place?"

"Yes. There's a storm cellar." Some of her color returned, and she appeared a bit calmer as they both rose to their feet. "Thank you, Lorenzo. Both for the incredible meal and the offer to pitch in. I really appreciate it."

An older couple hurried past them toward the exit, and Lorenzo hooked his arm around Valencia's waist to steady her. While there wasn't a sense of panic in the restaurant, anxiety buzzed in the air. With so many ranches in the area, many of the diners shared the same concerns as she did, and there was a flurry of activity as bills were quickly paid. Conversations grew louder as people speculated on the possibilities of the uncertain weather. One of the servers informed a table nearby that a funnel cloud had been spotted half an hour north of them. And at the hostess's stand, a woman read aloud from her phone about a series of tornado outbreaks across East Texas.

Lorenzo didn't question the need to tuck Valencia closer to his side, moving them quickly to the exit. Even if she hadn't gone pale, he would have felt responsible for her safety while they were together. But knowing that she was worried made him all the more protective.

Pushing open the door, he guided her toward the parking lot as a gust of wind swept past them, the air current strong enough to notch his concern higher. And although the sun had recently set, there was enough twilight to distinguish the greenish cast to the sky.

Not loosening his hold on her, he leaned closer to be sure she could hear him over the rush of squall. "I'd feel better if you'd let me drive you home."

She nodded. "I would, too. Thank you."

"Good. Come on." Relieved at her acquiescence, he led her to his truck. He opened the passenger door for her, helping her inside before jogging around the front to take a seat behind the wheel. "Is your storm cellar stocked?"

Before she had a chance to respond, he flipped on the headlights and pulled out of the parking lot, heading toward Valencia's place.

"It is." She'd rested her small leather clutch purse on the console between them, and she gripped it tightly now, her fingers digging into the material. "I'm actually very disciplined about emergency preparations, so I go through the provisions regularly to make sure nothing is expired and that I have everything I could possibly need."

Something struck him as a little off about her words, perhaps because they sounded so calm when her body language suggested she was extremely tense. Maybe she was trying to reassure herself with her measured words.

"That's excellent news. Hopefully, it won't come to that, but it's good to know the space is ready if we need it." He couldn't stop himself from reaching across the console to lay a hand over hers. Her skin was cold. "Now, walk me through what needs to happen with the animals. You have solid stables. I'm assuming you want the horses inside?"

He knew some owners allowed their animals

to remain outdoors in case a building was directly hit, but good stables could protect them from flying debris.

"Yes. We need to get them all in stalls, then secure the doors and windows. I'm not worried about halters or name tags as every animal is microchipped. Including Barkis, who will come to the storm cellar with us." She shifted in her seat, sliding her hand out from under his to retrieve her phone from her clutch. "I should look for weather updates."

"Of course. Let me know what you find out." He hoped for encouraging news, but the fact that the weather warning wasn't just because of one twister, but potentially several, didn't bode well.

He remembered a day two years before where thirty-nine tornadoes had broken out across four Southern states. But he didn't see the need to mention that to Valencia. Glancing sidelong at her as he reached a stop sign, he could see the worry etched in her pretty face.

"So far the National Weather Service has reported three. All of them have been EF-0 so far, although one of them was almost an EF-1." She rattled off the information, clearly well versed in the measurement scale that related a tornado's intensity. "And it looks like there's possible activity around Trinity Bay, too."

The site of Appaloosa Island and Soiree on the Bay.

Recognizing a whole new layer to Valencia's fears, Lorenzo knew the best thing he could do for her—the *only* thing he could do right now—was to get her home and make sure her horses were all safe.

Then, he'd make sure *she* was safe. Even if that meant riding out the storm together.

Four

Cold rain pelted Valencia's face as she climbed a ladder to close one of the high windows that provided extra air circulation in the barn. She'd exchanged her dress and heels for jeans and work boots before returning to the stables to secure the animals, and she was grateful for the sure-footed tread of the boots now with the wind whipping hard against her rain jacket.

At least the ladder was built-in, bolted to the side of the barn to make it easier to reach the area that used to be a hayloft. The rungs were slippery, though, and she needed to keep one hand anchored while she stretched her free arm to reach the wooden shutter that banged against the building.

Just a little farther…

Woof!

Below her, Barkis stood guard, sounding as edgy and impatient to be out of the weather as she felt. Latching the window was the last thing she needed to do since Lorenzo had taken care of the newest stable. Thankfully, he'd had work clothes stashed in his truck, so he'd been able to hit the ground running as quickly as she had.

Thank God he was here.

Especially when tonight was triggering haunting memories of another long-ago twister. Everything about the weather—from the plowed-earth smell in the air to the grit-filled gusts of wind—reminded her of the worst day of her life. One spent in a bathtub while her drunken birth parents argued over who was responsible for keeping Valencia safe. Neither one of them had wanted that chore, the memory forever twining the terror of tornadoes with the gut-sickening realization that she was unloved.

Just then, the wind slammed the shutter closed for her, whacking the back of her hand in the process, but at least making it easier for her to pull the latch into the locked position. Her last job complete, she started down the ladder as the rain turned to hail.

The barrage of ice pellets against the barn sounded like gunfire. And the pings against her back hurt through the thin windbreaker. Even worse? Her foot slipped on the next-to-last rung, the awkward flail of her body almost making her lose her grip.

Strong arms caught her lower body even as she wrenched her arm, trying to hold on.

"I've got you." Lorenzo's voice sounded beside her ear through her hood. "You can let go."

Her heart pounded wildly, from fear of the storm and panic at the memories, to gratitude toward this man who didn't owe her anything yet kept helping her anyhow.

Off balance in every way, Valencia did as he suggested, relinquishing her grip on the ladder to give him her full weight. For one heart-stopping moment, she hung suspended against him, her back pressed to the solid warmth of his chest. Her butt slid down the front of his hips as he set her on her feet, a sensation that made heat flare inside her despite the storm trauma threatening to topple her.

Before she could turn and face him—and maybe confront whatever that sizzling connection meant—a piercing siren wailed in the distance. A *tornado* siren.

Fear tore through her. She knew what that meant.

A funnel cloud must have been spotted nearby. The sirens didn't go off in Royal unless there was confirmed tornado activity.

Barkis whimpered at the same time Lorenzo

tucked her against him. She hadn't realized until that moment how much harder the rain-hail mix was pummeling her head and shoulders.

"We need to get in the shelter now." He led her toward the metal door she'd pointed out to him when he'd parked his pickup truck in front of her house.

The storm cellar entrance was a low mound between the house and main barn that the previous owner had surrounded with rock walls and bushes. The concrete shelter had been a strong point in favor of buying this property when Valencia had been searching for a spot that could double as a home and a horse rescue. Just knowing the large, steel-reinforced retreat was nearby had helped her sleep better, even though she'd never had to use it before.

A low rumble sounded like an incoming freight train, the noise growing higher and sharper as Lorenzo pulled open the low door. Dread ramped inside her as she looked around franticly for her dog.

Barkis didn't need to be told where to go. Her dog rushed down the carpeted steps into the dry, still air below. Valencia reached ahead and flipped on the switch for the interior lights, then followed him. She was grateful for the way the underground walls muffled the sounds of the sirens and the wailing wind, but still felt petrified at the thought of what a powerful storm could do to her horses.

To her *dream*. To her ability to help others with her precious animals that she loved more than anything on earth.

Heart in her throat, she stood immobile at the base of the shelter stairs while Lorenzo closed and locked the door behind him. He edged past her, taking in the space that consisted of two rooms with low-clearance ceilings—about six and a half feet. Fiberglass walls and storage benches wrapped the first room while a full-size bed dominated the adjoining one. There were pull-down benches in those walls, too, for when additional people needed shelter, but Valencia had added the regular bed for herself, knowing she would need every possible comfort if she ever had to use the space.

Her stomach dropped at the thought of using it now, of being trapped in here for hours.

Lorenzo's dark eyes shifted back to her. She hadn't noticed he'd already removed his jacket and boots. The cold dread weighing her down must have made her lose time, because she had no recollection of him doing either of those things.

"Valencia?" He approached her slowly. "Can I take your jacket? Help you dry off?"

Becoming aware of her behavior and how it must broadcast her unease, she tried to shake the suffocating memories off. Although she was grateful to Lorenzo for helping her secure the animals, she regretted the possibility that he might see her at her worst during the course of a storm.

"I can get it, thanks." She tugged down the sleeve of her windbreaker, water droplets sliding off the repellant fabric onto a rubber mat on the underground shelter's concrete floor. "There are towels under the first bench seat to the left."

Telling herself she was safe and that this is what she'd spent so much time preparing for, she tried to take comfort from going through a mental checklist of all they had at their disposal. Barkis padded over to the storage benches with Lorenzo, poking an interested nose inside the raised lid for a moment before moving off to sniff out a comfortable spot to lie.

"Wow." Lorenzo tugged two towels free from the bin, his gaze focused on the schematic taped to the inside of the lid where she had diagrammed the location of all her supplies. "You've got everything really organized in here."

"I—um." She knew her preparedness might appear over the top to some people. *Obsessive*, a former boyfriend had once phrased her need to be ready for any emergency situation. "Thank you. We should turn on the radio and see if there are any reports about the storm."

The eerie sound of the howling wind, even muted as it was in the cellar, unnerved her.

"Sure." Turning to pass her one of the towels,

Lorenzo narrowed his gaze. "What happened to your hand?"

Valencia glanced down to see the blood trickling along her knuckle, a small stain forming on the concrete floor from an earlier drip. The sight distracted her from the weather for a moment.

"Oh." She'd forgotten all about the injury amid her other worries, but she cradled the limb against her other arm now to try to stem the blood flow. "The barn shutter slammed onto my hand when I was trying to latch it closed. I didn't realize I got a cut."

Her voice sounded unnatural, even to her own ears. But although she told herself to snap out of it, she realized she was shaking. She could see her fingers trembling as she stared down at them.

Valencia didn't want to reveal so much weakness to the man in front of her, not when the fate of her rescue relied on him thinking she was completely competent. Yet, with the woozy sensation making her knees feel like liquid, she guessed she was moments away from an outright panic attack.

Lorenzo's concern grew in direct proportion to the increasing paleness of Valencia's skin. He didn't know if it was related to the storm, the injury or being in the more confined space underground, but the jitteriness he'd noted in her on the way back from the restaurant seemed to spiral into full-blown shock right before his eyes.

Her breathing was rapid, her pupils dilated, her skin almost ashen. Could she have sustained another injury she hadn't mentioned? A blow to the head even?

The idea made him more determined to check her over.

"Hey now." He shifted to put himself in her line of vision, even though he wasn't sure she focused on him even then. "Valencia? I'm worried about you. I'd like to take your boots off, and then we'll get your hand bandaged, okay?"

"I'm f-fine," she protested, teeth chattering on the words.

Yet she still hadn't moved from where they first entered the room, other than to remove her jacket.

He stepped toward her slowly, even though his own fears demanded he examine every inch of her to make sure she wasn't hurt more than she'd let on. But he couldn't startle her if she was already fearful and upset. He had no experience with people in shock, but he'd been with plenty of animals that'd shown those signs, so he hoped that the basic strategies still applied. Speak calmly and soothingly. Get them comfortable.

"Did you sustain any other injuries besides your hand?" he asked, wrapping the dry towel around her shoulders.

"No. At least I don't think so." Her answer was so soft, he wasn't sure he would have heard it if he hadn't been watching her mouth move at the same time.

But at least her breathing hadn't accelerated any more.

"I'm going to find the radio in a minute," he assured her as he dropped to his feet to unlace her boots. The fact that she didn't protest spoke volumes. "First, let's get you dry."

While he worked on the wet laces, the only sounds in the shelter were the moan of the wind, the pelt of hail on the metal door and Valencia's chattering teeth. Even Barkis was quiet, his big head resting on his paws on one of the benches in the next room.

Was it a good sign the dog didn't seem worried?

Easing off her boots, he set them aside. Then, he stood so he could tuck her against him and escort her deeper into the shelter. She trembled against him, her whole body shaking. But he thought her breath seemed more even than it had been a few moments ago.

"Have a seat here, okay?" He led her to the bed since it offered the most comfortable option, even though it amounted only to a utilitarian mattress on a metal frame, a clean sleeping bag for a cover. "I'm going to find the first-aid kit so we can take care of your hand. Would you feel better lying down?"

He wanted to wrap her in the flannel sleeping bag and hold her until she stopped quaking, but first he needed to figure out what had her so shook up. For now, he moved the towel to wrap her wounded hand.

"I'm s-sorry," Valencia murmured, her breath quickening again. "I think it's just the storm—" She broke off in a wheezing inhale, as if she couldn't draw enough air.

Damn it! He wished he knew what to do to help her. He left her side long enough to find a first-aid kit in the second bin. The schematic she'd drawn on a sheet of paper under the lid by the towels showed where every major item was located in the storage area, from sewing kit to pet care, flashlights to food.

The food supplies were all marked with expiration dates—every last one of them current. Water jugs lined a back wall. Fresh air circulated from vents high on the walls. Clearly Valencia had invested time and finances into a top-notch shelter. Because she was prepared, or were her efforts indicative of a deeper fear?

"Here we go." He brought the first-aid kit to the bed and sat down beside her, flipping on a small lamp clipped above the bed. "Let's get that cut cleaned up," he said aloud, compelled to narrate his actions as a way to keep her grounded in what was happening. Or, hell, maybe he needed to ground himself given how worried he was about her. He found the hydrogen peroxide and opened the bottle while he kept talking to her. “We’re going to weather this storm just fine, thanks to you.”

For a long moment, he didn’t think she was going to respond while he cleaned the cut, letting the excess solution fall onto the white towel. But as he re-capped the bottle and searched for antibiotic ointment, she said, “I was in a bad tornado once.” The words were gritty, as if her throat had gone dry. “I saw how much damage it could do if you aren’t prepared.”

Something in that softly uttered admission made him think that whatever had happened then was causing a lot of her distress right now. He wanted to see her expression, but she stared down at the cut as he worked on it, her damp hair falling over her face to further hide it.

At least her pallor wasn’t quite as ashen anymore. And her breathing seemed to have evened out once again. Still quick and shallow, but not as ragged.

“Well, you made sure that wouldn’t happen again,” he soothed as he tore open a bandage. “You’ve got everything we could possibly need down here. I can't think of any safer place to ride out a storm."

She remained quiet while he finished bandaging her wound, then set the kit on the floor near the now-sleeping dog. He left the light on long enough to tip her chin up so he could look her in the eyes. Her pupils were still wide, yet not as dilated as before. Overall, she seemed calmer. However, that didn't stop him from stroking a hand over her hair so he could feel her scalp beneath, to reassure himself she hadn't hit her head while they'd been preparing the horses.

"Are you sure you didn't get hurt anywhere else?" he asked, watching her face for any hint of reaction—a wince that could betray a bump or a cut.

Yet he saw only her eyelashes flutter, then fall closed. Her chest expanded with the first deep breath since they'd been inside the shelter, her breasts pressing against the heather-gray T-shirt she wore, adorned with the logo for Donovan Horse Rescue.

His body reacted to that in a wholly inappropriate way, considering she'd been on the verge of passing out just ten minutes before. But he couldn't have moved his hands away from her hair if he tried. He skimmed his fingers lower, tracing the back of her neck through the silky locks.

"I'm okay," she murmured, her eyes falling closed. "Just a little embarrassed, I guess."

"Why?" Genuinely perplexed, he ran his thumb along her cheekbone, telling himself he did it only to encourage her gaze. "I can't imagine anything you'd need to be embarrassed about."

Her eyes opened slowly, a momentary flash of awareness making him damn near catch his breath. Part of him felt grateful that her thoughts had shifted away from her worries, but he also knew better than to act on the feelings stirring up between them now. "I have tried so hard to put my best foot forward professionally with you," she began, twisting around enough to tug a plush blue lap blanket off the shelf that served as a headboard. "Only to completely fall apart after our dinner."

Her hands were still shaking as she spread the blanket over her legs. It took all of his restraint not to capture those trembling fingers in his and hold them. Hold *her* until she stopped shaking. But he couldn't afford to muddle his concern for her with the attraction he'd been feeling ever since they met.

He fisted his hands instead.

"You didn't fall apart," he argued, not sure why she thought that. "Anyone would be rattled by a storm like this."

Remembering that he'd never retrieved the

radio, he was only too glad for an excuse to stand, to stride away from the magnetic draw of her. Returning to her drawing of the supply layout, he traced the location of the device to the third bin. Flashlights, extra batteries and what might have been a satellite phone were neatly packaged near the radio with a hand crank and built-in charging station.

"It goes beyond the usual fears," she admitted as he returned to sit beside her.

"Because you were in a tornado before?" he asked softly, passing her the radio in case she wanted to turn it on for updates.

"When I was very young. Still living with my birth parents." She took the device, resting it in her lap on the blanket before glancing at him. "I was adopted when I was eight years old."

He knew this, of course, from the investigator's report. Recalled her biological father's unsavory past. But unwilling to admit how much he'd already learned about her history, he steered her back to whatever had happened during that long-ago storm. There was little about her early life in her file beyond simple dates.

"Would it help to talk about it?" His gaze wandered over her from her honey-brown eyes and long dark lashes, to the way her blond hair dried in waves. "Or should I try to distract you?"

Her pupils widened slightly at that last remark,

and he wished he could see into her mind to know what she'd envisioned at that moment. Her mouth fell open briefly, before she snapped it shut again and speared to her feet.

"First, I should find some dry clothes," she said abruptly, gathering up the blanket that had slid off her lap. "I'm feeling a little steadier, but it would help to get warm." She shuffled back a step in her socks, reaching overhead to pull a simple curtain that divided the shelter's two small rooms. "I'll find some clothes and a couple of waters for us. Do you want to change? I have men's things here, too."

"No, thank you." He didn't think it would be wise to get too comfortable in this intimate setting with Valencia. "I'll turn on the radio," he offered instead, already adjusting the tuning dial for a station. "See what's happening. Maybe this will all be over soon."

Although the harsh whine of the wind continued outside, the hail had stopped pelting the metal door to their shelter.

"I hope so." She rummaged through her bins, opening and closing plastic lids to find what she needed.

A moment later, the sound of a zipper in the enclosed quarters had his head wrenching up. Through the white curtain, he could see her shadow moving as she shimmied off her jeans.

He might have made a noise in response because she stopped midmotion, her head turning toward where he sat even though she couldn't possibly see him.

His throat went dry at the thought of her so close and half-dressed.

He pressed the volume button on the radio, cranking up the sound to cover the pregnant pause.

"…tornado outbreaks across all of eastern Texas, resulting in significant threats to life and property. Take shelter immediately." The message was a prerecorded standard tornado warning for their area, but that didn't make it any less terrifying.

From Valencia's side of the curtain, he heard a quiet exclamation, halfway between a sob and a wail. Cursing himself for turning the radio on, he tossed it aside and went to her, privacy be damned.

She needed him.

"Come here." He wrapped her in his arms, never dropping his eyes for a second even though she wore only a T-shirt now. "I've got you," he whispered into her ear, stroking her hair with one hand while pressing her to him with the other. "It's going to be okay."

He told himself it was true, and that he could make her believe it, too, even though she shook like a leaf now.

But a moment later, the lights in the shelter went out, leaving them in total blackness.

Five

The total darkness fell over Valencia like a smothering weight on her from all sides. As panic stole her breath, she clutched Lorenzo tighter, her fingers digging into his upper arms and silently demanding an anchor in a world gone black.

Right now, it didn't matter that she'd wanted to make a good impression on him, or that he held the future of the shelter in his hands. She knew only that her old fears would eat her alive if she couldn't find a way to battle them back. Having the lights go out when she was already shivering and half-dressed had catapulted her backward in time, ripping open wounds she'd kept long hidden.

"Valencia." He said her name with a sternness that made her think it wasn't the first time he'd spoken it. He still held her in his arms, but his whole body had gone tense.

"Yes?" She tipped her face up toward where his would be.

"I need to find the flashlights," he told her more gently, his fingers rubbing along her back through her T-shirt. "Let's get you settled with a blanket, then I'll retrieve a lantern from the bin."

"Okay. Sounds good," she agreed, even though she couldn't seem to ease her grip on his arms. Her fingers were still vise-locked on him, her nose buried in the soft flannel of the work shirt he'd changed into before he'd helped secure the horses. She breathed in his scent, pine and musk, and told herself to let go.

To no avail.

He waited a moment, probably giving her time to move away. When she didn't, he stroked a hand over her hair, his lips lowering so that he spoke close to her ear.

"Want me to go with you? Help you find the bed?" he asked, his words a raspy rumble that stirred something inside her.

Something that wasn't fear.

"Yes. Please." Her voice was small and soft. Tentative. The vulnerable parts she showed him now were a far cry from the strong face she normally presented to the world.

But she couldn't afford to care what he thought about her. Not when she could fall apart in a million tiny pieces if her old demons gained a toehold in her thoughts.

She'd been alone in the bathtub when the roof ripped off the house. The screech of the metal peeling away from the rafters mingled with the sound of her mother's screams.

Swallowing hard, she tried to tamp down rapidly encroaching memories as Lorenzo shuffled her sideways in the direction of the bed. Ignoring the angry thrash of the wind against the exterior door, she focused on the sounds within the storm cellar. The steady thrum of the rancher's heartbeat under her ear. The soft thunk of his leg meeting the resistance of the utilitarian metal frame a moment before he lowered her to the mattress. From near their feet, Barkis made a snuffling noise in his slumber.

"Here you go." He drew the fleece lap blanket around her, his denim-covered knee brushing her bare thigh as he shifted.

Once more, sizzling awareness stirred within her, offering a welcome distraction from rational thought and memories. And as the bright, clear flame of heated attraction flickered over the shadowy fears, scattering them, her breath caught. Held.

The inconvenient response almost made her regret that the power had gone out before she could finish changing into dry clothes, her clean T-shirt barely covering her hips. She hadn't had time to pull on a dry pair of sweats. Then again, if not for the hot flare of lust roaring inside her, she would be shaking from the chill of the past.

"Will you stay by me?" she asked, willing to sacrifice her pride for a chance to keep her anxiety at bay. "Just…wait a few minutes to get the flashlights?"

Beside her, she felt him tense as his body went still. He'd let go of her to wrap the blanket around her, but afterward his right arm had returned to the small of her back, where his palm rested, steady and strong.

"Of course," he answered after a long moment, then huffed out a slow breath between his teeth. "Are you sure you don't want to talk about whatever happened in the last tornado?"

She gave an involuntary shudder. "No. Distraction would help more."

His fingers flexed against her spine, the heat of his hand permeating the fleece.

"Valencia." Her name sounded like a warning and a plea at the same time.

Although maybe she heard those things only because she felt equal parts danger and desire herself. Just then, something heavy crashed into the metal door at the top of the stairs. A big tree limb, maybe. Or a part of the house?

The *roof*?

Her gut roiled.

"Please?" She clutched the blanket around her like a cape, wishing she could crawl into his lap and stay there until the tornado ran its course.

Instead, she pressed closer to him, hip to hip, her thigh squeezing against his.

He made a ragged sound of protest, but at the same time, he encircled her shoulders with his arm, tugging her nearer. For a moment, he rested his cheek against the top of her head.

"Maybe you could suggest an appropriate distraction," he urged, the words sounding like he gritted them out. "Because my thoughts are all running in the wrong direction."

Her heart picked up speed. Was *she* the wrong direction? She hoped he understood she wasn't trying to seduce him. She was scared, damn it!

"Let's play two truths and a lie," she suggested, desperate for anything to lighten the tension for them both while still keeping him next to her. She *needed* him by her. "You can tell me two true things about you and one false, then I'll guess which is which."

"Two truths and a lie," he repeated slowly. Musingly?

She wished she could see his face to help her

guess what he was thinking. Did he take her request seriously? Or did he find her frivolous?

"A game will help distract us." She hoped. "Besides, it helps to listen to your voice. It reminds me I'm not alone."

Without her conscious permission, her fingertips landed on the flat, hard plane of his pectoral muscle. She smoothed her hand over it, absorbing his warmth, savoring his strength. Feeling him, breathing him in, set this tornado apart from her past. Because having Lorenzo here with her, in *this* moment, gave her a physical reminder that she wasn't scared and alone while her world cracked apart.

Maybe he heard some of the residual fears in her voice because he relaxed a fraction, some of the tension easing from him.

"Right. Two truths and a lie." In the pause while he was thinking, a lightning crack vibrated through the storm cellar, making her jump. Lorenzo's lips went to her hair, pressing a comforting kiss there before he spoke again. "I play guitar in my free time. I hold the record for fastest calf roping among my brothers. I once shot the principal of my middle school with a BB gun."

In spite of everything, she couldn't help a surprised laugh. "Please say you didn't hit your principal with a BB gun. Although that's so specific, I feel like it has to be true."

She focused all her attention on the man beside her. His warmth. The scent of the outdoors on his work shirt. The flexing muscle in the arm wrapped around her. Right or wrong, his presence felt like a lifeline while the wind raged outside.

"I can't give you clues," he chided, his tone gently teasing. "You have to guess the lie."

"Okay. The lie is that you play guitar."

"Wrong. We should have made stakes for this game. What do I get if I win?" His voice was husky and low, rumbling between them in the dark.

"You can play guitar?" she asked, intrigued.

"My whole family is musical. Diego is the most talented, and he's a guitarist for a local band attracting some regional attention recently." Brotherly pride tinged his voice.

"That's so cool." She imagined Lorenzo playing guitar, his long fingers skillfully moving over the strings. "Do you ever all play together?"

"Sometimes on the holidays a bunch of us will break out instruments. But more often than not, we pass around a guitar and everyone takes a turn."

Having grown up an only child—both with her birth family and later with her adoptive parents—Valencia loved the idea of sharing a talent with siblings. "An invitation to your house at Christmas must be highly sought after."

She could almost hear the music in her ears. The mingled voices of five brothers. How lucky they were to have one another.

He chuckled. "I don't know about that. But we keep each other entertained." Pausing, he lowered his voice before speaking again. "So what do I win?"

A pleasurable shiver stole through her. Was he flirting with her? Or was she hearing suggestive intimacy just because she felt attracted to him? She knew he wasn't the kind of man who would flirt casually just to distract her.

Her pulse jumped.

But she knew better than to put too much stock in the awareness pinging through her, so she rerouted the conversation.

"I'm not sure we can declare a winner until I hear more about the BB gun incident." Her voice betrayed her breathlessness. She licked her lips and tried again. "Is that the lie?"

Outside the wind redoubled, making her edge back on the bed, inserting more space between her and the door.

But just as her old fears threatened to swallow her up again, Lorenzo moved with her, keeping her cradled against his side. His warm strength anchoring her. *Tempting* her.

"Wrong again, Valencia." His voice was a sexy vibration in her ear that put all her focus back on him and the way he made her feel. "We'll have to double the stakes since I've fooled you twice."

Her skin tingled at the idea of him claiming a prize from her in this dark, intimate hideaway. Just when she thought nothing could distract her from the storm, the heated image seared the edges of her fears.

The promise of forgetting was too tantalizing to ignore. Maybe that's how she was able to scrounge up the boldness to meet his challenge head-on. To walk toward the attraction instead of away from it.

"Never let it be said I didn't honor my debts," she murmured softly, her breathing shallow and quick. "Name your price."

Lorenzo knew better than to mix romance and business.

And yet.

These were *extraordinary* circumstances.

Valencia was a strong, independent woman who'd worked hard and sacrificed to build a rescue that would save animals, yet she'd shown him a decidedly vulnerable side when she'd admitted she was frightened and in need of distraction. Was it so wrong to offer her that when she shook against him every time the wind rattled the door? To scavenge a few moments of pleasure together when they could walk out of here to a gravely different world in the morning?

He didn't want to take advantage of her. Far from it. He wanted to shelter her in his arms. Offer her whatever escape he could. The attraction had been there from the moment they'd met.

Would it hurt to call on it now, just for a little while, to help them ride out the storm?

"What if I claimed a kiss?" He told himself that talking about it didn't mean it would happen.

Even just *mentioning* the idea was a better distraction than any game they might play—the possibility it enticed. He sat so close to her he could feel her interest as sharply as his own, the darkness heightening his other senses.

Valencia's soft gasp of surprise was too close to his ear for him to miss. Her back arched a fraction underneath his palm, as if she swayed toward him already.

"Just one?" Her breathless words held a note of expectation. Her hand shifted, landing briefly on his chest, then darting away again, as if she wasn't sure she should commit to the touch. "I thought we were going to double the stakes."

Ah, damn. He hadn't expected her to embrace the idea so fully, but here she was, calling him on his bluff.

Heat rippled through him at her bold words, the sultry promise behind them making him forget everything but pressing his mouth to hers. How could he have known that talking about a kiss would push them closer to the precipice over the hot attraction that bubbled between them?

Every heartbeat sent a hot surge of want through his veins, until the kisses were a foregone conclusion. He would make sure she never forgot them.

"That we are," he promised huskily, angling toward her in the dark, his free hand moving to her bare knee so he could brush light circles along her skin. "But I need you to agree to one before I take a second."

A small hum of pleasure vibrated up her throat, calling an answering growl from his. He had to taste her. *Now.*

"Valencia." He tightened his hold on her knee, his voice growing demanding as his need ratcheted higher. "Do you forfeit your lips to me?"

He felt her quick nod before she spoke. "Yes. That is—" The words cracked on a dry note. "Please."

With considerable effort, he made himself move slowly. He needed this to last, wanted this distraction to spin out for as long as possible. Not just to keep her from thinking about the storm, but because he craved a thorough taste that would leave her hungry for more. Already he knew one kiss wouldn't *ever* be enough for him.

Removing his hand from her knee, he lifted it to her face, brushing her shoulder on the way before landing on her jaw. He skimmed back and forth, tracing the gentle curve from her ear to her chin before laying his thumb over the plush softness of her mouth.

Her breath warmed the digit. He felt her inhale. Then the soft, shaky exhale.

Hunger for her surged, a primal need commanding he lay her down. Cover her. Distract them both in the best way possible.

Instead, he lowered his lips to hers, kissing her with a gentleness made possible only by ruthless restraint. Valencia sighed into him, her breasts pressing against his chest, the tight points of her nipples making him ache to undress her so he could taste her there, too. Shutting down the instinct, he refocused on the soft slide of her mouth over his, needing this kiss to last. He let her get used to him before teasing apart her lips with his tongue.

Then, things got out of control.

Valencia's needy moan went right through him, compelling him to give her more. To answer that primitive need. He sifted through her silky hair to cup the back of her head, holding her where he wanted her while he explored every inch of her mouth. He learned what kisses made her shiver and which ones made her whimper. The rose-and-vanilla scent of her skin teased his nose, beckoning him to sniff out more of it. To find the source of the fragrance.

She arched harder against him, her curves molding to his body. Reminding him she wore only a T-shirt over her panties, the lights having gone out before she could finish putting on dry clothes. That mental visual slammed him, nearly taking him down for the count. He waged a desperate internal battle with his hands not to touch more of her, not to test the softness of her skin where her hips curved or where her thighs shifted restlessly.

She'd agreed only to a kiss, he reminded himself. He would honor that, damn it. But as his restraint stretched thin, nearing the breaking point, he recognized he had to end the embrace before things went further.

Except before he could pull away, she twined her arms around his neck, hauling him down to the mattress with her.

He landed on top of her, barely getting an arm out in time to prevent all his weight from crushing her. Still, his hips pinned hers, his thigh sliding between her legs.

Desire scorched over him, dragging a guttural groan from his throat. The sound mingled with her sigh of satisfaction. And somehow, hearing the way she responded to that friction of their bodies, threatened to incinerate all his good intentions.

She felt so good against him, her body fitting to his perfectly. Visions of sinking inside her weren't helping him to get a handle on this situation.

If anything, every second they spent with their torsos pressed intimately together only made it tougher to pull away. One more minute and he would release her. He *had* to, damn it.

Thump!

The entire storm cellar vibrated as if an earthquake hit it, the bed rumbling beneath them.

Lorenzo broke the kiss, body tensing.

"What is that?" Valencia's fingers clenched tighter around his arms, her voice shaking.

Even as she spoke, the rumbling had ceased. The wind still howled, a constant angry shriek, but the vibrating had stopped.

He dragged in long, ragged breaths, trying to recover himself. His blood still ran hot, but he was almost grateful to the storm for reminding him he couldn't take things further. And how messed up was that thinking? The tornado could be wreaking destruction out there.

That thought finally helped cool him off.

Get a grip.

"Maybe a tree fell outside," he guessed, doing his best to speak calmly. He didn't want her to panic. "I should find the lantern and turn on the radio. It would help to hear a report on where the storm is moving."

He didn't mention that he needed to see her face, too. Without the visual cues of her expression, her skin color and her eyes, Lorenzo couldn't be sure how she fared. If she was on the verge of another panic attack, he needed to know.

And he needed to be in command of himself, too.

Because although he hadn't wanted to end their lip-lock because of potential danger from a tornado, it was fortunate things hadn't gone any further between them. The kiss might have been his idea, but he hadn't meant for it to get so out of hand. She tested the limits of his control unlike any other woman, no matter what he'd told himself about pulling away from her.

Lorenzo shot to his feet, needing to put some space between them. To focus on keeping her safe. He had a responsibility to this woman, especially when he knew that she'd been petrified of the storm. He might be able to justify their teasing around the attraction to distract her, but taking things beyond a kiss would have been wrong. Unethical.

"Okay. Good idea about the lantern." A rustling noise told him she was already sitting up on the mattress while he felt his way around the storage bins.

Fur brushed his right arm as he felt Barkis join

him, the dog's quiet panting a comfort as turmoil raged outside.

"I've got it." Lorenzo leaned back on his heels, then switched on a powerful flashlight.

The bright white beam gave him a glimpse of her standing beside the bed as she slid on a pair of navy blue sweatpants, her pale thigh disappearing under the knit cotton. He stifled a groan, returning the light to the bins. He found bottled water and poured one container into a dog dish for Barkis, then brought two others over to the bed to sit beside a now fully dressed Valencia.

His shaky restraint thanked her for putting clothes on, even as his baser thoughts lingered over the sight of her bare thigh.

Luckily for him, she seemed as intent as him on putting the kiss behind them, all of her attention now focused on the radio she'd pulled into her lap. Flicking on the power, she adjusted the tuner until they could hear the stock tornado warning again. Then, she spun the dial until she found a regional weather report listing towns that had already reported significant damage from the storm.

While they listened, Barkis lapped at his water, and the two of them drank from their bottles in the relative quiet. The wind had eased outside. At the moment, it was less of a shriek and more of a sustained moan.

Lorenzo remained on his feet while he chugged

down his water, knowing the temptation Valencia presented just being next to him. Her sweet, floral scent clung lightly to his clothes, or maybe it was on his skin. He didn't dare inhale more deeply to find out. Her fragrance was like an aphrodisiac.

"Should we look outside yet?" she asked, her cheeks a little flushed as she glanced up at him.

Her lips swollen from his kiss.

He swallowed hard at the visual. The sight made him want to kiss her again. To haul her against him and finish what they'd started. But he knew that couldn't happen. He'd allowed himself the pleasure of touching her only because she'd asked him to distract her, the request revealing a vulnerability that wouldn't allow him to refuse.

Right. As if he hadn't been *dying* for more of her.

"No, it's best to stay here for a while longer. We could be in the eye of the storm." He strode toward the stairs that led to the overhead door and stood still to listen.

A moment later, Valencia spoke again, her head bent over her cell phone. "My phone is still charged, but I'm not surprised there's no signal. Even on a clear day it's hard to get a connection down here."

Her comment reminded him how thoroughly prepared she'd been for a storm. "You don't need a cell signal to access outside information when the radio is working to give updates. The original tornado warning said there could be storm activity through midnight. It's not even eleven o'clock yet."

She shook her head, setting aside her device. "I can't believe that when it already feels like we've been down here forever." Her brown gaze darted to his, her already pink cheeks flushing deeper. "I mean, the first half hour we were in here was terrifying."

But the last half hour passed in a haze of heat and hunger, the time flying past while they kissed. She didn't need to articulate it for him to know they were both thinking it.

Remembering.

"Are you okay?" he asked in the heavy silence. "You were really rattled when we first came down here. I was worried about you."

Her fingers traced the outline of the emergency radio, a French manicure unspoiled by their rush to secure the horses.

"Bad memories settled on me like a toxic cloud. I couldn't seem to see outside of them, the past and the present tangling up because of the storm." She took a sip from her water bottle before recapping it. "I hadn't realized how triggering a tornado would be."

He wondered what had happened during the other storm. The one that haunted her. But he knew this wasn't the time to ask about it. Not when the second wave of the storm could still bring more destruction down on their heads.

"But you're feeling more steady now?" he asked instead. They might have another hour or more of storm to weather, and he'd prefer to understand her fears more before that happened.

"Thanks to you." A smile curved her lips for a moment as she met his gaze again. "I appreciate—" Her teeth sank into the plump fullness of her lower lip. "That is, I know you were distracting me because I asked you to. And it did help."

His heart slugged hard in his chest, his blood heating with the need to pull her against him again.

Damn it. He'd never survive being stranded here with her if he couldn't rein himself in.

Giving her a clipped nod, Lorenzo stalked back toward the stairs.

"If the wind doesn't pick up again in another ten minutes, I'll try the door," he assured her.

Because getting sucked into a tornado might be the only thing that would keep him from tasting her again.

Six

The next hour ticked by slowly for Valencia, waiting for news that the tornado had passed.

Her fears had calmed since the game she'd played with Lorenzo. Then, her fears had receded even more when they'd kissed. The memory of those smoldering embraces taunted her even now as she stroked Barkis's furry head and listened to the latest updates on the weather.

Many Texas and Oklahoma communities had been threatened—from Royal all the way to Appaloosa Island.

Valencia wished Lorenzo sat beside her now while they listened to the reports, but he'd pulled away after their kiss, making her wonder if he regretted what happened between them. He'd paced the small shelter for a few minutes when they'd started hearing the news. Then, he'd made himself at home on one of the storage bins that converted to a bench, leaving plenty of distance between them since she'd never left the comfort of the flannel-lined sleeping bag on the bed.

Now, Lorenzo entertained himself with a three-dimensional maze that had been a gift from the tornado shelter company when she'd upgraded some of the features in the storm cellar. The intricate marble maze lit up, helping her to see him tilting the small box to the right and left, the motion moving the marble through the obstacles. They'd turned a lantern on the lowest setting to illuminate the shelter, but they were both sitting just outside the pool of yellow light it threw. Lorenzo's strong features and dark eyes were visible, but shadowed.

"The news from Appaloosa Island sounds serious," Valencia remarked softly, more to herself than to the man who seemed determined to put thoughts of their kiss behind him.

No doubt he shared all her same reasons for resisting intimacy, considering they were doing business together. She understood why that was a bad idea.

She just wished his withdrawal hadn't been so complete that he needed to sit as far from her as possible while the storm continued outside. Things had certainly quieted down, but until they heard an all clear for the area, Valencia wouldn't be able to stop imagining the worst-case scenario.

"The take-cover warnings are standard procedure when the threat level is high." The maze box went still in his hands as he spoke. "But that doesn't mean they've been hit."

"I know." She nodded, trying to focus on Barkis's trusting face as she stroked his silky ears. "It just feels like one thing after another keeps thwarting the art and music festival. Somehow, even after the news of the missing money, I keep holding out hope that it will all come together."

Lorenzo set aside the maze. "With good reason. Usually, everything the Edmond family touches turns to gold. I'm sure this will be no different."

She sifted through his comment, wondering what it was about the handsome rancher's words that suggested he held some hidden resentment.

"You're not a fan of the Edmond family?"

"I like them well enough," he mused, as if considering the question for the first time. "I don't know Gina at all, but I consider Ross and Asher to be good men. Rusty, on the other hand—"

He hesitated, making Valencia wonder if there was a history between Lorenzo and the Edmond family's oft-divorced patriarch. But then he continued with a careless shrug.

"I have no beef with him. I'm just surprised that the head of such a wealthy family doesn't support more good causes. If not for Billy Holmes's influence, Soiree on the Bay wouldn't have even come together. I don't care that Rusty is considered cantankerous and unapproachable. But not doing more with his wealth is a strike against him in my book." Standing, Lorenzo walked closer, but his focus was on the radio, not her. "I think they're about to talk about Royal."

Her thoughts of Rusty Edmond evaporated at the prospect of news about the tornado. Although she did tuck away one piece of insight from the discussion. Clearly Lorenzo saw supporting charitable works as part of his community duty, something that only raised her opinion of him.

Another reason to regret they hadn't met under different circumstances. If her horse rescue hadn't been dependent on the Cortez-Williams family's goodwill, Valencia would already be thinking about ways to repeat that toe-curling kiss.

Lorenzo turned up the volume on the radio as the broadcast shifted to their county. They'd bounced back and forth between the weather service and local news for the last hour, hoping to keep current.

"...Local tornado warnings have been lifted," the announcer informed them. "But we've received reports of significant tornado damage from all over the county, so use extreme caution when exiting your home or driving on roads in the area. Be prepared for power outages, downed electric lines and fallen trees. And the National Weather Service has confirmed at least five tornadoes ripped through the area—"

Valencia didn't hear the rest of the broadcast. She felt almost dizzy with the news that *multiple* tornadoes had struck. A panicked buzzing started in her ears, not just because of the past, but also very firmly in the present, demanding she check on her horses now that the immediate danger had passed.

"I need to get outside," she blurted, shooting to her feet. She rushed toward the door, where Lorenzo had hung their coats to dry. "I've got to make sure the horses are safe."

To his credit, he was a step behind her.

Heart hammering, she shoved on her boots at the same time that she reached for her windbreaker. Meanwhile, Lorenzo snapped off the radio and retrieved two powerful flashlights.

"Take this," he demanded, passing her one of them. "The exterior lights won't be on unless you have a backup generator for the barn."

"It wouldn't come on automatically, but I do have one I can wheel out there later." Assuming she could still access it in her garage.

There was no telling how much damage they

might find when they opened the door of the storm cellar. The last tornado that swept through Royal had ripped the roof off the Texas Cattleman's Club and brought the town to a halt.

Some of her worry must have shown on her face because Lorenzo rubbed a soothing hand along her back.

"Try to relax. The calmer you are, the calmer your animals will be." His steady voice rumbled in her ears and hummed along her senses.

The practical advice helped her to breathe through the churn of anxiety, giving her the best possible motivation to stay focused.

"Thank you. I know you're right," she murmured, grateful all over again he'd been with her throughout this ordeal. She didn't even want to contemplate how terrified she would have been in the storm shelter by herself, without Lorenzo's patient, soothing presence to keep her grounded.

"Let me go ahead of you, okay?" He edged past her to mount the steps to the door. "That way I can clear a path if there's any fallen debris."

After her silent nod, she waited while he lifted the latch, hugging herself tight. At her feet, Barkis whimpered softly, wagging his tail as he gazed up at her.

A moment later, the plowed-earth scent of the storm filtered through the metal door as Lorenzo pushed it open. Moonlight shone weakly through a few leftover clouds, suffusing the night with a glow that seemed almost bright compared with the dimness of the shelter. A few wet leaves blew down the steps, covered with gritty mud.

Heart pounding, she tried to peer around Lorenzo's broad shoulders to assess the damage. And although she held the flashlight with one hand, her other had gripped the hem of his jacket at some point, her fingers seeking to touch any part of him for comfort. How had she gotten so close to this man so quickly?

With an effort, she unclasped her hand to relinquish her hold while she waited for his verdict.

"Well? Can you see the barn?" she asked as he stepped over the threshold into the night.

Valencia held her breath, her airway constricted tight. The moment seemed to draw out forever, her fear swelling, threatening to swallow her whole.

Then at last he turned back around, giving her a short nod over his shoulder.

"I see it. And from this side it looks unharmed." It was probably a good thing that he offered her a hand to help her the rest of the way out of the shelter, because her relief was so swift it was almost dizzying.

Thank God.

Scrambling out the door, she almost ran across the muddy yard to reach the barn, a horse's soft whinny the sweetest greeting she'd ever heard.

These animals were her whole world now, and she wouldn't let anything—or anyone—distract her from her mission to build a safe haven for them.

As a lifetime rancher, Lorenzo appreciated animals and respected people who did the same. So of all the things he found appealing about Valencia, it shouldn't have been a surprise that her transparent love and deep affection for the horses in her care topped the list.

He'd helped her settle down two nervous stallions and an old mare, turning them out to the smaller of two pastures after he'd secured a few places where the fence had been damaged. But seeing her coax one of her newest skittish rescues out of a stall, soothing the mustang's fears with soft, crooning words, had made some invisible band tighten around his chest.

Even now, drying his face and hands on a gray guest towel after he'd accepted her offer to wash up before heading home, he felt the tug toward her. His admiration for her was all the stronger after seeing her comfort that mare when he knew that no one had comforted her in whatever long-ago tornado she'd weathered.

Her resilience humbled him. Her appeal winding around him like a lover's touch. Tempting. Teasing.

Emerging from the downstairs bathroom inside

her minimalist ranch home, Lorenzo told himself he should bid Valencia goodbye and head home. It was past one in the morning, after all, and he'd already walked a knife's edge of wanting her after that kiss in the storm shelter. He had no restraint left, so he needed to put some distance between them until the world settled.

Decision made, he found her in the farmhouse-style kitchen, seated at a table on the wide-plank floors. The white cabinets and natural wood accents were free of clutter and decor, though a few worn cookbooks rested on a shelf over one counter. Under the glow of an industrial-style pendant light, her honey-blond hair had a warm luster as she bent over another small weather radio.

The announcer's voice became more distinct as he approached. "…an E2 tornado, but significant wind damage has been reported on the southern side of Royal."

"Everything okay?" he asked when she didn't look up from the radio. His hand itched to touch her, to rest between her shoulder blades where he suspected she'd be tense.

Not that he'd be able to stop touching her there if he had that opportunity. He remembered all too well how she felt against him. The need to claim her lips again vibrated through him like a physical imperative.

"Yes." She shot to her feet as if nervous. "Just

listening to the damage reports. Apparently County Route Twelve is washed out."

"Route Twelve?" The road between his place and hers.

Of course.

She nodded, nibbling her lower lip. "I'm sure you want to get home and check on your place, but you're more than welcome to stay here. It's late anyway. Maybe the road will be cleared in the morning."

His heart pounded a slow, warning thud as she stared back at him with concerned brown eyes.

He wasn't supposed to have feelings like this for her. But the time they'd spent together had been intense, escalating their relationship to something deeper. Still, he tried to hold back the need to ravish her.

"They're calling it an E2? Already?"

"Yes. So not as bad as it might have been, but it touched down less than a mile from here, so—" She exhaled a long breath, but it didn't fully hide the way her lower lip trembled.

Relief at the near miss washed over him, all but taking his knees out when he thought about how close a twister had been to demolishing this place she'd worked so hard to build.

"We were so damned lucky." He couldn't help but open his arms to her.

She didn't hesitate. Valencia threw herself into

him, her arms locking around his waist as she buried her head against his chest.

"I know." Her whisper was hoarse with emotion in the otherwise silent kitchen. "I've been sitting here going over and over it in my head. If it had been a direct hit, the horses would have—" She choked on the words and lifted her head, her brown eyes red-rimmed with unshed tears. "I should have left them outside where they could have run free to safety."

"No. You can't think like that." He framed her face in his hands, needing to impart the truth of the words. "They could have been hurt that way, too, caught up in mangled fences or hit by lightning, hail, flying debris. You know that. Your barn is strong, and they're fine."

Nodding tightly, she blinked away the tears, letting only one roll down her cheek. He thumbed it away, wishing he could swipe aside her old fears as easily.

"Thank you. I know you're right. I should be fine now that it's over, but I just feel so—" She seemed to search his gaze, as if looking to see if he felt it, too.

The relief. The adrenaline rush of getting through something life-threatening.

Lorenzo couldn't have said what she saw in his eyes. But he felt the moment that the relief morphed into desire. Heat roared through him, demanding an outlet. Or maybe it was a simple need to celebrate being alive. Whatever it was, he had zero chance of containing the need to kiss her again.

To lick and taste her. Claim her. Revel in the fact that they'd made it through the storm.

Their mouths fused together, heads tilting for better access, tongues tangling. The sounds she made—soft, hungry sighs—only added fuel to the fire inside him, driving him higher. Her palms splayed along his back, skimming and rubbing, as if she couldn't feel enough of him.

He lifted her against him, and she responded by curling her leg around his middle, climbing up his body until her ankles wound around his waist. Groaning at the feel of her lush curves against him, he cupped her ass in both hands, squeezing, directing her hips right where he needed her.

Cotton and denim didn't begin to dull the heated throb where her sex met his. And between the greedy way she kissed him and the way her thighs clamped around him, like she'd never let him go, Lorenzo guessed she wanted him every bit as badly as he craved her.

Still, he broke the kiss to be certain. He tipped his forehead to hers, raking in a breath.

"I need to be sure you want this—"

"*Please.* Yes. My bedroom is in the back of the house." She tipped her head in the direction she meant, and his boots were already charging over the wide-plank floors to find it.

He toed open a whitewashed door into a bedroom, visible only by dull moonlight slanting through plantation shutters above the king-size bed. The room had few furnishings save the cast-iron bedstead, and he headed toward it, spinning around so he could sit on the edge of the gray-duvet-covered mattress, keeping Valencia on his lap.

He skimmed his hands under her shirt and then stopped himself. "Do you have condoms? Mine are in the truck."

She helped him by tugging her shirt up and off, giving him a mouthwatering view of perfect breasts molded by a black satin bra, two tiny bows at the straps unnecessary decorations for so much beauty. "Lucky for us, yes."

Leaning to one side, she towed a wicker basket out from under the bed where an unopened box lay on top of a psychology textbook, a pair of fluffy socks and a bright pink case shaped like it probably held a sex toy.

A guess that seemed all the more probable by how fast she shoved the basket back under the bed. The thought only made him doubly determined to please her, the urge to satisfy her hammering through him with every pound of his pulse.

"You're so gorgeous." He raked the straps of the

bra off her shoulders, then ran his tongue along the two swells above the black satin cups. "I've wanted to touch you all night. Since dinner. Hell, before dinner."

Her back arched, bringing her breasts even closer to his mouth at the same time it pressed the V of her thighs against the rock-hard length of his erection. He didn't know which stole his breath faster, but the need to have her naked grew exponentially.

"Touch all you want," she urged him, her nails raking over his chest, scoring him right through the cotton T-shirt. "But I want to feel all of you, too."

She tunneled under his shirt and dragged it up and over his head. He used the moment to unhook her bra, releasing the soft weight of her into his palms. He lifted one mound to his mouth to tease over the dark nipple, circling and suckling until she whimpered. Then he moved to the other side to repeat the treatment.

She forgot about touching him for a long moment, her hands catching at his hair instead, holding him in place, showing him what she liked. Knowledge he would not waste.

Never stopping his worship of her breasts, he flicked open the button on her jeans and lowered the zipper enough to slide his hand inside, fingers sliding down the satin panties along one side. Dipping beneath the silky fabric to find her wet and ready for him.

She cried out at his touch, as if that one stroke was enough to bring her close to the edge. Releasing one of her nipples, he gazed up into her face, taking in her closed eyes, her head thrown back. Experimentally, he stroked her there again, savoring all her sweetness, and her fingers clenched his shoulders tighter.

He had a hundred things he longed to do to her, myriad ways he wanted to touch her and bring her to the pinnacle of pleasure. But he also yearned to do whatever she craved. What would make her feel best. So he watched, and stroked.

"You feel so good here." He palmed one breast with his free hand and licked over the nipple on the other. "I could touch you all night just like this."

"Don't stop." She breathed the words quietly, her nails digging into him deeper. "It's been so long for me, and—"

She broke off on a gasp as he slid two fingers inside her. Immediately, he felt her pulse around him, her body squeezing him tightly. He pressed deeper inside her, needing to feel every spasm, wanting to coax as much as she had to give him.

Lorenzo had never seen anything so beautiful as her riding his fingers, her soft cries filling the room as she found her pleasure.

The need to be inside her redoubled, filling his chest with a possessive fire so primal his hands shook with the effort to be gentle as he undressed her the rest of the way. But Valencia was having none of that. She about tore his jeans off, raking his boxers with them until they tangled in his boots and he had to help her free him.

"Please, please, *please.*" She murmured it like a chant, her silky long hair sliding over his body as she moved around him, undressing him. "Hurry."

Knowing that she needed him, too, cut the chains on his hunger. When they were both naked, he hauled her into the middle of her bed, his eyes roaming over her beautiful body while he tore open the box of condoms and rolled one onto place.

All for me.

The fierce need rode him hard, demanding more of her.

"Did that feel good?" He breathed the question into her ear as he stretched over her, making room for himself between her thighs.

"So good," she gasped, her hips lifting to meet his.

"There's more where that came from," he promised as he nudged his way inside her, her tight heat stealing his breath. "We're only just getting started."

Seven

This. Man.

Valencia stared up at him in her darkened room, wondering if he had any idea how much he turned her inside out. Her feelings for him had exploded in a hundred directions during the storm, leaving her utterly raw. She had no barriers now, all her nerve endings exposed to his skillful touch. His hypnotic words.

We're only just getting started.

She wasn't sure she'd escape this night with her heart intact.

For now, she could only cling to his strong shoulders to try to anchor herself as he filled her. Stretched her. Made her see stars behind her closed eyelids. It wasn't until he kissed her mouth—slowly, tenderly—that she realized she'd been holding her breath.

"You okay?" he asked, stroking her face.

Her eyes flew open as she realized he'd been holding back for her sake, giving her time to accommodate him.

A piece of her heart definitely chipped away at the thoughtful look in his chocolate-brown eyes.

"More," she demanded, writhing against him, wanting him to take as much pleasure as he'd already given.

Her word worked like a magic spell, setting his hips in motion and launching her into a higher plane of heat. The delicious friction built inside her, as if she hadn't just orgasmed all over his hand.

He seemed to sense that she was close all over again because he rolled her on top of him, his dark gaze missing nothing as he reached between them to stroke her.

"Oh." Her thighs clenched him, sensation rocking her core.

No one had ever propelled her body to heights like this before. Then again, had anyone ever tried? She stared down into his eyes as he worked that tight bundle of nerves exactly the way she needed. And she flew apart.

Absolutely *imploded*. Her release squeezed him over and over, her feminine muscles fluttering wildly.

Only then did he shift her to her back again, driving home between her thighs, again and again until he found his peak. He strained against her, his body tensing in a way that showed off every single muscle, delineating each masculine ridge and hollow. The sight affected her. The whole night had wrecked her, but seeing him find pleasure in her body made her want to curl against him and never let him go.

It was just as well that his eyes were closed at that moment because she guessed everything she was feeling would have been visible in her expression. She tried to tuck in all those feelings as he panted through the last of his release, his body slumping to one side while he kept the bulk of his weight off her.

He couldn't know that she would have welcomed it. Would have savored being pressed deeper into her mattress underneath him. So she tamped down the rush of tenderness that overcame her and turned her head to the side in time to see him settle beside her on the pillow.

She couldn't look away.

For long moments, they simply breathed each other in, and she wondered if he felt like his world was off its axis or if that was just her. But then he blinked, a slow closing of his eyes. When he reopened them, there was a distance there that hadn't been in place before. A guarded look that told her he planned on keeping the boundaries between them.

A moment later, he smoothed a strand of hair off her face, a sweet gesture she might have misinterpreted if she hadn't been watching him carefully. She'd seen the moment that he'd mentally pulled away from letting this night have any deeper meaning.

Valencia wasn't just being paranoid. She could feel him already retreating from her. From her point of view, the night had brought a monumental shift in her relationship with this man. But she understood Lorenzo saw her as a business associate first and foremost.

What had just happened between them didn't change that.

Maybe he was already regretting it even now. As he pulled the blankets over them and tucked her against him, he didn't reveal any other tangible sign of his retreat from her. But the heated touches of earlier had turned to cold comfort now, no matter how close they lay together when they finally fell asleep.

Valencia's fears about Lorenzo were confirmed when she woke up alone at daybreak.

She glanced over at him now—shortly after noon—as she sat beside him in the Cortez-Williams family's private helicopter. They were on their way to Appaloosa Island to assess the damage from a separate tornado that had ripped through the festival site the night before.

He'd already been on his cell phone arranging for the short helicopter flight while seated at her kitchen table when she'd emerged for breakfast that morning. And even though everything in Lorenzo's demeanor had told her he was resurrecting the old professional boundaries between them, he had still invited her to come along with him.

How could she refuse the offer when the future of her rescue was so entwined with the fate of Soiree on the Bay? So she'd agreed, and the roads in Royal had been cleared enough for them to drive over to the Cortez-Williams place where Lorenzo kept the family helicopter.

Now, the pilot of the small aircraft circled Appaloosa Island, giving them an overhead view of the destruction from the storm. In the middle of the blue waters of Trinity Bay, the island seemed to float like a shipwreck. Downed trees lay in every direction, the upturned roots exposing big gashes in the earth. Roofing tiles were scattered like confetti over the ground, while mangled fencing jutted from random dirt piles. And one of the temporary buildings erected for the festival was demolished on one side.

"Oh, no," Valencia murmured, peering out the window as the chopper neared the ground. "How will we ever clean this up in time for the festival to open at the end of the month?"

She was meeting members of the advisory committee here today. Would any of them have a clue how to proceed in the face of so much damage?

For that matter, did they even have enough of a budget to make repairs? The money woes hadn't disappeared.

Lorenzo swore softly. "I can't imagine how they'll ever clear it all. Although that looks like a truck from Bowden Construction down there giving it a valiant start."

He tapped the window to show her where he was looking, his strong arm reaching over her. A shiver went through her at his nearness, memories of their night together never far from her thoughts since she'd awoken alone. But she couldn't afford to think about that when Lorenzo had not acknowledged what had happened in any way, almost as if those sweltering stolen moments didn't exist. So she forced herself to find the oversize pickup for Jack Bowden's construction company.

"Maybe that's a good sign," Valencia tried to assure herself, even though hope felt like a scarce commodity today.

Between Lorenzo's defection, the rumors about the vanishing festival funds and seeing the festival grounds in ruins, Valencia felt everything she'd worked so hard for slipping away.

"It has to be." He unfastened his seat restraint as soon as the helicopter touched down on a rough patch of torn-up grass, the loud *whap*, *whap* of the rotor blade sounding even louder as the door opened for their exit. "There are a lot of good people backing Soiree on the Bay. They'll make it come together."

Valencia hurried to unbuckle from her seat as Lorenzo offered her a hand out of the aircraft. Flashbacks of his hot, searing touch shivered through her as she braced herself for the feel of his skin on hers.

"You know as well as I do their money has gone missing," she reminded him, needing to contradict him to keep herself from relishing the warmth of his fingers around hers. She couldn't help that his touch, and his proximity, were still deeply arousing to her, even though he'd decided to resurrect all the boundaries of professionalism between them.

"I do. But the Edmond family isn't the only sponsor of the event. My brother Rafe has invested heavily in Soiree on the Bay." Lorenzo released her hand as soon as they were out of range of the chopper blades.

"Rafe. He's the one after Matias?" She tried to recall what he'd told her about the five Cortez-Williams brothers, a conversation they'd had at Sheen last night before all hell had broken loose.

So much had happened since then. Her whole life had been turned upside down along with Appaloosa Island.

"That's right. Rafe owns RCW Steakhouse."

Once again, she didn't miss the note of pride in his voice at the mention of his brother's accomplishments. But any response she might have made was halted as Lorenzo gestured toward a small group of people gathered under one of the giant live oaks still standing near a demolished stage. A man and a woman stood close together, arms looped around each other, while two other women peered down at a shared tablet, heads almost touching.

Festival advisory board member Lila Jones was one of the women, and Valencia thought the other lady who held the tablet worked with Lila at the Royal Chamber of Commerce. The couple was Brett Harston and Sarabeth Edmond, one of Rusty's exes. Brett had been an advisory board member until the Edmond family patriarch booted Brett off for seeing Sarabeth. Valencia had enjoyed getting to know them over the last few months planning the Soiree, and at the sight of her busi-

ness associates, she tried to swallow the ache of hopelessness she'd been battling all morning.

Greetings were exchanged all around. Lorenzo already knew Brett from the Texas Cattleman's Club, but he hadn't met Lila before. Lila's new assistant, Megan, said a quick hello before excusing herself to take a call. Lila, with her intensely blue eyes and long, dark hair, had recently become a social media star thanks to a romance with a notable online influencer, Zach Benning.

The brunette's pretty smile was nowhere to be seen today, however. She appeared as gutted as Valencia felt inside.

"Has anyone spoken to Jack Bowden?" Lorenzo asked, his dark eyes moving slowly over the damaged festival preparations. "We could see from the air that one of his construction crew's trucks is already on-site."

Lila nodded as she tucked her tablet under her arm. "We saw him a few minutes ago. He said he's assessed the destruction and is sure he can repair the stage and the buildings in time for the festival."

Valencia's breath caught. Hope flared.

"That's good news, right?" she asked, peering around at the other faces, wondering why they weren't more excited to hear it.

"It would be," Lila admitted, flipping her long ponytail over her shoulder. "Except that when he called Edmond Ranch with an estimate for the cost of repairs, he was told there is no money."

No money? And more important, *why not?*

Speechless, Valencia could only shake her head. She refused to speculate about the Edmond family in front of Sarabeth, unwilling to make Gina and Ross's mother uncomfortable. But what on earth was going on?

Sarabeth cleared her throat, a few strands of shoulder-length blond hair blowing over her cheek as she spoke. "I called Ross to ask him about the missing funds, but he told me the same thing I'm sure he's told all of you." Her gaze darted to Brett and then back to the group. "A great deal of money is missing from the account with the funds from the ticket sales. Ross says they're still trying to track it, but his meeting with the bank was delayed by the tornado."

Lila made a soothing comment about the delay being unavoidable, but Valencia couldn't suppress the heat of anger building inside her. The accounting for something like the festival wouldn't be elaborate. If money was missing and a reasonable explanation hadn't been found yet, that meant something underhanded was going on.

She didn't want to think the worst of anyone, but what other reason could there be? Ross Edmond was a smart man. If he couldn't find a paper trail, there was no hope of recovering what they'd lost. The money was gone.

And so were her dreams for the rescue.

A knot twisted inside her chest, raw and chafing.

"Excuse me," she murmured, overcome with so much frustration she didn't know where to put it all.

Turning her back on the group, she walked away from Lorenzo and her friends on the advisory board, needing to collect herself. She strode quickly toward the water, the beach not too far from any location on Appaloosa Island.

She wished she'd brought Barkis with her. The solid presence and unconditional love of her dog would help unfasten the tangle of emotions tightening inside her. Picking up her pace, she'd almost reached the water's edge when a voice from behind her left shoulder raked over her senses.

"Talk to me, Valencia. How can I help?" A strong masculine hand wrapped around her elbow, stopping her short with the gentlest of tugs.

Blinking back her surprise, she spun on her heel to face Lorenzo, all of the hurt and anger from the storm bearing down on her. And now, seeing his face when she was reeling from the news that the money for the Soiree on the Bay festival really was gone, she couldn't help but remember how he'd tried to shut her out this morning.

"How can you help?" she repeated coolly, folding her arms around herself as she stopped at the edge of the beach where the surf rolled to the tips of her toes. "Are you sure you want to? You've made it clear you're only interested in a business relationship, so there's no need for you to get tangled up in my personal disappointments."

She gazed out over the waves, powerless to rein in her words when she was exhausted from the emotional roller coaster she'd been on over the last twenty-four hours. Reliving the fears from her childhood—and having Lorenzo there to witness them—had taken more out of her than she'd realized. She felt like she didn't have the strength to hold herself together any longer.

"That's not fair." He came shoulder to shoulder with her where she stood, but he made no move to touch her. "I'm here, aren't I?"

Valencia shivered at the distance between them. He might be only inches away from her, but it was telling that he didn't lay a finger on her after everything they'd experienced together the night before.

That hurt.

"Not for me, you're not."

Lorenzo dragged in deep breaths of the air blowing in off Trinity Bay, reminding himself he hadn't done anything to deserve Valencia's anger today.

She'd been through a lot, and he understood her frustration at the possibility of not being able to grow her horse rescue the way she'd dreamed now that the arts festival might be a bust.

But he truly had flown out to Appaloosa Island mostly for her sake. He'd wanted to do something nice for her after pulling away from her following their night together. He had hoped seeing the festival site for herself would alleviate some of her worries. Instead, it had only confirmed them.

That wasn't his fault, though.

"I realize this is a disappointment for you." He turned toward her, taking in the delicate contours of her face as she stared out over the water, her honey-brown eyes focused on some distant point. "This is a setback, but you'll find another way to support the rescue. You've accomplished so much already."

Pursing her lips, Valencia darted her gaze briefly toward him, then back to the glittering expanse of blue water. "Have you ever known what it's like to struggle? To be denied something you've worked so hard for?"

He ground his teeth together, ignoring a question that wasn't relevant. "The Soiree could still happen. The Edmond family might still pull this off."

She nodded slowly before turning thoughtful eyes on him. "It could. But neither of us believes that anymore."

Lorenzo couldn't argue with her. Hell, he didn't want to. He hated that their time together had been tainted. First by his recognition that he'd broken his own cardinal rule not to get involved with someone he did business with, and then later by the unraveling of Valencia's plans for the ticket sale money from Soiree on the Bay.

"Today definitely didn't turn out the way we'd hoped," he acknowledged, not sure how else to comfort her.

Still, the weight of regret seemed to anchor his feet in place on the beach beside her.

"Maybe we should cut our losses." She looked him in the eye, squaring her shoulders to his. "I can get a ride home with Lila or one of the other board members."

He blinked in the face of her...*dismissal*?

"I don't mind waiting for you to finish up—" he began, but she was already shaking her head.

"I know that. You're too much of a gentleman to leave me stranded." She gave him a gentle smile, and he remembered how they'd touched and held each other in that dark shelter. Her lips had been so soft beneath his. But she definitely wasn't remembering their shared kisses now. "What I mean is, I'll be okay on my own, Lorenzo. You can go now, and you certainly don't need to feel badly about it."

A knowing glint in her brown eyes told him they weren't just talking about the helicopter ride.

Somehow that got under his skin. That she would suggest he didn't need to feel guilty about sleeping with her and then walking away. He wanted to deny that he had done any such thing, because of course he'd prefer to see her again. To take her to his bed over and over.

But unless she planned to refuse the support of the Cortez-Williams family for her horse rescue, he couldn't continue to see her since they had business dealings. And he'd never ask her to renounce that support so that she could be with him.

Regret burned hotter. Deeper.

Yet he wouldn't compromise what was right.

"Are you sure you'll be okay?" he asked finally, hating to end their time together like this.

"I'll be fine." She gave a clipped nod. "Bye, Lorenzo. And thank you, for everything."

It was wrong to walk away without another kiss. Without another touch. But that's exactly what he did. Leaving Valencia and the beach behind, he headed toward the family's helicopter still parked in open grassland near the staging area.

The only positive thing about ending their liaison now was that at least Valencia would never know how thoroughly he'd investigated her personal life as part of awarding her the grant money. She wouldn't like knowing that he'd glimpsed some of her secrets before they'd ever met.

With the hole burning in his chest at her impending absence, however, Lorenzo wondered if it would have been worth her learning the truth for a chance to be with her again.

Eight

Safety goggles sealed to her face, Valencia lined up the laser guide on her table saw, then lowered the blade. Sawdust flew as the metal teeth seared through another board to repair her paddock fence, the scent of new lumber swelling in the muggy July heat. She'd kept the big barn doors open to begin her project that morning, wanting the fresh air to keep the dust at a minimum, but now that the sun had risen to its peak, she was ready to call it a day.

Her shoulders ached from hunching over the boards while she worked, and she stretched as she straightened. A full day had passed since she'd visited the Appaloosa Island and things had unraveled fast with Lorenzo. She'd tried to focus on tornado cleanup around her property so as not to spend too much time thinking about their falling-out and what it might mean for the rescue. Backbreaking labor was good for wearing her out so thoroughly she couldn't be too stressed.

Except today, as she added the last cut plank to a pile in her truck bed for a round of fence repairs later, she couldn't hide her head in the sand anymore. She needed to call Asher Edmond and see what was happening with the festival. To find out if her chance of receiving any money from the Soiree on the Bay ticket sales was gone, or if there was still some hope that the event would come together.

For all Valencia knew, her disagreement with Lorenzo—and sleeping with him before that—had pulled her rescue off the list of the Cortez-Williams family's approved charities. Which could mean her horses might not receive a single cent in donation from either of the groups that had once seemed so promising.

That would be painful enough in itself. But Valencia couldn't deny another persistent ache since her argument with Lorenzo. She missed him. She'd thought about him countless times since her return home from Appaloosa Island without him. Now that he'd spent time in her world—meeting all her horses, helping her to care for them before and after the tornado—she had memories of him here. She could look out over her paddock and picture him coaxing in her most stubborn and moody old mare when the storm had been brewing. Inside the stable, she remembered how he'd laughed when one of the docile draft horses had nuzzled his shirt pocket, hoping for a treat.

And in her bedroom alone the night before, she'd remembered how it felt to have Lorenzo there with her, too. He'd worked his way into her life so quickly she hadn't had time to consider how much it might hurt if things didn't work out between them. But there was no "them" and it was foolish of her to think otherwise.

Peeling off her leather work gloves in exasperation, Valencia rested a hip on the tailgate, then pulled her phone from the back pocket of her jeans.

The sound of cicadas filled the air, an audible reminder of the summer heat even as she stood under the shade of a bald cypress tree. She pressed the contact button next to Asher Edmond's name on her screen. One ring later, the call went to voice mail, the same way it had done for days. Disconnecting, Valencia ground her teeth in frustration and moved down her contacts list to try Asher's stepsister, Gina Edmond. At twenty-six years old, Gina was four years younger than Valencia, but they'd moved in enough common social circles over the years that they were friends.

The call rang twice before Gina answered.

"Hello?" The young woman's voice sounded hoarse with emotion.

Valencia stilled, her senses all focused on the call.

"Gina? It's Valencia. Is everything okay?" She straightened from where she'd been leaning against the tailgate.

"Oh, my God, no. Things are not okay at all." Her friend's voice broke, her pitch high and breathless.

"What's wrong?" Valencia's stomach knotted, foreboding stirring. "Should I come over? Do you need someone to be with you?"

She'd never been to Gina's home, but the woman sounded too upset to be alone.

"No. That's okay. It's just that—" She paused, as if sucking in a deep breath. "Asher has been arrested. On embezzlement charges linked to Soiree on the Bay. I just can't believe this is happening."

"Asher?" Valencia shook her head, certain Gina must have said the wrong thing. The wrong name.

Asher Edmond was a good man. Rusty had adopted him when he married Asher's mother, Stephanie Davidson. Rusty had since divorced her, but Asher remained an integral part of the Edmond family.

"Yes. Asher. And I can't believe it, either. How could he do such a thing?" There was a note of despair in Gina's voice, and Valencia's gut churned in sympathy.

She glanced around at the projects she had in progress around the rescue today, but told herself it could all wait if Gina needed a friend.

"He might not have," she said carefully, hoping the words brought comfort and not false expectations. "Just because the police arrested him doesn't mean he did it."

"I know you're right, but they must have had convincing evidence to arrest him in the first place." Gina sniffled once, then again before continuing. "I'm so sorry to unload all this on you. You didn't call to hear about my problems."

"Don't be sorry. It's no wonder you're upset. And I only called because I've wondered how things are going with the festival," she admitted, scraping some damp hair from the back of her neck. "Gina, it's no trouble to come over if you need a friend. I want to be there for you—"

"No. I'll be all right. I appreciate the offer, though." She spoke with a bit more composure, her voice softer now. "I should probably talk with Ross and figure out what this means for the festival. Maybe there's a chance it will still happen if—"

Valencia hung on to her words. Yes, for her

friend, but also because the future of the rescue and the equine therapy camp were riding on the festival. "If what?"

"I was going to say maybe the festival will happen if the police have traced the money from the ticket sales, but I guess a part of me doesn't want that to be true because it would mean Asher really *is* guilty," she admitted.

Valencia's heart ached for what Gina must be going through. Of course she would worry about her brother. And the scandal of having an Edmond arrested was going to hurt the whole family. She understood the shame of that better than anyone knew. Because while her adoptive parents were wonderful people, Valencia had never felt free of the taint of her biological relations, especially her father with his long history of fraud, forgery and identity theft. Logically, she knew that shouldn't reflect on her, but that didn't stop her from sometimes feeling like an imposter in the privileged world she inhabited now.

"Please know you can call me anytime," she told her. "If you need anything…"

"Thank you." Gina sniffed again. "I appreciate that more than you know. Bye, Valencia."

The call ended and she slumped back against her truck fender. The day had gone from bad to worse in a hurry, but with her horses counting on her, she couldn't waste a day for a pity party.

Returning her phone to her pocket, she tried not to think about Lorenzo or what he thought of the latest developments with Soiree on the Bay. Instead, she slid behind the wheel of her truck to drive the perimeter of her fence so she could patch the broken areas.

Too bad there wasn't a patch job for her aching heart.

Two days after Asher Edmond's arrest, Lorenzo took the ferry back to Appaloosa Island. He'd had family ranch business in Houston, so he'd taken the helicopter to Mustang Point, splitting the difference between Appaloosa Island and the city. Now that he'd finished his business, he wanted to see if any preparations were happening toward the festival. Just because he was curious, of course.

Not because he wouldn't stop thinking about Valencia.

A breeze blew in off Trinity Bay as the ferry moved through the water. Lorenzo tipped his face into a light spray kicking up, remembering the way the rain had pelted them the night of the tornado before he'd taken shelter with Valencia. So much had happened in such a short time. Learning more about her fears and her hard work, seeing her commitment to her horse rescue with his own eyes. Then, later, he'd lost himself in her arms, tasting and touching every delectable inch of her beautiful body.

Memories of the time in her bed had filled his dreams every night since. Again and again he undressed her, peeling away the layers that kept her from him. Again and again, he heard her soft whimpers in his ear, then woke up aching.

Alone.

Logically, he knew he'd done the right thing in walking away. He'd been burned before by crossing the boundaries between romance and business, and he refused to take that risk ever again. For her sake as well as his own. But knowing he'd made the only possible choice didn't stop the churn of regrets where she was concerned about what might have been. And it sure as hell didn't prevent him from missing her.

It would be one thing if all he missed was the sizzling intimacy. But he also wondered how she was faring with repairs at her rescue. How she was dealing with the news of Asher Edmond's arrest. He couldn't remember the last time a woman had so thoroughly preoccupied him. Maybe because no one else ever had.

When the ferry reached Appaloosa Island, Lorenzo stepped onto the pier along with a couple dozen other people. He didn't know what he'd expected to see once they docked, but it definitely wasn't the mayhem unfolding in front of his eyes.

A group of network news vans were parked on the grass outside the festival headquarters—a small public building requisitioned by the Soiree on the Bay coordinators to oversee preparations. And, to add to the pandemonium, protestors crowded the parking area near the beach. They were carrying signs that read I Demand a Refund and I Paid for a Soiree Scam, and there were also a few photos of Asher Edmond with the caption Swindler on the Bay.

The atmosphere was raucous, with reporters standing at various points in the crowd to obtain video footage while others broadcast live updates. Between the shouting demands of the unruly protest groups and the private island's lack of public facilities to maintain the visitors on the eastern undeveloped side, it seemed like a disaster waiting to happen. While there was a resort on the western side with some amenities, a business catering to tourists surely wouldn't want to host the unhappy protestors if they could help it.

"Lorenzo?"

A familiar voice called to him from a group of people standing off to one side of the protestors.

Searching the faces, Lorenzo spotted his brother breaking off from the group and heading toward him.

"Rafe." He clapped his sibling on the shoulder. "I'm surprised to see you here."

Dressed in black jeans and boots, Rafe wore a silver-gray button-down. His years in the restaurant business had given him a more cosmopolitan air than the rest of the Cortez-Williams brothers. But he didn't have any of his usual genial charm around him today. He looked downright grave.

"I don't know why I keep showing up here, either," Rafe admitted, his dark gaze roaming the unhappy protestors. "I invested heavily in the festival and I keep hoping that this nightmare will end. That it will all be a mistake, and they'll find the missing money—"

He broke off, shaking his head in disgust. Before Lorenzo could speak, Rafe turned toward him, continuing, "*Missing money.* Who am I kidding? It's a poor turn of phrase for funds that were clearly stolen."

The venom in his voice was unlike anything Lorenzo had ever heard from his younger brother before. Concerned, he lowered his voice before asking, "How much did you invest?"

"Too much," Rafe spat out. "Not enough to ruin me personally, but enough to bankrupt the business."

Lorenzo swore. "You know I'll help—"

Rafe was already shaking his head. "And you know I'd never ask. Thanks just the same."

For a moment, both men were quiet. Lorenzo understood his brother's pride. No doubt, he'd feel the same way if their positions were reversed. But that still didn't stop him from wanting to offer any assistance he could.

Rafe rocked back on his heels and said, "It's unbelievable how fast things soured. Or were we just that naive to trust the Edmond family?"

"I still can't see Asher doing something like this," Lorenzo muttered, his gaze going to the cutouts of Asher's face on the signs the protestors were waving around.

"I always liked the guy."

"Me, too," Rafe acknowledged. "But sometimes people only show you what they want you to see."

Lorenzo couldn't deny the truth of the words.

They spoke for a few more minutes before his brother left to see if he could find Ross Edmond. Lorenzo hoped Ross would have answers for his brother, but wasn't holding his breath. Seeing the Soiree on the Bay festival fall apart was hurting a lot of people. Not quite ready to make the ferry trip back to the mainland, he headed toward the beach to take a walk. The sun was setting, turning the water a shade of greenish blue while the sky was streaked with violet.

Normally, he didn't take the time to appreciate that kind of thing. But back home, he knew he'd have only thoughts of Valencia waiting for him. So he headed away from the crowds toward the quieter part of the beach to clear his head for a little while. There were a few cabanas dotting the sand along the tree line, but for the most part, the view was unspoiled here. Maybe if he walked far enough he'd leave behind the raised voices of the protestors, too.

Too bad he couldn't outrun his regrets while he was at it.

Cursing his attempt to vanquish his own demons, Lorenzo stopped. He had responsibilities back home in Royal. A ranch to run. Family that counted on him. He shouldn't be wasting time at the site of a doomed festival that was bringing his brother financial trouble. Lorenzo turned on his heel to head back to the ferry when he spotted a female figure he recognized well.

Tall and willowy, the woman stood at the edge of the water, a pair of sandals in one hand while her fair hair blew behind her. A pink pencil skirt hugged her curves while the sheer sleeves of a filmy white blouse skimmed her shoulders.

His breath caught. Held. And it was almost as if she could feel his attention on her because at the same moment the woman turned to face him, her pretty features lit by the setting sun.

"Lorenzo." She said it almost as if she wasn't surprised to see him, but he knew that couldn't be the case.

Maybe it simply felt inevitable to run into each other again.

"Hello, Valencia." He stalked toward her, boots silent in the soft sand.

She straightened as he came toward her, shoulders tensing.

The fact that he made her anxious was one more thing he'd regret. He'd never intended that. Now, he weighed his approach while the water lapped softly at the beach.

"Last time we were here, I was so sure the festival wouldn't happen," she observed, keeping her attention on the water where streaks of purple light glowed on the waves. "But I guess I couldn't help hoping I was wrong."

He didn't like the self-deprecating note in her voice. Hated that her hard work on the rescue wasn't going to be rewarded with the festival donations she deserved.

"We all had every reason to hope the festival would still take place." He'd encouraged her to think positively, in fact.

Did she hold that against him?

"You have to admit things look bleaker today." Turning toward him, she ran a weary hand through her loose hair. "I'm not sure who is worse, the protestors or the reporters."

His gaze tracked the movement of her fingers even as he imagined the stroke of those silky strands through his own hands. "You can't blame folks for trying to hold the Edmond family accountable."

"I don't." She shook her head and heaved a sigh as a small wave washed over her toes. She stared down at her feet disappearing into the sand as the water receded. "But their presence is a sign of how much things are falling apart. If the festival was happening, the Edmond family would have coordinated some kind of response to the protests. A PR person would be talking to the crowds and the news, spinning a narrative."

"Right." He understood her point. "The lack of response speaks for itself."

Echoes of their argument returned to his ears as they stood in silence for a long moment. She'd accused him of never having known struggle. While he didn't think that had been fair, he also recognized that she'd been dealing with a lot. Yet he wasn't certain he knew how to navigate that conversation now any better than he had been before.

So, for the moment, he sidestepped it for a topic where he could be more proactive. Make some kind of impact instead of feeling so damn helpless.

"How are you doing with cleanup at the rescue?" he asked instead.

He'd missed her voice. Her intelligence. Her passion for her work. He wanted to keep her talking. To extend this unexpected time together.

"I just finished the fence repairs today," she answered, never missing a beat. Maybe she was as eager to avoid the topic of their argument as he'd been. "The horses romped around like new colts once they had access to the big field again. They were ready to run."

"I'll bet." He grinned at the image, understanding well how it felt to throw off restraints put on by the world. "I'm sure the restoration work has been keeping you busy." He knew firsthand how many hours could disappear into efforts like that without dedicated ranch hands to help. "You'll be ready to play like a new colt, too, when you have a day away from fence repair."

She laughed, lifting one foot to drag a toe through the wet sand, the pattern she made disappearing when another wave lapped against the shore. "Maybe I will be."

The music of her laugh still whispering through his head, he had the overwhelming urge to ask her to spend that day of relaxing with him, but that negated every guideline he'd put in place for mixing business and pleasure. He'd backed off for good reason. But reason never spoke as loud as attraction and desire when it came to Valencia.

"How were things at your place after the tornado?" she asked, turning her light brown eyes on him.

She was so lovely. Her high cheekbones and easy smile. Her athletic strength honed day in and day out with physical labor. The bright banner of fair hair.

Realizing he'd been staring, he cleared his throat.

"Not bad, all things considered. The animal areas didn't receive much damage, but an old windmill looked worse for wear." He backed up a step to keep his boots away the surf and Valencia followed him up the sand.

"Do you still use it?" She stopped as they neared the tree line, her face in shadow as she turned to face him again.

"We have a few new turbines set up for irrigation and generating power, so the old mill from my great-great-grandfather's time is more nostalgic than anything." He'd devoted a day to reattaching a broken sail, then found himself ordering other parts to keep the machinery in working order. "It sits in a picturesque spot along the river near the original cabin. The cabin is in disrepair, but I'd like to maintain the windmill."

"Good. Nothing says 'welcome to the country' like a weathered barn and a fantail windmill. I like spotting them on road trips." She bent to slide on her sandals.

Was she getting ready to leave?

Lorenzo couldn't deny that it had been good to see her again.

What if there was a way to maintain their

friendship without letting the attraction take over? Shouldn't he at least explore the possibility?

"Valencia." He reached for her, just to put a hand on her arm and encourage her attention.

But as his fingertips slid over the silky material of her thin blouse along her forearm, he was swamped by the need to feel more of her. Her skin was cool beneath the fabric, and he ached to touch it without a barrier.

Her gaze fixed on his. Awareness of her filled his senses, drawing him in, pulling him closer…

"I should probably go," she murmured, though she didn't pull away. "It's a long drive back to Royal. I rode over with Lila and Zach, and I'm sure they'll be ready to leave soon."

Lorenzo forced himself to release her. Still, he couldn't help but make a case for what he wanted to happen next.

"My helicopter is in Mustang Point. Fly home with me and you can be in Royal in a third of the time."

In the silence that followed, he could hear the protestors' voices in the distance. He really wanted to make sure Valencia got home safely.

"I'm not sure that's a good idea after—" She shook her head impatiently. "That is, I don't want to blur the boundaries that I know are important to you. To me, too."

"A ride home won't blur any boundaries," he

promised, recognizing that she deserved better from him than how abruptly he'd pulled away before. "Besides, I owe you a return trip after the way we parted company last time."

He'd regretted that, even though Valencia had been the one to suggest they go home separately.

She nibbled her lip for a moment, making his pulse stutter with the memory of how her lips had felt on his. But then she wrapped her arms around herself as she peered up at him.

"Just a return trip?"

"One return trip only," he agreed, trying to ignore the swell of victory over winning her over. "I can even have the pilot put the chopper down near the rescue if you want to be delivered to your doorstep."

"I don't think my horses would forgive me for that. But if you don't mind me tagging along with you as far as your ranch, I'd be glad for the ride."

The fresh rush of pleasure he felt at her acceptance nearly stole his breath.

But could he trust her in a way he'd never been able to trust his former fiancée? He dismissed the question since it couldn't come to that anyway. For tonight, he'd simply escort her home and enjoy her company.

"Good. Should we get on the ferry?" He offered her his arm.

She rested her hand there as she nodded. "Okay.

I'll text Lila to let her know I'm going with you. As a newly engaged couple, she and Zach will probably be just as glad for the time alone."

Wincing at her choice of words, Lorenzo found it a challenge not to crave "alone time" with the woman who'd starred in his dreams every night since the tornado—the same woman who walked beside him now, her arm trustingly wound through his.

One way or another, he would make good on his promise to deliver her back to Royal without taking another taste of her lips.

Nine

Valencia gazed through the helicopter window to the ground below, the lights of Royal piercing the night. The flight was long enough for conversing through the headset microphones—but she'd been glad to keep the exchanges limited and focused instead on the sights along the way.

A lit-up baseball diamond where a local game was in progress. A summer festival on a town square. A drive-in movie theater. They'd spotted a few places with tornado damage, but overall, the destruction had been minimal outside of Appaloosa Island.

Better to stick to small talk about the sights

than to let herself think about how it felt to have him beside her again after their disagreement and the ensuing days apart. Seeing him on the beach at Appaloosa Island had been like a moment straight out of a fantasy. She'd been musing about him and suddenly, he was *right there*.

Now, seated in such close proximity that his knee brushed her bare one, she struggled to keep her expression neutral while seized with the urge to lean into his big, strong presence. To tip her head against his shoulder and close her eyes long enough to forget how her dreams for the equine therapy camp were vanishing more every day.

And based on how strong the urge grew, Valencia knew she should head back home for the night as soon as the helicopter touched down. She couldn't risk falling back into Lorenzo's arms, no matter how enticing that might be.

"We're home," he announced a moment later, the low rumble of his voice through the headset stirring memories of the night they were stormbound together, his deep baritone a comfort in the dark. "There's the Cortez-Williams ranch."

He pointed to a spot out the window, and she looked out to see two well-lit gated entrances on either side of a palatial main home. While the surrounding ranch acreage remained mostly in darkness, the security lights along the driveways illuminated the main house, a pool and separate cottage. With stone walls, deep wooden porches and aluminum roofs, the buildings were a blend of modern farmhouse and Spanish influences. A large horse barn and paddock were visible near the house, although she guessed there were more stables for such a large working ranch, but they might not be lighted at night.

"What a beautiful home," she murmured as the helicopter descended in a nearby field. "And I envy those stables."

Lorenzo's laugh came through the headset. "Why am I not surprised you'd appreciate the horse lodgings more than anything else?"

She smiled, warmed to think he knew her so well. Perhaps she shouldn't feel pleased about that, when sleeping together had probably ruined her chance of securing the donation she'd counted on for Donovan Horse Rescue. But she'd striven her whole life to be viewed on her own merits. It was a relief to think Lorenzo recognized what was most important to her.

"I have spent a lot of time reviewing stable plans this year," she admitted. "If there's any chance that one day I'll have camp goers entering my horse barns to work with the animals, I want to be sure they're spacious and high-functioning."

"Would you like to see them?" he asked as the aircraft landed, pulling off his headset. "A quick tour before I drive you home?"

The invitation in his dark eyes wasn't what drew her in. If anything, it made her warier of spending time together since she knew how vulnerable she felt where this man was concerned.

But she really couldn't turn down his offer to show her the stables. Not when she'd poured so much thought and time into crafting her plans for the next phase of building at the horse rescue. She didn't have many opportunities to walk through facilities like his.

"If you don't mind showing me," she said as she pulled off her headset and unbuckled her seat belt. "I'd be glad to see them and dream about the future."

A few moments later, Valencia strolled through the field beside Lorenzo, the helicopter rotor slowing behind them.

"Will you be okay in those shoes?" he asked, his palm grazing the small of her back to guide her toward the path to the stables. "I didn't think about that, but you're not dressed for the barns."

How could a touch so subtle give her so many shivers?

"I had a meeting with the festival advisory board," she explained, her words a little breathless thanks to his nearness. "So it gave me an excuse to break out some of my old wardrobe from my days in the corporate world. But at least the sandals are flat. I'll be fine."

He shot her a sideways glance. "Do you ever miss that work? Your lifestyle must have done a one-eighty."

Now that the helicopter had shut down, the night seemed all the more quiet. The soft cadence of crickets mingled with the rustle of the leaves in a mild breeze. Enticing. Romantic.

Risky.

"It did, but I was ready for the change. I'd rather spend the days on horseback in jeans than chasing the next big account in a designer skirt." She slowed as they reached the sliding double doors in front of the tall, cream-colored stone barn. Sighing appreciatively, she skimmed a hand along the pale rocks, tracing her fingers through the mortar seams. "This is really beautiful. I would have loved to do my stables in stonework. Especially having just been through a tornado."

The dark thoughts of worst-case scenarios had circled her head for days afterward. Stone buildings were safest. If only she could build such sturdy walls around her emotions.

He paused in front of the doors and then turned to face her. Shadows faded, the concern in his expression easily visible now that they'd neared the security lights that illuminated the roads between buildings.

"The workmanship on your new stable is excellent," he reminded her gently. "I thought that the first day you showed me around. And it did weather the storm with almost no damage."

She appreciated his reassurance, knowing it was well intended.

"You're right. Although there's always room for improvement." She attempted a smile, recognizing he couldn't possibly know the extent of her personal fears after the tornado she'd been in with her birth parents. Besides, it wasn't a good idea to revisit her more recent memory of a tornado since Lorenzo figured so prominently in it. "Let's see the rest."

She was grateful when he slid open the heavy door on the right, admitting them into the dimness. He hit a switch on the wall to turn on the lights along the center aisle, leaving off the fixtures over the individual stalls. There was a swell of horse greetings at their arrival, surely more subdued than usual given the hour. A couple of whinnies. Some stomping of feet and tossing of heads. And one long snort.

Lorenzo walked to the closest stall first, greeting an alert-looking black paint with a pat on the neck. But Valencia's main attention was fixed on the wide aisle and immaculate stalls, the familiar scent of fresh hay and leather tack permeating the place even though the building housed ten animals. There were empty stalls on either end of the barn, with movable partitions to make larger stalls for foaling. A spacious tack room in the back beckoned, but she was tempted to say hello to all of the animals first.

"I am all the more impressed with your stables now that I've seen the inside," she announced, extending a hand to a pretty strawberry roan quarter horse peering over its stall door at her. "But how am I going to focus on the building when you have all these beauties in here?"

Encouraged by the animal's greeting as it nudged a nose under her palm, Valencia stroked a hand over the glossy coat.

"You're really good with horses," he observed quietly, his voice sounding closer than he'd been a moment ago.

Glancing over her shoulder, she saw him pause a few feet away, watching her. Awareness stirred, tingling through her bloodstream and dancing along her nerve endings. She hoped it didn't show as she swallowed back the feelings.

"They saved me," she told him simply, confessing a truth she didn't trust to many people. But she realized she wanted him to know this about her. She trusted him with that piece of herself. "I felt more heard and understood talking to a horse for the first time than I ever had by anyone before then."

When he remained silent, she rushed to speak, to smooth over the awkwardness of the admission.

"It might sound strange to someone who doesn't know horses. But you do." Her gaze flicked to his face briefly before she tipped her forehead to the roan's cheek. "I was overwhelmed by how easily a horse can offer trust. How simple and straightforward it could be to form a bond with a big, powerful animal."

She knew her explanation might stir more questions than answers, but she really wasn't ready to share more than that about how painful her early childhood had been. For her, it was enough that she'd worked past those memories to live a life on her own terms. Trust, however, was still hard to come by.

"They trust you, too," Lorenzo observed simply, moving to the next stall to soothe a gray Arabian that head-butted his door. "It's easy to see how they gravitate to your calm demeanor. We used to offer boarding services on the ranch, and I can remember nervous owners visiting their mounts, agitated about every little thing, and convinced their horses were high-strung. But those same animals would be relaxed as can be as soon as the whirlwind of nervous energy was out of the stable."

Grateful to him for keeping the conversation light despite what she'd shared, Valencia laughed appreciatively.

"Funny how that works." She had observed

the same phenomenon herself. And now that she thought about it, maybe that was some of what drew her to this man walking through the stable with her.

She'd recognized his ease with the animals when he'd visited her rescue. She'd gravitated toward it then.

Even after all that had passed between them, she couldn't deny the pull of that quality in him. Was it weird that she trusted what a horse thought of a man?

Get it together, Valencia.

Of course it was weird.

But she wasn't relying solely on the equine endorsement. She liked him, too. The fact that a temperamental Arabian was nuzzling his hair affectionately was just icing on the proverbial cake.

"I should go." She hadn't meant to blurt the words, but a sort of panic seized her as she acknowledged how much she still wanted Lorenzo. It wouldn't be wise to give in to that combustible attraction again when it had already come back to bite her after the tornado. "That is, I'm sure you have things to do and you've already been kind enough to give me this much of your time. I should just—" ger gaze locked onto his dark eyes "—go."

It wasn't a graceful exit. But when the alternative might be plastering herself against his chest and whispering all the secret longings of her heart, she figured it was better to make the awkward retreat.

She hastened outside into the moonlit night, her heart pounding as she heard his step behind her a second before his hand slid around her wrist.

"Valencia." He held her only a moment before letting go. Just enough to claim her attention. "Please wait."

Lorenzo watched Valencia as she hesitated, her feminine figure silhouetted in the full moon sitting low on the horizon. He wasn't ready to let her go.

He'd known the magnetic pull between them wasn't finished, but the electric current that sparked from just the brush of his hand over her arm underscored how quickly the attraction could ignite.

"This—" She gestured back and forth between them. "Whatever is happening between us isn't wise. You know it as well as I do."

Of course he knew. He'd been fighting the urge to kiss her every second they'd spent together almost from that first meeting.

"That doesn't make it any easier to walk away." Even now, he battled the need to sift his fingers through her hair and cradle the back of her head so he could taste her. Slowly.

Thoroughly.

Not just because he wanted her. But because of a connection that kept flourishing every time they were together.

Her words from inside the barn kept chasing around his head. *They saved me.*

Valencia had trusted him with that much of her past, a piece that he guessed she'd rarely shown to anyone. She'd allowed him a glimpse beyond the polished, successful woman she'd become to the vulnerable girl born into a family that clearly hadn't deserved her.

I felt more heard and understood talking to a horse than I ever had by anyone before then.

With those heartfelt words, she'd made him regret every time he'd suspected her of unscrupulous motives for fundraising on behalf of the rescue. The knowledge of her father's criminal history weighed on him since it had been obtained by a paid investigation into her past, cheating him of having her confide in him on her own terms.

More important, he'd robbed Valencia of the trust she'd deserved from the start. Instead, he'd been one more person in her life to let her down. She didn't even know how fully he'd failed her yet, a thought that felt like lead in his gut. Especially since he now knew that she was *nothing* like his ex-fiancée, and he'd let his prejudices color all of his decisions with Valencia because of them.

Pacing, she wrapped her arms around herself,

her body language defensive. "Sometimes it's better to walk away than to keep making the same mistakes."

He hated that he'd inspired the wariness.

"Is that we're doing?" Maybe he should have just let her go, but he really wanted to know. "Making mistakes?"

In the distance, a coyote howled, stirring answering calls in the night. The sound echoed every lonely, hungry impulse inside him.

"You must have thought so, Lorenzo, given how fast you retreated the day after the tornado."

He ground his teeth against the exasperation of how wrong he'd been. But she deserved to know he regretted his actions, whether or not it made any difference to her now. So he forced his jaw to unclench and met her gaze.

"No. I never thought it was a mistake—"

She raised an eyebrow. "Do you mean to tell me it was a coincidence that you dodged morning-after awkwardness by being glued to your phone when I woke up alone that day?"

Even when he was the target of her cool anger, he couldn't deny a flash of admiration for the way she called him out for his role in what had happened. He owed her an explanation.

"I will admit I worried about sacrificing our professional relationship when we'd just come to terms for how my family's charitable program could benefit the rescue." He'd resorted to work instead of confronting the gray area of his relationship with Valencia. "And you have to admit we'd been on an emotional roller coaster the night before. Was it any wonder if I was still reeling a bit?"

Her expression softened a fraction. She swayed toward him.

"I may have been reeling a little, too," she admitted, blinking fast. "The tornado was a lot to process."

The note of fragility in her voice brought him closer. He couldn't help the urge to protect her, even if that meant he needed to keep her safe from any distress he might cause.

"I should have talked to you about what happened. And I regret how I handled that. But believe me, not for a minute did I regret being with you." He'd thought of little else since then. He missed seeing her. Talking to her. Kissing her.

Hell, he just missed *her.*

And having her here beside him now, seeing the favorable way she looked over his ranch and his horses, filled him with a sense of rightness. Like she belonged here.

For a long moment, she remained quiet. Thinking. Her gaze roamed over the main ranch house and some of the outbuildings while she seemed to ruminate over what he'd said. When at last her focus returned to him, her look was still guarded.

"Then don't keep me in suspense," she said finally, tilting her chin up at him. "What would you have said if you had the chance to go back and talk to me about our night together?"

His lips quirked for the briefest instant, registering some amusement that she wanted an accounting. But just as quickly, he acknowledged that this might be his one and only chance for a do-over, and he'd better not mess it up.

Dragging in a breath, he dug deep for the right words. Scratch that. He couldn't worry about the best phrasing. He owed her the truth.

"I would have told you that the night we shared was the most memorable one I'd ever spent with any woman. Period."

She made a small gasp, but pressed her lips tight around the sound as if trying to hide it.

He let the truth of that statement sit with her for a moment, allowing her to hear and see how deeply it resonated for him. Then, he continued.

"Considering the short time we've known one another, that realization rattled the hell out of me—then and now—but it has to mean something."

She gave a wordless shake of the head, so subtle he wondered if she realized she was doing it.

Only because of that, he finally permitted himself to touch her. Just enough to capture her chin. Tilt her face up to his.

"You disagree?" he asked, running a fingertip under her jaw. Noting the way her lips parted at just that simple caress. "Our time together didn't mean anything?"

"We can't allow it to." Her words were a quiet whisper, but there was a thread of desperation in it, almost as if she'd made the same argument to herself a few times. "My work is too important for me—and to future generations of troubled kids who need the kind of help I can offer—and I can't afford to choose a personal relationship over a professional connection that could be the difference maker in getting an equine therapy camp off the ground."

Disappointment stabbed him. How could he argue with her passionate commitment to a good cause?

He forced his fingers away from the temptation of her skin, his hands falling to his sides.

"I respect whatever you want, but you don't have to choose between them."

Her breath hitched. He could hear it through the sound of the crickets breaking into multipart harmonies in the live oaks sheltering the driveway.

"What do you mean?" she asked.

"I mean the donation is beyond my control now. The office of my family's charitable giving has already approved the funds. I couldn't revoke that even if I wanted to. But I assure you, I don't."

It shocked him to see the relief go through her in a visible wave. Had she been stressed about that this whole week?

He cursed himself all over again for not clearing things up better with her after their night together. But before he could apologize for not making that perfectly apparent, Valencia wound her arms around his neck.

The feel of her suddenly in his arms chased away everything else. Reason. Logic. Boundaries.

There was only the trace of roses and vanilla from her skin. The soft weight of her breasts pressed to his chest. The hypnotic pull of her dark eyes as she stared up at him in the moonlight.

"Are you saying that if I kiss you tonight, there's no chance I'm going to blur any boundaries?" Her fingernails clenched at his shoulders, a gentle scrape that stirred him like nothing else.

"Zero." He articulated the word clearly even though his breath rushed in and out of his lung like a bellows.

Her lips pursed. She gave a nod—all business—like they'd just concluded an important negotiation.

Then, fingers tunneling through his hair, she pulled his head down to hers and kissed him like she didn't plan on coming up for air for a long, long time.

Ten

Valencia had restrained herself as long as humanly possible.

But then she'd gone and spent too long under the influence of a hypnotic full moon listening to Lorenzo methodically break through all her boundaries. Who could resist a man who said things like: *The night we shared was the most memorable one I'd ever spent with any woman. Period.*

Her knees had been a little wobbly ever since, the desire for him so strong she couldn't draw a breath without anticipating the way he would taste. Then, once he'd insisted there were no boundaries to blur anymore—no way what they were doing would affect the status of the rescue with his family's foundation—how could she hold back?

Especially when she so rarely let herself act on an impulse, afraid of somehow revealing her unsavory roots.

Tonight, she was shoving all that aside to embrace the way Lorenzo made her feel fully alive and present to the moment.

Wanted.

Breaking the kiss to peer up at him through half-closed lids, Valencia hauled in gulps of air to try to catch her breath.

His voice rumbled low and warm against her ear. "I'm hoping that means you want to come inside the house with me."

"Yes. Please."

Pivoting on his heel, he took her hand and drew her toward the massive two-story house that wrapped, L-shaped, around a pool and cottage. Except he didn't pause by the back entrance of the main home. Instead, his boots charged unerringly across the stone path toward the smaller, separate residence on the opposite end of the pool.

"You live *here*?" she asked, taking in the more modest building that was about the size of her own home, whereas the main house had to be close to ten thousand square feet.

"I do." He led her onto the covered porch and

unlocked the front door while she vaguely noted gray-painted rocking chairs and a wooden map of Texas that served as wall art between black-shuttered windows.

"Then who lives in the main house?" She hoped it wasn't a nosy question, but since Lorenzo ran the Cortez-Williams ranch, it seemed only natural he'd live in the dwelling clearly built for the owner.

"My parents." He didn't seem to mind her question, holding the door wide for her while she stepped into the cool interior of a Spanish Colonial–style home, the terra-cotta floors and exposed beam ceiling visible by the glow of a wrought iron pendant lamp that hung in the foyer. "They raised six kids there, and my brothers still come home most weekends for barbecues. For as long as my mother enjoys the extra space, I want her to be comfortable there. She makes better use of it than I would."

She followed him through the living area, where leather couches were surrounded by low wood bookshelves filled with old volumes. Her eyes drifted to a silver-framed photo on the mantel that must be his whole family standing near an outdoor fireplace. Flanked on both sides by dark-haired sons, an older couple stood in the center.

"How lucky for you all to get along so well that you can live in close proximity like that," she observed.

Abruptly, Lorenzo stopped in front of her and turned, his hands finding her waist. This close to her, she was reminded how much bigger he was. Taller. Wider. Stronger.

"Thank you. But I'm hoping that's the last we talk about my family tonight." His fathomless gaze locked on hers as the heat of his palms stroked lower, settling on her hips. "Or anything that's not you and me."

"Oh." She made a shaky exhale, the sound emerging like a half-stifled moan as anticipation stirred. "Good idea."

Heart hammering, she canted closer, ready for more.

Heat flared in his eyes. His chest expanded with a breath, making that strong wall of muscle brush lightly against her breasts. Her skin tingled everywhere.

"Come with me." His eyes smoky with need, he took hold of her hand, pulling her toward the hallway to the left. Leading her through the first arched door, then closing it behind them, Lorenzo sealed them in a big master suite dominated by a king-size bed draped in all-white linens.

A moment later, his mouth claimed hers again. The intensity of his kiss made her realize how much he'd been holding back before. Because now, he didn't just taste and explore. He *devoured* her.

Backing her up against the door, he pinned her

in place with his powerful body, a welcome weight she'd longed to feel every day they'd been apart. She tipped her head against the unforgiving oak, submitting to his hunger, letting it stoke hers.

Heat raced all over her body, like a small blaze following a path of accelerant, every place it touched turning to an inferno. His hands molded to her body, tracing her curves through her clothes before tunneling under her skirt to grip the backs of her thighs. Lifting her.

She twined her arms around his neck and locked her heels behind his waist as he walked her toward the bed. Every step rocked his hips against hers. The hard ridge in his jeans pressed between her thighs with such friction that it made her see stars behind her eyelids.

When he settled her on the edge of the bed, he relinquished her to unfasten the buttons of his shirt. She tried to do the same, but the visual of the bronzed muscles he exposed along his abs kept distracting her as he worked. Finally, after he yanked his shirt off, he knelt between her thighs to finish unfastening the buttons on her blouse.

They both watched his progress, their foreheads bent together, breath mingling.

She pressed her knees against his sides, the fiery warmth of his skin tantalizing her. In another moment, he had her last fastening undone, and he skimmed the top off until she sat on his bed in a skimpy lace bra and the wrinkled pink skirt already rucked up her legs. She felt entirely wanton, craving every delectable sensation he could wring from her body.

"I've been dreaming of this. Of you." He sketched a finger down one strap of her bra, then traced the lace edge of the cups. "Having you here in my bed."

"I've dreamed about you, too," she admitted, unable to stifle the impulse to arch her back in offering. "Every night."

He tugged down the lace with his finger, exposing a nipple already tightened to an aching point. When he bent his head to flick his tongue over the tip, she gripped his shoulders and held him there, needing more.

"Lorenzo." His name was a plea on her lips.

His only answer was to shift to the other breast, repeating the same exquisite kiss there. She speared her fingers into his thick, dark hair, keeping him close. Only then did his hands shift to her thighs, traveling slowly up from her knees.

Higher.

She rocked her hips, craving the pressure and friction of him at the juncture of her thighs. But his hands continued their maddening crawl, his splayed fingers caressing every inch of her on their way up her legs.

When he reached the band of white lace at last,

she thought she might come out of her skin. He leaned back to look at her, his dark eyes scanning her body until his gaze positively smoldered. She thought she might combust.

Instead, she skimmed her palms along his shoulders and contented herself with soaking up the feel of him. His warmth. His strength. His potent masculinity. She stroked two fingers up his corded neck, delighting in the heavy swallow beneath the skin. Did she affect him as much as he affected her?

She couldn't possibly if he could afford to take so much time teasing along the sensitive flesh of her inner thighs that her legs began to tremble. Maybe he felt the quivers of her muscles because a moment later, his hand was inside her panties and his tongue was in her mouth.

A moan tore through her, but he captured it, their lips sealed together. His touch was sure. Steady. As if he knew exactly how to drive her higher, his fingers playing over her slick folds. For a fleeting instant, she wondered how he'd learned her body so well the last time they were together, but then all her thoughts scattered as tension knotted inside her. Tighter. *Hotter.*

Pleasure built to a fever pitch, the sensations so delicious she could only hold still for the onslaught. Then, all at once, her release broke over like a rogue wave. Her feminine muscles clenched hard while a gasp tore from her throat. She clung to him, arms wrapped around his neck and clutching him to her. He felt like the center of her whole world for those long moments as she came, his hand anchoring her in the rough sea of her pleasure.

Oh. My.

Rattled and still buzzing with the aftershocks, she wasn't ready to let go of his neck, but he gently pried her arms free, pausing to drop a kiss on her lips before he stood to undress.

Their eyes met briefly as she watched him, then her gaze dipped to his rigid erection, the sight reminding her how much she wanted to please him in return. That put her into motion again, shimmying out of her lacy underwear before she slid off the bed to kneel in front of him.

He'd never seen anything so sexy.

Still flushed pink from her orgasm, her lips swollen from his kiss, Valencia blinked up at him from her spot on the floor. He wanted to make her feel good. To make this night about her after the way he'd pulled back from her the last time.

But when he reached for her, thinking he would lay her back on the bed and come inside her, he found his fingers sifting through her silky hair instead. Petting. Stroking.

Savoring.

And heaven help him, her tongue peeped out of her mouth then, running around the rim of her lips as if to ease him into her, and he was lost. His control shredded. Instead of lifting her up, he drew her nearer. The soft moan she made was something he knew he'd replay over and over again forever, the note of anticipation in it as difficult to miss as her distended nipples.

Or her lust-dazed dark eyes.

So when her lips parted around him, he sank inside her sweetness, his brain blanking to anything but her plush mouth and the tentative fingers holding him steady. Desire scorched over him, burning up everything except for this red-hot connection. Her head bobbed, knees inching closer, one hand splayed on his thigh to steady herself, and he'd never experienced anything hotter.

Too soon, he teetered so close to the edge he didn't know how much longer he could hold back. And he *had* to finish between her legs. Needed to feel her there after he'd given her an orgasm. And yeah, maybe he wanted to make sure she felt him there, too.

"Come here." Somehow, he found the willpower to lean over her and lift her to her feet. "I have to be inside you. *Now.*"

She gave a wordless nod, looping her arms around his neck to drag him down to the bed with her so he stretched out over her. Honey-brown eyes locked on his, she arched up, grazing her hips to his.

He was so far gone he nearly sank into her at the blatant invitation. But he didn't even have a condom on. And damn, he'd never been so wound up that he'd been in danger of forgetting. Heart thudding, he pulled away to retrieve a condom from the nightstand drawer.

Lids at half-mast, she watched him tear open the wrapper and roll the protection into place. Her one foot teased up and down his leg while she waited, almost as if she craved contact with him every moment. Or maybe that was what he wished, and he was projecting it onto her. Because damn, he never wanted to stop touching her.

When he was ready, he put one knee on the bed, his arms bracketing her shoulders. She shivered beneath him, a sensual little undulation of her body that made him long to discover every single thing that affected her that way.

Cupping her chin, he kissed her until they were both panting.

"Are you still ready for me?" He remembered how she'd felt coming apart around his fingers.

"So ready." She gave a fast nod. "Hurry."

With that encouragement, he slid a hand around her hip, holding her in place. Then, tipping his forehead to hers, he sank inside her inch by incredible inch, until they were fused together. Their satisfied groans twined together in the still room.

Damn.

His heart pounded like it wanted to burst out of his chest, and he'd only just gotten inside her. She disarmed all of his restraints, stripping him bare.

He wanted to think about something else, any possible distraction, to make this time with her last longer. But he'd been hungering for her for days on end. Having her in his bed now, real and honest, sweet and sexy at the same time, was too much. Besides, she deserved for him to be right there with her every moment of this extraordinary encounter. He couldn't pretend that being with her was anything less than earth-shattering.

Because this woman was rocking his whole world.

"You feel so good," she chanted softly, her fingers flexing against his chest. "So, so good."

Valencia rolled her hips and locked her ankles around his waist, as if letting him go wasn't even an option.

Something about that act—the possessiveness of it—shoved him even closer to the ledge. Heat shot up his spine, his release hovering. He reached between them to touch her, to tease the tight bud of her sex, wanting to take her over the edge with him.

Her breath caught. Her teeth clamped down on her lip.

Then she shuddered. Hard. She squeezed all around him, the spasms pulsing.

A shout tore from his throat as he came, his hips pumping into her as the release shook him to the core. The heat of it raked through him for long moments until he was all but light-headed from it. He slumped to her side, trying to regain his breath.

Failing.

He closed his eyes for a long moment, willing himself to recover. No easy feat when being with her was the best feeling he'd ever experienced. Hands down.

As his skin began to cool and they gently disentangled themselves, he tried not to think about *why* being with her affected him that way. Wasn't ready to look beyond the physical when he'd only just patched things up with her after the way he'd failed her the first time.

For now, he could focus on the physical, couldn't he? Especially since that's all she appeared to want from him.

This time, he'd hold her. Talk to her. Let her know he wasn't checking out on her just because their passions had been spent.

He dragged a pillow closer to tuck it under her head, then hauled a light blanket up from the foot of the bed to cover them. Afterward, he lay down beside her again while the wrought iron ceiling fan spun slowly overhead, stirring the air.

He combed through her hair with his fingers while he made himself comfortable next to her. "So I think we proved in no uncertain terms that our first time together was *not* a fluke."

The corners of her mouth kicked up and a sound suspiciously close to a giggle tripped from her. "You sound almost disappointed. Were you *hoping* the first time was a fluke?"

It amazed him that making this beautiful woman laugh could feel even more rewarding than making her come. Another sign that merely enjoying the physical side of this relationship might not be as simple as it sounded.

"Hell no. If anything, I couldn't wait for a chance to test the theory." He traced the delicate arch of her eyebrow. "But the question is, now that we know the chemistry isn't going away, how do we handle that?"

The question was one he'd been posing to himself, of course. But he hadn't meant to share it with her. Certainly not tonight, anyhow.

A tiny furrow appeared between her brows as she seemed to consider. "I don't know. But at least we don't have to worry about having business dealings anymore. You said that wasn't a concern now that the horse rescue has been approved by the foundation."

He smoothed the small indent between her brows, regretting that he'd made it appear.

"It's not a concern," he assured her. Then, realizing he'd never shared anything about his former fiancée with Valencia, he wondered if knowing about the other woman would help explain his actions. He didn't want to give her any more reasons to worry about his family's support of her rescue. She deserved to rest easy about that. "I may have been overzealous about distinguishing between my business and personal lives after my ex-fiancée convinced me to give her restaurant company a substantial discount on my family's meat for five years."

The story still embarrassed him. But Valencia seemed to key in on different details than what upset him.

"You were engaged?" She went still.

"Unfortunately." The bitterness was still there, but for the first time in a long time, he felt a bit... *less* resentful. Was it because of Valencia? "She targeted me for my wealth, and I failed to see it until she'd run up my credit cards and disappeared."

"What a horrible woman." The indignation in her voice surprised him as she levered herself up onto one elbow. "No wonder you have a difficult time trusting."

Valencia's dark eyes flashed with anger, and he couldn't deny a surge of tenderness for someone who would be so defensive of him.

Would she feel the same if she understood his inability to trust was what had driven him to investigate Valencia's past? No doubt she would consider it a violation of her privacy. Guilt swelled.

"I just figured it was a better practice to keep my private life far from work," he explained, his hand settling on her hip through the blanket. "And it served me well enough until I met you."

Her eyes narrowed as she caught his hand in hers, threading their fingers together. A playful gleam lit her gaze.

"Are you suggesting I messed up your plans?" Her voice was warm and teasing.

The blanket shifted lower on her breasts, and he wanted her all over again. Not just because she was way sexier than any fantasy. Because she was kind and good.

His voice thickened when he spoke again. "I'm saying you are worth breaking the rules for, Valencia. Meeting you made me realize I'd be foolish to pass up the chance to know you just because of some worn-out commitment to keeping my personal life separate from work."

Her breathing quickened, her chest rising and falling faster. Her dark eyes softened.

Damn but he needed her once more. This time, he'd take as long as he wanted to make her feel good. To show her that he wasn't playing around.

So he covered her body with his, and showed her everything he wasn't ready to put into words.

Eleven

Stealing out of Lorenzo's bed in the middle of the night, Valencia scooped up a black T-shirt off the floor. He'd offered it to her to sleep in…and then had promptly pulled it back off to make love again. Falling almost to the middle of her thigh, the fabric was impossibly soft and smelled like clean laundry with a hint of the pine and musk scent that usually accompanied him.

She lowered her nose to her shoulder to breathe in the scent of the fabric again as she peeked back at his big, sleeping form in the moonlight slanting in through the blinds. So strong and male, the muscles of his shoulders and arms apparent even when he was at rest. And as much as she'd like to be sleeping now, too—especially since he'd worn her out in the most delicious of ways—she'd awoken feeling a little antsy. Restless.

Quietly, she slipped out the door of the master suite and into the living room. She felt too anxious to remain indoors, but she hesitated to exit the front door, where she might be visible to anyone looking out of the main house. It might be four in the morning, but still she knew her relationship with Lorenzo wasn't to the point where they were ready to share it with friends and family.

Were they?

The question told her exactly what had her too revved up to sleep. Her relationship with Lorenzo had gone hurtling forward tonight, but she wasn't sure what she wanted that to mean. Worse, she wasn't sure what *he* wanted from it, either. But the night had been too amazing to do anything other than simply enjoy the connection. To revisit all the comfort and pleasure he'd given her the night of the tornado.

And he was right, the chemistry had been no fluke.

Spying a back door off the kitchen, Valencia padded toward it in her bare feet. Then, pushing it open, she stepped outside onto a private patio where a wicker couch with deep cushions faced a cold fire pit. No one would see her out here since there were only fields and four rail fences in the distance—or at least as far as she could see in the moonlight.

Dropping into the cushion with a sigh, she had just tipped her head back to stargaze when the door to the house opened again.

"Valencia?"

The sound of his voice shimmied through her, all of her senses going on high alert just from his nearness. It wasn't fair how much he affected her.

"I'm out here." She lifted a hand to make it easier for him to see her in the dark. "Sorry if I woke you."

He was already closing the distance between them. And she felt her heart rate quicken, her defenses falling fast.

"That's okay. I'm a light sleeper." He dropped into the cushion beside her, dressed in a pair of gray cotton gym shorts and a white T-shirt. "Everything all right?"

His hand landed on her knee since she had her legs tucked up underneath her. She shivered in spite of the warm night, remembering the ways he'd touched her and how quickly she'd unraveled.

She was falling for him.

The realization hit her all at once. Not just because of his mesmerizing touch. But because of the concern in his eyes right now as he looked at her.

"I'm fine," she said a shade too brightly, not sure what to do with this new knowledge. "Just a little trouble sleeping."

His gaze wandered over her for a moment before he seemed to accept this answer. Reaching toward her, he drew her against him so she could lay her head on his chest.

"Talk to me," he ordered softly, arranging her hair so she could settle comfortably against him. "Tell me whatever's going through that pretty head of yours."

She smiled. Did he have any idea how lovely it felt to have her cheek rest on his warm chest? To feel the rumble of his voice beneath her ear as he spoke? Breathing in his delicious pine-and-musk scent, she nuzzled closer.

His invitation to confide in him touched her deeply. Gave her courage. He'd told her something of his past earlier. Perhaps it was time for her to share more of herself if she wanted any chance of building a real relationship with him. And with a fresh wave of tenderness welling inside her, she couldn't deny that was exactly what she hoped for.

"You know how much I want to launch the equine therapy camp," she began slowly, tracing circles along his chest with her fingertip as a cooling night breeze stirred her hair. "But I haven't fully explained why."

"In the barn tonight, you mentioned something

about horses saving you." He continued to smooth his palm over her hair, a comforting gesture.

"My adoptive parents put me in an equine therapy camp when I first came to live with them. A counselor recommended it for me because I'd been…neglected. Earlier in life." She still stumbled over saying she'd been *abused*, finding the word personally triggering. It felt at odds with her determination never to see herself as a victim, but she knew that was a very personal hang-up.

If she'd learned one thing in her personal journey, it was that no two people reacted to trauma the same way. The things that had worked for her, and had been healing for her, wouldn't necessarily help someone else. But it was important to respect each path and let people find the tools that worked best for their emotional recovery.

"I'm so sorry, Valencia." His fingers never quit stroking. "When you said that you'd felt understood by a horse, I wondered what that meant about your family."

"They were awful people." She was grateful that most of her memories had grown dim with the passing years, but there were still some that remained as jagged as ever. "My mother didn't have a nurturing bone in her body, and she seemed to think it was a game to taunt my father when he was angry. Which was most of the time."

Echoes of old fights, ugly screaming accusations, could still give her nightmares. Not often, thank goodness. But the past seemed like a dark stain in her mind that would never fully fade.

Lorenzo went motionless now. Tense.

"You don't have to tell me. Especially if it upsets you." His voice sounded strangled.

She closed her eyes for a long moment, examining her feelings. But she felt close to him. Safe in his arms. And she wanted to share something after he'd confided in her about his unhappy engagement.

When she opened her eyes again, she murmured, "It's okay. I want to tell you."

Sinking into the comfort of the darkness and the steady slug of his heartbeat beneath her ear, she continued, "They were a volatile couple, young and poor. My mother was a teenage runaway when she met my father. In a *bus station*. That was where he taught her how to panhandle to distract people so he could pick their pockets. My earliest memory is of being in my birth mother's arms while we—while *she*—ran from the cops."

Counseling had taught Valencia how to separate herself from the actions of her parents. But no amount of therapy had taken away the sudden awful gut clench she felt to this day upon seeing uniformed police officers. Or the guilt that went hand in hand with the reaction.

Lorenzo's hand slid to her shoulder and gave a gentle squeeze. "Valencia—"

"Just let me get through this, okay?" she pleaded, wanting to have the basics shared so she didn't have to revisit the memory. "The last time I spent with them was in a tornado. Locked in a bathroom while they fought over who should have to stay with me. Neither of them wanted to." The snippets she recalled from that argument were the most vivid of her childhood. "But the angry words stopped when the tornado ripped most of the house away."

Lorenzo's arms wrapped around her. He murmured some quiet words of comfort against her hair.

"They were both injured, I think." The aftermath was hazy for her, the timeline less linear. "I remember my mother saying she was going to find help afterward, and for me to stay there—in the bathtub. But she didn't come back. Rescue workers found me two days later and that's how I ended up in foster care briefly until I was adopted."

She didn't dwell on those two days alone. The period spent in the eerily quiet remnants of their small mobile home was frightening, but at least the time seemed to pass quickly. Perhaps because she'd been in shock and numb to everything. She wouldn't have been able to leave the old cast-iron tub even if she'd wanted to since debris had fallen over it, trapping her there.

For a moment, they remained in silence. The night sky had lightened by degrees while they spoke, a pinkish-gold glow warming the horizon.

"My God," he said finally, huffing out a rough exhale. "No wonder you were terrified in the storm last week. I can't imagine how traumatizing that must have been after what you went through."

His words soothed her. Yet, beneath her ear, his pulse sped faster. Was he troubled about what she'd confided? She tried not to be defensive, but she was all too aware of how many people judged her for her parents' sins.

She straightened from where she'd been curled against him, looking into his dark eyes for the first time since she'd began her story. His gaze darted away from hers.

"It wasn't as bad as it could have been," she assured him, not wanting to linger on that aspect since the tornado was in the past, and her horses were all safe. "Having you with me really helped."

"I'm glad I could be there with you." He sounded sincere enough, but something about his demeanor seemed…off.

Was he contemplating another retreat?

That didn't seem quite right considering he'd sought her out to talk to her.

"The storm anxiety doesn't happen very often,"

she admitted. "So it's less problematic for me on a day-to-day basis. More often, I struggle with feeling tainted by my father's criminal past—"

"But I remember when that massive twister hit Era," he said quickly, steering her back to the storm. Almost as if he wanted to avoid talking about her father. "The damage was catastrophic."

Surprised he recalled that, she started to nod.

Then, a thought occurred to her. She froze.

"Did I mention I lived in Era?" The small town north of Fort Worth wasn't well-known.

A shadow crossed his eyes. His whole face changed as his mouth worked silently for a moment.

A cold knot tightened in her gut. She'd missed something in this exchange and her brain slammed into high gear to pinpoint it.

"No. But it was the biggest—" He began to speak, but at the same time, her mind filled in the blanks about how he'd identified where she'd lived as a child.

Disbelief warred with a deep sense of betrayal.

"You knew all of that already?" The question was rhetorical, so she didn't wait for an answer. "How?"

"Please." He straightened on the patio sofa, shifting so he faced her. "I wasn't aware of most of it—"

"How. Did. You. Know?" She spit each word

like a bullet, anger roaring to life that he would mince words with her when she had a question that required an immediate answer.

He jammed his fingers in his hair and tugged on the strands, his agitation clear. But when he answered her, he met her gaze again.

“A private investigation.” He seemed to allow that a moment to sink in before he continued. “I told you that I am thorough when I vet potential charities for donations from the ranch’s foundation.”

His words chilled her.

He’d had her investigated? Without ever mentioning it, despite all the time they’d spent together?

Anger simmered.

What the hell had it revealed? She was uncomfortable enough with her past without having it typed up in a report for Lorenzo’s personal review. Something he should have told her already, damn it.

“You never mentioned a personal investigation was part of the process.” Standing, she needed to pace away some of this frustrated energy. It angered her to realize she was barefoot and wearing his T-shirt.

She’d slept with the man who had her investigated and never bothered to mention a thing about it.

“I should have told you.” At least he had the

courtesy to acknowledge it. Too bad the confession came too late to make a difference.

Her chest burned with the realization of how foolish she'd been. How she'd thought they were getting close. In reality, all that had happened was that she'd embarrassed herself in front of this man. She'd laid herself—her heart—bare.

"Yes. You should have. Especially before I poured out my personal stories for you, thinking I was—" She blinked away the sudden liquid heat in her eyes, horrified when two fat tears rolled down her cheeks.

She turned to swipe them furiously away.

"Thinking what?" he asked softly from behind her.

"You don't get to ask questions." She turned on him, pointing an agitated finger. "You already paid to have your questions answered."

"It's been hard for me to trust." His quiet admission, the reminder of the way his ex-fiancée had treated him, softened her heart.

Until she remembered the way he'd let her prattle on about her past without telling her he already knew it. A fresh surge of anger made her recognize she'd been wrong about him.

He wasn't the man she'd believed him to be. Only now that he'd broken her trust did she realize how much she'd placed in him. How much fragile hope she'd already built up in her mind about a relationship. A future.

"I understand why you'd want to protect yourself against false women." She almost wavered when she saw the flash of desolation in his eyes. "But I've done nothing to betray you. Who is going to protect me from false men who can't be honest?"

Whatever raw, unshuttered emotion she'd thought she saw in his gaze died a moment later. She'd probably misread him. Again.

His jaw flexed, his stony silence speaking volumes. Pain and disillusionment cracked her apart that he had no words to reassure her. Nothing else to say.

Mustering as much dignity as she could manage while wearing only his T-shirt, she drew in a deep breath as she turned toward the house. "I'm going to call a car—"

"I can take you home, Valencia." He moved to follow her, his long strides eating up the distance between them, his voice full of frustration.

Well, she was *more* than frustrated. She was crushed. Heartbroken. And so very angry.

"No. Thank you." She was close to breaking, her emotions in turmoil. She didn't want to be anywhere near the man responsible for the deep ache in her chest. "I can't be with you right now."

Maybe never.

Pivoting away from him, she hurried inside the house to find her phone and get dressed. Whatever she and Lorenzo had shared, it was over now.

Twelve

Ten days later, Lorenzo plowed down a dirt road in a shortcut toward Elegance Ranch, taking every pothole so hard it challenged even the top-notch suspension of his truck. But there just weren't enough potholes in Texas to help him get over the pain of losing Valencia.

He'd known that she'd meant it when she said she needed to be alone. But he'd still tried to contact her. Four times, damn it. He still wanted to frame an apology in a way that would make her understand why he'd hadn't been more up-front with her.

But when ten days had passed without her taking his calls, he knew she wasn't interested in hearing from him. Maybe the feelings that had taken root in him hadn't been reciprocated. Because he missed Valencia more than he'd ever dreamed it would be possible to miss someone who'd been in his life for such a short time. And that stung so much worse than he'd expected. Far more than even when Lindsey had tried to wipe him out of every last cent.

Now, he tried to channel the hurt of losing her—the anger at *himself* for losing her—into something more productive. Like finding out how the Edmond family was going to make it up to the people whose lives they'd ruined with the sham music and arts festival that never got off the ground. He steered the truck off the back road onto the finely paved private road that would take him to the Edmond family compound.

Soon, he parked his pickup truck in front of the security gates at Elegance Ranch, then let the engine idle while he pressed the intercom button and waited. He'd tried contacting Ross or Rusty, but they never returned his calls. It seemed the world was ignoring him these days.

Impatient with the lack of response, Lorenzo stabbed the button again, waiting for an attendant or someone from the main house to answer him.

"Hello?" A woman's voice finally answered.

Unfortunately, it didn't sound like Gina Edmond's voice.

"It's Lorenzo Cortez-Williams. I'm here to see Ross," he said evenly, willing to play nice to obtain an audience.

"Ross isn't here, sir," the woman replied. "The whole family is away."

"Away?" Irritation laced his voice. The July heat wafting in through his open window only added to it. "What about Rusty? Or Gina?"

"I'm sorry, sir, there's no one here today but staff. If you'd like to leave a message—"

"How about Billy Holmes? He's not family." Lorenzo recalled Ross's college friend Billy Holmes was one of the organizers of Soiree on the Bay, and the guy had been living in a guest cottage on the ranch property for the past two years.

"I'm sorry, sir," the woman repeated more firmly. "No one is allowed on the premises when the family is away."

Refusing to bother staffers who'd surely fielded flak from the media already, Lorenzo thanked the woman and put the truck in Reverse. Driving away from Elegance Ranch, he headed toward the Texas Cattleman's Club, too keyed up to return home, where thoughts of Valencia bombarded him around every corner.

His house was crammed full of memories of her from their last night together. He'd hardly slept in the days that followed their breakup, finally changing bedrooms so he didn't keep seeing her hair spread over his pillow, or recall her smile as she pulled on his old T-shirt before lying down with him for the night.

Hands fisting around the steering wheel, he was grateful to pull into the lot for the Texas Cattleman's Club a few minutes later, needing something to distract him from the way he'd failed her. She was nothing like his former fiancée, but his prejudices had allowed him to paint her with the same brush, seeing dishonesty that wasn't there. And now it seemed there was no repairing the damage he'd done with his lack of trust.

With a nod to an older rancher exiting the stone building beside his wife, Lorenzo stepped inside the cool interior of the historic clubhouse. He could count on one hand the number of times he'd shown up here by himself, using it only as a meeting place for business. But going home alone right now wasn't an option.

"Can I get you a table, sir?" the young hostess asked, reviewing her electronic tablet.

"Yes. It's just me today—" he began when his gaze shifted to the bar behind her.

Where Billy Holmes sat alone at the far end, tipping a glass to his lips.

Unbelievable. He'd looked all over town for any of the Edmond family, and here was Billy Holmes, dressed in an impeccable blue suit and hiding in plain sight at the Texas Cattleman's Club. Perhaps, because the club was private, it was one of the few places in town where media didn't have access.

Still, it ticked Lorenzo off to see the guy having a drink in the middle of the day, casual as you please, when his failed festival had hurt so many people. News broadcasts for the past week had focused on a series of vendors who'd invested heavily in Soiree on the Bay and wouldn't recoup their losses. Just thinking about it made his blood boil. And, of course, it upset him more than he could say that Valencia would be struggling to make her dream of an equine therapy camp happen. Not to mention that Rafe could still lose his restaurant...

Lorenzo turned back to the hostess.

"Actually, no table for me." He slid her a tip just the same since he recalled the woman was a college student. "I'm going to have a seat at the bar."

He strode through the cool interior, passing a few tables that included people he knew. He nodded to the other ranchers politely, but kept his eye on his quarry.

"Billy." Lorenzo greeted the man as he took a seat nearby, leaving one bar stool free between them.

As he glanced up from his now-empty glass, Billy moved a bit slowly, and Lorenzo guessed he'd been drinking for a while.

"Lorenzo." He nodded cordially, then flagged down the bartender, signaling for another drink.

Grinding his teeth together to hold back the accusations he wanted to let fly, Lorenzo waited until he'd ordered a drink for himself—bourbon, neat—then pivoted hard to face Billy.

"You have a lot of nerve coming around here today, leisurely drinking when the Edmond family has ruined the lives of so many people." His anger ran hot. And yes, it felt good to have an outlet for his own defeat with Valencia. For screwing up something really special.

"Is that right?" Billy Holmes was well-known for his charm. Rumor had it that he'd sidled into Rusty Edmond's world almost immediately when Ross brought his friend home from college. Apparently Billy had the cantankerous billionaire's ear better than Rusty's own kids did.

Either way, there was little evidence of that charm now.

"One hundred percent," Lorenzo continued. "Do you just not give a damn about the victims of this festival scheme?"

"I do, actually." He went silent when the bartender returned with their drinks, setting the glasses on the bar in front of each of them. When the guy left, Billy lifted his bourbon but didn't take a sip. "I'm as much of a victim as anyone. No one knows how much I've lost."

The dark bitterness behind the words was unmistakable. But that didn't stop Lorenzo's jaw from dropping at the guy's audacity.

"Excuse me?"

Billy continued, almost as if he hadn't heard the question, "I should have suspected that Asher was up to no good," he muttered, swiping condensation off his glass. "I always sensed a rivalry between Asher and Ross. That Asher felt Rusty favored his biological son over his stepson. Don't you think?"

"I never noticed anything," Lorenzo argued, wondering where this was going.

Clearly, Billy didn't take any ownership for the crisis. And maybe he didn't deserve any. But it seemed wrong of the festival organizers to just disappear when so many people had lost money to the farce of Soiree on the Bay.

"I guess blood is thicker than water," Billy continued, sloshing some of his drink over the edge of his glass before it reached his lips. "Biology is destiny, right?"

"I've got to call BS on that," Lorenzo disagreed, not comfortable with the idea that Ross Edmond had received preferential treatment over Asher. It just wasn't true from what he'd witnessed over the years. "Just look at how close Rusty is to you, and you're not his son."

Billy went still. Then nodded slowly. "An astute observation. Maybe Asher was as jealous of me as he was of Ross. Perhaps that's why he took down the festival."

Lorenzo thought that was missing the point, but arguing with a guy who was already a few drinks in was probably a waste of his time. Still, he couldn't help asking, "What do you think the Edmond family will do to make it up to people who've lost so much because of this?"

Obviously, no one was going to give Rafe his money back or Valencia the donation she'd been promised, but he wondered if they'd at least thought about a plan.

"I have a good feeling that in the end, everyone will get what they deserve." Billy lifted his glass in a toast to that, but Lorenzo had no cause to drink to it.

He didn't believe that was true, for one thing. And for another, it only ticked him off more that Billy didn't seem to take the festival failure seriously. Shaking his head, he stood, ready to leave.

But the sight of Valencia crossing the dining room, deep in conversation with Lila Jones, stopped him dead in his tracks.

Damn, but she looked so lovely she stole the air right out of his lungs. She wore a black pencil skirt and pale gray blouse with full, feminine sleeves. Her hair was loose around her shoulders, reminding him of how she'd looked on the beach at Appaloosa Island when she'd held her sandals in one hand, dipping her toes in the sand.

He could have sworn time suspended for a minute as he watched her in animated conversation with Lila. He felt a physical ache so strong it rooted him to the spot. Still, she must have felt his stare somehow because she glanced over her shoulder just then, turning back to look behind her before leaving the club.

Their eyes met. Held. He could have sworn he saw an ache in her gaze that echoed his own.

And a moment later, she was gone.

The crushing weight of knowing she didn't want to see him felt like more than he could stand. Beside him, Billy whistled low. Lorenzo turned, realizing the guy had observed the exchange somehow.

"Is she someone special to you?" Billy asked, rattling the ice cubes in a now-empty glass.

Lorenzo didn't need to think twice about that one. Because something inside him had shifted this week. And seeing Valencia just now only confirmed what he'd suspected for the past several days.

He was in love with Valencia.

"Yes. She is special." He regretted that he hadn't realized it sooner, but it couldn't be too late. "And she's one of many people suffering because of that damned festival."

Slamming his glass onto the bar, he stalked away from Billy, fueled by a new determination to see Valencia again. To convince her to hear him out. He noticed that Lila Jones had lingered behind Valencia, who'd already departed.

Hastening his pace, he intercepted Lila just as she left the hostess's stand.

"Lila," he called out before he joined her near the door. "Do you have a minute?"

"Well, hello, Lorenzo." The brunette's gaze went to the window overlooking the parking area where they could both see Valencia closing the door of her pickup. Her attention then returned to him. "Sure. What's up?"

"How are things going with the festival? Have you heard from the Edmond family?"

She adjusted her purse strap on her shoulder. "Unfortunately, no. I think they're just waiting for things to blow over."

"Which they won't." He wondered how Valencia was doing, but knew he had no right to ask. "The festival was supposed to be in two days. Have you heard how any of the performers are responding to the canceled event? How they're handling things?"

He'd read online that many fans were unhappy that they wouldn't be seeing the popular musicians they'd paid to hear live. There was a lot of backlash on the bands, who couldn't help that there was nowhere for them to perform.

"A couple of them have decided to do some local shows as a way to connect with fans. Two of them will be performing at the Silver Saddle on Saturday when the festival was supposed to begin."

"Really?" His gaze tracked the progress of Valencia's truck as she backed out of her parking spot, powerless to keep his eyes off her.

"For what it's worth, I think Valencia will be there."

His head whipped back to the woman beside him. Lila's lips curved in a small smile. Ah, he had an ally after all. A good thing, since he needed all the help he could get.

"I have been trying to find a way to talk to her," he said carefully, unwilling to intrude on a friendship in a way that might further risk Valencia's trust, but he was grateful for any other hint this gracious lady cared to drop. "I owe her an apology."

Lila tapped her chin thoughtfully for a moment, then she leaned closer, her long dark hair slithering off her shoulder as she spoke.

"She's been busy trying to find accommodations for some new rescues. The tornado left a rancher without a barn near Mustang Point. It's been in the news, and she's been working to coordinate a way to get them all here."

While Lorenzo hated the idea of Valencia being upset or stressed, he couldn't deny that this news gave him an opportunity to help her. And he needed something constructive to do. Even if she never spoke to him again, his heart belonged to her. He wanted the best for her.

"You've given me an excellent idea for an apology." If she threw it in his face, then so be it. He still owed her the words. "I can't thank you enough."

Straightening, Lila winked at him. "Good luck, Lorenzo. Maybe I'll see you Saturday?"

Filled with new purpose mixed with wary hope, he nodded. "Count on it."

He might not be able to replace the funds Valencia had lost to the missing ticket money from Soiree on the Bay. But he knew how to transport and board horses. He had the equipment, the manpower and the means.

Now, he just hoped Valencia would hear him out. Because he couldn't escape the feeling that this was his last chance to win back the woman of his dreams.

"I'm sorry, I don't understand." Valencia sighed with exasperation into her cell phone as she slid off Sapphire's back and led the Belgian to the paddock by her reins. She needed to cut their morning ride short in order to take this call from a farm in Mustang Point. The spread had been hit hard in the recent tornadoes and she'd been trying to help them by taking in some of their displaced animals. "Did you say your horses are *gone*?"

She'd been running Sapphire at a full canter when she'd taken the call, so she was a bit out of breath now. Maybe she'd misheard? Poor Sapphire could have run for another hour, but Valencia really did need to return to work.

For three days, she'd been calling all her local resources to see who could accept those five horses left stranded by the same tornado that had ripped through Appaloosa Island. The animals were beautiful. Well cared for. Well mannered.

But the farmer who'd been keeping them had lost everything. Including his favorite mount—a young gelding quarter horse. He'd been so distressed that it was hard for him to think about rebuilding for the remaining animals in his care. Valencia empathized. And she wanted to take the animals because she suspected they could be great fits for the therapy camp. Plus, they would be somewhat local in case the farmer changed his mind once he was done grieving.

So it made no sense that the farmer's daughter

was telling her the horses had already been taken care of. How could that be? What had happened to them? Were they safe?

"A man came yesterday with two big horse trailers," the younger woman explained, and in the background Valencia could hear her shuffling papers. "I have the paperwork here, somewhere, but it was a rancher my father knew from the Texas Cattleman's Club. And we were so grateful because we have nothing here to feed the horses. Even the hay was ruined."

"I know about the hay," she reminded her, putting the cell phone on speaker, then clipping the device to her belt before tugging off Sapphire's bridle once they reached the paddock. "That's why I've been in a hurry to get everything coordinated. I was planning to get the first of the horses myself this afternoon."

"Well, your friend saved you a trip. The man who loaded them up said he was holding them for Donovan Horse Rescue."

Her *friend*?

Valencia stopped her trek toward the tack room, where she'd been headed to hang the bridle.

"He's holding them for me? Did you get his name?" It must have been someone she'd called in the last few days. Although no one had said they were prepared to take on the boarding, even if they'd been willing to help her with the transportation.

And actually, no one had agreed to that, either. She was perplexed.

"It was a long name. Lorenzo something. He was really, really good-looking."

Valencia dropped the bridle. It couldn't possibly be him! Surely the woman misheard.

Valencia breathed through the tension, the grief, knotting in her chest. She was probably just missing him so much—even though he'd hurt her, damn it—that she was hearing his name when no one had said it.

"Lorenzo?" she repeated softly, still liking the way it flowed from her lips.

Still missing saying it aloud since she'd refused to speak to him. She hadn't even told anyone that he'd broken her heart. Although Lila might have guessed over their lunch the day before.

"Yes, that's right. I have it on the paperwork he left with us," the farmer's daughter continued. "He said he was going to stable them for you until you were ready to house them. I think he lives near you. He was from Royal."

The air whooshed right out of her lungs. Lorenzo. Somehow managing to be a part of her life even when he wasn't present.

Bending to retrieve the bridle, Valencia didn't know what to make of the news. Was it a good sign? Had he wanted to do something kind for her? Or was he simply using it as a way to speak to her because she'd refused to answer his calls?

Either way, it was kind. Tremendously so. He'd always been so supportive of her passion for rescue and equine therapy. He deserved a thanks for his thoughtfulness. And she intended to do so.

Right after she figured out how he'd managed to find out——

Lila.

Valencia sagged back against the tack room wall, her legs shaky at the thought of facing Lorenzo. She'd told Lila about the horse dilemma over lunch yesterday, and then she'd seen Lorenzo on her way out. He must have stopped to speak to the woman. It hadn't taken him long to act. She couldn't deny that she was touched.

"I'll have to talk to him, then," Valencia managed finally, straightening from the wall and draping the bridle over the proper hook. "I'll be sure to let you know how they're doing once I've got them settled," she promised. "Call anytime if your father changes his mind."

The woman's gratitude echoed after Valencia disconnected. She clutched the phone to her chest as she stepped back outside under the shade of the live oak. Barkis trotted over to greet her, nosing her hand for a pet.

What did Lorenzo's gesture mean?

So many nights she'd lain awake in her bed, her eyes gritty from crying, asking herself if she'd done the right thing walking away from Lorenzo. Yes, he'd hurt her by not telling her about the background check. But it wasn't that she minded his looking into her personal background. From a business perspective, she understood, and would have gladly welcomed it for the sake of securing the donation from the Cortez-Williams family.

It was that he hadn't told her about it once they'd started to get intimate. To trust him not only with her body, but with an emotional piece of her past… Only to find out he'd known all along and hadn't mentioned it—that had been what hurt. Still, would it sting so much if she hadn't begun to care for him deeply?

Her phone buzzed against her hand, while she mulled that over. Even with her screen brightness turned all the way up, she had to shade her eyes to see the incoming text message.

From Lorenzo.

I'll be at the Silver Saddle tomorrow at 4 p.m. I really need to talk to you.

Her breath caught as she read the words. And she knew from the way her heart skipped a beat that she couldn't possibly refuse. She needed—no, she *ached*—to see him.

And for the first time in nearly two weeks, a tendril of hope sprouted inside her.

Thirteen

Had he scared off Valencia for good with that text message?

Heart hammering double time in his chest, Lorenzo searched the crowd for her from a private table inside The Silver Saddle bar and tapas restaurant, a Royal hotspot inside the luxurious Bellamy resort property. The place was filling rapidly for the promised entertainment, a popular band that had been booked for Soiree on the Bay. For now, a deejay spun upbeat country music from a booth by the dance floor, but the instruments for the band were in place on a nearby stage. A few couples were already two-stepping, and the volume from nearby conversations picked up as the crowd grew.

In the ten minutes since he'd sat down, Lorenzo had already spotted Abby Carmichael, the documentary filmmaker who'd been following the festival debacle. Lila Jones sat at the bar with Zach Benning, the social media influencer whose online platforms had attracted a lot of interest in the festival. Lorenzo wondered how the implosion of the event affected him, but the guy seemed fully focused on Lila right now, his arm wrapped possessively around her.

The sight shot a pang through Lorenzo, making him miss Valencia even more. Would she really skip this event altogether just because he'd let her know he would be there? He sighed. But the bigger question was… Had he finally found the woman meant for him, his *soul mate*, only to lose her? And if he had, he knew he had only himself to blame.

He waved away his server, not ready to order anything yet. His stomach was in knots anyway. As the male waiter hustled off to another table, Lorenzo finally caught sight of the woman he'd been waiting for as she entered the bar. His breath hitched.

Hope burned with a reminder of just how high the stakes were. Had his gesture with moving the horses been enough to win her back? Or was she simply here to issue an obligatory thank-you? Each long-legged step brought her closer to giving him his heart's desire…or dashing his hopes for a future with this incredible woman.

Dressed in a simple blue wrap dress that hugged her feminine curves, Valencia smiled and waved to friends as she wove her way through the packed bar. Part of him longed to go to her so he could clear her path, but he knew he didn't have the right to escort her.

Something he hoped like hell would change after he had the chance to speak to her. For now, he contented himself with watching her, acknowledging the overwhelming pleasure of seeing her again. Then, when her honey-brown eyes found his, awakening memories of how it had felt to be the center of attention, he shot to his feet to wait for her.

Nerves jumping, he thought his heart might break right through his chest with the way it knocked around inside him.

"Valencia. I'm glad you're here." He held a chair for her as she neared the table. "Won't you have a seat?"

He couldn't read her gaze, her face revealing nothing except for the high color in her cheeks. Was she agitated? He hoped this meeting didn't cause her any stress or unhappiness, but it was too much to hope that the rush of pink in her skin could be from the same awareness that never failed to stir inside him whenever she was near.

"Thank you," she said softly, brushing past him to accept the seat, leaving a hint of rose-and-vanilla fragrance in the air as she lowered herself into the high-backed leather chair tucked into the private corner.

Grateful to have her here, to know she was granting him this audience after how he'd hurt her, he did his best to situate her comfortably before taking the seat opposite her. With their backs to the wall, they could have a good view of the room, but right now, he had eyes only for her.

"Thank you for joining me," he began, his heart in his throat as he thought about all that was riding on this conversation.

Before he could begin, however, a woman hurried over to their table. She was dressed in black pants and a white blouse, simple clothes similar to the attire of the staff, but Lorenzo knew she wasn't their server. Besides, her handbag was tucked under her arm as she edged around a tray of drinks balanced on a high table nearby.

"Excuse me." The woman held up a finger as if to indicate she needed only a moment. "I'm so sorry to interrupt you, but I'm trying to set up some appointments with people about the festival debacle." Reaching in her bag, she withdrew a white business card and laid it on the table between them. “Lani Li, private investigator.”

Lorenzo exchanged looks with Valencia, wondering what she thought of the intrusion. But his companion’s expression was difficult to read as she reached for the card and read it over.

“Who hired you?” Valencia asked the newcomer as she looked up from the card and passed it to Lorenzo.

The woman—mid- to late-twenties, he guessed—scooped her long, sleek ponytail off her shoulder and shoved it impatiently behind her back.

“I’m not at liberty to say. But I assure you, my client is prepared to get to the bottom of who is responsible for the failed event.” Lani crouched closer so she could lower her voice, as if she didn’t want anyone to overhear.

Interesting.

“Besides Asher Edmond?” Lorenzo asked, curious to learn if someone else had suspicions about a bigger cover-up at work. Something about Asher’s arrest made him uneasy.

“I plan to review all of the evidence from start to finish,” she returned, sidestepping what he knew had been a loaded question. “I’m making no assumptions. I’m only interested in learning the truth.” She turned her gaze toward Valencia. “I’ve been hoping to speak with you, Ms. Donovan, as I know you were on the advisory board.

Would you be willing to talk to me about your experience with the festival? I'd be glad to come to you to make it easy."

Valencia didn't hesitate. "Please call me Valencia. And assuming you are who you say you are, I would be happy to speak to you. I can be reached at Donovan Horse Rescue anytime. I think we can both agree that this isn't the right time or place for further discussion."

The private investigator nodded. "Fair enough. I'll be in touch, Valencia. And thank you."

Lorenzo echoed the thanks over the woman leaving as he watched her bustling away, withdrawing another business card from her bag as she made a beeline for Lila Jones. Then his focus returned to the beautiful woman across from him.

A woman who deserved so much more from him than he'd given her.

Valencia slid a finger under the tiny horseshoe pendant she wore on a gold chain at her neck, then slid the charm back and forth while she studied him across the table.

"So? You must know I'm curious why you wanted to see me."

The suspense was killing her.

She'd been a few minutes late to this meeting with Lorenzo because she'd been nervous and unsure how to proceed. Should she ask him about the horses he'd transported on her behalf? *Thank* him?

As grateful as she felt about what he'd done, she wanted to hear him out first. She needed to know how he felt about what had happened between them. Did he take any ownership for it, or understand how his actions had hurt her? She was nervous about the outcome of this conversation, fearing it could be the last time they spoke. Fear… anxiety…and yes, love, welled inside her.

As she searched his dark eyes for answers, the rest of the noisy bar fell away for her.

Until a server appeared.

Thankfully, Lorenzo seemed as eager to be done with their drink order as she was, and the waiter disappeared a moment later.

"Valencia." His voice was a warm rumble across their table as he met her gaze once more. "You asked me why I wanted to see you," he began, his expression earnest. "And the truth is I've never stopped wanting to see you. I've missed being with you every single day—every hour—that we've been apart."

His admission made her tingly inside. She couldn't deny it. But she could hardly confess to missing him, too, if he didn't understand why she'd left in the first place. The nervousness she'd felt going into this meeting was still there.

He continued, however, laying both hands on

the polished tabletop as he spoke. "But I know you deserve better than someone who is anything less than fully honest with you. I had a responsibility to tell you about the private investigation before we got involved romantically, and I failed you. I'm so incredibly sorry for letting you down like that."

She appreciated his directness, and some of her anxiety eased a fraction. She forced herself to let go of her horseshoe good-luck charm.

"I know things escalated quickly between us with the tornado," she acknowledged, recognizing that her uncomfortable past had been part of the reason she'd taken comfort in his arms that first night. "But even if you'd told me after the storm, I would have been more understanding."

It wouldn't have hurt so very much.

Nearby, the musicians started to play. The gentle twang of a country love song filled the bar, the crowd quieting a fraction to enjoy the strains of the fiddle.

Lorenzo's face was solemn. Sad, perhaps. "I have no excuse, and, again, I'm sorry. I allowed my experience with Lindsey to taint my feelings so much I've had a hard time trusting anyone, much less my own judgment."

Even his words sounded pained. Could the ache he felt over their split be as agonizing as her own? She leaned over the table a bit at the private nature of their conversation. Also, maybe because she found it almost impossible to resist the magnetic pull that she'd felt toward him from their very first meeting.

"I know how past hurts can color your choices," she admitted, wanting to share a conclusion she'd reached in the last two lonely weeks without him. "I've spent a long time trying to shed the taint of my birth family. But I'm not them, and I'm tired of trying to be the best at all times just to set myself apart from them. It's exhausting."

His brows furrowed with what looked like concern. "You're a good person with a warm, giving heart. A charitable nature. Anyone who can't recognize that doesn't deserve your time."

The passionate inflection behind the words touched her. And stirred a hope that Lorenzo's feelings for her hadn't faded.

She wanted to hear more, but she spied the server heading toward them with their drinks and wondered if she'd ever have Lorenzo to herself for more than five minutes at a time.

"Would you like to dance?" he asked, extending his hand to her as he pushed away from the table.

He was dressed in a dark suit with a white shirt left unbuttoned at his neck, though his expensive leather boots still marked him as a Texas rancher. An extraordinarily compelling one, at that.

Valencia nodded. "It might be our only chance to speak privately here." She placed her palm in his and allowed him to draw her to her feet, her blood rushing in her ears at the feel of his skin warming hers.

His touch brought back so many memories.

For now, she followed him onto the dance floor, her breath catching when he stopped to pull her into his arms.

With one hand settled on the small of her back, the other wrapped around hers, he led her to the spot farthest from any other dancers while the music wrapped around her.

"I deeply regret hurting you, Valencia." Lorenzo's gruffly spoken words picked up right where he'd left off earlier. "I knew as soon as you left my house that night that I owed you an apology. And I don't blame you for not wanting to hear it. But I can't rest until you know how sorry I am. I hope you can accept my apology."

She saw the sincerity in his eyes. Felt his concern for her in a hundred little ways, from how he looked at her like she was the only woman in the room to the way he hadn't pressed her into meeting with him.

And he hadn't once brought up the kindness he'd done her by securing the horses she'd been anguished about rescuing all week.

"I forgive you." She stroked her hand lightly along his shoulder where it rested on his tailored suit. The warmth of his body beneath it sent a shiver of awareness through her that he must feel.

His hand flexed on the small of her back, a slight clenching of his fingers. But he didn't pull her closer.

"You do?" he rasped.

"Yes. Of course I do." She felt sure of it to the depths of her being. Sure of *him*. "I was so hurt that night. Not just by what you'd done, but also that you barely seemed to acknowledge it. But I've searched my heart, and I know you're a better man than that. A mistake is just that—a mistake."

A long breath shuddered through him as he wrapped his arms around her fully. Tightly. She felt his relief at her answer, and knowing how tense he'd been about this conversation soothed any last fragments of frayed pride she might have been feeling.

The song ended and another began as he held her. They were out of the way of dance traffic, however, and no one seemed to mind that they clung together to one side of the floor.

"You're an amazing woman, Valencia Donovan." Lorenzo's words were for her ears alone, spoken into her hair as they swayed together to the new duet sung over the strains of a steel guitar. "I would give anything for a second chance to show you how much I care for you."

The tender feelings she had for him swelled

stronger as her new hopes took root. She couldn't imagine any place she'd rather be than right here in his strong arms, his heart pounding so hard that she felt it against her breast.

"Like transporting five beautiful horses all the way from Mustang Point?" she asked, reaching up to stroke his jaw.

"No. I'd give far, far more than that."

Her lips lifted in a half smile as her hand dropped back to his shoulder. "Well, the horses were a wonderful place to start. Thank you so much."

"It was my pleasure to do something for you, but I hope it was only the beginning." He speared a hand through her hair to cradle the back of her head, then tipped her face up to his.

Electricity seemed to crackle through her, zinging its way to all her nerve endings until she hummed with it.

"A beginning?" Her tongue darted out to moisten her lips gone suddenly dry. She probably gazed up at him like a woman under a spell, but she couldn't find it in her to care about anything other than this man in front of her right now.

Her feet stopped moving.

All her attention solely on Lorenzo.

"Yes." There was a fierceness in his voice. A new determination. "It took my head a while to catch up with my heart, Valencia, but I know now that I love you. And I'm going to do everything I can to prove to you how much."

The intensity of his gaze made her knees go weak.

Happiness soared inside her so high she felt light-headed. Although his mouth now hovered so close to hers that the promise of a kiss might have contributed to that light-headed feeling.

"Then take me home," she whispered, her breath coming fast as her emotions threatened to spill over for the whole world to see. "Because I love you, too, Lorenzo. And I think we need to start showing each other how much."

His lips claimed hers as if he wanted to taste the words for himself. Seal them between them. And she wanted that, too, because she could have lost herself in that kiss for hours. Days.

A lifetime.

"We're going to do that," he assured her when he broke away, breathing heavily. "Because I'm going to love every minute of showing each other how we feel. But I want you to know that you don't have to prove a thing to me. You're a woman of your word, and I will never question that again."

He stroked a fingertip over her still-quivering lip. Around them, the song ended, and the other couples applauded for the band. But Valencia could think only about her new beginning, and the man who loved her.

So she didn't mind, not even a little bit, when he swept her off her feet and into his arms where anyone in the Silver Saddle bar could see them. Happy laughter bubbled out of her as she wound her arms around his neck, delighting in the romantic gesture from this ruggedly handsome, pragmatic man who would never give his heart lightly.

They earned a few wolf whistles, and she thought that Lorenzo got a couple of slaps on the back on his way out of the crowded bar. But Valencia had eyes only for the man who held her, the rancher whose strong arms would shelter her through any storm.

* * * * *

Look for the next book in the
Texas Cattleman's Club: Heir Apparent series:

How to Catch a Bad Boy
by Cat Schield

After one hot night with a handsome stranger, business executive Mycah Hill doesn't expect to see him again. Then she starts her new job and he's her boss, CEO Achilles Farrell. But keeping things professional is hard when she learns she's having his child...

Read on for a sneak peek at
Secrets of a One Night Stand
by USA TODAY *bestselling author Naima Simone.*

"You're staring again."

"I am." Mycah switched her legs, recrossing them. And damn his too-observant gaze, he didn't miss the gesture. Probably knew why she did it, too. Not that the action alleviated the sweet pain pulsing inside her. "Does it still bother you?"

"Depends."

"On?"

"Why you're staring."

She slicked the tip of her tongue over her lips, an unfamiliar case of nerves making themselves known. Again, his eyes caught the tell, dropping to her mouth, resting there, and the blast of heat that exploded inside her damn near fused her to the bar stool. What he did with one look… Jesus, it wasn't fair. Not to her. Not to humankind.

"Because you're so stareable. Don't do that," she insisted, no, *implored* when he stiffened, his eyes going glacial. Frustration stormed inside her, swirling and releasing in a sharp clap of laughter. She huffed out a breath, shaking her head. "You should grant me leeway because you don't know me, and I don't know you. And you, all of you—" she waved her hand up and down, encompassing his long, below-the-shoulder-length hair, his massive shoulders, his thick thighs and his large booted feet "—are a lot."

"A lot of what?" His body didn't loosen, his face remaining shuttered. But that voice…

She shivered. It had deepened to a growl, and her breath caught.

"A lot of—" she spread out her arms the length of his shoulders "—mass. A lot of attitude." She exhaled, her hands dropping to her thighs. "A lot of beauty," she murmured, and it contained a slight tremble she hated but couldn't erase. "A lot of pride. A lot of…" Fire. Darkness. Danger. Shelter.

Her fingers curled into her palm.

"A lot of intensity," she finished. Lamely. Jesus, so lamely.

Achilles stared at her. And she fought not to fidget under his hooded gaze. Struggled to remain still as he leaned forward and that tantalizing, woodsy scent beckoned her closer seconds before he did.

"Mycah, come here."

She should be rebelling; she should be stiffening in offense at that rumbled order. Should be. But no. Instead, a weight she hadn't consciously been aware of tumbled off her shoulders. Allowing her to breathe deeper…freer. Because as Achilles gripped the lapel of her jacket and drew her closer, wrinkling the silk, he also slowly peeled away Mycah Hill, the business executive who helmed and carried the responsibilities of several departments… Mycah Hill, the eldest daughter of Laurence and Cherise Hill, who bore the burden of their financial irresponsibility and unrealistic expectations.

In their place stood Mycah, the vulnerable stripped-bare woman who wanted to let go. Who *could* let go. Just this once.

So as he reeled her in, she went, willingly, until their faces hovered barely an inch apart. Until their breaths mingled. Until his bright gaze heated her skin.

This close, she glimpsed the faint smattering of freckles across the tops of his lean cheeks and the high bridge of his nose. The light cinnamon spots should've detracted from the sensual brutality of his features. But they didn't. In an odd way, they enhanced it.

Had her wanting to dot each one with the top of her tongue.

"What?" she whispered.

"Say it again." He released her jacket and trailed surprisingly gentle fingers up her throat. "I want to find out for myself what the lie tastes like on your mouth."

Lust flashed inside her, hot, searing. Consuming.

God, she liked it. This…*consuming*.

If she wasn't careful, she could easily come to crave it.